The Complete
Aaron Sans Erotica Collection
Volumes 1-7

66 Stories about MILFs, Gangbangs, BDSM, Fantasy & Sci-Fi, Cuckolds, LGBT, and Anal

Aaron Sans

Contents

BDSM, Bondage, Discipline, Domination, Submission, Sadochism, and Masochism

Fantasy, Sci-fi, Surrealism, Religion, and the Just Plain Weird

MILFs, Cougars, and Mature Women

My Best Friend's MILF and Our Smoking Fetish, Anal Sex, and Squirting

Sandy was so sexy. And my best friend's mother, twenty-some years my senior. Always flirting with her son's friends, trying to get a rise out of us. About 5'6" 100 lbs, Sandy had a sexy deep smoker's voice and perky tits she wasn't afraid to go braless with. On more than one occasion I recall her sitting on my lap at their house, leaning in asking me to light her 120 cigarettes. She was so fucking sexy smoking, always taking long deliberate drags. Sandy enjoyed every cigarette she smoked, often switching brands and talking about how she enjoyed the flavors. Sometimes I would have to almost rush home or into their bathroom and jerk off right then, wishing I was lighting her cigarette for her to suck my needy cock off while exhaling smoke all over me.

Some years later I ran into Sandy at the mall, being the very touchy affectionate type when I said hello she gave me a big hug. Her jeans were so tight they hugged her ass perfectly, her tits slightly protruding from the sleeveless button up shirt she had on. She had no idea I had been jerking off to her for years, wishing I could cum inside her. Her smell was incredible when she hugged me, that of perfume masking the cigarette smell. I made sure she saw me look her top to bottom, several times, and I expressed to her I hadn't seen her son in a few years… I would love to have lunch and catch up. We chatted for a few more minutes, and then hugged again, this time she gave me a kiss on the cheek, which I returned just as quick, getting rather close to her mouth.

A week later, Sandy called. She said she was running some errands if I wanted to meet that afternoon for lunch, which I excitedly agreed too. I was so fucking horny heading to meet her, not really expecting much just proud of the fact this was happening. Lunch went good, and some flirting ensued. As we were leaving the restaurant, as soon as we exited, she immediately put a cigarette to her mouth. "I'll light that," I insisted. holding the lighter slightly back so she had to come to it. We each had a few drinks, and she could tell I was enjoying her lighting up. Then she said it. Asked me if I enjoyed watching her smoke. Like an over excited puppy, I said that I loved it. It was my fantasy to light her cigarettes. Surprised, she laughed and said I could light all her cigarettes, now turning so her ass pressed against my pulsating rock hard cock. I pushed gently up against her, feeling as if I could cum right then.

"I will call you" she said as she exhaled and flicked her cigarette, giving me one last long hug before she left. Thankfully Sandy wasted no time, and the next night we were on our way a bar. We had to go quite a distance away so she didn't have to worry about her husband or being seen by any family. We joked and flirted the whole way. Several times she would reach over and rub the inside of my legs, coming close to the head of my dick. The night pressed on, into the wee morning hours, and Sandy decided we should get a hotel. She had been dancing and grinding on me all night, every head in the bar watching us more than likely thinking she was my mother when we first arrived.

Inside the hotel room she pushed me on the bed, opening my pants up revealing my swollen cock. She took her leather cigarette case, rubbing it up and down the shaft of my prick, meanwhile kissing up the insides of my legs. Before I knew it she was stroking me and licking my asshole. I had never had that done, at first I squirmed then I started working my ass hole into her tongue, moving my hips up and down as she tugged my cock.

"Is this my cock now?" she asked kissing my balls. I confessed to her how I had jerked off so many times to her… how I had jerked off in her panties in their bathroom, just the smell of her sweet pussy made me cum. I had to taste her pussy, every piece of her. I licked her freckled skin from shoulders down to her slightly hairy crotch. Mounting my face, Sandy ground her clit on my mouth as I used my hands to feel every inch of her body, unsure if this would be my only chance to fuck her. She rode my tongue faster, threatening me that she was going to cum, until she went from my mouth to my prick that was standing up. She immediately came all over me, sitting down to my balls squirting a stream of cum up to my belly button. I held her tiny ass in one hand, pulling her hair with the other as we stared in each other's eyes, almost angrily fucking. I had to pull my cock out to cum. I couldn't take it and exploded all over her, only for Sandy to push my dick back in her before I was done cumming. I grunted in pleasure feeling the last few pumps of my jizz fill her.

"I want it fucking rough, give me that young cock! It's mine now," Sandy whispered to me as I flipped her doggy style taking my belt and putting it around her hips. Using the belt I thrust her hips into me, using my fingers to open her tight asshole and massage it, spitting on her ass crack telling her she better cum again for daddy. She loved it, proceeding to cum again. This time I got my face down there helping her squirt while she was on all fours. I sank my prick back in her, telling her I wasn't done… that I was going to fill her with cum. She begged for me to unload in her ass, so I rode her as hard as I could, in pure ecstasy awaiting another thick load. Feeling my cock working itself full of cum, Sandy leaned her head back for me to light her cigarette while I fucked her. Her tight body and long cigarette drags forced me too cum, letting my cock glide between her ass crack until it pumped another hot cum load on her. Sandy wiggled her ass around on me as I shuddered in disbelief how incredible that was.

"Does this mean from now on this is my cock?" she said exhaling smoke. I furiously kissed her, telling her I was hers anytime.

How I Seduced the MILF Next Door

This is the story of my first sexual encounter. My name is Romi, and I live in India. This story goes back to fifteen years ago, when I was just an 18 year old and still in junior college. I had this very sexy woman living in my neighbor hood. Her name was Archana and she was married with a five-year-old son. She used to stay alone with her kid as her husband was in the army, and he was posted in Kashmir. So you can see she was on the radar of many a person. I too used to try and take advantage of her.

I used to climb the roof of my house and tried to stalk her. My roof and hers were a common one, and if I would climb up at night I could see her washroom without her noticing that someone can watch her. Therefore, I used to climb the roof every night just to get a glimpse of her sexy body. My parents would query why I climbed the roof every night, and then I would have to say that I was feeling hot and wanted some fresh air. You know back then the concept of an air conditioner was not that popular in India. Besides, buying one was a very expensive thing.

So coming back to my story, I would wait for her to use her washroom every night, but all the effort would go in vain, as I could never catch a glimpse of her using it. But I still persisted and very religiously every night would set my eye trap to have a glimpse of her nude body using her washroom. Finally, my patience paid and that day came when I got to see her peeing in her washroom. That day, I do not know but for some very strange reason, she was having a bath and during the entire process she had left her washroom door open.

For me that was a jackpot, because finally I could watch her nude. She started the shower and the water started sprinkling on her. I could see the water droplets falling on her huge boobs and then trickling down her brown nipples. I just wanted to drink those water drops by sucking her tits hard. My cock started to harden and I just wanted to break into her house and fuck her hard, but controlled my self because that would be inappropriate.

I kept looking at her taking a bath. The water was flowing all over her body. It was flowing over her large round, milky white ass, her pink colored pussy. I just wanted to suck her pussy and all her juice that was available down below.

Suddenly she sat down on her hunches and started peeing. I just wanted to drink that pee of hers. It was getting impossible to control. My imaginations of fucking her got wilder and I started masturbating hard while watching her bathing. After a while she stopped bathing and started wiping her wet body, but for me it was impossible to control my excitement, and I continued to masturbate to the extent that I got so weak in my legs that I eventually sat down tired. I was completely drenched in my sweat and my hands were full with my cum and sperms.

After a while I slowly climbed down my house roof in such a manner so that my parents would not catch me, had a bath and entered my room. That night I could not sleep as the very thoughts of my neighbor Archana kept me engaged. My imaginations grew wilder and I decided to have a real fuck session somehow.

We were not on talking terms, and I started thinking as to how I should get her talking to me. To my surprise the opportunity came without me needing to try. Her kid was not well, and she had to take him to the doctor, but was finding it difficult to do it alone. She came and started knocking on my door and by sheer coincidence I was the one who opened it. It was a pleasant surprise for me. I never expected her to come knocking. I quickly realized the sensitivity of the situation and controlled my surprise. Without any further delay, I got my car out and took them to the nearby doctor. The doctor checked her son and advised her to take special care of him as he was suffering from malaria. I told her not to worry and said to her that I would be around till her son recovered. She gleefully accepted my help and thanked me. We came back home and I stayed back at her place to help her.

Some days passed by and her son was recovering. I would diligently visit her place everyday and would run errands. She was mighty impressed by my antics and this was pretty visible in her eyes. It seemed that she had started liking me. As you know when husbands are not around then wives try to find support in other people. I was younger than her by at least 10 years, and it is human nature to find young people attractive. The same was happening to her, and I could feel it.

One day when I entered her house, I realized that she had gone for a bath. Her son was sleeping in the other room and somehow she had not bolted her front door. Thinking this was an opportunity I removed my clothes and got naked, and in this naked position I stood in front of the bathroom door waiting for her. I thought enough was enough and decided to fuck her at any cost. After a while she finished bathing and opened the bathroom door just to realize that I was standing naked. She was surprised and tried to close the bathroom door on me, but it was too late. Slowly she reopened it, still naked, and gave me a strange look that I took as a sign to take control.

I followed her bathroom and took her to her bedroom. Next, I started licking her boobs. They were succulent and delicious. I was sucking her nipples so hard that she would moan in pain, but that was not stopping me from enjoying her body. I then pressed her boobs hard and started licking her neck. I then went down on her cleavage and slowly started going down on her navel. I kissed it hard and realized that she was moaning in excitement. Next, I went to her pubic hair. The hair was black and dense, and I was liking it. I started licking it more and I could hear her moaning hard. I had always imagined she'd do so in my fantasies of her, and with every moan of hers I was getting more excited. I then went further down oh her clit only to realize that it was absolutely wet and was ejaculating precum. The juices were just flowing, and I started to suck her clit and spread her legs to see her pussy. Her pink pussy was getting more pink, and I suddenly realized that she was completely wiling.

She was moaning and said that she was wiling to get fucked by me and there was no need for me to forcefully fuck her. I continued to do what I was doing. I kept licking her pussy and clit and kept sucking her juices to the point that she said that it was getting uncontrollable and she wanted my cock.

I picked her legs up and put them on my shoulders. She said she liked this position. I then put my cock in her wet pussy and started thumping her hard. It was a dream come true for me. I kept fucking her only to cum quickly out of sheer excitement. She said it was ok, as it was the first time for me and it happens like this. She told me to relax and began to suck my cock. I readily agreed. All these days I had seen blowjobs in movies and here it was happening for real. She then tied my hands with a towel and continued to suck my cock and my balls slowly. I was loving each and every bit of it as she kept moving her mouth on my cock. Slowly, my cock started getting harder again. She realized this and sat on it, and started riding slowly. She got hold of my hands and told me to press her boobs hard. I indulged and could see her getting more excited. I kept fucking her like this and felt more control over my ejaculation. She was seemingly enjoying more and kept riding my cock hard. After sometime she untied me and told me that she wanted to try doggy position. I indulged again and started fucking her. This seemed more enjoyable than the missionary position. I kept entering deep in her pussy and she kept moaning hard, shaking and convulsing in her orgasm.

We then fell of each other and she caught my cock and said that she would help me cum. She started to suck my cock again and did it vigorously. I was getting more excited and caught hold of her hair and started pumping my cock deep into her mouth. Finally, I could not hold much longer and cummed in her mouth. We then lay beside each other on her bed. Finally, after sometime we had a bath together and I left only to return to fuck her again.

So this was how my first sexual encounter happened and following this I had many more sessions with her, but this was probably the best fuck I ever had.

A MILF's Journey into Sexting: Mutual Masturbation in a Digital Age

I met Reggie totally by chance, via a free dating site that a co-worker told me about. When I signed up my user profile and uploaded my photo unto the site, little did I know that I was in for the best sexual experience of my life.

I was a little nervous at first because I was a little rusty when it comes to playing the dating game. I didn't know what to say or what I expected to find out there in the dating pool. As a single mother of three beautiful girls, I found myself totally submerged in the task of raising these precious gifts and inevitably ended up neglecting my own personal needs. I totally shut down the dating game, mainly because I didn't want to expose my daughters to different men, or "uncles" as some women like to call them. As far as I was concerned, uncles could wreak havoc on a household too. So, unfortunately, I embarked on a celibacy hiatus for 10 years. No sexual contact at all with anyone besides myself.

Even though I was starving for human touch, longing to feel a man's hot body all over mine, I managed to keep myself satisfied by perfecting the art of "getting myself off." Sometimes, I would use toys to help me reach my climax. My favorite toy is called a "jackrabbit." The jackrabbit that I had was one that had a setting that pulsated and throbbed. I was able to set that jackrabbit to perform to meet my taste at the time. If I was in the mood for soft kisses and light caresses, in other words, if I were in the mood to "make love" I would set the throb and thrust to a low setting. Sometimes, this setting was what I wanted. Just like making love to a man, a slow thrust and throb was just what was needed to make me cum and the orgasms sometimes were really intense.

I don't always like that low setting. There are times that a woman wants that hardcore sex….that hair pulling action…..bodies slamming against bodies. My jackrabbit could handle that challenge too. I would set that speed on high, full throttle and let it rip. In this mode, it felt like a hard cock pounding into me and twisting and turning and pulsating, too. Usually, when I put the jackrabbit on this setting, I have to brace myself for a powerful, intense orgasm. That pulsating jackrabbit felt like the real thing to me, only better, when I had it set on high mode. Orgasms would usually cum very quickly and would sometimes cause me to literally arch my back high off the bed as I rode that orgasmic rollercoaster. I call it an orgasmic rollercoaster when I have multiple orgasms and cum at least 3 times in one session.

Perhaps the best feature of my beloved jackrabbit is the two little rabbit ears that massage and work my clit. When set on high speed, that jackrabbit can really send a girl to the moon and back. So, this went on for ten years. I became so good at "doing" myself that I didn't seem to miss the human aspect of sex. As a matter of fact, I actually preferred flying "solo" for a number of reasons. Perhaps, the number one reason why I preferred to do me was that I didn't have to deal with another person. The jackrabbit would deliver outstanding results without actually having to deal with being in a relationship. It's a beautiful feeling to experience pure, sweet sexual satisfaction without the problems that come with being in a relationship. Plus, the jackrabbit eliminated the cleanup factor. I've never been fond of having to clean up after having sex with a man. I hated how sometimes, hours after you've had sex, you experience that post-sex drip. When gravity gets ahold of the situation, cum tends to drain out of me and that is something that I don't care for.

But about six months ago, a co-worker convinced me to sign up for a free dating site. I actually looked forward to hooking up with someone who I might be compatible with. Also, the jackrabbit was starting to lose its power and I couldn't get off like I had in the past. One thing that crossed my mind is that I might have become frigid. I was past menopause and sometimes the onset of menopause causes the sex drive in a woman to diminish. This was absolutely terrifying to me. I decided to try out the free dating service in hopes that I could find someone who could give me what the jackrabbit had given me all of these years.

I met Reggie on the 3rd day of being on the site. What prompted me to respond to his profile was that he was claiming to be a highly sexual person with some very refined skills in bed. He boasted about how he was sure to please any women in bed and that anyone interested in him should make sure that they bring their "A" game. Needless to say, I was up for the challenge. I sent him a message to tell him that I was interested in getting to know him better. I had no idea what I was in for. Reggie and I exchanged phone numbers and were talking on the phone to each other within 30 minutes.

Reggie was by no means shy. He seemed to be a very confident person who was very sure of his sexual capabilities. Our conversations quickly escalated to one full of passion and desire. We exchanged pictures and were immediately attracted to each other. After Reggie and I had become very comfortable with each other, he convinced me to send him some "adult" pictures… pictures that were for his eyes only. I was very shy about sending erotic pictures, however, it was second nature to Reggie. The very first time that he sent me a picture of his hard cock, I couldn't resist the urge to masturbate while looking at that picture. I imagined myself sliding down on that hardness and slow-grinding until I cum. I imagined how it would feel to have that thick, hot pipe deep inside of me.

Needless to say, I went from zero to 100 real quick and came hard while using just my fingers. (I didn't have time to get the jackrabbit out for the job.) After I got off, I told Reggie about it and he immediately got hard as a rock. He told me to hang on a minute and he would send me something that he wanted me to watch. After about 20 minutes of waiting, I finally get a text with a media file attached. When I opened it, I saw a short clip that Reggie had made of himself cumming. He was jacking off so fast that the images on the screen were a blur. After about 2 minutes of hardcore jacking off, he let go of a healthy load of thick, white, creamy cum. When I saw that, it caused me to get off again. I watched the video clip that he had sent 3 times and on the third time, I timed it just right so that I could cum at the same time that he did. Needless to say, that was one of the best, intense orgasms I have ever had in my life.

So began our secret sex sessions. I was amazed at how someone could get me off so intensely without even touching me. I looked forward to his calls each night because I knew that I would sleep well after getting a good nut and being totally satisfied. We spent a lot of time sexting, having sex through text messages. During the course of our erotic sexual adventures, we discovered a lot of sexual secrets about each other, some of them really kinky. I introduced him to the art of cumming without making a sound. This was something that I found to be very arousing. It also was great for our situation because neither one of us lived alone. He lives with his older sister and I live with my kids. The last thing that either of us wanted was for someone to hear us getting off. When Reggie tried to do the silent thing the first time, he wasn't so successful. When he started cumming, he let out a loud moan because he said it felt so good. To my surprise, the second time was much better. When he started cumming, the only sound he let out was some heavy breathing. He recorded himself getting off without making a sound and sent it to me. Needless to say, I had an earth shaking orgasm when I saw him do it the way that I had instructed him. I watched intensely as his cock resembled a pit bull on a leash, trying to get away from its owner. I thought it had a mind of its own when I watched him cum really hard. Even though Reggie had advertised himself as a sexual god, it was I that conquered the art of sexting. I became very good at pleasuring myself while talking to him. Reggie was very good at sexting too. I never got bored listening to him and I ALWAYS got off!!! Reggie was not at all shy about sending me pictures and/or videos. It was I, on the other hand, who was extremely shy about sending pictures. I actually sent him one boob shot after several requests. He was surprised to see that I am a 46DDD. That's right! I have had big boobs for as long as I can remember. I have naturally what other women have paid lots of money for.

After several requests, I finally gave in and sent Reggie a picture of my kitty cat (as he calls it). It was very difficult to take that picture because women are not in the position to just whip it out and start recording. After several attempts, I did manage to get a good shot to send to him. Reggie gave me the task of finding a name for his cock. He was packing pretty well with about 7 and ½ inches to boot. In addition to being longer than average, he was also hung thick. I always like to watch how the head swells up really fat right before he spits his load. I can't watch that without cumming myself. I came up with the name "lucky 7" for my new friend and needless to say, I was in love. Reggie and I continued to have our little fling for 6 months. He worked overnight with a major shipping company and he was on graveyard shift for a while. This worked out well for us because he would call or text me every morning when he would get home from work, around 9 a.m. He claimed to have a special delivery for me and I looked forward to that early morning sex. It was also good because everyone else in my house would either be at work or at school. This meant that I didn't have to be quiet while cumming. It felt really good to scream and get loud while I'm getting off without the fear of being heard.

Over the course of our six month affair, Reggie and I got to know each other very well. Unfortunately, we never had the opportunity to get together for some real sex. This was partly due to the fact that we lived 250 miles apart from each other. Needless to say, even though we never met in person, even though I never got the opportunity to ride him like I wanted to, Reggie still manages to light my fire just like he did when we first met. I still find it hard to watch a video of him getting off without having an orgasm. I think he has me dickmatized!

13

Anal Sex for Two 70-Year-Old Ladies at the RV Park

It's always been interesting listening to other people talk about their relationships with their wives, girlfriends and so forth, but I always thought that it was far better to participate than to listen or read what was going on. My life and experiences took place all over the world when it came to women, and I thought I was more than proficient when it came to being intimate with a woman.

About two years ago I decided to buy an RV and tour the country. One of my stops took me to a little town in New Mexico that was devoted to senior citizens . . . but ones that were active. After about a week in my park, walking around and saying hello to all, I noticed how open and friendly folks were. My neighbors on both sides were attractive, well-kempt women in their late 70's who showered me with baked goods and dinner plates with wonderful items that I'd never be able to cook myself. Frankly, I thought I'd really landed in a wonderful place.

My two "ladies" were out in the shade during the day, and at night they'd be at one home or the other while their husbands were off for the evening at the local Casinos. One evening, Doris came to the door and asked if she could come in. I asked her in and as I was making coffee for us noticed that she wasn't shy about letting my see that she had nothing on under her dress. She had sat back in my captain's chair and allowed me a full and long look at the lovely bush that resided between her slim athletic legs.

When I offered her coffee, she made it a point to lean over excessively and allow me to see that her pert little breasts were not contained in a bra as one would expect from most women her age. She mentioned that she'd be more comfortable on the couch and as she got up, made it a point to rub her breasts against me in a most delicious and delightful manner. As she sat down she noticed a slight bulge in my pants and with a girlish giggle asked, "Are you a little excited?"

I told her that I was and that I hadn't been with a woman for a few months as I was travelling around the country in my newly acquired RV. She coyly brushed her hand against my pants where my cock was and said that it seemed I needed a little attention. I told her that her being married and her husband coming home in a bit might pose a problem. She told me that he usually stayed in town for the weekends when he went to the Casino, as he drank a bit and it was far safer that way.

She no sooner finished her sentence than her cell rang and her husband announced in a thick slurred voice that coming home would be out of the question tonight. I made a weak complaint about her being married, but she already had the zipper down in my trousers and was pulling my cock out and fondling it gently. As my cock grew she began to lick and tongue the tip of it and gently suck on just the head until I came to a full erection.

At that point I felt I was going to explode and she suddenly slapped the head of my cock. "Not so fast" she said softly. "I need a little work on my pussy, and I mean to get what I need." At that she slipped rapidly out of her skirt and relaxed on her back holding her pussy open with both hands and said ... "Suck my clit slowly and softly."

I was amazed at how sweet and succulent her cunt was. It wasn't old smelling or nasty as I thought an old broad's pussy would be. She moaned and groaned and moved around and then suddenly erupted and came in my mouth. I was surprised and just about to get up when I felt someone gently holding me in place. I turned to see Alice, my other "lady," standing above me completely naked and rubbing her pussy that was already glistening with come. I turned to Alice and she spread her legs around my face and gently lowered my head back on the couch and let me suck on her clit until she came all over my face. At this point, I was delirious but nothing had happened to my now gorged cock.

Doris was first and she bent me over to suck on my balls my Alice softly played with my cock. I started to say something about their husbands coming back and was quickly told to shut up and, "Go with the flow!"

It didn't take long for Alice to take my cock in her mouth, stand up and let Doris start tonguing her pussy. Meanwhile Doris gently repositioned herself and lowered her pussy over my mouth and let me tongue her again. Within minutes I came and not a drop came out of Alice's mouth. She kept sucking until I thought I was full of air and brought me to another erection.

The two ladies then repositioned so that one was sucking on ones cunt and the other had her ass in the air. I didn't know whose ass was up, but I heard Doris say fuck my ass. I slowly slid my cock in to her waiting ass and slowly fucked her until she started moaning and telling me that she loved ass fucking more than pussy fucking.

Meanwhile Alice was busy sucking on Doris's clit and getting her to come over and over while I built to a climax that ended with a rupture of come that started oozing out of Doris's asshole. As she slowly lowered herself to the floor, Alice starting licking the come out her ass and bending over in a position that only said . . . fuck me like that.

My cock was aching and I knew there wasn't another drop of come in me but the "ladies" kept moaning, kissing one another and me and begging for hard massaging of their tits, ass and pussy. I could feel the slippery wetness of come from both of them and the jism that I had put in Doris's ass and pussy, and the two of them just kept kissing and sucking on one another and myself. After a slow relaxing time laying together, I felt my cock begin to twitch and I ran my hand over Alice's ass and pussy and she simply rolled over, got up on her elbows and put her nicely turned ass into the air.

Doris licked Alice's asshole until it was nice and wet, jerked on my cock and got it slippery and then helped me slowly bury it all the way into Alice's hot little ass hole. She squeezed as I slowly buried it completely in her ass hole and then squeezed my cock as I slowly withdrew it until just the tip was left in. This went on for several wonderful moment s and then I buried it fully in her asshole and filled her with come, which immediately began to ooze out of her hole around my cock. Doris quickly got up under us to lick both of us clean.

On and on we went all night fucking and sucking in so many positions that I thought I'd pass out. In the morning as we fucked and sucked ourselves in to awareness I knew that many a night would come in the future for me to enjoy more of these lovely "ladies" and their penchant for anything kinky and rough.

From Voyeur to Stud: An Erotic Story with Group Sex and Cougars

I was just eighteen. A lanky awkward lad that had no objectives or ambitions in life. All I could do was try to concentrate hard on my school work when my mind wandered in such of female bodies. Being awkward I had no girl friends to name. This raised my curiosity and huger as well for opposite members of sex. I had acquired a telescope of good quality and had narrowed down on neighboring houses that had young females. I had even gone far to check locations of the rooms and bathrooms of such females from various optional edge holds of my big house. Believe me I was ingenious enough to find six vantage points. At appointed hours of the day I would perch on these watch places and watch the neighboring females undress to change, take showers, pee and even fuck around with guys or various kinds.

As bonus I could get to see parents and brothers of such females do similar activities with their counterparts. My focus, however, were always these girls of my attention. I, thus, had a ready sample of three preferred females around me. I would mention them in order of their worth.

The first one was not a girl but a woman who had divorced and was living alone. She was Jennifer. Around 28 years in age Jennifer was a stunner. If looks and body could kill it was hers. She had a height of 5' 6" and had a boob size of at least 37. She had a waist of about 26 and hips around 35-almost hour glass. Every morning I saw her undress and shower and ditto in the nights at around 11. Her nipples were like long grapes and cherry red. She had heavy set hips that invited you in their warmth. I always wondered who was fool enough to divorce her. Then I saw her aloofness and her loneliness which made me believe that she had some attitude problems. In the last six months I had not seen her in male company though young persons of locality sighed and moaned behind her back.

While Jennifer was voluptuous, the same could not be said about Mary. She was a girl all right and she had the thinnest body that I could voyeur on. She was plain plaited, 5' 3" in height and may be just around 65 pounds in weight. Her boobs were firm and small white globules and they formed perfect protuberances with her neat and tiny hips. She had a strange lure and passion in her eyes and her voice was the huskiest that I had ever heard. I used to watch her after I had done Jennifer watch.

Third and last was the girl my own age. It was nature's wonder that at my age she had grown to full size and had competing figure to that of Jennifer, however, she lacked the refined and passionate looks of Jennifer and appeared like an over grown careless student who was bubbly and carefree. She had full boobs and a very full set of hips. She wore skirts and tees and her two sets of soft flesh moved invitingly whether she walked or ran. She was a flirtatious girl and I had seen her pet and even fuck with three boys locally. She was Cynthia. I used to watch her as my third choice on most days. I still cannot forget that day when my voyeur set up was busted.

It was a hot afternoon and I was perched atop my small roof house and had setup my telescope right there and was enjoying an afternoon watch. Cynthia's mother was in bed with her boyfriend and he was humping her for a quickee before her father got home. Just when I was wondering where Cynthia was I was tapped on shoulder. I startled and turned around to see Cynthia. I got frightened to see the look of disgust and anger on her face. She screamed, "So you are up to this!"

My lips were locked and I shook all over. My eyes were downcast. Suddenly Cynthia' soft voice comforted me and I found her hands on my crotch. She whispered she would not utter a word to anyone if I did what she said. Before long I hardened in her palms. She massaged me fast and good and then took the lollipop inside. She sucked like a pro. I rubbed and kneaded her boobs and sucked her nipples hard as she lay down on the nearby haystack spreading her legs wide. Soon I had undressed her and was riding her in missionary position. I fucked her mad and came twice inside her. She squealed and, moaned and sighed a lot as we ravaged each other.

As I removed my member from inside her we heard footsteps and watching us like that was Mary. Cynthia and Mary were close buddies and Mary had come looking for Cynthia. Before I could say anything Cynthia giggled and pointed a crooked finger at Mary asking her to join the action. Mary began taking off her clothes. Her slender body came nude. She jumped on me like a panther. She literally began raping me. Her hands massaged my dick hard and fast and she sucked and licked balls and shaft. She made me hard again as Cynthia took shorter turns in between. Mary rode me and got my member nail in her hole. She hopped on me for God knows how many minutes but she made me come fully again. She had a hole that fitted my member so snug that I felt like the two -my dick and her hole were made for each other.

I was screaming with exhaustion as I was inched to my last drops of cum. then Mary wanted to lie down so that I could ride her but I begged them to leave me as I had had enough already. They both agreed but warned me that they would use my services anytime they like or they will expose me to all. I never voyeured the two again as they came regularly for live show till I stayed in that locality. I had no other option but to bow to their warnings.

The very next day. I was exhausted by having two hours of sex with the two girls, and I immediately fell asleep. It was a nice lulling sleep and I slept like a child. My shy virginity had been broken after all and not too late at eighteen. I had experienced two rather young females and while I had some memories of their act my mind immediately compared their bodies and attitudes to those of Jennifer who was at least 15 years their senior. I remembered how I had watched her full beauty undress and her ripe and full body parts spring out. How that maddeningly shapely nudity excited my mind began irking me.

I had a feeling that I had a second class sex while the first class waited next door. I began hatching a plot. My plan was simple. I told my parents that I would be gone for the night to my friend's house some 15 miles off coming Thursday as I had observed that Jennifer left for some kind of work every alternate day starting Tuesday. She probably had an off on Monday. Instead of going to friend's house my plan was to sneak in the house of Jennifer and then in her bedroom so that I could watch her closely as she undressed.

The rest I wanted to leave for the chances to happen as they might. I did just that. Jennifer was out. It was three in afternoon. I had been gone from my neighboring house for twenty minutes. I sneaked in the house and examined it. I found a closet in bedroom that appeared unused as my watching spot. I waited for Jennifer to come back. In the meanwhile I ate from the packet that I had brought along. Nothing happened till 6. Around that time door knob turned and Jennifer came in. She was dressed in a small skirt and a Tee. Her boobs juggled as she moved and I wanted to lift that skirt. She came in bedroom and began to undress. Her skirt fell her tee was taken off and she unhooked her bra. The rosy nipples screamed for my lips as I hardened in the closet. She had her back to me. Her panties came off and full hips came in view. I wanted to snuggle my member in between the divide. I opened the closet more and was on my toes. Suddenly a mouse surprised me and I fell out on floor flat with a loud thump.

Jennifer startled and almost screamed. She subdued it when she saw it was me. Her look was 'what the hell are you doing here at this time?' Our eyes met and she helped me up. Her palms immediately began caressing my hard member. She whispered I knew you would come one day. She freed my member from my pants and began sucking. She sucked well and then she got up and fed her nipples in my lips she fed me like a baby as she continued to stroke me down there. Soon we began deep kissing and tongues got interlaced and then inside. I pushed her to her water bed. Fucking n water bed is rather tough as more stamina is needed. I was a young lad so I began ravaging her hole. She was much wider than the other two girls and she made husky and delicate sounds urging me on. I entered her roughly and began almost raping her. Squeezing her boobs hard and fucking her simultaneously. We made love for 35 minutes before we both came hard. I departed with the promise that every Thursday I would do the same visit her and have her. I was no longer a voyeur.

An Older Woman's Bliss and My First Rim Job: Mature Fetish

The conversation drifted from details about our histories, goals, and current states of affairs. Spanning the better part of an hour it was safe to say things were going well. I had learned that she was less than 6 months removed from a long term marriage. I asked myself, "Is it really going to be this easy? Rebound GILF action, I'll take this."

She left the table to take a phone call, and returned a few minutes later. "Fuck him, fuck him, fuck him. If he were anything like you I would have already had my needs met. Piece of shit. If he thinks he has any chance of landing a new broad with half as tight of a pussy or the sexual appetite I have, he is genuinely insane."

I was taken aback by her comments, but suddenly very intrigued. "So what kind of things are you into, sexually speaking?" I asked in anticipation of what she would be holding back.

"Let me show you a video tonight, it will show you better than I could describe it," she responded with a playful smile. Whatever the surprise was going to be, I knew I was going to be all for it. I've never done anything too wild by Internet standards, but her pure sex appeal and obvious libido had me craving to satisfy Cat's every desire. Our coffee date ended. Enthused, I rushed home to satisfy the need to release my built up load of cum before my balls got any more painful. Fucking blue balls. It used to be prude high school cheerleaders, now it's eager and mature older women. After a quick nap I beat my meat again to my favorite porno I have ever encountered. It involves this greying, aging mother of about 50 years old caressing the cock of her supposed son's best friend. Lasting 25 minutes, she teases him and teases him to keep him on the edge of orgasm. As he shouts in pain, pleasure, whatever it is I can't help but wish for a woman to make me feel like this. Dominated. Controlled. A woman who knows what she is doing and isn't afraid to make me submit to her desires. I continue to watch the video until I find myself on the edge of ejaculation once again, seeing the cum dribble out of the actor's beautiful cock. He wishes to get the orgasm over, to return to a state of normalcy, but the older woman won't let it happen. Knowing what she is doing, his orgasm lasts 5 intense minutes, at the end of which I must clean myself up. Fuck socks. Some guys use those. I use a wife beater. Feels right to me.

I jump into the shower, noticing it is 6:30 pm and I need to be at Cat's house by 7:00. The plan is to feed me. When I arrive there is no food. Slightly upset that I had not eaten since getting coffee I began to feel nervous. These feelings were soon allayed as Cat told me to follow her to the bedroom. What is this, breakfast in bed? Cat turned out the TV located facing her bedroom, an extravagant room surely paid for by the ex-husband. She mentions that she has no jobs, but seems to be doing alright. Before I can complete my thought I see the image of a man getting pounded in the ass by a transsexual woman while he sucks the balls and licks the taint of another man. What the fuck did I just get into? Giggling, Cat says, "Oops, that one just gets me gushing. Don't worry, I don't have a cock, that's why I need you. This is the actual video I wanted to show you."

With a few quick clicks of the remote I saw a man lying down to get a blowjob. His smoking hot wife was at his hips, hands on balls, sucking off him off. She was smoking hot. Maybe this old lady isn't so crazy after all. I started to wonder what the big deal was as the sucking continued. I thought to myself, "Seems pretty vanilla, what's the big deal?"

"Just wait," Cat replied as if she were reading my mind. Sure enough, not 30 seconds later the man had his legs lifted up getting his salad tossed by this blond bombshell. She seemed to be ferociously attacking his ass, balls, and anything that could get the poor man to moan. I thought, "Either this man is a damn good actor or he sure is enjoying himself."

"Has a woman ever given you a rimjob, Steve."

"No, I've never thought about it to be honest with you. Would it be gay if I did?" She dismissed my juvenile thought with a laugh and instructed me to continue watching. What soon unfolded on the screen was the insertion of a rather large black dildo of some sort into the man's ass. Wow. Didn't see that coming. Starting slowly, the woman began working up the speed, depth, and ferocity of the anal pounding. When she was satisfied with this foreplay, she stuck the dildo in, left it there, then jumped onto his cock and rode it like only a porn star knows how. The scene ended with a rather milky, energetic cream pie into the woman's slightly bushy pussy. It was beautiful. I half expected him to stick his face into her crotch and lick up his cum.

"Let's start." Cat knew I was interested and could not tell her no. We kissed, fondled, and held each other's entire bodies in a passionate embrace. We moved into a 69 position. Neither of us wanted to sacrifice our partner's pleasure so it seemed most logical. Her pussy was something else. A sweet aroma, completely bald, nice small lips encasing her vagina. She would probably have a sexy camel toe was one thing I was thinking as I lay there face deep in her womanhood. This was when I noticed her working her way to my balls. Jesus Christ her lips and tongue. I felt like crying as she captured my entire ballsack in her wet mouth. Swishing them around like a quality mouthwash, my body shivered. I could no longer focus on pleasing her. Moving back and forth between my balls and shaft she stroked and sucked on me for at least 10 straight minutes before heading further south. Gently, softly she kissed and tongued around my butt. Slowly working toward the hole itself, I got excited. My rod became even more hard than it already was as she full on made out with my ass. I was in heaven. Pure. Carnal. Heaven. As a 21 year old man trying this for the first time, I wondered what else I was missing in life. Naturally I could not resist as she began working my tight rectum open with her middle finger. She worked it slowly and steadily until it was surprisingly comfortable.

"Have you ever heard of the prostate," she asked?

"What, about cancer?" I asked, barely able to keep my thoughts straight.

"No silly, this." What followed was amazing. Waves crashed through my body as my pleasure receptors became overloaded with feelings. I had no idea what this prostate was, but soon enough I found out as she continuously massaged it while she sucked my throbbing member. Working her way up to two fingers she asked me if I would let her ride my cock. She didn't have to ask twice, but before riding me she did just want the porn star did: she put an anal plug in my ass. It had an extra edge at the bottom, I guess to prevent it from getting lost up there, and it had coarse veins that I could feel bulging against the inside of my ass. But by God it felt good. There I was being fucked by a sex toy while passionately fucking my new sex mentor. It was the best sex ever. We took turns trading positions, complimenting each other's stamina along the way. Her body was something else. A soft, pale white. She had light brown, small nipples affixed onto large fake breasts. Not too fake, and definitely better than any I ever had the pleasure of caressing. With curves like a winding mountain road she continued to blow my mind for what seemed like eternity. It seemed she had brought herself to orgasm a dozen times. Playing with her clit, licking the pussy juice off of her fingers, grabbing my balls and begging me to fuck her harder. It was perfect.

Then she begged me to cum. I had pleasure flowing through my body, and the added sensation of knowing she wanted to please me so bad gave me all the encouragement I need. To send me over the edge she quickly switched holes, shoving my steel-hard penis into her ass. Anal sex was new to me, and the sudden sensation and change in texture riddled me with excitement. Quickly I realized I was wearing no condom. I thought to myself, "Fuck it, we'll try another new thing tonight." What had begun as a tickle coursing from depths of my prostate to the tip of my engorged cock was now turning into an explosion as I shot my seedy load deep into the sweet, soft ass of my new-found lover. Wow. Didn't see that coming. It was safe to say I would be coming back for more, and the look of pure satisfaction in her eyes as she lit up a night-cap cigarette ensured me that she would be wanting it again. As I gently removed the anal plug and went to wash it, Cat asked me to come to her. Briefly, she deep throated the plug, looked me seductively in the eyes and said, "I want to keep your cum protected in me all night with your new toy" as she slid the plug into her asshole. I was instantly erect again, fancying the look of contentment on her face and enjoying her beautiful naked body.

"Not tonight, babe, she remarked, you need to go home. I sleep alone and we're not going to get things mixed up. Put your clothes on. This is sex only, and I approve. Tomorrow I'll show you what I call the blue monster and maybe you can see what my ass tastes like." She kissed me good night as I showed myself to the front door. I think I will have to check out some videos on rimjobs and prostates when I get home, maybe it looks as hot as it feels.

Unexpected Pickup at a Fancy Bar: Getting it on with a Cougar

She had a very strange personality. She was fifty two and still looked as if she was just 32. She had wavy blondes that fell pertly on her shoulders, and she had a lip pout that made her instantaneously a sex oozing puppy. She had blue eyes and a determined chin. Her breasts sagged a little, but they were just the size that would shape out alluringly in her tee. She had a pair of hips that were unusually ripe and full, and she had the uncanny ability to work them... maddening gyrations of that the flesh that seemed to invite you. She had a laugh that almost implied that I am open and you can have me. She was a very good conversationalist and engaged men just like that in deep and warm conversation. She wore rich dress and also displayed a good amount of expensive jewelry. Whenever you passed by her she smelled of a heavenly perfume and when drunk her slurs became so seductive that it was hard for the men around to control themselves.

The moment she landed from the expensive car that she used, she was drowned in a mad rush of men. Each night, she would stagger out with a new and handsome guy who had a very high profile. In fact all those who could take a drink or two in that very expensive bar belonged to very well off backgrounds. She obviously came from a very rich background but no one had ever seen a male accompany her when she arrived. She always came alone. She sat at her prefixed table and ordered two drinks to start with and then it was a merry go round for her as she was widely hosted by men present.

I had recently got promoted in my organization and as a reward for my hard work they had given me a reward cum gift membership of this bar for two months. I was a moderately placed individual. Both in looks and resources. Generally, I would not have ever thought of crossing my class divide and try and date a woman so above my class. But this lady, who was called Annette, entered my dreams. Her ways had seduced me in only one week of my observation of her. I badly pined to uncover her tee and unhook her bra and massage her boobs that hung so alluringly. I wished hard to kiss and suckle those luscious lips that pouted sex. I wished to hug her tight as my hard-on rummaged and made its way between her hip parting. In short I felt that having her would provide me with so much satisfaction that nothing else would ever would. But she was surrounded by a fortress of rich and formidable blokes. Some of them towered inches above me. Others had God like personalities and yet others displayed so much wealth that I was reduced to a mute spectator.

South gets a blast of winter. This was a full blasted winter night. Snow was already five inches thick and the neons that shone at night had a bleary effect about them. I got out of my car and jaunted inside the bar. To my surprise there were only three occupants inside. One was a very old man in his seventies and other a sixty year old woman and the third one ,also a woman, sat with her back to me. She had unfamiliar winter hat on her head and she sat with a glass of champagne. In order to get a glimpse of her I ordered my glass and sat on the stool that was bang opposite her. She was still head down and sipping quietly in the cave of her hairs. Bar lights were dim and it was not possible to see more. Then she suddenly looked up and I almost sprang from my stool as it was none other than Annette. My heart beat hastened as he was looking such a sexy woman in that winter blight. Her warm clothes were not able to hide her ripe and lush curves, and I suddenly grew active in my groin. My loin was firming up more and she smiled with her open lips. She purred me to join her. With hesitation I joined her. She was such a good conversationalist that she had me eating out of her hand very soon. For the next hour she entertained me with volley of small tone questions and anecdotes and I almost refreshed. I had ordered five drinks by the time she held out her hand and languorously invited me,"Come, let us go".

I could not refuse her and went her way. Outside, her chauffeur drove in and we made a speedy exit to her mansion. She lived in a sprawling home and I could only see two rooms in it. One was the living room where I was made to sit and the other was the room where I was called upon to go. Annette had vanished. When I entered that room it was a royal bedroom with a teak double post bed. In that bed lay a nude woman who was just like Annette. I thought it was her, but as yet there was something strange about that women which made me feel that it was not Annette. She was same age, more beautiful and had firmer boobs and riper hips. She looked at me with innocent eyes. I was very hungry for a beautiful woman's body and simply lunged inside the bed covers. I hungrily kissed her and my hands cupped her boobs. Her hands slid to my hard on and she began to massage it slow and good. The more I kissed her the more my hard on grew as she was returning the kisses with full passion. My tongue entered her mouth and went deep inside and she swallowed it like a candy and relished my occupation of her mouth. Then I got to her nipples and I sucked then wet and red. My rasping tongue made them ache and swell like stones.

In passion I began squeezing her boobs as if they had milk in them as I sucked. She kept stroking me unmoving from her face up position. I fingered her pussy for long till it became very wet. Her upper body parts began to heave. Her satiated boobs juggled like hell. Shaking widely with perspiration. Her face became flushed and eyes shone in naked desire. She whispered she wanted to carrot me with her mouth and love me with deep sucks and tongue caresses till I came. She gesticulated with an open mouth to mouth fuck her. I slowly rose and inserted my hard on in her mouth and began wobbling it in and out. Her lips were already thick and she had the passion as if she had not been satiated for long. She tongued shaft and tip to drive me mad. When I bent down to kiss her, her mouth smelt of my man smell, which was strangely languid and exciting. It indicated that the woman had loved you most privately and she has allowed you to do something which is down right special. She kept at it for good 15 minutes and my dick was total bathed in her saliva. Her red lipstick had come off and could be seen smeared on my dick all over. This sight made me go very crazy. I was too full to control it any longer. But then she pinched my tip just a bit to have me quieted.

She slowly and with care threw me out of her mouth. Her eyes were now pleading darting forth from my hard on to her pussy. Her hand invited me to get her down there. By now I was back in the state where I needed a bit more excitement to water her. She seemed very very thirtsy and her hands almost adjusted me down. Her sighs and moans became very loud and she screamed that she wanted me to fuck her hard. I slowly rode her and rammed her hard. I was merciless and it was amazing for me to discover how nicely my engorged member fitted her enlivened pussy. I fucked her so hard that she screamed for more and begged me to remain inside her for long after we had finished. Her wetness indicated to me that I have to do work very fast. I slid inside and outside her. I had never erupted as good in life as this time around. I fucked her two more times and each time I had to ride her and she got screwed in missionary position. I had never observed that she never ever moved during our three fucking sessions. Finally when I wanted to leave, the car came to drop me back. Next night I met a guy at the bar who had gone three or four times with Annette. The secret came out then. Annette came sourcing males for her twin who had been paralyzed below her waist since birth.

She herself had a very handsome husband who was very rich, and she never ever used any males from the bar.

Gangbang, Group Sex, and Double Penetration

Foursome at the Bachelor Party

She looked at the information on the note again. Hotel room 142. She rolled her eyes and hefted her bag on her shoulder as she pressed the doorbell. A man at least six feet tall opened the door. He leaned a well muscled arm against the door frame and smiled down at her. "You the stripper?"

Lynn smirked. "No. I'm here to deliver pizza."

His grin hitched up a notch. "So you're the stripper." She nodded and he pulled back to let her in.

"Are you the groom?" He shook his head and pointed into the room with his thumb.

"Nope," he said, directing her attention to a guy with dark blonde hair. "He is. I'm the best man." He held out his hand for her to shake. "Edward." She cocked an eyebrow.

"Most people don't shake the hand of a stripper, but I'll bite." She took his hand in hers and was surprised by the heat coming from his palm. "Lynn."

"No last name?"

She pushed her way past him, releasing his hand. "No last name. Where's the bathroom? I've got to get changed."

"You couldn't wear your costume over here?"

Lynn shook her head. "I would've been arrested in a heart beat." Edward scanned her up and down. She was wearing a pair of low-rise jeans with a shirt that showed her mid drift. Her high tight breasts had the thin shirt drifting a few inches above her belly button. A pair of flip flops peeked from beneath her pants legs.

A corner of his mouth went up. "I bet you would have. I want to arrest you, and you're dressed like this." He looked into her soft brown eyes. "Looking like you should be a felony." She flipped her hair over her shoulder, used to guys flirting with her.

"Bathroom? I've got to get changed and start dancing, or else there's going to be a riot." Edward scanned the room of eager men and chuckled.

"Down the hall and to your left." Lynn thanked him and walked away, putting an extra swing in her step because she knew every man's eye was on her ass. Edward shook his head appreciatively, watching her heart shaped behind disappear around the corner.

The groom came over and clapped him on the shoulder. "I recognize that look." Edward sank down into a recliner, propping his chin in his palm, waiting for the stripper to reappear.

"You're going to be even more familiar with it after tonight." James smirked.

"It seems like I'm going to have to end my bachelor party earlier than I thought. I want to get back to my fiance anyway. There are a few things I want to test out before the honeymoon anyway." Edward laughed. "If we're wearing the same expression right now, the rest of the guys are going to be disappointed." James shrugged.

"There's a bar only a few minutes from here. I bet they'll be thanking us after we see that girl dance."

"Lynn."

"What?"

"The girl's name is Lynn. And she'll have mine memorized before her night is over. I promise you that." Lynn stepped out from the hallway, a long wrap dress concealing what she would soon reveal.

"I think you might forget what yours is after calling out mine," she said challengingly. Edward's eyes traveled up and down her slim body appreciatively. She was tall, and her long legs took up a good portion of her physique. The dress belted at her waist emphasized a well-muscled, but still slim and narrow rib cage. Sitting above that were breasts that at first seemed too large for such an athletic frame until you got a look at her back view. That heart-shaped, firm bottom, paired with those bouncing c-cups made her the perfect woman in Edward's eyes. The fact that she had seductively tilted brown eyes in an innocent sweet heart face only added to her attractiveness, and the hard on he had making his blue jeans a little too uncomfortable. Lynn gave him a knowing grin and sashayed over to the stereo. She slid a disk into the top and pressed play. She kept her back to the room as the first strains of music dripped from the speakers. The slow beats of rhythmic jazz filled the ears of the eager men as she raised her arms up above her head. She smiled and shook her hair back, letting the tips brush against her bottom.

The thin silk of her pink dress showed every twitch of her muscle as she began to sway side to side. She suddenly turned toward the many eyes watching her.

"Which one of you is the lucky groom?" James raised his hand. She stalked toward him on a pair of black stilettos. She leaned over him, letting him catch a glimpse of her breasts. He sucked in a deep breath when she pushed them toward him in a slow body roll. Edward was having a hard time himself, and he was only getting the back end of the show. But that view was better than the front in his opinion. The light washed through her thin dress, so when she parted her thighs, he could see the space between very clearly. He shifted in his seat as she climbed into James's lap, her thighs parted on each side of his. She slowly leaned her head back until she could see all of the men in the room. Her dark hair was so long that it brushed against the floor.

All he could think about was how powerful her thighs must be if she could hold herself in that position for so long as she undid the ribbon holding her dress together. She let it fall from her shoulders as she thrust her breasts up into the air. Lynn smiled and leaned up into James's lap.

"I don't usually do this, but your friend over there is turning me on." She tossed her hair over her shoulder and pressed her lips against his ear. "I hope your future wife won't be too jealous for what's about to happen, but I think the rest of the guys will enjoy the show." Lynn ran a finger slowly down his neck and hooked it in the collar of his shirt.

"You're not the type to embarrass easily, are you?" James shook his head. "Just think of this as a bonus then." He nodded and Lynn's mischievous smile grew to downright evil. Edward's brow lowered when he noticed the odd exchange between the stripper and his best friend. Then his eyebrows darted right back up to his hairline when Lynn leaned in and kissed James. He expected his friend to move away, but James pushed his tongue into the stripper's mouth. He grabbed her thick hair and pulled her head back, running his mouth down her long neck, biting at her skin. He heard cheers and some startled noises of surprise from some of the other men in the room.

Edward was a bit surprised himself. He'd expected James and his future wife to give up their adventuresome ways when they got married, but from the way James was kissing the stripper, he suspected they would always be the type to have a few extra guests in the bedroom.

Lynn chuckled, slightly startled when James completely stripped her of the wrap dress, tossing it to the floor. "Wow, you really aren't shy are you?"

James shook his head. "I've had my fiancé in rooms even more crowded than this." She raised an eyebrow.

"Really? And are you planning to have me tonight?"

"Depends on how far you're willing to go. Of course, I'll have to call my fiancée first." She felt an unexpected rush of heat and the possibility crossed her mind. She'd never been with a woman before.

"You'd really call her?"

James nodded. "She'll love this as her wedding present. It's nothing like I have prepared for her honeymoon, but I guess it's best to get her warmed up." Lynn nodded excitedly and James reached into his pocket. He grinned up at Lynn as he spoke to his fiancée.

"Hi, baby. I hope you're not having too much fun at your party, because I have something that you might like over here. Remember when we had that blonde and that redhead?" He listened to her response. "What if I told you that I've found you a brunette with those chocolate brown eyes that you like so much?" He laughed. "I knew you'd love it. And wait until you see her. She'll put your yoga teacher to shame."

"James, what's going on?" Edward asked when his friend hung up the phone. James smiled at his best friend, then all of the rest of the guys. "My fiancée is coming over, for a little bit of fun with Lynn here." Edward couldn't help the surge of jealousy that ran through him at the glitter in Lynn's eye when she looked over her shoulder at him.

"I guess we'll leave and give you guys some privacy." Lynn pouted.

"I think the lady wants you to stay." A slow grin spread across Edwards face. The rest of the guys chuckled and one of the men stepped forward. "As much as I like to watch a good show, I like to experience it myself once in awhile."

A couple of the other men nodded. "Come on. I saw a strip joint a few miles up the road." Edward sank back into his seat as the rest of the guys filed out.

"How long is it going to take Jessica to get here?"

"Impatient?" James stroked Lynn's hair back from her shoulder and let his hand drift down to her breasts. He started to slowly grind up against her. "Jessica won't mind if we start without her." He grabbed Lynn by the hips and pressed her down against his erection. He increased the speed of his actions as her body started to roll against his, her breasts pushing up into the air.

"Are you going to let me do all the work?" He asked Edward. Edward shook his head and moved across the room. He stepped behind Lynn so her head rested against his abdomen. He removed her bra, then moved his hands onto her shoulders and down her body until he held a breast in each hand. He slowly rolled her nipples between his fingers, pinching and pulling them until she moaned softly. He bent down and took one in his mouth. Licking it slow at first, then increasing the tempo. The actions of her hips echoed it. She pumped against James while Edward dipped his fingers into her mouth, feeling her tongue roll over his fingers as she panted in pleasure. He suddenly pulled away from her, leaving her gasping for more when he heard a knock at the door. He smiled.

"Wow, she got here fast."

James smiled. "She always moves quickly when it comes to sex." Edward went to the door and opened it for the petite blonde. Her blue eyes sparkled with excitement. She stepped into the room and took in the scene. Her eyes traveled over Lynn's long, athletic body.

"You know exactly what I like, James."

"Is that why you said yes when I asked you to marry me?" She nodded and moved over to him, taking his lips in a fierce kiss.

"Now, let's get this started. We only have a few hours until you make an honest woman out of me. Take your clothes off. You too, Eddy," she threw over her shoulder. James stood up, depositing Lynn into the couch.

"Always so impatient." He was out of his clothes in moments, as was Edward. Jessica slowly stripped herself while Lynn stood mesmerized.

"Do you like what you see?" She smiled at Lynn's inexperienced expression as her eyes travelled over Jessica's body. "Is this your first time with a woman?"

Lynn nodded.

"Alright then. I'm going to have to ask the boys to step back while I help you get rid of that sweet shyness in your eyes." Lynn swallowed hard as Jessica made her way over to her. The petite woman was barely five feet tall and had bouncy, blond curls. With her china blue eyes, she looked just like a doll. But there was nothing doll like about her when she climbed into Lynn's lap. She smiled and started running her hands down herself, letting them linger on her breasts. For a tiny woman, she was well-endowed. Her breasts over filled her hands. She leaned forward and planted a swift kiss against Lynn's lips. Fleeting, almost like the touch of a butterfly. She dropped her breasts and leaned in to do it again. This time Lynn was a little more prepared for her. She opened her mouth when the kiss came and was startled by the shock of pleasure she felt when Jessica's tongue darted into her mouth. Jessica slid her hands behind Lynn's neck as she deepened the kiss, tangling her fingers in the taller woman's chestnut hair. She began to moan when her breasts brushed against Lynn's. James looked over and grinned at the size of Edward's erection. He ran his hand along his own.

"I don't see how you can stand there so still." The muscle worked in Edward's jaw from the effort of not moving across the room and letting one of the women relieve the ache in his dick. Jessica suddenly jerked her head away from Lynn's and grabbed fistfulls of Lynn's hair, shoving her mouth onto her breast. She rolled her body against Lynn until she took the initiative and sucked the swollen bud into her mouth. Lynn was amazed by how fulfilling it was to begin to hear Jessica pant. She grabbed the small woman in her strong arms and pulled at the nipple until she knew it was painful. But being a woman, she knew how much Jessica would like that. Jessica gasped as the pain sent sparks of lust straight to her vagina, striking her with heat.

"I think it's time to call the boys over, don't you?" Lynn nodded and Jessica looked over, crooking her finger at James. He got behind her, ready, knowing what she liked. Jessica smiled at Edward.

"Take my position." His brows scrunched together.

"Kneeling in the chair?" She slid herself down into a kneeling position on the floor.

"Trust me. Your dick will thank you." Edward looked at James and James swept his hand toward Lynn. "Your dick will thank you." Edward knelt in the couch with some trepidation. Jessica parted Lynn's thighs and leaned in, smelling the scent of her heated pussy.

"I know you've been tongued before. No one can resist this." She watched Lynn's vagina twitch at her words and smiled. She heard James kneel on the floor behind her and felt her own pussy begin to drip in anticipation. Her breath begin to come in short little spurts and her hips begin to move before he could even touch her. She loved being so easy to turn on.

"Take me before I come!" James grabbed her hips and shoved himself into her moist vagina, almost losing it himself when she clenched around him. Her fingernails pierced Lynn's thighs, shooting waves up pleasure up into Lynn's cunt. Jessica rocked forward, pressing her breasts between Lynn's knees as James shoved into her powerfully, rocking her small body. The sounds of sex made it impossible for Edward to just sit there. He grabbed Lynn's head and shoved his dick into her panting mouth. She latched onto it eagerly. She leaned her head back against the couch as Edward pumped into her mouth. She could feel the tip of his dick pressing against her throat, and she swallowed, letting the muscles of her throat ripple against him. Edward groaned in ecstasy. He never would have thought fucking a mouth could feel just as good as a cunt. The hot wetness of her mouth created a slick pocket for his straining dick. Jessica salivated as she watched the thick cream seep from between Lynn's legs and soak into the fabric of the couch. She couldn't resist anymore. She licked her tongue out, letting the power of James's thrusts push her forward into Jessica's vagina. "Ahhh. Ahhh. Ah!!"

The sounds of each of their pleasure only amplified it for everyone else. Edward rammed his dick into Lynn's mouth so hard that it rocked her head back while her hips thrust up against Jessica's skillfull tongue. She couldn't describe the pleasure of being filled in both ends. She spread her thighs wide, letting Jessica's tongue slip into the very depths of her center. James rode his fiancee harder than he ever had before, leaning over her back and gripping her waist hard so he could shove into her to the hilt. When that didn't seem to be enough, he grabbed the backs of Lynn's knees, giving himself more leverage.

"Unh!! Unnnnnnn." He pumped in, then pulled all the way out, then shoved into her with such force she screamed in pain against Lynn's swollen vagina.

"Ahhh!!!!!!!!!!" Edward pulled himself out of Lynn's mouth and stepped off of the couch, his legs almost too weak to support him. White cum mixed with saliva dripped from Lynn's wanting mouth. He grabbed her arm and tugged her from the sofa. He threw her across the arm of the couch and took her from behind, grinding her pelvis into the plush of the sofa. He grabbed her legs and lifted her all the way off of the ground, wrapping her legs around him while she still faced away from him. She had to grab the other arm of the couch for support. When he drove into her, she could feel the pressure from the sofa pushing against the front of her vagina, tightening her so that she felt more pleasure than she ever had before.

"Ohhh. Ohh. Ahhhhhhhhhh. Fuck. Fuck me. Fuck me harder." Jessica's pleas blended with her own.

"Fuuuckkkk Meeeeee!!!" James grabbed her legs and spun her around, without removing his dick from her clenching vagina. His hips pumped so quickly that she just bounced in his arms, her breasts slapping against her rib cage.

"Ooooh! Oooh!" Before she could come, James suddenly thrust her away.

"Show me!" She spread her legs out wide for him, shoving her fingers into herself as she kept her eyes on his. "Show me, bitch!!!" She rocked into her fingers. She laid back against the floor so her hips could rise off of the floor. She inserted one finger, then two. Then three. James slid his hand up and down his thick dick, jacking off as Jessica pleasured herself. Edward looked down at the writhing Jessica as Lynn clenched around his dick, an orgasm causing her hips to pump and roll around him. He gasped and collapsed as he released into her, resting against her back as they both turned their heads to watch Jessica make herself come while James's hand worked faster and faster. When Jessica's body started to spasm uncontrollably, he let go of himself and thrust into her, holding himself perfectly still while she convulsed around him, tossing her head from side to side. When she was done, James rammed into her hard, causing her to scream out again.

"Take her." Edward looked at him in confusion. "What?"

"Take her. Roll that bitch over and fuck her from behind."

"But-"

Jessica's bright blue eyes flared open and she rolled onto her stomach. "Take me!" Edward looked at James for permission before he laid his body on top of Jessica's. James nodded as Jessica lifted her ass until he could see the pink of her anus.

"In her ass."

"But-"

"Do it!!" Lynn pulled herself from her exhaustion to watch as Edward slowly slid his dick into Jessica's ass. It was well lubricated from her drenched vagina.

"Get under her Lynn!" James commanded. He'd pulled a bag from a drawer next to the nightstand and now held a riding crop and a fake dick in his hand. The strap on dick had a smaller penis on the side that would rest against her vagina. She licked her lips and walked across the room on shaky legs. James smacked her across the breasts with the riding crop. She flinched in pain, but was surprised that her nipples rose in excited response. Heat pooled between her legs.

"Put this on and get under her." She hesitantly took the dick from him and slid it up onto her legs. She bit her lips in pleasure as the smaller dick slid into her cunt.

Her vagina clenched and unclenched around it. James's eyes scanned up and down her lean body and he came to a decision.

"Edward. Lift my fiancée up. Let her kneel in front of you, but keep fucking her." Edward did what he said, pushing into her until his dick was buried to the hilt in her ass.

"Kneel in front of her, Lynn. What she's feeling, you're going to feel too. I'm going to fuck you so hard that Ed's going to feel it." Lynn found herself panting again. Moving with the small dick in her vagina brought her to her knees.

"Oooh!!" She moaned and grunted as she got on her knees in front of Jessica.

"Ahh. Ahh." She couldn't help grabbing the fake dick and pulling it out a little and pushing it back into herself.

"Ahhhhhhh!" James knelt behind her. He slipped a hand between her legs and drew his slick fingers from her cunt to her anus, moistening her before he took her.

"Have you ever been fucked in the ass before." Lynn shook her head, her long hair brushing against his dick. He closed his eyes in pleasure as he put his dick against her tight little ass. She spread her legs so he could enter more easily. Panting, Jessica leaned forward and licked at Lynn's breasts. She bit the tips, pulling and sucking at them in turn. Edward grunted as he tried to keep up with her eager body, his thighs bumping against hers as fucked her. James was now all the way in Lynn's ass, holding still so she could spread to get used to him. He smacked her thigh with the riding crop, causing her to twitch as she dropped her head back onto his shoulder.

"Do you like that?" She nodded. "Then put your dick in my fiance if you want more." Her tilted brown eyes opened slowly, smoldering as they looked down into the blue ones of the blonde. She lifted her hands and rubbed them down Jessica's body. She hesitated, then slid them between Jessica's legs. She massaged Jessica's cunt with both of her hands, squeezing with her fingers and running her hands over the moist recesses. She slid her hands out and rubbed the scented liquid on to Jessica's pale thighs.

"She's dripping wet," Lynn gasped.

"That's why I'm marrying her," James said proudly.

"She's always dripping wet. Now fuck her." Lynn needed no more prompting. She'd always wondered what it would feel like to stick a dick in a woman. Jessica spread her thighs for her, also giving Edward greater access to her ass. Lynn locked eyes with Edward over Jessica's head as she slid her dick into the gasping woman. God! It felt like she was fucking him and being fucked by him too.

"Ahhh. Ahhhhhhhhhhhhhhhhhhhhhhhh!!" She wrapped her arms around Jessica, their breasts grinding and slapping together as she pounded into her, the small dick on the back of the dildo sending shocks of pleasure through her body as James rode her slowly from behind. She bit into Jessica's shoulder, her hips rotating as she pleasured herself on the small dildo, barely even thinking about how good it felt to Jessica. Grunts and groans filled the air as they each increased the speed of their humping.

"Shit! Ahhh, fuck. That feels so gooooooooood!" Jessica screamed. James kissed her hard, slipping his tongue into her mouth, darting it in and out as he rose up onto his knees to possess Lynn's ass.

"Un! Unnh!"

"Haaa! Haa!" The wet sound of Lynn's dick slipping in and out of Jessica's vagina almost brought them to climax as their hard nipples scraped against the soft flesh of their chests. James smacked his own thigh with the riding crop to bring himself to new heights.

"Ummm! Umg!!" Jessica was the first to come. Her scream filled the air as she collapsed against Lynn. Edward was next, exploding into Jessica. White ejaculation ran from her ass and down her thighs. James collapsed too, pulling his dick out of Lynn so he could drip his ejaculation over her sweet ass. He pulled her back against him and removed the dick from her, replacing it with his fingers. He thrust them in and out of her until her hips began to move against his palm, her crisp pubic curls rubbing against his hand. He dipped two fingers in her, then three. He knocked her legs apart, then slipped in his forth finger, cupping her inside and out.

Edward could only watch in amazement while Jessica slipped her head between Lynn's legs so she could look up and watch Lynn be brought to her culmination. James's ejaculation and Lynn's moisture ran down into her face and she lapped it up, slipping her own hand between her legs. She slipped in two fingers and fucked herself slowly as Lynn began to scream and climax, James's fingers wiggling and rubbing against the smooth walls of her vagina as she rode his palm.

"Ahhh. Fuck. Fuck. Fuuuck!!" Lynn came in a wave of ecstasy. She'd never been so fulfilled. She collapsed to the floor. She couldn't stop touching herself, keeping her nerve endings alive. James moved over to Jessica, pulling her unto his arms and sinking his dick between her thighs, warming it until it rose to his third erection of the night. Edward, breathing hard, moved over to Lynn.

"The night isn't over until you're calling out my name." Lynn laughed weakly, her whole body relaxed from the intense sex.

"I don't know what positions there are left after this."

Edward smiled.

"Trust me. I've been friends with these two for a long time. There's plenty left for us to do. Have you ever scissored?"

"What's that?"

"Have you ever been fucked upside down?" She cocked a slender eyebrow, her tilted eyes beginning to glow with arousal.

"Underwater? Against the wall?"

"That one, yes."

"While your wrists were tied to the ceiling?" She bit her lip, her hand drifting down to see if she was wet again. She gasped. She was. James's eyes glittered as he watched Edward seduce the stripper. He slowly begin to push his dick in and out of the hot space between his fiancee's legs. She let her vagina slide along the top of his dick, knowing that he would take her whenever he wanted. That only increased the anticipation. Her pants began to fill the room, exciting Lynn even more.

"Show him, Lynn. Show him what you want," James encouraged. Lynn grabbed the fake dick by the hilt and rammed it into herself, thrusting her hips so hard that the sound of her flesh hitting the floor filled the room. She rolled onto her stomach so she could have more control of her movements. She pressed her face into the floor as she worked her hips around in a circle, then downwards, grunting and gasping as the dick slid in and out of her wet cunt. James spread his fiance's legs and took her like an animal, humping her so fast all she could do was lie still and take it. Flup. Flup. Slup. The sounds of their sex was so loud that Lynn had to fuck herself even harder to be heard above them.

"Ahh!" She grunted. "Ahhhhhh. Un. Unnnnn. Un!!"

"God, that feels so good," Jessica moaned. "Ahh, fuck. Harder, James. Harder." Lynn's stomach muscles contracted as her cunt ground down onto the dick. Edward could only watch in amazement as her long hair whipped back and forth over her tan shoulders and back. His dick sprang out into the air. He never knew he had the energy to have so much sex in one night. He grabbed Lynn roughly by the arm. She slid the dick out of her vagina and his hot, ready one replaced it. He fucked her in the same animalistic way James took Jessica, pounding her hips against the floor. They both came to climax quickly this time because their nerves had already been waiting for it. They both threw their heads back, grunting as they road it out together.

James shoved hard into Jessica a final time and pulled out of her, knowing how she liked him to watch her orgasm to completion. She slipped her fingers into herself and shivered and quaked until she breathed out hard.

"Best fucking wedding present ever, James." He smiled.

"I'm just glad Edward called that stripper. I've never seen this side of him. He was starting to seem like a little choir boy." Edward was surprised he had the strength left to chuckle.

"Now I can see why you never work out." He laid a hand against his chest.

"Best cardio ever." James slugged his friend in the shoulder and lifted Jessica up onto his lap.

"There's strength training too." Edward raised an eyebrow. James nodded.

"If your little stripper is willing, I've got some books you two might light to see, and this little shop you both might like to visit." Edward looked at Lynn and she smiled that seductive smile, her brown eyes looked like she was ready to go again already.

"I'm willing if you are." He grabbed her wrists. "I can't wait to see you in handcuffs."

Is My Wife A Lesbian?: Threesome with the Face Sitting Swimming Instructor

Matthew decided to take the day off work. He knew his wife would be at home, and he hoped she would finally have sex with him. For the last two months, Layla had been turning away from his advances. Each time, she would feign a headache. Just the thought of sex anymore made Matthew swell. His need was intense.

As Matthew pulled up to the house, he noticed the Chevy Impala that belonged to the swim instructor, Shay, was parked in the driveway. Matthew knew his son was at school, so he was curious why Shay would be at his house right then.

When Matthew walked into the house, he noticed it was eerily quiet. The house was large and often echoed even the smallest of sounds. He thought, maybe Layla and Shay were out by the pool. However, he was unable to find them outside. So, Matthew went up the stairs in search of his wife.

As he stepped near his bedroom door, he could hear laughter from behind the shut door. Matthew's curiosity began to peak. He slowly opened the door, unsure what the women could possibly be doing in the bedroom.

As he slowly opened the door, he could hear the shower running. More giggles quickly filled the room. The thought of Layla or Shay in the shower made his cock swell and pulse. He quickly tried to erase the thought from his mind. Matthew was sure there was a more logical explanation. As he walked toward the bathroom door, he could hear more giggling coming from inside. Matthew reached his hand up to knock on the door, but stopped when he heard his wife, Layla moan in pleasure.

Matthew gently opened the door and peeked inside. He could make out the figures of the two women inside the shower stall. Both were breathing heavily, and Layla was still moaning with pleasure. With little thought, Matthew walked over to the shower door and quickly pulled it open.

In the shower, his wife had her arms tied around the shower head. Shay was kneeled on the floor eating Layla's cunt. Neither Shay nor Layla at first noticed Matthew watching. Layla's nipples were hard and erect, water flowing off them.

She was standing with her eyes closed, lost in satisfaction that Shay was providing. Shay slowly began to crawl along Layla's body, trailing along it with her tongue until she found Layla's nipples. When she began to suck on her nipples, she inserted her finger deep into Layla. Layla gave out a cry and opened her eyes.

Matthew sucked in a gasp and looked Layla in the eyes. Layla did not seem disturbed. Instead she whispered in Shay's ear. Shay untied Layla's arms, then quickly turned around and reached her arms out toward Matthew. He stood in disbelief at the scene he was witnessing, all the while aware of his bulging erection. Shay stared deeply into Matthew's eyes and began to unbutton his shirt. Layla, meanwhile, had begun to pleasure herself, all without taking her eyes off the situation unfolding with her husband and Shay.

When Shay reached down to unbutton Matthew's pants, she whispered into his ear, "I see you've enjoyed the show." Then she ran her tongue down his ear and down his chest, all while unbuttoning his pants. When Matthew's pants fell to the ground, Shay firmly grabbed his rock-hard cock and slowly placed her wet lips upon it. She ran her tongue round and round the tip before plunging it deeply into her throat. Matthew let out a low, deep moan. His eyes wide open, he met the gaze of his wife. Layla was licking her lips and moaning at the scene.

Much to Matthew's surprise, Layla knelt beside Shay and said, "I want a turn." Shay slowly removed her lips from around Matthew's shaft and began to rub the tip of it around her wet face. Layla leaned over and proceeded to lick Matthew's hard, bulging cock. Shay leaned over to Layla and began to French kiss. When they finished, Shay rubbed Matthew's dick on Layla's lips. Layla looked up at her husband and inquired, "Are you having as much fun as we are?" Matthew could not form a reply before Layla placed her wet, warm mouth around his dick. Matthew let out another moan of pleasure. Shay knelt behind Layla and simultaneously licked her cunt. The girls were moving together in a slow, deliberate motion.

Matthew realized if he didn't calm the situation down a bit, it would be over too soon. So, he stepped back from the women, both barely noticing his absence in their own pleasure and told them both, "Follow me!" He walked into the bedroom, rock hard cock leading the way. Both women ran and jumped on the bed, their wet bodies glistening in the afternoon sunlight. Both were staring straight at Matthew as he approached the bed.

Layla reached into the nightstand and pulls out a dildo. She begins to rub it all over her body before placing it inside herself. She let out a groan as Shay began to suck her nipples. Feeling left out, Matthew jumps onto the bed and licks his way up to Shay's cunt. It is warm, wet, and welcoming. Layla pushes him away from Shay, wagging her finger at him. She tells Matthew, "You are mine, dear husband." Layla then takes the dildo slowly from her cunt and rubs it on Matthew's lips. "Want a taste?" she asked. Shay takes the dildo and says, "My turn." She lays flat on the bed and slowly rubs it down her body to her perfectly shaved cunt. Layla straddles Shay and begins to suck and pull on her nipples, eliciting a moan from everyone. Matthew climbs behind Layla and quickly inserts himself. Before he can manage to thrust twice inside of his wife, she quickly rises and pushes Matthew down on the bed. Shay climbs on top of Matthew's head, placing her cunt within tongue reach for him.

At the same time, Matthew felt Layla mount him from top. Matthew tried to concentrate on trying to please Shay, but it was near impossible with the things Layla was doing to him. She leaned back and placed Matthew's balls in her hand. She began to massage them as she rode up and down on his cock. Meanwhile, Shay was screaming out with pleasure. Just as Matthew was about to cum, he heard both girls scream out simultaneously in orgasm. Matthew felt the wet juices of his wife sliding down his balls and the sweet juices from Shay's cunt covering his face. Matthew thrust hard and deep, finally reaching orgasm. His body twitched and his toes curled. Both girls were taking turns licking the cum off of his cock.

Matthew almost passed out with delight. Shay casually got up from the bed and began putting her clothes back on. Layla continued to lick and suck on Matthew's cock until it finally fell limp. Shay waved bye and said, "We should do this again." Then she quickly exited the house. Layla and Matthew looked at each other, both a little surprised and embarrassed. "What just happened?" said Matthew. Layla smiled brightly and winked at Matthew as she got up out of the bed.

"I need a shower. Want to join me?" asked Layla. Matthew jumped out of the bed and followed her back into the bathroom.

Barely Legal Beginnings: Graduation Party Jacuzzi Hand Jobs

I closed the door slowly behind us as we stepped into the room. She looked at me gingerly with a slight curl in her smile and I knew she was just as ready as I was. With the party in full swing downstairs we had the perfect cover to do absolutely whatever we wanted in this room of Jake's house, and the bulge in my pants couldn't wait much longer. I had been waiting for this chance with Courtney ever since I accidentally dropped my macaroni on her at lunch sophomore year in college. At the time I was such a quiet kid and could never see myself even speaking to her, and to her I was just that weird guy who hit her with macaroni. I tried my best to become more outgoing in the years to come and branch out to different friend groups and by the end of high school I had finally made it into the group of popular kids.

Well, really all I did was get brought into the group by Tony, one of my friends who was incredibly athletic and just exuded confidence. This was the night of graduation, and the first graduation party. As soon as I arrived at the party, I knew what my only plan for the night was. Courtney was one of my closest friends now. We started talking at the beginning of senior year and since then we just really clicked and had so much in common. Unfortunately, she had a boyfriend for most of the year and I was just like a brother to her and nothing else.

Over the past month, I've been helping Courtney through a terrible breakup (without letting her know how excited that made me) and trying to tell her everything would be okay. We've had some drunken nights together that never really led to much, but I've heard from some of her friends that she always thought I was cute but not really her type. This party was going to change all of that. As soon as I walked in, I headed straight for the group that Courtney was standing in. Everyone was about to do their second round of shots and Courtney was clearly already very tipsy. I walked up behind her and tapped her shoulder, her eyes bulging when she saw that I had shown up.

"I had no idea you were coming!" she exclaimed while throwing her hands in to the air and resting them around my head. Her embrace was warm and all I could focus on was her firm breasts pressing against my chest and the smell of liquor coming from her.

"I couldn't miss our first graduation party. What am I? A loser?" She gave me a cheeky grin knowing that the drinking scene wasn't my favorite and that I wasn't a regular attendee of most parties. After we caught up and had a few drinks, everyone slowly moved outside where the rest of the party was taking place. Jake had plenty of space for a great party considering both of his parents were lawyers. The open backyard contained a huge pool with a Jacuzzi as well as a volleyball court and grill.

"Last one in is cleaning up the kitchen!" I hear Courtney scream out behind me, before quickly throwing off her jean shorts revealing a lacy thong bikini and jumping into the pool with her shirt on. Not wanting to give any other guys the chance, I quickly cannonballed in after her without even taking off my shirt. As I hit the water, I feel the rush of freezing water and quickly tried to surface to catch my breath. As I wiped the water from my eyes, I see Courtney in front of me taking off her white laced t-shirt. When I first met her during the macaroni incident, she was a B-cup at the most. After a whole lot of puberty later she had two voluptuous D-cups that other girls could only dream of. She slid off her soaked t-shirt to reveal the smallest no-strap bikini top I have ever seen, lacy and pink to match her thong. The moonlight perfectly accentuated her perky breasts as they bounced around in the water, seemingly about to burst out of the tight bikini top if Courtney weren't careful.

Two of the football guys both screamed out that they were coming in and jumped on either side of me and Courtney, causing us to both move towards each other to avoid the splash. As we get closer my hand slightly brushed against her ass, sending a shock through my entire body. Courtney was a conservative girl, so seeing her in such little clothing was such a huge surprise that I couldn't help but get a little hard from having touched her exposed ass like that. Courtney was a swimmer and caught all the guys attention with how much she went to the gym and toned her legs (and obviously her ass). Soon the pool got crowded with plenty more guys and girls jumping into the freezing water. Jake put on some music and everyone was having a great time hanging out in the water.

Ever since I got in, I couldn't ignore the bulge in my pants that just seemed to get bigger and bigger as time passed, every time I stood next to Courtney. One of the girls shouts "Chicken!" and everyone runs around in chaos looking for a partner. Before I know it, I have two hands on my shoulder as Courtney screams "Let me up!" and I have no choice but to bend down and let her on. Courtney wasn't the lightest girl but after two years of conditioning for football it wasn't much trouble to lift her on my shoulders. With each of my hands I gave her thighs a firm grip and was taken aback by how fit she was. I was instantly distracted by the warm heat of her pussy against the back of my neck, which seemed odd for how freezing the pool was. Courtney must have noticed where my attention was because she leaned down to whisper in my ear and said, "Sorry, the alcohol is kicking in and I'm a little wet."

My brain instantly lost all control. Never in our relationship had we ever shared anything sexual about each other, especially when she had a boyfriend and always treated me like a brother. Was she wet because of me? Was it just the alcohol? I feel an instant rush of adrenaline and can't focus. Everyone starts the game of Chicken and begins running headfirst into each other trying to knock the opposing team over. Surprisingly, Courtney and I lasted until the last three teams, but I was no match for some of the more muscular football guys who almost immediately tipped us over. I lost my balance and Courtney and I went tumbling backwards, and I managed to turn myself around to try and catch her and make sure she didn't hit anyone, in the chaos we both ended up under the water and my head was resting in between her amazing breasts.

Time froze and I forgot where I was, my entire focus was on her amazing body and how this was the closest I had ever been to her. I quickly snap awake and rise to the surface pulling Courtney along with me. "Like what you see?" Courtney teased as my entire face glowed tomato red. I turned away, looking embarrassed and let out a defeated, "I don't know what you're talking about," but it was very clear she knew that I was staring.

After all, she was one of the hottest girls at our entire high school and she knew it. After the game of chicken ended, everyone moved to the Jacuzzi to recuperate. I was one of the first to move so I made sure to get a seat next to Courtney who was being much quieter now than before when we were in the pool. Everyone was talking and drinking beers when suddenly, I glance to my left to see Courtney's beautiful green eyes staring right at mine. As soon as our eyes lock, she quickly looks away with a slight blush on each cheek, and I asked, "You okay?"

She leaned in close to my ear and said, "I've got something I have to do." Not knowing what she could have meant by that, I sank back into my seat keeping a close eye on her every movement. The Jacuzzi was full and the backyard was dark after the clouds covered the little moonlight that was outside, so I couldn't really see Courtney enough to know what she was doing. She sinks down into the water until the water is up to her breasts, and I feel a hand graze over mine. Completely dumbfounded, I didn't even know what to say. Was she making a move on me? Before I even had the time to rationalize the situation her hand continued past my hand and started to creep across my lap. Her hand brushed across my now throbbing cock and I jolted a little bit, not knowing what was about to happen. Her hand stopped abruptly for a moment, then continued to grasp my hard cock that was resting up against my left leg. The entire time we were both staring deeply at each other and ignoring the entire Jacuzzi full of people around us.

I felt her hand start to slowly stroke my cock up and down, every single movement feeling amazing. She smiled shyly and gave me a wink as she shifted her body position. Her hand left my cock and started moving up my waist to go under my trunks, and I used my hand to grab hers. I looked at her intently and say "Not yet" to let her know that I wanted this but not in a Jacuzzi with a bunch of other people. She nodded in agreement and motioned towards the door with her head. Silently, we both raised ourselves out of the water and made our way inside, unnoticed by the crowd of people we left behind.

She grabbed my hand and led me to the stairs on the other side of the kitchen, flashing me a quick smile as we passed two other girls who had absolutely no clue what was happening. We made our way up the stairs, my eyes focused heavily on the sway of her ass as she moved up each step. Still leading my hand, she moved it towards her hip and guided my fingers across her thong and on to her ass as I give it a squeeze. I heard a soft moan escape her as we continued moving upstairs. We quickly made our way into what seemed to be a relatively unused room that was most likely a guest room. As she moved towards the bed, I make sure to close and lock the door behind me, refusing to look away from her body for even a second. As she reached the foot of the bed, she turned around while fumbling behind her back at the straps to her bikini. Without saying a word, I quickly walk up to her and run a hand down her shoulder and on to the straps to undo them for her.

In front of both of us, a full-length mirror revealed the most beautiful moment I've ever seen as the tight bikini top started to give way. Her huge breasts break free from the grip of the top sending it straight to the floor as her clearly hard nipples bounce free. She turns to me, one hand reaching out for the rim of my trunks and the other grasping my hand to lead me to her nipple. I reach out and give a firm grip to her amazing breast, feeling so victorious of finally achieving this moment I had waited for so long. Her other hands ran down past the waistband of my trunks, gripping the base of my bare and throbbing cock between her fingers. My gaze left her beautiful green eyes and moved towards her breasts as well as her soft hand slowly rubbing my cock, a sight I had only dreamed of days before.

Business Conference Threesome: Two Girls, One Guy, Three Orgasms

Looking back at it now, it was just a business trip. That was all it was supposed to be. I had no idea what this seemingly innocent trip was going to turn into. My company (one of those internet companies, where no one really knows how they make their money, nor did I for that matter) was sending me to Atlantic City for some sort of business. I did not really know how or what I supposed to do, outside of a presentation I had worked on several months earlier.

The trip, like all traveling these days, had taken a lot out of me. All I really wanted to do was check into my room and get some rest. After getting out of my cab from the airport, the hotel seemed inviting enough. Many people were out on the streets, given the time of day. The sun had not yet set, and people were out doing what people do in Atlantic City. I had no idea of what was going to come my way.

As I walked up to the front desk, I noticed the hotel bar off to my right. It seemed like every other hotel bar I had ever seemed before. A fire place in the middle of the room had a fire going. A sign mentioning some convention caught my eye. Some sort of other convention was going on this same week. In the back of my mind, I caught myself thinking that surely there would be at least one single girl attending this convention. She would probably be looking for some sort of one-nighter here in Atlantic City. This thought quickly left my mind when the desk worker started talking.

The attendant was a woman in her mid-40s. She was one of those women who looked like she was hot back in her day. However, the fast living of Atlantic City had taken its toll on her. She tried to small talk, mentioning that I had been upgraded to the king size bed. This was an added bonus given my 6 foot, 5 inch, 280 pound frame. I was always told that women liked tall, big men, but I never found this to be true. After getting my room key, I proceeded to the elevator, and headed to my room.

The room was alright as far as rooms go. Nothing fancy, but decent for a room in Atlantic City. I figured I was due a shower before grabbing a drink down at the hotel bar. I unbuttoned my Brooks Brother button up and undid my pants. The feeling of the air conditioner on my body felt good. It was a hot, muggy day here.

Not bad for the middle of July, but still hot. I started the shower, making it hot for such a hot day. The steam rose from the shower and filled the bath room. The thought of some single broad looking for her one night stand filled my head again.

I decided to go with cargos and a t-shirt, nothing too fancy given that my plan was just to grab a drink and head to bed. On the elevator, two middle aged women mentioned that they were there for the convention. Something about business women in 2016 or something. I shrugged them off and exited the elevator. I walked by the front desk, where that same woman was in the back doing something. Probably trying to look busy, when actually she was just wasting time.

I sat down at the bar, and the bartender asked what I would like. He was probably 30-something, the sun aging him more than that. Whisky sour is my favorite. Today seemed like a whisky sour kind of day. And that's when I noticed those two. Two women sitting down the row of chairs from me. One of them looked to be 25 or so. She was a blonde. Her hair was long and flowing over her shoulders. She was pretty by anyone's definition. The other had dark hair. She was pretty too. They both seemed flirty with the bartender. That kind of flirty that is looking for a free drink.

All of sudden, I caught the blonde staring at me. At least I thought so. She said, "What are you doing here this week?"

"Business," I said, "business for work." She looked at me like I had a giant dick on my forehead. Then she did something I did not expect. She slowly turned in her chair towards me. She had on a little black skirt. She did not try to keep her legs together. From my view, I could see her little yellow underwear. Her crotch looked delicious. Her panties pressed against her pussy, and I could make out the outline of her lips. The other girl seemed to know what was going on. She playfully looked over the other's shoulder.

"Do you see anything you like?" she asked.

"Yes, yes I do," I replied. She then came over and grabbed me by the hand.

"Then we should all go to our room," she said. Once in the room, their clothes were off. I grabbed the blonde by her shoulders and ran my finger across her underwear. I could feel the warmth from her as I ran my fingers along her pussy. The brunette joined us. I felt her crotch too. Next thing I knew, she was on top of me. My dick was in her pussy. The brunette sat on my face.

The room smelled like sex as she rode me up and down. Within a few minutes I could feel her cream running down my dick. The other girl's pussy was grinding my face. Her juice was flowing onto my mouth. She was moaning more and more as she went faster. I did not how much longer I could go. None of us were concerned that I did not have a condom on. Within seconds, I was about to cum. I came inside of her. The brunette continued riding myself, announcing she was going to cum.

All three of us had an orgasm. The room smelled like freshly fucked pussy. The girls simply put their clothes on and left. It was over. As fast as it started, it was over. My business trip was a success. It was off for my presentation in the morning.

Threesome with Two Women: DP with a Strap-On

I got into the hobby with a goal in mind; to have my first duo. I didn't want just any duo though, so I began "auditions" if you will, to find the perfect girls for me. Ashley has a sexy petite body and a knack for detail and knowing what you need. Lily has a killer body and an appetite for sex while looking deceivingly demure.

I first met Ashley back in August, and she immediately became the focus of all my thoughts. Her attention to detail is what sets her apart from the rest. Then I met Lily in September, and I knew they would fit perfectly together even though they had never met.

So in the months that followed several attempts were made to get the two of them together, but our schedules never quite lined up. Finally everything lined up last month and it was everything I'd hoped it would be and then some.

Ashley is a world traveler, each meeting is an investment in time and the dividends are her undivided attention to your every desire. Based on other times I've seen her, I believe she has the ability to become anyone you want her to be, and she pulls off the slutty rocker chic look and personality that I love so well. Ok, enough preamble.

Setting up with Lily & Ashley was actually pretty easy, I booked a room for us to play in so once we all committed to a date and time I knew I could count on them. They are both very communicative in the time leading up to the date so you are never left in the dark.

I met Ashley at the hotel bar at the set time and Lily was scheduled to arrive a half hour later. Being that it was Thursday afternoon, the bar was almost empty. Ashley greeted me as always, with a sexy smile, bright eyes and a very sensual long kiss. She has the softest tongue but isn't shy about using it. She was dressed in mostly black as I like and even remembered to wear a cute pink collar that I had jokingly mentioned the last time we met. Since we were waiting on Lily, we ordered some drinks. We both got Jack & Coke, she took some in her mouth and let me suck it out as we sat there and she swayed to the rock music I had playing on the jukebox.

We moved to a dark corner of the bar and I pulled her top down to play with her perky pink nipples. After some more swapping Jack, she got under the table and gave me a very aggressive but quick blowjob, let me tell you, this girl has absolutely no gag reflex. In a previous meeting I face-fucked her pretty hard and came straight down her throat, she never gagged, I was in heaven. A text from Lily and a few minutes later we all went to the room.

Ashley let her in as I followed, I had a raging hard on in anticipation of the events about to unfold. They introduced themselves and shared a sexy kiss before coming to me. We had a short 3-way kiss, Lily quickly got naked and Ashley and I commented about her beautiful Venus De Milo type body. Soon they were both on their knees sharing my cock. Both are aggressive deep throaters and they took turns.

They followed my every direction, both swirling their tongues around the head of my cock as if they were making love to it with their mouths. I was already on visual and sensory over load at this point, so we took a break to all get naked and in bed. Something I had heard about in college, champagne waterfalls, sounds fun, but in practice it's awkward and messy, but still fun. I had Lily sit over my face as Ashley dribbled Jack & Coke down Lily's body from her chest into my mouth, problem was just as much got into my eyes so we quickly abandoned that idea. The next several hours were a blur.

I made sure to check off the few things I wanted to do, Lily riding my face and Ashley riding my cock while they both made out. I heard Ashley ask her if my tongue was in her ass, she said yea, then Ashley came around and said 'does her ass taste good?' then sucked my tongue. Damn I love that dirty girl.

Ashley brought some various dildos, she doesn't do anal but Lily loves it, so I thought some double penetration was in order. Lily got on top of me in reverse cowgirl and Ashley slowly guided my cock into Lily's creamy white ass while Ashley was playing with her strap on and entered her pussy. Several times I could feel what Ashley was doing inside Lily on my cock, incredible!

Lily laid back on me and started saying 'Im gonna cum', I squeezed her tits tight as Ashley and I worked her over front and back until she was a hot sweaty mess laying on top of me. We took a short breather, had some more Jack swapping, now it was time for the finale, double throat job with them sharing my cum. We worked up to it, one doing deep throat while sloppily kissing the other and them switching places. I was way over stimulated, so I really had to focus to get off. I think Ashley sensed that and started with some hot dirty talk to get me there. When I finally got close, Ashley joined her between my legs and they both went porn star crazy sharing my cum, tongues and cum sliding all over their faces.

The time of my life. We slept a little while in a sticky pile, Lily had other obligations so she got dressed and left, but Ashley and I enjoyed winding down together. She cleaned me up but we left that room a mess.

Rompero: Nearly Fucked to Death by Latinas

It was a Saturday afternoon – one of those pointless lazy days which seem to drag on forever, hot outside but grey, muggy, and overcast. Without money. The day just seemed lifeless. *What is the point of a Saturday afternoon with no cash to spend? I couldn't even go to my local bar to check out the talent, all my amigos and girlfriends were out of town… after all, who wants to hang with a guy like me who's broke and pissed off?* I thought angrily. Why let this empty afternoon get me down when I could go out and make myself something to do? Such as finding some gorgeous Latino ladies with huge tits to talk with? I knew the day would eventually pass into evening, and if by then I was still sitting down staring at the TV, I would become depressed as well as start suffering that aching pain from overloaded love cream which had been building up in my ballsack since Friday. I was aching for a decent fuck.

Anyway, I'm telling you this so you know, whenever you are bored or unhappy or "overloaded," OK fine, let off some steam with a copy of *your magazine here,* but hey why not rather go out and find yourself some sweet pumpum to let your steam off for you? And if she pays for the drinks, then so much the better! Walking down a nice suburban promenade by the sea is always a good spot to find beautiful women; they tend to walk their dogs alone if they've broken up with a boyfriend and you can tell by the look in their eyes that they haven't had a decent fuck for ages, sometimes not even for years if their partner was a loser. The road along the sea-front was long, a wide walkway with lots of trees, flowerbeds and the usual jam of parked cars sitting outside sea-side apartments, hotels, restaurants, and big shore-houses – just the place to find myself a pretty, intelligent woman with the same thoughts on her mind as mine. There must have been many people passing through, visiting from out of town this afternoon since the cars belied their owners' statuses. BMWs, Mercedes, Bentleys, Aston Martins, and people-carriers stuffed into parking spaces end-to-end. Perfect! There were plenty of hotties and shorties about, anxious, stressing their exes for cash, putting the kids to bed and watching TV with a bottle of wine, putting their vy on charge, or just waiting for someone horny and good-looking chap like me to come along and rescue their day.

"Excuse me, I'm lost. Do you know the Institute for the Study of the Americas? I'm late and my friends told me it was nearby, next to one of these hotels?"

Her question went almost uncomprehended as I turned towards her heavily accented voice, expecting to see an elderly lady in a gown, holding a bible. Instead, my jaw dropped as I noticed her near-flawless curves, bare midriff, massive cleavage, and strong yet delicately balanced features with the trademark Hispanic pout formed by exotic cupid-bow lips. Early 20s, I guessed, an academic or wealthy city-girl on a weekend journey to the sea-side to break the monotony of the grimy city streets and their inbred inhabitants. But her eyes! As they reached mine, the light flashed within for just a fraction of a second and the daylight became fleetingly gloomy and dark, and in her face I beheld her inner aura, the power of a creature divine, searching my heart and soul with fingers of pure spirit for bad intentions. She found none, but detected a vague mirroring of her own life and desires. Our mutual surprise mellowed to a calmness inside, the knowing of what was to come... the understanding that we would walk and explore the unknown together... at least until the next sunrise. My heart pounded at the thought of these hours to come.

Take it slowly, I thought to myself. *Don't rush this one. Savour the time and company that fate or the powers-that-be have blessed you with.* I saw the tell-tale giveaway signs of her lust, her issue of a deathly boring Sunday now solved, her nipples becoming erect and poking through her thin blouse like exquisite buttons created by a Divine designer who knew and appreciated real beauty. I could smell her musky scent of sex carried on the humid air; it wafted at my senses as it dawned on us that I was one of the few males who was her sexual equal, perhaps even superior.

"Umm. actually I don't know the place, but I'd be happy to help you find it..." I replied, "Uhhh you wanted, uhh, a ummm the..." My voice faltered totally, and I felt ashamed at forcing her to take the upper hand. I was thrown off-guard by thoughts of giving her sex, "Esta loca... dale heuvo...," and I nearly blurted it out loud. This lady could read me like a book, and I had hardly started communicating with her. A sudden pang of doubt gnawed at me. Would she play with me like a cat toying with a piece of string, until she became bored and discarded me? It wasn't usually this way. I had proved to myself time and time again that I was a veritable expert at connecting with the opposite sex. This one was different however, not your average rich-bitch with a BMW and a phony PhD in economics looking for some wealthy do-gooders to hang with, to earn some brownie-points for her next women's lib conference. No. Just one glance told me what I needed to know. She was a real gal, a chavabella, a bad senorita who had somehow made it good, a nena who knew the streets, maybe had even run them, who had discovered her bruja muchacha powers and mastered them. OK, not a gang-leader, but still a lady who knew how to work people, maybe more so than a lot of so-called alpha-males. A Real Puta. And she was gorgeous.

She flashed a grin at the sound of my halting voice, showing pearly-white teeth and the beauty of her cocoa-complexion matched that unmistakable facial profile . A Latina! A bona-fide South American Goddess – Hispanic with just a touch of indigenous Aztec or Afro-Caribbean, her trademark black hair flowing behind her like a dark river as she tossed her head back with that Amazonian 110%-in-control poise. 5"10, tall for a Latina girl, but still not lanky. She was perfectly formed, with a straight stance, wide hips, slim mid-riff, and a perfect pair of guanabanas; nipples poking through her skin-tight top like riveting eye-magnets. Skin the colour of light chocolate. A vision of beauty, old enough to know it; but young enough still to be taught a lesson or two by someone who knew how to handle her the right way. By someone who knew how to press all her right buttons. Someone who knew the lingo, the reality of trying to make it good in a world gone bad, who knew the code of the streets. Me.

"Hey guey!" my eyes had been fixed on those bulging chiches for so long, I hadn't noticed my amigo Tonio strolling towards us, probably with the exact intent as I had: to check out this piece of work, this Chica, this Puta. "Where's the party, man?" Only he hadn't been invited to any party, yet. Tonio spoke the Colombian and Brazilian tongues like a native, and he was the type of man who could never grow bored with a pair of tetas. As much as I needed company, three was a crowd, yet I might have to bring him in for the cash. I was horny, desperate for a fuck, but I was broke and brokesters don't tend to gain access to the Chocha until they've proven their prowess with their arma and correrse.

"This your lady friend? What's a beautiful senora like you doing with Marco here? Won't you introduce us?" Tonio tried the direct approach, but he had missed the earlier connection between myself and my mysterious Tía buena. We didn't even know each other's names. We probably didn't need to. "That won't be necessary. Marco and I are heading to the Institute to meet my sisters, and I'm late." Trying to hide his envy, Tonio's eyes were speedily undressing my muchacha. I nearly laughed out loud at his gawping mouth as he clocked her chichis bulging through her blouse. The outline of her underwear could be seen in the daylight, and her thin black leggings did nothing but accentuate her culo; I noticed the lips of her raja as she waggled her ass from side to side while she strolled off, arm locked with mine. Tagging alongside, Tonio was chatting to me. "What is it about hot and spicy brown ass chicks?! Can't resist em'. My lil' bro was not at his absolute best the other day, and then there was this hot ass Puta passing by, all of a sudden I got a boner." My new companiana smiled coyly at me and remained silent. All three of us would be going to meet the sisterhood at this Institute; it didn't take a genius to work that out.

There were 9 women in the Institute of the Americas. Nine young senoras who were politically active in working for the emancipation of Latina women. Nine members of the sisterhood, my senora, Tonio and myself. The building was otherwise empty, apart from the security guard, another senora from Cuba who had a tight black uniform and a night-stick. She looked to be the most dangerous person in the room, 13 in all. Most of the buffet had been eaten or taken away, but in the corner of the hall I spotted a sight for sore eyes, bottles of wine chilling in a cooler cabinet or waiting to be enjoyed with the evening's entertainment. What was puzzling was how there was only us 13 and not the usual milling throng of older financiers, politicians, and academics dragging along their reluctant spouses, the kind of people whose only job is to be asked for money for one cause or another. This was definitely not your usual political function, whether the invites had not been sent properly or because nobody wanted to know, and these senoras were not happy at having their evening wasted. The gleam in their eyes as they spotted myself and Tonio spoke volumes about how their day had gone wrong, and they wanted to make up for lost time. These chicas, supposedly political social feminists, were all for supporting women on top that's for sure — on top all night long!

"You've read my book, right?" I was introduced to the senora closest to me, Anita. "The Fight for Freedom and Equal Rights for oppressed women in the Latin Americas?"

"Lo siento, I haven't, Anita..."

"Here, have a look. We've all contributed our stories, my sisters and I. Women in places like Cuba, Mexico, Colombia, Peru, we are united against the injustices we face every day. I'm sure you'd know this already if you came here with my sister

Daniela – she's our youngest. She started us all up in the academic world, since she's the smartest."

I looked at the book. All nine authors were listed in the cover. They were sisters all right – the real deal, a complete family of senoras, all gorgeous and for some reason I couldn't work out, seemingly free from the usual stresses of having to work like crazy to support their family. "They must be working hard with these books," I thought out loud, and straight away Daniela, still escorting me around the room, snatched the book away and laughed.

"Let's not worry about the books. Let's have a drink!" Glasses filled, we toasted each other "Salud!" It was only a matter of time before the inevitable happened, my dick by now was aching with pain and felt like it was going to burst if he didn't feel some action. Half-running, half-dragging me alone into an office, Daniela's blouse slipped off in a single fluid movement revealing to my eyes at last her perfect pair, her chiches supported in a white push-up bra. I had seen many a pair of pumpkins in my time, but her's were perfection. It was all I could do to stop myself there and then from having a tit-wank off them and leaving her with a lovely pearl necklace to deal with. Then her leggings came off, like a second skin they revealed her sculptured curves, her culo-cheeks making a line of passion going right up to her lower back, with tattooed angel's wings on her shoulder-blades. That was it. I could wait no longer. Eyes closed, I felt her ease her pechos over the bulge of my now naked cock and start to move, rocking gently at first and then gaining momentum.

"Slowly!" I gasped "Despacio!" I had to beg her. This was going to be a long night.

While she was using her guanabanas the best way she could, I realized that even if I eased my load all over her, once, twice, three times, she was so hot, my angel, my Puta, that I could easily go on and on all night. It didn't occur me for an instant that I could switch off the energy and the passion of her heart and soul, I was a mere rag-doll caught up in the release of divine energies, the natural desires and the feminine bruja powers that Daniela knew how to exploit and turn into never-ending waves of pure pleasure and joy. Her neck was swiftly and eagerly covered with huge dollops of my sack-cream as I came. I knew then that this was just the beginning. It took a whole minute for my eyes to come back into focus so I could see her, and not just feel her lithe beauty. The smell of her perfume mixed with the salty creaminess of my spunk as she spooned handfuls of it into her mouth, using it as a lubricant as she went down on me, cupid-bow lips spread wide as my cock quickly regained its strength. Her tongue was what made me gasp the most, it was pierced and in a slightly odd way, I felt myself almost from the outside, as if I'd left my body. I nearly couldn't handle the agony of the ecstatic waves pulsing through me. With expert hands, Daniela used a technique I thought only older madrinas knew: channeling the energies of our fucking with her hands into parts of my body to enhance our sex. I began to vibrate, nearly convulsing like an epileptic with the power of her movements. The power. I'd never felt anything like this before. I could feel the electric sparks in the air as she expertly arched her groin, cat-like and lithe, so she could accommodate my ever-growing stem right down into her throat. It was an almost absurd laugh which helped me to slow down as I saw her gag slightly from my sheer size. My cock was nearly too big for her throat and she had to work hard to maintain her rhythm.

We were caught, Daniela and I, in a moment of complete abandon. As she moved up I caught her hair with a jet of my mecos. Immediately I thrust her back against the computer cabinet and she howled with delight, grabbing my bare ass with her clawed hands as I heaved myself quickly inside her panocha. "No mames!" she moaned "You're kidding me!" The feeling was completeness, a coupling of the spirit as well as the flesh. She obviously hadn't anticipated my stamina, It was clear no Latino man had ever pleasured her with such intensity. I was surprised myself at how we felt, there was hardly any talking, only the sounds of our frantic movements, not just our groins but our entire bodies were locked in total passion. She begged for more as I gradually moved up a gear, gaining confidence rapidly at the sight of her glistening sweat-soaked skin touching mine. Head thrust backwards, jet-black hair dangling to the ground in streams, we had little time for talk. Our contacts were now becoming more and more physical. As I moved to her rhythm, I let her take control for a while, as I had to regain some of my composure. "¡Olé! This Puta is an expert, a real pro" I mused, after all, I had scored a proper banger. I could feel her relaxing now, the slow preparation of her body, the gathering of her strength before her correrse. As she shuddered in ecstasy, I noticed how much she was enjoying herself. "Daniela, you haven't been fucked this way for a long time!"

All she could do was grunt "Si", I marvelled at her skills as a dancer, all Latina Putas are excellent dancers, but she was magic, moving me with seemingly no effort to take her mamey from behind. "Singar de mira quien viene"

"Doggy-style?" I replied, knowing only too well what Daniela wanted now.

"Pronto."

In the throes of ecstasy and becoming slightly worried about the trashed office, I found it hard to make out exactly where the scream came from. "Daniela?" We were satiated, now reached the point of mutual fulfilment. Every movement now became a blessing, there was no longer the pain of urgency, yet my focus remained unnaturally high. Cool. Detached even. About two hours must have passed, another two hours of now-gentle sexing one another. There was no robotics, every action seemed perfect as though meant to be, preordained in the greater scheme of things.

"Si, mango?"

"Shall we move on to the casa?" I could have stayed in her arms until sunrise, but this was impossible, the thought of the security-guard in her black uniform flashed into my now pleasured mind, but could not interrupt our montaro. I was under her spell. Daniela was now my Madrina. My Puta. Then louder still. Was this pleasure? Or pain? Or something else?

Lovers entwined, still breathing each other's perfumes, we strode out of our nest into the world beyond. I had to see what was going on, besides I didn't want anything interrupting my plans for Daniela, and her obvious plans for me. It was better for me to stay with the Puta I knew and loved. Especially when I had a chucha cuerera like Daniela. Her tonto. Her rulacho. Her raja, trained to please in a thousand ways of la regarse.

"Tonio?" I couldn't believe my eyes. As I moved out through the door, a reluctant spell weaved by hours of bombearo, I saw my amigo in the main hall, butt naked, with Anita, the eldest sister, the final 10th elder hermosa of my Puta lifting herself off his still-erect heubo. He looked kinda funny lying askew on the floor, with 9 senoras now fully clothed and one pulling her skirt expertly up grinning at him with obvious pleasure. His head bobbed and sagged to his chest, smiling in ecstatic bliss, moving as though with the same rag-doll feeling I had, only this was different. Nine Putas in a row!. He looked dazed as though he had fought in many awful wars, but he had won them all. A conqueror of his own domain, drunk on the power of his vanquished foes. With a smirk and smoothness born of arrogance and control, Anita threw me a small key. "Unlock his handcuffs." I noticed how she moved with the grace of royalty, a sex-queen now revealed in her true realm. Her sisters seemed locked to her command, warriors all, victors of men's morrongo and of men's souls. And Tonio... his eyes never lost that distant stare, as though time for him had stood still and his heaven had become hell.

All rose. "It is time for our departure. I trust you enjoyed your romper el tambor?" What was this older senora saying? She couldn't have meant me? How the fuck did Daniela know that stuff? The moves? The words? She was the embodiment of sex itself. The Divine Puta. There was no way I was a rompero here, I would have known. As they strolled out to the convoy waiting in the night, the family of bruja-sex gave us one final dismissive look. "You were not sacrificed. I made sure of this as soon as my sisters laid eyes on you. My first time to hechar un casquet, and you were the only one who could cope..." called my Puta.

Even to this day I walk in a daze. At times I look for her, I remember her smell, Her hair. The way she moved. The way she took my verga. Her eyes. Her skin. Her conejo. I wonder if that day was nothing more than a crazy hallucination, a figment of my dreams and nightmares? Then I remember Tonio's visiting schedule. The doctors have put him on a combination of nine antipsychotics... he still doesn't know where he is. The light has gone out of his eyes these days. He no longer speaks of crica or enjoys the company of anyone. The doctors say he has lost his mind – "too much moto", but I believe he has lost his soul.

The Bouncer, Bartender, and Client: An Erotic Threesome with Bondage, Lesbians, Oral Sex, Titty Sex, and Cream Pies

It was after the bar had closed, the smell of beer and cigarettes filled Nick's nostrils, a dirty smell. Normally, that always made him think about taking advantage of the girls at closing time. Girls always like the bouncer after a few drinks. Unfortunately, he was off his game tonight. The woman he had been working on all night ended up in the bathroom—probably throwing up all the Jack and Coke that he had poured for her. She had tested her long nails across his thigh throughout the night, leaving him unsatisfied. He became surprisingly attracted to her because of her tattoos and colored hair. She had bright red lips and nails to match, in his mind he had called her Scarlett. Just another fish in the sea, he thought woefully.

"Hey, I need you to take this trash out so we can get the fuck outta here, already!" Said Felicity from behind the bar. She always wore denim mini-skirts on Friday nights, and tonight she was looking particularly good, must be that old familiar smell, thought Nick. It also probably helped that she was wearing a skin-tight white t-shirt, he could see her bra was lacy and barely large enough to contain her breasts. Her dark hair was pulled back into a ponytail, her thick eye makeup had begun to run a little in the summer heat. Nick just happened to love a messy face on a petite body, with a nice set of curves. Generally speaking, though, it is never a good idea to get involved with people you work with. Little did he know that Felicity had been interested in him for months but was afraid to say anything to him because she knew he was the type that picked up on the bar flies that often visited the bar on the nights they worked together. She certainly wasn't looking for anything but owning him for a night.

He took the trash from her with a smirk.

"What do you mean we can get the fuck outta here? You taking me home tonight?" he said teasing her.

"No one is going home if we can't get this place cleaned up so come on!" She playfully whipped him with her bar towel, something that certainly didn't help his level of arousal.

As he walked himself into the summer evening's air, he caught a whiff of an alarming smell coming from the trees a few yards away from the dumpster. It smelled like something had died, like a squirrel or raccoon. Felicity followed a few steps behind Nick, also bothered by the odd smell in the air. Nick absentmindedly tossed the bags into the dumpster and slowly approached the trees. He saw what appeared to be a heap of denim in the trees. Felicity's eye grew big and she put her hands to her face in disgust and fear. There appeared to be a man's body under the denim. She recognized him from several hours earlier in the night—she had served him several drinks even though he appeared to be homeless. She felt her stomach sink.

"Forget it, maybe he is just sleeping it off, come on let's just go inside and worry about it later." Nick said, turning towards her and trying to lead her back into the bar. She allowed him to steer her back from where they came, but Felicity stopped just beside the dumpster.

"What is it? Come on, let's just go." Nick said, getting somewhat aroused by her big eyes looking to him for comfort. Felicity looked up at him waiting for him to say something to comfort her, but Nick didn't know what to say. He was conflicted by his carnal desires that were instantly amplified by her vulnerability in that moment. Her lips were especially seductive, even in the dark.

Felicity was overcome with clarity and a need to cling onto something, someone. She tried convincing herself that the man by the tress was not dead, but in the pit of her stomach she knew. As she was looking up at Nick, she was reminded that one of the best things in life is spontaneity. "We only live once, you know." She looked up at Nick through her long eyelashes, feeling herself get wrapped in his big arm as he drew her close. Felicity didn't hesitate to pull her lips close to his neck and ear, where she began to run her tongue up and down his neck lightly.

Nick could barely contain his excitement. He ran his hands down just below her skirt, then ran them right back up onto her ass, under the denim and squeezed hard lifting her into the air. He pushed her back onto the side of the dumpster, she wrapped her legs around his waist and very slowly unbuckled his belt. Nick ran his thumbs up and down her lacy panties, feeling the moisture from within. He slipped his finger inside of her, just enough to get her excited too. Felicity squeezed her hand through his zipper carefully, reaching for his already hard and very large cock. Her other hand was firmly wrapped around his neck, pulling his face right into her breasts, still impeded by her t-shirt.

Nick lifted her into the air again and walked into the backdoor of the bar. He knew exactly what he wanted to do, that smell of beer and cigarettes helped him find his way to the bar itself. He sat her up on the bar, their tongues entwined as he slid her lacy panties off. She placed her dark blue stilettos on the shelf just below the bar, her legs barely spread as if to challenge Nick to seek out the thing he really wanted. He ripped off her top and pulled her tits out of her black and blue bra, her nipples hard and erect. He pressed his mouth over her left nipple, teasing her with his tongue. This made her feel a little impatient as it aroused her enough to really get her juices flowing. Felicity ran her fingers through his hair, then directed his head towards her pussy, throwing her head back and spreading her legs further apart. As Nick made his way using nothing but his fingers and tongue around the soft and wet folds of her cleanly shaven pussy. She moaned as he teased her clit just enough to make her want more. She came quickly, her tits bouncing together as she moaned and threw herself back onto the bar. Nick stood and grabbed her off the bar, setting her on the floor.

She led him towards the women's restroom, looking over her shoulder, back at him as she walked. Felicity had always wanted to try out one of the vibrating cock rings for $0.50 and she intended to take this as far as she wanted. Nick followed her, curious of what was to come next. He stopped just outside the bathroom door, and leaned up against the pool table as Felicity disappeared inside. He heard a metallic clank and something drop. Then, he heard Felicity talking to someone in the bathroom. He stood and approached the door, opening it slowly.

It clearly was another woman's voice, and one he was familiar with. As he looked inside, he saw bright colors and immediately knew it was the girl from earlier in the night. Scarlett. She had clearly been sick, but had somewhat recovered because she looked as though she was excited to see him. She stood next to Felicity, taller and leaner. Her dark and playful style excited him back to his original state of arousal. Her chest was delicately tattooed and her arms were covered in ink, her multi-colored dreadlocks rested just above her perky breasts. Nick realized she had already removed her top, it was lying next to the toilet where she had been sick. Now, she wore a simple black bra, her smooth stomach leading his eye right down her long legs, her thigh-high boots covering tight leather pants.

As Nick stared at Scarlett in disbelief, Felicity turned towards him and knelt, reaching for what was now a throbbing cock contained only by his already undone belt and jeans. She pulled him out and looked up to Scarlett so she could see exactly what he had to offer. She carefully and sensually wet his shaft with her tongue before she shoved him deep into the back of her throat. Felicity's mouth was salivating at the corners of her lips, she was hungry to take him into her as much as she could. He could tell she wanted it badly, and relaxed as she pulled Nick in and out of her petite little mouth. Scarlett watched and began to undress herself slowly for him to watch. Felicity slid the vibrating cock ring onto Nick's member, it was lime green and gave Nick a particularly odd sensation at first. After it slid down towards the base of his enlargement, Felicity allowed her tongue to help make the sensation more enjoyable. Scarlett turned away from Nick as she began tugging at her pants, revealing that underneath she had on lacy black panties. She looked at him from behind her shoulder, her red lips enticing and her pink tongue beckoning him. She bent forward slowly, arching her back so that her ass was right in front of Nick, a gesture that he found almost too much for him to contain himself. He stopped Felicity and reached for Scarlett as she stood and made eye contact with him.

Scarlett squeezed herself between Nick and the bathroom door, taking Felicity's hand and led her out to the pool table. She cleared it off, and instructed Felicity to grab the microphones from the karaoke stage. She looked up at Nick and patted her hand on the green felt of the pool table, showing Nick that she was ready for him. She carefully removed her bra, dangled it in the air for a moment, then let it drop to the floor. Scarlett began crawling on all fours towards him on the table. He came towards her with anticipation, he could feel her fingers dance along his neck as she pulled him close to her ruby red lips. She worked her magic along his ear and he could smell her mildly sweet perfume coming from her wrist. In these few moments, he blindly followed her bodily movements that caused him to end up under her. He realized she had gotten him on his back, lying on the pool table, as she mounted herself on top of his chest. Her weight was somewhat heavy as she focused it on his shoulders, pinning him to the table. Felicity handed her the microphones and their cords. Scarlett began tying his wrists in the cords—tightly.

Nick had never been tied up before, the sense of losing control was new to him. It was arousing and somewhat unsettling, he could feel himself becoming detached from the situation. Scarlett edged her way off the pool table to fasten the cords to the legs of the table. Felicity caught on and tied his feet to the other end of the table. As she finished, she sat at a table off to the side of the pool table, with the vibrating cock ring. She licked her fingers and pushed them inside herself, then rubbed the ring on the outside of her clit. Scarlett had disappeared for a moment and returned with a bottle of whiskey in her hand.

Scarlett motioned for Felicity to get up on the pool table, which she did enthusiastically. Felicity stood above Nick's chest, her own fluid barely rolling down her inner thigh. Scarlett leaned Felicity's back between Nick's legs on the table, and lifted her legs into the air with one arm to hold them steady. She poured the whiskey into Felicity's creamy hole, filling it. Felicity squeezed herself tightly, but liquid still ran down her legs as she positioned herself against his lips and let it gush inside his mouth. Nick swallowed hard and pushed his face into her hard, driven mad from feeling like a caged animal, nibbling at her clit. The smell of her moist, soft skin on his face encouraged him to try and reach for her tits, but he was reminded of the cords that kept him from moving. As he struggled, Felicity rubbed herself on his face harder, greedily supplementing her arousal with her toy she hadn't neglected to bring over. Scarlett made her way onto the table, behind Felicity, and pulled her back by her large, bouncing breasts. They hung out of her bra still from earlier, the blue and black folds barely visible under her swollen tits. Scarlett pinched Felicity's nipples hard as Felicity began to come again. This time, more creamy whiskey flavor dribbled into Nick's mouth as Felicity cried out in pleasure, heaving and trying to catch her breath. Nick could feel her smooth and silky legs as they began to spasm on either side of his chest. Felicity fumbled around her skin folds, trying to prolong her initial climax. Scarlett reached down and assisted her with her bright red nails delicately brushing Felicity's clit. Nick pushed his head forward and plunged his tongue directly in and out of her as she came for the third time. Liquid ran down his tongue and into his throat. He felt long nails dance readily along his thigh, he knew it was Scarlett's other hand as she firmly gripped his member, her thumb carefully rubbing the head of his cock.

Felicity rolled off of Nick's chest onto the floor, taking a seat in a nearby chair. Scarlett had him right where she wanted him—at least for the time being. He wanted nothing more than to touch her on any part of her body. She teased him with her hands and her tongue intermittently. He sat with his head up when he could muster the additional muscle control. His senses were being overloaded with pleasure and his inability to move made it difficult for him to control how stimulated he felt with each stroke from Scarlett's hands and mouth. Felicity crept up behind Scarlett and circled around to Nick's feet. She climbed up between his legs, Scarlett moved to the side still holding him in her hand. Felicity bent down and pushed her tits on either side of his cock. Scarlett puffed her lips outward as her spit rolled down her chin onto his tip, Felicity looked at him through her thick eyelashes and pulsed herself up and down his shaft, her tits gripped tightly in each of her hands. Nipples erect and pink, the color of Felicity's flushed cheeks. He couldn't stand it any longer as Scarlett began to touch herself and breathing heavily while watching Felicity work him over. Nick couldn't control himself any longer, he erupted in a sudden burst of unbridled pleasure. Felicity's mouth caught what it could, the rest of her chest and face was covered in his creamy glory. He threw his head back as Scarlett's red lips enclosed the tip of him and she sucked what was left right into her throat. She cleaned the rest of his cock with her skilled tongue cleaning it off, slowly, leaving lipstick on him here and there. Scarlett leaned over with her lips pouting and wanting onto Felicity's cum covered chest. She slowly licked the creaminess from her right nipple and worked her way towards the center of Felicity's chest and up her neck. Felicity sighed lightly as she moved her head towards the ceiling.

Felicity stayed on her knees as Scarlett straddled Nick's torso, standing upright. Her thigh-high leather boots made Nick question the reality of the situation. Felicity pulled Scarlett's panties to the side and began rubbing her fingers in and out of Scarlett's swollen pussy. Nick could only see from behind Scarlett, her small and perfectly rounded ass, right in his line of view. He could see Felicity's fingers protrude between Scarlett's lips. Her dreadlocks hung down her slender back, another tattoo on her shoulder blade. Felicity leaned her face into Scarlett and wrapped her hands around her hips, grabbing her ass and pulling at her panties, ripping the delicate lace apart. Felicity's breasts hung down and bounced together as she began licking and fingering Scarlett with purpose. Nick could see her right leg begin to quiver and she lost balance for a second as she began feeling the intensity of stimulation. Scarlett grabbed her own nipple and squeezed down hard. She lost control of her leg ever so slightly, knocking the bottle of whiskey onto the floor where it shattered. Felicity, startled, stopped what she was doing. Scarlett moved herself off the pool table and began to loosen Nick's restraints just enough for him to get himself free whenever he chose to. Felicity made her way back behind the bar, and pulled out the soda gun. Scarlett was preoccupied with the microphone cords as Felicity sprayed her.

Nick was hit with some of the additional splashing as the liquid barely reached Scarlett's right arm. Felicity giggled and ducked behind the bar quickly after Scarlett gave her a look of playful intrigue. Scarlett gasped, then gave a subtle laugh meant for Felicity as she ran to the other side of the bar, her ass and tits bouncing as she reached behind the bar and grabbed the other spray nozzle. Felicity tried to get her again but was not prepared instead hitting a bottle of vodka, knocking it to the floor mat. Nick unraveled the mess of cords at his hands and feet as the girls engaged in guerilla tactics on either side of the bar. He found his way toward his pile of clothes to find his leather belt. He owed Felicity one for the towel shenanigans earlier in the night. The girls didn't even notice him moving about, much less did they see him sneak up behind Felicity. Scarlett noticed at the last minute, as she stood just over the bar to shoot Felicity with the soda sprayer one last time.

As the water hit Felicity's face and chest, Nick gave a light smack to Felicity's left ass cheek. She stood up and spun around to see Nick—whom she sprayed with more water as she backed away from him towards Scarlett. Luckily for Nick, Scarlett was on his side. She slid herself over the top of the bar and back behind as Felicity backed up. Scarlett grabbed the sprayer from her and wrapped it around her waist, bending her over the back shelving of the bar. From the mirror, Scarlett could see Nick getting very hard from this display. Scarlett took the belt from him and exchanged the sprayer hose. Felicity was now ready for mounting, and she anticipated it greatly as she had not yet had the pleasure of feeling Nick inside of her. Scarlett stepped out of Nick's way and positioned herself between him and Felicity just long enough to give him a few wet pumps in and out of her perfect mouth. Nick was tired of waiting for his turn with Scarlett, she had teased him enough that night. He was not going to miss the chance to take what he wanted. He took the belt from her hand, spinning her around and wraping the belt around her waist. He had a perfect view of himself and Scarlett in the mirror. He synched the belt around her perfectly sculpted stomach and pulled back.

Felicity moved herself underneath Scarlett, lightly grasping at her breasts licking her nipples. Nick was very focused on Scarlett's perfectly round ass, pulling back on the belt with one hand. The other hand pulled back on her puffy, moist, and sensitive pussy revealing just how welcoming her insides were going to be for his penetration. Scarlett's heart raced as she anticipated Nick's entrance inside of her, she knew that the build up of her own desires was reaching a climactic end. She felt Nick's angry expulsion of saliva splatter on her, waiting impatiently for him to feed the hunger that had manifested. Nick wanted to return the favor of anticipation to Scarlett, rubbing himself just outside of her access, lightly enough that he could tell it was driving her crazy. She demanded that he fuck her and do it now! Nick made a gesture as though he was going to plunge deep inside of her right as Felicity began lapping at Scarlett's clit. Scarlett moaned and her knees gave a few inches. As she was coming, Nick finally gave her what she wanted. He could feel her pulsate and twitch a silky moisture around him as she screamed in pleasure. Mid-climax, Nick reached back and gave her a quick spank. Her knees gave way again, Nick catching her with the belt around her waist. Felicity continued to wildly lick at Scarlett's clit and using one hand to squeeze her own breasts.

Nick pulled himself in and out of Scarlett's tight hole, occasionally feeling Felicity's tongue brush against him. He could feel the moist buildup inside of Scarlett make its way down her leg, mixed with Felicity's saliva. Nick glanced up and saw in the mirror, how he had Scarlett bent over and defeated as she consumed all that he had to offer for her in that moment. Scarlett was out of breath and felt a sensation of fatigue throughout her body, but her pussy was still hungry for more, she could feel that this was going to be one of her most enjoyable encounters so far. Nick felt so perfect inside of her, so long and robust that it filled her up. She thought of how badly she wanted him to come inside of her. Nick noticed a slight change in Scarlett's posture, like she wanted to challenge him for more. He again spanked her just before inserting his finger into her unusually tight ass. Scarlett's body jolted from the surprise but clearly enjoyed it. Felicity reasserted herself with Nick's balls, cupping and licking them as he pushed himself into Scarlett.

Nick gripped Scarlett's ass tightly and forced himself deeper and deeper inside of her with every movement. He could feel the building up of sensation in the tip of himself as it smashed itself inside of the tight and wet environment he found himself enjoying immensely. Felicity's tongue and hands firmly staying in synch with his movements as he felt the pressure growing inside himself at an uncontrollable rate. Felicity reached up and teased Nick's ass lightly smearing her own spit around his rim. At that moment, the floodgates released themselves for Nick. As he plunged inside her one last time, Scarlett's sensational floodgates also opened. In a brief but intense moment, the two of them lost themselves in pleasure. Nick mustered a deep growl and gritted his teeth tightly as he left himself explode inside Scarlett. She could feel the pressure releasing inside her wildly pulsating pussy. She had lost complete control of herself, her body had taken what it wanted from Nick's in a greedy and unforgiving gulp. Nick felt exhausted and exhilarated, but not ready to pull away from Scarlett. Felicity backed off the two of them as she knew her work was done.

As Felicity turned to get out from under Scarlett's bent over body, she looked towards the doorway and saw a figure. She stopped dead in her tracks, and squealed. Scarlett and Nick became alarmed, and looked down at Felicity. They followed her eyes to the door and saw a figure dressed in dirty denim, a particular smell came from him as well. He smelled faintly like a dead animal which rose above the smell of the many fluids present from Nick, Felicity, and Scarlett. A gruff clearing of his throat and a brief sniffle proceeded the once thought dead man's words.

"I knew sleeping outside would have its perks one of these days."

Surprise Birthday Threesome: Blindfolded Tara Shares Her Husband With Another Woman

Tara was wet. Tara had been wet all day. She couldn't stop thinking about what her husband Enzo had told her before she left for work. "Tonight when you get home, your sweet tight snatch is going to be licked and fucked harder than you have ever had it".

Sitting at her desk, Tara had been fantasizing all day. She day-dreamed about Enzo's hard thick cock deep inside her. Her boss left early so she was just there to answer the phones until 5 o'clock, and she had an hour left. Her pussy felt so wet and slick, she just had to touch it. Tara pulled down her white lace panties just a little and touched her already swollen clit. She let out a small moan and started rubbing her clit very softly and tenderly. Her fingers were very wet and she needed just a taste of her own yummy juices. After putting her finger deep inside her wet snatch, she pulled it out and licked it clean. She was so close to cumming; her whole body seemed to ache.

But she stopped, she couldn't cum, not yet.

Tara was thinking about Enzo and waiting to cum on his hard shaft. After a minute or so she stopped rubbing her pussy and started to pull up her panties, but she stopped and with a smile on her face, she placed her panties into her purse. It was five. She could now get home and see what her husband had planned for her. Tara only lived about 15 minutes away from work, but to her it felt like forever. She was hot, horny, and still dripping wet.

As she pulled into the driveway, she noticed all the lights were out and only a faint glow was showing. Candles, she thought, and was getting even wetter. The door was opened, and when she shut it behind her, she called "Enzo, I'm home, baby."

Enzo was standing there naked and his cock was rock hard. "Hey baby, happy 35th birthday," he took her in his arms and kissed her hard on the lips. Tara almost came when he kissed her it was so intense and full of lust. Enzo said, "Honey, I have a very special night planned, but first I need you to put this on." Enzo handed her a lacy black scarf.

Tara laughed and said, "You want me to be blind-folded?"

"Yes, dear, just for tonight," Enzo replied. Tara took off her clothes, and standing naked by the front door she put the blind fold on. Enzo tied it tight, to the point that it almost hurt. "There, now take my hand and I want you to sit on the couch."

Tara did exactly what Enzo said, her whole body felt tingly from excitement. "Now sit back and spread your sexy legs wide open baby," Tara could hear the lust in his voice. There was no sound or movement, but all of a sudden, Tara felt Enzo's tongue gently lick her throbbing clit. Tara let out a startled scream before she settled back down. The lick and kisses were soft and wet and slow, so painfully slow. She was almost screaming... she needed to cum so bad. The lick and the kisses were getting ever so faster and his hot breath coming out of his mouth was driving her crazy with lust. She could feel herself about to cum when Enzo must have sensed it too because he slid in two fingers and Tara exploded all over them. Her body rocked. She screamed and bucked and quivered. After a few moment, she was trying to catch her breath because she knew she had never came so hard before in her whole life.

In the afterglow of her wonderful orgasm she noticed she could see just a tiny bit from the lace in her blindfold. Enzo was standing up about 5 feet from her and then she felt a tongue lick her freshly cummed pussy. She got very nervous and noticed long red hair. The only woman she knew that had long red hair was her best friend Lynn. Tara was mad, but just for a second, she realized that Lynn had made her cum so sinfully sweet that she just settled back down and played along. The soft licking started again and this time it was even hotter, as she knew a woman was licking her. She was so turned on she came again almost instantly, but this time she reached out and touched Lynn's hair. Acting surprised she yanked the blindfold off of her and said in a slight amused confused voice. "Lynn"?

Lynn said, "Hey girl you have no idea how long I have wanted to lick this sweet pussy of yours, and since it's your birthday, Enzo and I thought this would be a great present." Tara was instantly pissed and got up, stormed out of the living room, went to bathroom, and slammed the door. As she sat on the edge of the tub naked and with her pussy juice trailing down her leg, she thought, "What in the hell am I so pissed about?" She sat at there for a few more minutes and there was a knock on the door.

"Hey hun, can I come in?" Enzo asked.

"Sure."

Enzo opened the door and sat down on the toilet, he had put on some shorts and was looking like a deer in the headlights. "Hunny, I'm so sorry" Enzo said.

"Stop! Just stop. I get it and thank you," Tara mumbled. "I'm over it I was just shocked at first is all. Wheres Lynn?" asked Tara.

"Um. . . I think she's getting dressed". Enzo said sheepishly.

Tara stuck her head out of the bathroom and yelled, "Lynn can you come here for a sec, please?"

Tara could tell Lynn was very ashamed and on the verge of tears. Lynn looked so fine and hot in that moment Tara realized.

 "Lynn" Tara said. "Would you like to fuck me and my husband tonight?"

Lynn looked up at Tara and with her smile said yes. Tara grabbed Enzo's cock and grabbed Lynn's hand and demanded, "Make him hard."

Lynn grabbed Enzo's cock and started sucking him fast. Enzo's cock grew in her mouth and Lynn was getting so turned on feeling him swell up. While Lynn was on her knees sucking Enzo's cock, Tara had put her twat right at Enzo's mouth. He was licking her deep and fast. After a few sexy moments of this, Tara again commanded, "To the bedroom."

As they walked naked to the bed, Tara said, "Babe sit right here for a sec, stroke your cock and just watch."

Enzo sat down slowly stroking his hard swollen dick and watched his wife go down on Lynn. Tara licked her fast and sloppy, making Lynn cum and squirt all over Tara's glazed face and mouth. Tara glanced over at Enzo and saw how hard he was.

"Fuck her," she demanded.

Enzo got up and onto the bed and slid very slowly inside Lynn's tight cooze. He almost came. She was so wet and almost too tight. He started pounding her love hole and she came so hard on his cock. Tara was stroking his balls and kissing Lynn's tits and Enzo said, "I have to stop a sec I'm about to cum."

"Go ahead baby," Tara said, "cum in her, cum in her deep." After hearing those words from his wife he couldn't hold it any longer and filled Lynn's tight cooze up with his hot sticky jizz. Enzo stayed inside Lynn until his cock went limp and slowly pulled it out with a nice trail of cum seeping out if her pussy. As Enzo lay beside Lynn, Tara was very turned on seeing her man's cum dripping out of her best friend's pussy. Before she even realized what she was doing she was licking every drop of jizz from Lynn's snatch and some of it had made its way down Lynn's ass crack and Tara was hungrily licking it there also. Tara's pussy was so wet and her clit was throbbing. She lay on her back and took Enzo's hand and placed it on her snatch. Enzo understood, and started kissing and finger fucking his wife.

As Lynn rolled over, Enzo's hot cum was still leaking out of her pussy. She began issing and licking Tara's nice tits and rubbing the top of her clit. Enzo's cock starting to get hard again, and with an aggressive thrust, he forced his way inside his wife's warm and welcoming pussy. Lynn rubbed Tara's clit faster and faster, getting turned on again herself watching Enzo fuck her friend. A massive orgasm was boiling up in Tara's loins, and she grabbed Lynn, "Sit on my face and face Enzo."

Lynn arches her ass just right so Tara can have easy access to both of her wet holes, and as Enzo is fucking Tara's wet clam, Tara is tongue fucking Lynn's warm sweet asshole. Tara hears Enzo and Lynn kissing as she's being fucked and while she's tongue fucking Lynn. Her moment comes, she cums so hard and squirts her warm cum all over her husband and the bed.

Lynn feels an orgasm coming also and gets off Tara's face and bends over doggie style with her hands spreading her ass and tells Enzo, "Fuck my ass." Enzo pulls out of his wife's freshly cummed twat and slides slowly into Lynn's hot asshole. Lynn lets out a moan of pleasure aaron pain and surprise, but starts to slowly move her hips and press her ass against Enzo's body. Lynn feels her ass tighten around his shaft and feels herself about to cum when she Tara's fingers slide into her snatch. Lynn cums so hard and so fast she lets out a long and loud scream.

Enzo slowly pulls his cock out and to his surprise Tara says, "Let me suck it." Enzo almost cums as his wife starts sucking on the tip of his cock. Fighting not to cum with every fiber of his being, Enzo starts face-fucking his wife's wet mouth. Lynn is watching them and moves so she can place her whole face between Tara's legs. As Lynn is sucking and slurping Tara's hot mound, Tara has a hard and deep orgasm. Enzo can't stop himself from cumming this time, and splurts hard in his wife's mouth. Enzo pulls out and let's just a little bit drip onto his wife's pussy, where Lynn hungrily licks it up.

The three are spent, and there is some small kisses and light petting lingering after the moment. The three lie there for about half an hour. Lynn is the first to get up and laughs and says, "Damn! You need to have a birthday every week! I can barely walk my pussy is so swollen and sore."

Tara smiles and says, "You never know, hun."

As Lynn is in the bathroom, Tara smiles at Enzo and says "Dear this was the best birthday present ever."

"I think Lynn is in the shower, should we join her?" Enzo asks.

The Threesome with a Hooker that Fixed Their Marriage

"Want to fuck or are you scared that your wife will walk in on us?" questioned Lola, looking at Sadmon with enquiring eyes.

"She won't be home for at least two hours, so we have plenty of time to fool around my darling." Knowing that time was of the essence, Lola wasted none of it and proceeded to unbuckle Sadmon's belt. She dipped her hand inside of his boxers. She felt his hefty, warm meat. She never wanted him more than she did now.

"You have a really huge cock," she uttered.

"I know, and you will get the full 10inches of it in just a few minutes." She grabbed his dick by the neck and led it through the front of the boxers. She knelt down before him and gently placed her lips over its huge head. It felt like she was sucking on a warm cucumber. "Fuck, you are good at this game, Lola."

"I know, Sadmon! I've had a lot of experiences." Sadmon chuckled. Lola was a great blowjob artist. She sucked better than any good vacuum cleaner. Her tongue swept over his dick better than the most expensive broom that was sold in the most expensive stores. Fuck, she was so good that he wouldn't mind if his wife would walk in at this moment. He thought to himself, maybe wifey would learn a trick or two if she would walk in at this point in time.

"I want to see you naked, Lola. I want to see if your body is as sexy as your lips are!" Lola got up off her knees. She unbuttoned her blouse, slowly and meticulously removed her bra and her pants. She was not wearing any underwear. "Bring your ass here, Lola."

She cleared her throat, "Aren't you forgetting something?" She gestured with her hand that he needed to remove his clothes as well. He was not as diligent as her; he quickly took off his clothes. He wanted her pussy and he wanted it badly. He wanted to massage it with his fingers, eat that pussy, and pound it. He had so much to do, and all before his wife got home.

He advanced towards her. Picked her up, lifted her pussy towards his face and laid on the bed. She knew exactly what to do. She grinded her pussy against his lips, gently at first. Fuck, her crutch was so warm and tasty. He enjoyed tasting her moisture, and she enjoyed the massage of his tongue. She was quite aroused at this time that she was on the verge of exploding. She pressed herself harder down on his lips and rode over his face even harder and faster. "I'm cumming," she announced. She oozed inside of his mouth. He enjoyed this and swallowed every single drop.

After eating her pussy, he decided to take command. He rolled her off his face and onto the bed. He caressed both of her nipples between his fingers. Her nipple stuck out as pointy as his hard dick. Caressing from her neck, he worked his way down to her nipples. He started to nibble them with his teeth. He moved his right hand downwards, towards the hips and between her thighs. He rubbed his hand against her pussy. She was so fucking wet. He poked his index finger inside of her. She shivered from all the excitement. He shoved his middle finger inside as well to test her reaction. She shivered again. He knew that her body was begging him to put his wet cock inside. He led his cock between her thighs and pushed his full length and breadth inside. To her surprise, he did not push it in her pussy. Instead, he pushed it straight in her ass.

Nevertheless, Lola enjoyed this and groaned a little. He fucked her in the ass for about five minutes. When he had gotten enough, he decided that he wanted her pussy. After all, there was nothing more satisfying in sex than being inside of a hot and sticky pussy. Yes. He wanted her pussy so badly and he wanted it now. Besides, his wife would soon be home and he knew that Lola had to be gone before she got home, or that would be the end of his marriage that was already falling apart. There was no more time to waste. Sadmon took his dick out of Lola's ass, and placed his fingers inside of her pussy again. She was still really wet. "Alright," he thought to himself, "she is now ready for my anaconda!"

He held his dick with his right hand. Paying attention to his own desire rather than tenderness, he shoved his entire plus-sized cock inside of her. It did hurt Lola a bit because of the force that it was done with, but for her it was more pleasurable than painful. Lola really enjoyed having sex, so for her it was no big deal whether or not the guy was gentle. As Sadmon entered her pussy, he could feel that it was so warm and so fucking wet, he knew he was at home now, and he was ready to hit his homerun. He pounded her slowly at first so he could savor the moment as much as possible. Lola got wetter and wetter with each of his stroke. He was enjoying being inside of her pussy and making her more moist, so he intensified his speed, so much so that she felt like she was going to lose consciousness. He grabbed her by her hips and forced her legs above his shoulders so that he could penetrate her even better.

He whispered in her ears, "Gosh, your pussy is so fucking wet. It's fantastic!" They were both enjoying grinding against each other's bodies and dabbling in each other's liquids. "Fuck, this woman is amazing," Sadmon thought to himself, "I don't remember the last time having this much fun during sex." Sadmon wanted to change position; he turned her sideward, he turned sideward as well. He inserted his cock once more, and continued pounding her pussy. He briefly fucked her in that manner. Then, he wanted it in a different way.

"Get on your knees, Lola. I want to get it doggystyle." She willingly complied. He entered her kitchen in quite a rush, and pulverized her. His cock was so hard and warm, and he really knew how to fuck. Gosh, she could easily see herself as his mistress, but as a prostitute it would be best to leave things as they were for business reasons. "Are you enjoying this big cock, Lola? Do you want it harder?" Lola just nodded her head.

"All right, let me put it all on you. Here it is!" He fucked her harder and harder. Inside of her felt warmer and wetter with each stroke. He felt couldn't help it; he exploded inside of her.

"Okay, here is the money that I owe you. You were worth every single penny, Lola. I really wish that you could stay longer, but my wife will be home really soon, and she cannot meet you..." The door of the bedroom started to turn. Before Sadmon could tell Lola to hide, his wife entered the room. At this point, Lola and Sadmon were still both butt naked. Sadmon stood there stunned as if he had just seen a ghost, and he became a little puzzled when his wife smiled and said, "Hey, honey. Hey, Lola."

He asked, "You two know each other?"

Both women chucked, "Of course, we do. Janet and I have been having sex for the past three months now. She pays me to have sex with her. I am bisexual too you know," Lola replied, "but I had no idea that she was your wife, not that it would have made any difference to me whether or not she is married to you."

"Ladies, I don't know if I'm supposed to be happy or grossed out, but at the moment I'm fucking horny. Janet, please get your ass over here and join the party. We are all going to fuck each other right now!" Janet complied. She moved towards them. Lola took off Janet's blouse and bra and sucked on her nipples. Sadmon removed her skirt and panties and played with her pussy for a while. Sadmon, then, motioned for her to proceed towards the bed. She did so and laid down. She opened her legs. Lola went straight down on her. She started to suck her pussy. When Janet started to get really really wet, Lola inserted her tongue and proceeded to tongue fuck her. At this point, Sadmon was sucking from one breast to the other.

He lifted his head and exclaimed, "I'm going to punish both of you for not telling me about your little love affair by banging both of you really fucking hard!" He laid on the bed directly between Lola's legs and started to suck her. Lola was still kneeling down and was tongue fucking Janet. Both Lola and Sadmon enjoyed what they were tasting, the salty taste of pussy.

"Alright, I want to taste some dick now," Janet said. Janet got off the bed, and Sadmon laid down. Both women took turns licking his chest and sucking on his delicious popsicle. He felt like a prince among two beautiful princesses. He wanted to fuck both of them so badly, but he wanted to eat them out first. He made both of them lie on the bed and he alternated between both of them. While he was sucking on one pussy, he was playing inside of the other with his fingers. He wanted the women to get really wet for him so that he could have his way with them.

When they were both soaking wet, he said, "Maybe, I should leave you two to go at it alone, since you guy have been doing it without me for so long." The women objected. They did not want each other; they wanted more. They wanted cock. They wanted Sadmon's cock. He was only teasing them because he wanted their pussy really badly as well. He made it known to them that he wanted it doggystyle. He entered Janet's cunny first. While he was pounding her, Lola's head was between his tights. She was licking off their fluids as it drained from his dick to his balls to his tights. Next, it was Lola's turn to give her pussy to him. Likewise, Janet licked their fluids. Sadmon really enjoyed pounding both women, and the harder he pounded them, the more the women tend to enjoy it. He rotated between women three times. Then, he felt like he was about to cum. He grabbed on to his cock really hard. He didn't want to cum in either of them; he wanted to come in their mouths.

"Get on the bed, lie next to each other and open your mouths." The women opened their mouths, anxiously waiting for their reward. He started to jerk off. As he intensifed this action, he started to cum. The women were really close to each other that they were practically kissing. He sprayed in their mouths. The women willingly swallowed his release. He smiled at them, "Great job, ladies. Lola, how do I owe you for this round?" "No, Honey, I got this one. I will pay her!" exclaimed Janet. Janet paid her the usual price. Before Lola had a chance to leave, Sadmon and Janet invited her over for another threesome in two weeks' time. Lola indicated that she would come. For the rest of the afternoon, Sadmon and Janet laid beside each other in bed, without uttering a word to each other about the day's activities, but both of them were indeed blissful. The couple, who was having some marital problems lately and hadn't had sex in more than six months, was so happy that they finally did it. Who would have thought that being unfaithful to each other would actually bring them much closer?

Threesome in the Girl's Dorm

It was my first year of college. I had never had much luck with girls in high school but now my luck was going to change. Due to a screw-up with room assignment, I stayed in the girls' corridor. Even better, I had a private room since I couldn't live with a girl. Yep, my life was pretty good, but I had still never had a girlfriend or even sex. I received a handjob once, but I didn't even cum.

One night while studying, two of the girls from down the hall asked me to help them move their beds. I worked out quite a bit and my physique was fairly good. I agreed and went to help them. I heard them whispering as I moved the beds, but couldn't make out what they were saying. After I finished I started towards the door but one of them stopped me.

"We'll pay you for this, we promise," one said. I told them it was ok and that I was glad to help. The other girl went to the door, closed and locked it. They begin to strip off their clothes revealing luscious breasts and perfect, round asses.

One stepped up to me and said "Would you like a show?" I froze in anticipation and simply nodded my head. They wasted no time and laid on the bed, kissing each other passionately. I could feel my dick getting harder as I watched in amazement. One girl spread her legs while the other gently licked her clit and fingered her. Loud moans began resonating through the room. Luckily, the dorms had very thick walls and no one could hear. They noticed my hard on and beckoned me to join them. I took off my clothes and sat on the edge of the bed. They giggled at my shyness and pulled me on the bed. One began kissing me while the other took my dick in her hand and began sucking it. It felt exquisite. Her warm mouth was milking my cock. I looked down to see her drooling all over my dick, and licking my balls. I was in heaven, but I knew I wouldn't last long. I told her I was about to cum and they switched places. The girl who was kissing me began to suck my dick with more force than the previous girl.

I yelled "I'm CUMMMIIINNNG" but she didn't budge. I shot rope after rope of hot white cum into her mouth. "Sorry," I said, but she laughed. The two girls began to kiss and swap my cum.

"Wow," was all I could say. They cleaned themselves up and I started to get dressed. "Where are you going?" one asked.

"To my room."

She looked disappointed and told me to sit down. "Won't you stay the night with us?" ...College is going to be great.

Getting Out of the Ticket: Foreign Object Penetration and Double Penetration with Two Cops in Belize

Jodi was new to Belize, and unfamiliar with the customs. So when she was stopped at a road check, she had no idea what to expect. The officer who approached her vehicle was young, very young. Jodi thought of her wrinkles beginning to etch into her face. At 40, she felt like she looked pretty good, but she longed for the days when she would wrap this traffic stop up with just a wink of her deep brown eyes.

"May I have your driver's license, please?" asked the officer. Jodi hesitated.

"Well, I've only been in this country for a few weeks. I have my license from the States..."

"That'll be fine." The officer examined the license, and Jodi examined the officer. He was just what she had been hoping for... young, strong, and...black. Jodi had spent her first 40 years playing it safe, and had come to Belize to leave the boring behind.

"Are you aware that this is expired?" the young officer flashed her a smile. "That's a $50 fine."

"Awe...isn't there something we could do?" Jodi rubbed her inner thigh. "I really don't want a ticket in my new country."

The youngn officer licked hid lips. "Even if I could help you out... what about my partner over there? How will we get away from him?"

"We won't. I like it when we all play together." Jodi suggested. The young officer called his partner over to the car window. The second officer was middle aged and broad in the middle. He was chomping at the bit for a chance with a hot lady like Jodi. The three of them pulled their cars into the orange grove, and the middle aged police man was the first out of his vehicle. He started to speak, but Jodi silenced him with s sexy "Shhhh". Slowly Jodi pulled her top off and exposed her round breasts. She cupped one and licked her nipple as if to lead by example. The men obliged, and each took one nipple between their lips. Jodi loved the feeling of holding the backs of their heads, as they licked and bit and sucked her. She reached for both men's cocks through their uniform trousers.

Hard already, Jodi would not be disappointed today. Rubbing hard at their cocks, she slowly unzipped both men. Stepping out of their pants, Jodi could see that the middle aged man had the larger manhood. She went at his cock first. Hitting her knees in the grass, she took the tip of his dick and licked it. Not putting it in her mouth just yet, she wanted first to lick off the pre come she knew she could goad from this cock. A crystal clear drip appeared at the tip, and Jodi thrust his cock deep into her throat. She took the cock deeply for a few strong strokes then went back to teasing the tip with her tongue. The younger policeman, not to be left out, slid Jodi's skirt over her full ass and tore off her panties! He spanked her ass leaving it red and hot. Jodi moaned in pleasure. Then he put his fingers into her...deep. Jodi was begging for more, and the young man thought he would put his cock inside her. Jodi had other plans.

Feeling around on the ground, she had come up with an ear of corn. She pulled it from it's husk and began rubbing her pussy with it. Taking her cue, the older officer started to put the corn inside Jodi. She absolutely loved it! Riding the foreign object for the entertainment of these guys was incredible! Just the sort of think Jodi had wanted to get out of her comfort zone. The look of shock and pleasure for the men sent Jodi over the edge and she came, hard, on the bumpy ear of corn she rode. Now, she wanted to give pleasure!

She grabbed the larger cock and guided it to her wet with come pussy. She dipped it, and got it wet and juicy, then she used it to rub her juicy lubricating come all over her ass. Flipping the man onto his back, Jodi mounted the hard, large cock. Then she reached around and pulled open her ass crack, giving a longing look to the younger officer. She was not disappointed. He immediately entered her from behind.

The pain of two cocks was paled by the pleasure Jodi felt. Finally full. Finally feeling what she had fantasized about. She knew the men could feel their cocks rubbing together as well. She drew everyone into a long sexy tongue kiss and took this fucking like she had done it a million times. She knew she would be doing this again. Her mount was bucking, almost at his peak. Jodi wanted to have another orgasm before it was through, so she bucked harder. She took the hand of the anal officer and added it to the fucking fray. He rubbed her clit while she came all over again. When the older man climaxed, the threesome felt the hot come rush! He lay, still inside her while the younger man fucked her ass until she felt she would be sore! Finally, he pulled his cock and finished coming all over her full red ass. Jodi left without a word. She didn't even know their names... and that was satisfying.

Another Man for My Wife's Birthday: Anal Threesome Fun

We had been together 10 years, so when it came time for my wife's birthday that particular year, I was kind of stumped on what she wanted that I hadn't already got her. All the times she used to ride me until I came inside her, I found myself frequently whispering to her if she would be turned on with another hard dick to hold on to while she fucked me. Seeing her become excited when we were out and another prick entertained her dirty thoughts, and with how much she loved sucking cock, sometimes it turned me on thinking about her fantasies coming to life.

When her 30th birthday was coming around I asked her what she wanted, and she giggled confessing to me she really wanted to bring a partner in the bedroom… another man, and to suck and fuck him while I watched. I obliged, and on the night of her birthday we responded to an ad on a local web site after some searching for the right candidates. She picked him out, a semi muscular man with a thick rock hard cock, its throbbing head curved upwards. Several pictures of his cock accompanied his profile, and she became very excited. After exchanging emails, he was on his way, and the fantasy was taking shape.

Slipping into a silk button up dress shirt and silk tight pants, she answered the door for him, pulling the stud inside and demanding he take a seat before sticking her tits in his face, grinding her wet pussy through her pants on his cock. He grasped her tits through the smooth silk, soaking it with spit as he gently took playful bites at her rock solid nipples. I couldn't take it. When I got up to sit next to them she pushed me down, "You're going to look, NOT fucking touch" she snarled.

I sat back down hurriedly, not before she took leather restraints and locked my hands to the chair. She told him to get up, and pulled his big dick out to start licking it, pulling it straight up and slowly teasing it with her tongue from his balls to his tip, his knees shuddering in pleasure. "This is how you suck cock," she said, "you feel the tip in my mouth and my tongue. I want to taste cum," she told him.

"How does his hard dick taste?" she asked me, using her tongue to lick the inside of my mouth before pulling my head back and slowly letting her spit run into my mouth. Pulsing my hips into the air she could tell I was yearning for her to taste my shaft, and she pulled it out, excitedly giving both of us head. Making him sit on my lap naked, stroking his needy cock, she got underneath him and cleaned his asshole, sucking his balls and pleasing his ass while he stroked his shaft.

"Fuck my ass," she told him as he stood up and picked her small frame into the air, holding her completely up, his dick disappearing up her ass. Grinding her ass up him against roughly, it's how she always liked it, her asshole taken when you fucked. Rubbing her slit now facing me while he rode her from behind, she held my shoulders as I was seated while he tried his best not to cum.

"I'm fucking cumming!" she yelled. "Don't you fucking stop!" Her cunt began squirting cum all over my legs as she squeezed her tits and glared at me with a nasty grin, laughing.

"Is this what you needed baby? Is this what you wanted for your present?" I asked.

"Oh fuck yes! I'm your filthy fucking whore; fill my fucking asshole full of cum," she told him as he grunted and groaned, squirts of his hot cum no doubt slipping out in her, until he threw his head back and exploded inside her ass, filling it up with cum.

"Good boy," she told him, the pleasure on both their faces as she slowly still worked up and down, back and forth gyrating on his dick. She wasn't done… no not even close. Leading him into the bedroom, she fit him into a latex bodysuit and mask, the only exposed part of his body was his long curved prick. She lay him on his back on the bed, and sank her pussy down on him, riding his dick even harder, cum leaking from her fucked asshole slowly drizzled out on the latex suit. Now unhooked, I stood in front of her stroking my dick, twisting my hand around the head needing to cum so bad. I couldn't get it out fast enough. I couldn't decide if i wanted to fuck her or jerk off as hard and fast as I could with her urging me to cum in her mouth.

Pulling her hair back, I jacked myself off, spraying hot cum up her chest and into her mouth, in her excitement she came again, squirting cum all over the latex suit he was in. She pulled his dick out of her, soaking wet with cum everywhere and sucked him until he shot a 2nd load into the air. She giggled and unzipped his mask, covered in cum rubbing herself all over him. It was so fucking hot after a few minutes I couldn't take it, and came from behind entering her tight ass.

"Ohhhh fuck yes," she threw he head back, succumbing to another shaft filling her ass. "Fuck my ass until you cum you dirty fucker," she taunted me, sprawled out on top of his cum covered suit. His flaccid dick hanging there, all cummed out, as he continued holding her hips steady so I could fill her up. I felt another load coming so hard it hurt, the first squirt I let go into her ass, then I pulled out and quickly shot the rest in her needy pussy hole, shrieking in ecstasy.

"Was that the best birthday ever?" I asked her after we escorted the man out.

"Yes, baby," she replied, "how will you top this next year?"

Five Person Gangbang in an Airplane: A Captain, Three Stewardesses, and Passenger Swap Fluids

I'm starting my day as any other: read my email, print-off today's flight plan, and head over to the plane. That's right, I'm a captain for a major European airline and fly the Boeing 747 to Cancun, Mexico, today. As I got on the plane, the most gorgeous flight attendant greeted me. I guess she's about 25 years old and has beautiful blond hair and blue eyes. I was completely speechless and couldn't stop staring at her boobs. Her boobs were enormous, and were too big for her sexy blue flight attendant uniform.

"Hi, good morning captain. I'm Jessica and I'll be your purser today. Can I get you something to drink?" she said while I tried to look the other way so she wouldn't see me staring at her boobs.

"Yeah, my name is Steve, just some water for me," I said. She bended forward to grab the can of water from one of the trolleys and I felt my dick getting rock hard. All I could think about was how nice it would be to take of that skirt of hers and fuck her right here in the galley. As I put my suitcase in one of the overhead bins, and I walk up to the cockpit, the other sexy 7 flight attendants walk down the jet way. I opened the cockpit door immediately as my boner was visible through my uniform pants.

"Hi Steve, how are you doing?" It was my co-pilot Bill who I've been flying with for over 6 years now. I get settled in my seat, and Jessica comes over to do the briefing with us and serve me my water, which I totally forgot about as I was way too busy thinking about other stuff. As Jessica walks out and closes the door, Bill says to me: "Trust me, your secret is safe with me."

I look with a frizzled face at him and ask what he means. "I saw the way you were looking at her. Trust me, she's amazing, I fucked her hard on my last layover, and I bet she'll enjoy it again." I looked at him and didn't know what to say. Was he really serious about this or could this just be a joke?

I replied to him, "I know she's very hot, but I've got my wife waiting for our anniversary. Happy marriage means you can look at other hot girls, but you can't touch them."

Bill laughs as we we're pulling away from the gate. Little did I know that this was going to be one of the most exciting trips in my entire piloting career! We were about 6 hours in-flight, and it was time for me to take an hour nap. I've always loved flying the 747 as it has a private crew rest right above the economy class section. As I walk through the cabin, I see most of the passengers sleeping or watching movies on their little TV screens. I open the door to the crew rest and one of the flight attendants was sleeping.

It was Alexa, she's one of the Spanish speaking flight attendants. She was lying so peacefully in the bed and I couldn't stop my horny thoughts. I take off my uniform and as I was about to take off my pants she woke up. "I'm so sorry," I said.

"Don't worry captain, I couldn't really sleep anyway," she says.

"Can I get you some coffee?" I ask her as we have this little coffee maker in the crew rest area.

"Sure, why not" she says. As I was pouring the coffee, one of the cups falls and drenched my pants full of coffee. Alexa runs over to me to make sure I'm doing okay and while she's sitting on the floor to grab the cup and dry off the floor I had a perfect sight from above right in her top were I could see a nice set of boobs.

As it's usually cold in the crew rest her top showed two nipples sticking out. "Let's get you out of these pants so we can clean them," she says while looking up to me. So I take off my belt and drop my pants. She looks up and I see that she was looking at my boxer short that I was wearing. She slowly moves her hands over my legs all the way up to my boxer shorts.

I couldn't resist the temptation and my cock started to grow like crazy. I haven't had sex for quite some time, so I couldn't leave an opportunity like this. "You can grab my cock if you like," I said while I was almost certain she wouldn't say no to that. Before I could even finish my sentence she pulls down my boxer shorts and grabs my hard cock. A shock of excitement went straight through my body when I saw how horny she looked at it. Slowly, she started to jerk me off, but it didn't take long before she jerked me off even faster. Suddenly, she opened her mouth and put my cock in it. Her mouth felt so nice and warm around my cock. This was the best I've had in years I thought by myself. While she was sucking me off, I pulled her black silky hair out of her face so I could see her beautiful hazel brown eyes. I pull my cock out of her mouth and push her on the bed.

"Oh captain your cock is so good in my mouth," she says while I take off her top. I grab her boobs and start licking the nipples while she still jerks me off. "Captain kiss me, please," she says while holding my face right in front of her. I kissed her and it felt amazing. My tongue and hers were going all over the place while my hands were still holding her boobs. My hands were gliding down towards her vagina. It was very nicely shaved and as my finger was slowly going in she started to moan from pleasure.

After a few minutes I realized that we had to hurry, because soon some other flight attendants would come over for their break. As I was looking at the clock Alexa got up and said that I shouldn't worry about the others. I didn't really understand what she was trying to say with this. However, I kept on fingering her nice tight vagina.

"Slide your big hard cock in me," Alexa says while still enjoying the fingering I did to her. As she was getting herself ready to sit on my cock. the door opened and two other flight attendants walked in. I didn't know what to do as I really wanted to fuck Alexa, but I knew my job was on the line here. Instead of walking away, the two flight attendants walked into the very small crew rest area and kept the door open. Another guy walked in and closed the door. "I think we can really start to have fun now," the guy says.

It took some time for me to figure out who he was, but then it got to me, he was a passenger from the business class cabin, from seat 2A. Alexa gets from the bed and walks up to Brenda, a blond 30-year-old girl and started to kiss her very passionately. The other guy was right next to them and got kissed by both girls one at a time. For me it was amazing to see so many sexy girls in the very small area at 40,000 ft. in the air. Gloria the third flight attendant takes off her uniform and walks over to me and puts her sexy body on top of mine and we both look at the live sex play that was going on in front of us. Alexa and the other flight attendant kneel in front of the guy at the same level of his underwear. She takes it off and pulls out his muscled cock. Slowly she opens her mouth while the guy holds on to the back of her head and pushes his cock in her mouth. The girl moans in pleasure and starts to suck his dick. Also Alexa starts to join in and suck his cock at the same time. "Go join them," I say to Brenda who was still enjoying the view from the bed I was lying on. She walks up to her co-workers and start to suck off the passenger. The guy moans every time another girl grabs his dick and shove it down their mouths. The view I had from my bed was amazing. I grabbed my cock and started to jerk it off and twist my right nipple. Alexa walks up to me and says, "Let's continue where we left off." I took my chance and grabbed her middle and shoved my cock down her wet fuck hole.

"Oh captain yeah," she screams it out of pleasure. The guy enjoyed the sight so he pulled one of the other flight attendants towards the little table, bents her forward and puts his cock in her nice shaved vagina. Alexa, in the mea time, stills moves up and down my cock and the third flight attendant joins us and starts kissing me. Alexa steps off my cock and tells the other girl it's her turn. It was so hot to hear a girl say that to another. The girl puts her tight vagina over my cock and as it was going deeper and deeper in her I realized she was extremely tight!

"Go on, go on," the girl says. I grab her boobs and make sure I didn't let my dick go out of her wet hole. The guy got very close to cum and right before he wanted to shoot his load, the girl pulled his cock out of her so he wouldn't cum. I stop fucking the flight attendant so I could walk up to the one that was having some fun with the passenger and put my cock, which was so hard and wet, in her. I made her bend forward so she could suck the passenger's cock at the same time. Alexa and Brenda started to kiss each other. I fucked the girl so hard and saw how the other guy enjoyed his blowjob. I really wanted to cum, but I wanted to try Brenda's wet vagina, as I haven't tried her yet. I pull out my cock of the girl and I walk up to Brenda.

"I'm going to cum in you and make you my slut for this trip," I said to Brenda. The guy walks up to Alexa and decided to fuck her right next to me. We both shoved our dicks in our girls, and we looked at each other as we knew this was going to be the hole we were going to cum in. We fucked our girls so hard and they were screaming off pleasure, sometimes I was curious to know if the passengers underneath us in the economy class cabin could hear them. I feel getting very close and the girl says: "Captain I want you to cum in me, make me your slut!"

I grabbed her hair and bent over her and I couldn't hold it any more. I feel the sperm shooting out of my cock into her hole and I moan like I've never done before. At the same time I see the passenger getting close as well. He pulls out his cock and yells to the girl to sit down in front of him. She does it right away and he shoots all over her face. He kept on shooting like there was no ending coming to it. I quickly grab my uniform that was full of coffee to clean myself and put on a new uniform. "I'm so sorry, but we're just about to start our landing so I have to go back," I said. "But let's continue this in the hotel if you like, because trust me I want to cum in all of you girls before heading back to Europe," I continued.

As I was trying to walk out, Alexa walks up to me and kisses me one final time. "Thanks captain, I want to fly with you all the time. You brought us to heights we've never been before," Alexa says.

I walk out and enter the cockpit. Bill, the co-pilot looked at me and says, "I was afraid you would never return. We're about to start our landing."

We both put our headphones on and Bill contacts the tower. Right before landing Bill says, "Did you see Alexa before you got to the crew rest?" All I could think about was what an amazing thing just happened in the crew rest. I can't wait for my flight back!

My Girlfriend's Slutty Roommate

This story I am about to tell you happened some years ago. I'm still a young guy but I was younger still and in college at the time of this story, and I must admit that to this day I am still both a little ashamed and a little turned on by what happened. Also, as a matter of privacy, I will be changing the names around of some of these individuals. So let's go back, shall we?

I'm 20 something years old and in good physical condition. Am I an Olympic athlete? Hell no. But I've got a good physique with nice solid arms and a six pack that definitely gets me glances from all genders when I take my shirt off. Not only that but I have fairly tan skin and a dark complexion, the latter of which has been complimented on more than one occasion as being "sexy and brooding". Personally, I don't know why some people find the brooding thing so sexy, but whatever.

At this time in my life I'm dating a beautiful girl named, let's say, Olivia. Olivia has deep brown eyes, sandy brown hair, and a fairly small frame. Despite her small frame she still goes around rocking it with a pair of 30Ds, or just shy of that size at least. Now Olivia and I have a pretty damn good sex life by most accounts. It's fast, it's fun, and sometimes really fucking messy which is okay with the both of us. More than that we are both up for a little experimenting from time to time, although granted up to this point in our relationship we had only ever really experimented with locations, positions, and a few toys (I think there might have been a little role playing one night when we got really drunk. I was Vegeta and she was Bulma from DragonBall Z but that's an altogether different story.)

At any rate, things are going great, sex is great, and all things considered we are a fairly typical couple. There was really only one problem; I had a massive, raging, fucking hard on for her roommate Natalie. She had at least the same sized breasts as my girlfriend's, if not larger, and a wonderfully shaped ass that practically seemed to shout at me every time I walked past her. Throw in the fact that she had nice, long, blonde hair (perfect for tugging on) and a set of gorgeous blue eyes, and she was definitely a pleasing sight.

Of course it didn't help that my girlfriend's roommates all became increasingly more comfortable around me the longer I hung around, so I saw Natalie in her underwear on more than one occasion. Worse still, Natalie was a bit of a floosy (no slut shaming here, just stating a fact), so lucky dudes were regularly coming in and out of her. Sorry, in and out of *her room*.

Of course I tried to broach the subject with my girlfriend, as any horny, 20 something year old college male would probably do. Naturally, I requested a threesome. Naturally the answer ended up being no, though Olivia did say she didn't mind me checking her roommate out or even flirting with her. With Olivia's blessing I began to do just that. It started out being kind of childish at first, but gradually became more heated and erotic as Natalie responded well over time. Initially it was just little teases here and there about someone's clothes, or someone's hair, or something stupid that one or the other did in a given moment. But when she started flirting with me when she was wearing nothing but a pair of panties and a tight t-shirt it became much more difficult to keep the flirting innocent.

By the time I realized it had gone too far she was regularly cuddling with me on the couch, usually half naked, with her legs draped across my lap. Despite my uncomfortable attraction to her roommate, Olivia never really seemed to mind, and indeed at times seemed to be encouraging it by giving us more private time, or never really bothering to confront either one of us about it. So, naturally, I allowed it to continue until one fine evening about three weeks later when we were all enjoying a few drinks. Now I'm a beer man myself, but that night tequila and vodka were making the rounds and I generally don't say no to free booze being thrust at me.

That night it was my girlfriend, all three of her roommates, including Nat, two guys from next door that Olivia's roommates knew pretty well, and a good buddy I had brought with me. The extra people aren't important really, or their names. What is important, though, is that after several hours of drinking the night eventually escalated into a friendly game of strip poker. I suck dick at poker, and especially so when titties are popping out every which way right at my face. Still I wasn't complaining, not even when my buddy helped my girlfriend get out of her shirt, or when I was out 20 bucks. I wasn't complaining because with each article of clothing remove I got to see a little more of Natalie. Even better Nat was sitting directly to my left, so it wasn't difficult for me to sneak glances at her exposed flesh whenever I felt the need. By the time everyone at the table was down to their skivvies, I could not deny how horny I was getting for Nat, or how broke I was. Better still the other players at the table were starting to get tired or bored with the game, including my girlfriend. It wasn't long after the last game ended that Olivia gave a good yawn, grabbed her clothes, and said goodnight to everyone before heading up the stairs for bed.

The moment Olivia was out of sight, I felt a hand slide up my leg and give my penis a gentle squeeze under the table. I looked to my left and saw Nat looking right at me, perfect blue eyes above a set of gorgeous breasts resting in a blue push up bra. The others began to migrate to the kitchen or the living room, and somebody said something about watching a movie, but the only thing I noticed was Nat's subtle but unmistakeable nod toward the stairs. With alcohol coursing through me, I let Nat practically lead me by the dick up the stairs.

The light was off in my girlfriend's room when we went by and I immediately felt a pang of regret for what I was doing. We stopped just outside Nat's room, which was directly beside my girlfriend's, when I quietly said, "I can't cheat on Olivia. I'm really sorry and I feel like a tool." Nat turned around, and with a sly little smile said, "Oh don't worry, I already asked for Olivia's permission. We wouldn't be here if she hadn't given me a 'yes'."

It took me about five seconds to absorb what I had heard. It took about another 10-15 more before we were bursting through Nat's bedroom door and I was tossing her on the bed, ripping off her panties. Now personally I have always enjoyed eating a woman out. I think it's sexy and one of the best ways to show a woman that you can reciprocate. But eating Nat out was pure fucking ecstasy. Her pussy was nice and clean shaven, maybe even waxed though it was hard to tell in the dark, but it was warm and surprisingly sweet. I say surprisingly because it wasn't, but I didn't want to sound like a dick. Needless to say my cock was pressing painfully against the seams of my boxers. Thankfully it wasn't long before Nat gave me a little push and she dropped to her knees in front of me around the same second my boxers dropped to the floor. She took me full in her mouth. I actually felt her tonsils before I felt her tongue. She stayed on her knees like that for probably a good five minutes until I turned on the lamp next to her bed to get a better view. Gorgeous blue eyes looking up at me, I quickly adjusted her hair to get the best view possible. She moved her head up and down, alternating working the shaft with her tongue and then with her whole mouth before moving on to the head. Sadly I have super ticklish balls, so when she tried to lick those I fucking kicked like a mule and poked her in the eye. I apologized profusely and she gave a good laugh so it was all cool.

She stood up in front of me, turned around, and unhooked her bra in what has to be one of the sexiest things I have ever seen in my life. Not able to contain myself any longer I pushed her down onto the bed frontwards and lifted her ass up into the air. I settled myself onto the bed, just between her legs, and stuffed her pussy with my cock. In retrospect I felt kind of bad because I rammed it in there so hard, but I was too fucking horny and too fucking drunk to really care. I'm above average in case anyone is wondering. 6 ½ inches. And I wear it fucking proudly. The first thing I noticed once I was inside her was how incredibly wet she was. Like significantly more wet than my girlfriend ever got. The next thing I noticed was she was already squeezing my cock as if she were cumming. I railed away at her for what felt like the better part of an hour before she asked me to switch positions. I was loathe to do so, as I had spent months ogling that ass and I was finally giving it the punishment it deserved. Still, I was eager to see her in other positions, too, so I let her take the reigns for a while.

Fortunately for me, she was very experienced and she hopped up on my cock as if she was born to it. She bounced up and down, nice and slow at first, settling into a good rhythm, but before long I felt like I was about to break a hip. It was then I also realized we were making a fuck ton of noise. I suggested quieting down but she just laughed and said, "I don't care if the others hear, and I want Olivia to hear. I want her to hear me fucking her man so that she understands it's not her cock anymore." I about burst a load just hearing her say that. Rather than spoil the fun prematurely though, I sat up and pushed her on to her back so that her head was hanging off the side of the bed. Seeing her like that, with the lighting perfectly bouncing of her breasts, and her head dangling off the side of the bed, made me feel like a fucking animal.

Once I was back inside her I knew that I wasn't going to last much longer so I pumped her hard and fast, all the while enjoying that wonderful squeezing of her pussy before finally pulling out and shooting a load so hard it reached to the underside of her breasts. I fell backwards off her onto the pillows and looked over at the clock to discover that eight minutes had gone by. Still, I felt touched by the hand of God in that moment and incredibly happy. Except it wasn't actually God it was a 22 year old female with an incredibly hot body. It wasn't God. She siddled up next to me and rested her head down on a pillow. I helped her get cleaned up and we had a nice chat about whatever came to mind.

After about 20 minutes I decided I should probably go check on Olivia, and potentially beg for forgiveness. When I sat up and swung my legs over the edge of the bed Nat said behind me, "Hey. . . You know I didn't get off right?"

I looked at her, stunned, before finally saying, "Not my problem." I then grabbed my clothes and left. I went into the next room, which was completely dark, and stumbled my way to Olivia's bed in the far corner. Once in bed next to her she reached over, slapped me, then gave me an incredibly impassioned kiss. Then she said, "I could hear you both next door through the walls... I couldn't resist touching myself to the sound of it. I think next time I want to watch." With that I realized three things: my girlfriend was naked and incredibly wet; my girlfriend was a bit of a cuck; and my girlfriend had just made me horny all over again. What happened next? I'm sure you can figure it out... Yes. Yes, I rolled over and went to sleep.

BDSM, Bondage, Discipline, Domination, Submission, Sadochism, and Masochism

Locked Up and Bound:
My First Memory As Her Slave

I force my eyes to open. Murky black is all my eyes will allow in. I try to pull my hand to my face just to feel it being held to a cold, damp wall. I struggle, trying to free myself. Kicking and screaming. My legs jerk back as I try to pull them up to me. Shooting pain goes up my leg, into my thigh, my ankles raw from the rope binding them to the floor.

My head is filled with fog, and bits of what seems like a movie starring myself. My lungs filled with dirty air. My mouth filled with the fading taste of blood and mildew. All I hear is the dripping of what I can only pray to be water. There is no light were I am. There is no fresh air were I am. There is only myself, confusion, and pain. I try to remember what has happened to me. I try to remember who I even am. I have no idea how long I have been here or will be here in this room.

I hear faint pats of bare feet against a concrete floor. They get closer and closer to me. The louder they become, the more I can make out a faint glow around what I assume to be a door. The fear in me bubbles up to my eyes, and it slowly starts to slide down my cheek. Whoever or whatever is coming toward me is almost here. The soft glow is now lighting the room to a point where I can make out concrete walls and a roof. There is a leak dripping down the wall. Thank god it is water. The slapping of feet stops just outside my prison's door. I hear a heavy lock turn over, and a faint blow as the light goes out. The room is dark again, silent, but I can feel someone there. I can hear their breaths entering and leaving their lips. I know they are near me, and I know they relish in my fear.

I hear an ever so slight giggle echo off the walls around me. It is a woman's voice. She hums a song that in any other time or place would almost be enjoyable.

I feel a warm hand touch above the rope on my ankle. I flinch and try to pull away only to be pulled back in place by the rope. "Play nice with me," she whispers. "I don't want to hurt you again."

Again? I ask myself. I froze. The fear I thought I had known was nothing to this. Her hand creeps up my leg. I can feel her at my feet; I can hear her breaths grow fast. She reaches up between my thighs and grabs hold of my dick. She starts sliding her hand up and down on it. Gently sliding her thumb over the tip every time she gets to the top. I feel myself growing in her hands. I cannot help it. The slower she goes, the more I harden, the more I can feel my blood pumping.

Her hand slips away from me, only for me to feel her legs crawl onto my lap. I can feel the soft hair of her moist pussy teasing me. Almost as if she is hovering over me making her hips go in little circles. I feel her soft lips kiss my neck. Her hands pull my face to her breast. "Suck," is all I hear. Suck is all I can do. I feel her hard nipple rub against my lips, begging for my tongue to come out. I open my mouth and begin to suckle like a newborn child. I run my tongue around it. I kiss her breast leading to them. I hear her heavy breaths turn to soft moans. The harder I suck, the more I can feel her pussy drip on to me. I am throbbing. I can feel just between the lips now. She lowers her body more. The tip of my dick can feel her clit going in those little circles .

I bite down on her nipple lightly. She moans louder and begins running herself back and forth on top of me now.

"HARDER," she demands. I bite down almost bringing blood to my mouth. "OH GOD YES, AGAIN," she screams. I begin to feel her warm blood flow into my mouth, and I bite down on her hard nipples another time. And with the blood flow, I feel her allowing me inside of her.

I can hear her legs hitting my own as she picks up speed. I feel my dick ramming her insides, begging for more. Her moans grow louder and louder until they are screams of pleasure. Her hands are now on my shoulders for support. I can feel her ass bounce off of my legs. Every breath she takes grows louder and louder. Her pussy so tight, so ready for me. Every time she slams down on me, I can feel my dick forcing its way into her.

She is screaming out now, no more moans. "OH GOD, OH GOD, YES, YES!"

She slows down . I can feel her teasing herself. I can feel my own breath growing fast. I let out moans of pleasure. I want more. She hovers above me only allowing the head to go in and out slowly. Getting deeper and deeper as she goes on. She finally thrust back down. I feel the warmth around it. It is holding on to me ,not wanting to let it go out again. It is tightening. I can feel my cum building up inside me. She is riding me at such a pace I know it won't be long before she is done.

I am about to burst inside her. I can no longer think. I no longer care where I am or how I got there. I can smell her sweat, and I can feel her pussy tighten around my dick as she cums with me. She moans as every pump of my cum goes into her. One last thrust before she stands up.

I am out of breath now. It is hot in this room now. I am exhausted. I hear her footsteps walking away. I hear a heavy door pull to and a lock click. With a strike of a match the glow of light is once again streaming through the outline of the door. I hear that same song, that humming, and she walks away from me. Leaving me again in this dark room. I know now why I am here. I know now that she will be back.

Blindfolded and Whipped

I could hear her stilettos clicking against the hardwood floors. I could only imagine her wearing those red ones I liked on her. I had gifted them to her on her birthday. She had never worn them. Now, I know what you must be thinking. When do girls ever say no to shoes? And on top of that, I am not the type of man to gift her expensive gifts. But one of my colleagues had given his wife the same pair and his wife, with happiness, had turned all wild in bed. I could only hope I would get the same.

"Oh yes, you wanted me to wear them, didn't you? Especially in bed. How you always complain about me never valuing you. Well, you got your wish..." Her soft voice touched my ears silently. I gulped.

"So sad that you can't see me wear them though. Especially when you are tied down and blindfolded," she continued as the clicking of her shoes stopped. They resumed as I could feel her presence on me now. She was rubbing her leg against mine. Her lips were so close to my ears. I could feel her hot breath on me. "Oh, and of course I have fulfilled your top fantasy today... I am wearing only my shoes..." That was it for my penis as it sprang to life like a hungry leopard smelling his prey. She then proceeded to climb on to me and she sat on my chest. I could see her hands moving to slap me through the satin cloth covering my eyes. Instead, it was a whip. She whipped me as I cried out in pain. This was my first time. It was a different type of pain.

"Do you want more?" she asked seductively as she touched the tip of the whip on my dick, which was already secreting love juices.

"Yes, Mistress," I said.

And she gave a quick blow to my dick. It was pain laced with pleasure. My cock wanted it. Wanted more. I could not believe this. I was in pain and nearly all of my body knew it, except my dick. She then proceeded to take my dick in her mouth. I was in heaven. I was tied to the floor, helpless, in pain and yet I found this experience strangely erotic. She was suckling on it like never before. Bouts of pleasure coursed through my veins as I begged for more. But just as I was about to come, she retracted her lips. She got up and sat on my face. The wetness between her legs was oddly sweet.

"Lick," she ordered and I obeyed. I licked her clean as she bit into my nipples hard. When I would stop because of the pain, she would start flogging me again. It was an amazing feeling. I would continue to lick her. As her moans became louder, I could feel her body contract in pleasure as she bit into my nipples, pulling my balls artistically as I moaned too. Her wet pussy exploded with juice in my mouth as I slopped it clean like a faithful dog.

And then it was her turn. She got up and then started literally sucking on my dick so hard that I had to bite my lips to keep my body from exploding. It was pleasure I had never felt. I came into her mouth as she continued to give me a blowjob.

"Next time, keep the toilet seat down. Honey..." She said as she got up and walked away.

"Wait! Untie me," I said but it went unheard. But I wasn't complaining. At least the shoes helped.

The Sluttiest Slut in Slut Town: An Erotica Gangbang, Bukkake, and Double Penetration Story

A group of naked and half-dressed men milled around. Some getting dressed, some cleaning the spunk off their spent boners, others just kicking back and enjoying a beer while watching the huge-titted slut they had just used and abused repeatedly. Sitting naked on the hotel room floor, her breasts a reddish tint from excessively rough handling, her mascara smeared all around her face, cum dripping from her gaping pussy and another globby string of sloppy cum balanced precariously on the tip of her nose, Sally asked herself, "How the hell did I get myself into this situation?"

And the answer was simple enough. She was a slut. A true blue, cock-guzzling, pussy-licking, fucked-silly slut. Now, granted, she wasn't a whore. Sally never took money for the multitude of cocks she regularly took into her mouth, pussy, and asshole. No, no, no. She was no whore. She was just a woman who loved to fuck, cash money optional. It seemed somehow wrong to her, ethically, to take payment for something she was going to do for free anyway. Besides, why did she need any more money? As a power-broking head of an upstart internet company well on its way to Fortune 500 status, she had all the green stuff she needed.

But it was the white stuff she wanted. White hot jizz splattered all over her body. A creamy, tasty treat force-fed down her throat and hand-delivered right from the end of a throbbing young cock. Or old cock. It didn't matter. She liked them all. Things just work out that way sometimes. It started with her eagerly accepting the advances of a hot young college kid in the dive bar down the street – flattered by the attention, more than glad to accept his invitation back to his hotel room. And it ended with her satisfied, knees weak and wobbly, gasping for breath and sitting on the hotel room floor having just been fucked by ten, count them TEN, young cocks.

What Sally didn't know was that when Ted invited her back to his hotel room, he didn't just want to fuck her. He wanted to fuck her and share her with his nine closest frat buddies. Of course, being the sluttiest slut in Slut Town, this would have only made Sally the Slut want to go to the hotel with him even more.

But he didn't know that, so she acted surprised and aghast at the thought of taking on that many men at once. But in her head, she knew she could take on at least twice that many. And take them on she did. She delighted herself that night taking all she could. Never a slow starter, she got right to work upon seeing the surprise group Ted had arranged for her. Her clothes were barely off before she was grunting and wailing as one stud fucked her ass and another thrust in and out of her pussy. Always good at math, Sally realized that left eight unused cocks to do with as she pleased. So she pulled over two of them and guided them both into her wet mouth. She was an all-night sucker, Sally the Slut.

"Mmmmmph, mmmphhh, mm-zzzgrph" she murmured, unable to properly articulate her thought as her mouth seemed to be jammed full with two thrusting cocks. Her inner mathematician went back to work.

"Let's see," she thought, "there are ten men here. I have one cock in my pussy. One cock in my ass. Which kind of hurts, by the way, but I'm not complaining. And two in my mouth. I need more." She motioned a couple more of the inexperienced but eager to learn college boys over because her hands just weren't busy enough. One cock for rightie and one engorged pecker for leftie would occupy them for a while. Her tits bounced wildly as she was pulled every direction and fucked hard, jerking the cocks in her hands, sucking the cocks in her mouth, her pussy stretched to the limit by a particularly thick one, and her asshole stinging and tingling simultaneously as the cock of the redheaded kid mounting her beat a steady thump, thump, thump rhythm right up her butt end. The boys fucking her mouth pulled out.

"Not fair," she thought, "I wasn't through with those cocks."

"Wait a minute, guys," she said, ready to complain about the total and utter lack of cocks in her mouth. But she was barely halfway through her sentence when she felt a gushy, salty spurt hit the back of her throat, catching her with her mouth fully open. Another followed, and then another. She laughed, hadn't seen that cumming coming.

"Okay," she giggled, "Good shot, fella." She loved the salty taste of a man's cum. It was one of her favorite tastes, and one she seemed to taste a lot. And now she had a good, solid mouthful of it.

"Hooray!" she thought. She swished it around, savoring that wonderful taste. "But wait," she thought,

"Maybe I can get another shot of that good stuff." And she turned to the other guy who she had in her mouth for that delightful double-suck, the guy she had affectionately nicknamed Cock #2. But she was out of luck with her oral desires there. Because his aim wasn't so good. Or maybe it was and she just didn't know what he was aiming for. The first sticky stream blasted her right on the cheek. But that which followed painted her face pretty good. What a fucking mess. What a lovely, lovely fucking mess.

Her right eye was pretty much plastered shut by the gooey glob of jizz congealed about it. Her cheek was just dripping with it. Her nose decorated with huge gobs of it. Fun! That was the start of her night. And before she was done, there were eight more satisfied bros and who knows how many pints of jizz covering her naked, writhing body in strategic positions from head to toe. She asked Ted, the smooth-talker from the bar and the last to cum – dropping a healthy load deep into her ass – if he'd like to meet up for a second date.

"No way!" he replied, "You just fucked all of my friends. You're far too much of a slut for me!"

Bound by Rope then Teased and Ravaged

Devin could feel the roughness of the ropes around his wrists. He had been wanting this for a long time now. But he didn't know how nervous he would be. The whip stung his bare flesh. This excited him more than he thought it would. His cock was so very hard, but she wouldn't touch him. He moaned in pleasure, in pain. This was all so new to him. Jessica was tall with long black hair. She wore shiny black heels and a mesh dress that showed her pink perky nipples. He wanted to touch her. To be inside of her, but he couldn't, and that was the excitement of this game they were playing.

Jessica picked up a candle from the many sitting on the waxy dresser and began to pour it down his chest. Devin bit his lip trying not to scream in pain. At first it was a burning sensation. But soon it cooled and he was relieved. Precum was now dripping from his cock. He wasn't sure how much more he could take. He was about to blow.

Jessica gently pressed down her heel onto his balls. Knowing just what he needed but wanting to tease him more. She began rubbing her cunt in front of him. Rubbing her clit in small circles, moaning in front of him. Devin's eyes widened as he thrusted towards her. Precum running down his cock and onto her heels. She licked her wet fingers and put them in her pussy, moving them slowly in and out, making sure he could see everything she was doing. Teasing him made her so wet. She wanted his dick just as bad as he wanted her.

While untying him, she pressed herself against him. He could feel her moist pussy through her mesh dress and rubbed his dick against her. The sensation was more than he anticipated. Devin picked Jessica up and set her down on the edge of the bed. He got down on his knee and began licking her wet, wanting cunt. He licked his pointer finger and put in her ass. She moaned in pleasure and surprise. She rocked back and forth, thrusting at his mouth. Shaking, she gripped her legs around his head. He pinched and pulled at her harden nipples sending her into more screams of pleasure. He licked up and down her pussy, from her clit down to the opening, licking circles around it and sticking his tongue inside of her, feeling the tightness of it and her pulsating. He needed her now more than before. Devin got up and pushed himself inside of her, thrusting himself deep and fast.

She moaned and grabbed at him, clawing at his back. He held her tightly, ramming her deep, her wetness running down his balls. He wasn't sure how long he could hold back his cum. He grabbed her shaking tits and slowed down a bit. Then Ddevin took his thumb and started rubbing Jessica's clit. Her legs began to shake harder, and so he sped up again. She began screaming, and he could feel her tight pussy throbbing around his cock. He couldn't hold it in any longer. She pressed her legs around him and he blew his load inside of her. Both of them screaming and moaning together.

Becoming Her Slave: A Fetish Story

I was a kind of guy who hated being in the company of girls. If ever I come across a corridor at college full of girls, or maybe even three or four of them, I would just turn back, slyly trying not to catch their attention, and would follow another route to my classroom. Hitherto, I haven't tried to investigate further into my strange demeanor; nor have I felt it being strange.

But with the porn, my cup of coffee was a little deviant. Instead of hard core milf fucking websites, I usually roamed around more in the Dominant/ Submissive ones, and I really enjoyed femdom.

I completed my college evading all those hurdles. The problem was that, after the freshman year of my post-graduation, college was unusually brimming with hotties, those kinds of hot gorgeous girls who would give you an instant erection even by the way they look at you. Even though mesmerized, I still had that feeling lingering inside me, a feeling of fright towards the opposite gender.

But it all changed one day. The day Rachel Rowlands sat beside me. I hadn't noticed her till now, and I was wondering why. She was hot, and beautiful. Unlike the other loads that seemed like spending hours on their makeups, which were evident from the pale look on their faces, Rachel looked simple. The only kind of makeup I could see on her face was that the thin black eyeliner she had used, which was rendering her an unworldly grace. The trail of smell that hanged around her was that of lavenders. Hot indeed. For me. The strips of her bra was barely visible through the semi-transparent T-Shirt she had been wearing, and the second I visualized in my mind how I would do in the bed with her, a bump rose on my pants.

I would be chained to the pole of my bed, with a slave collar around my neck, with her standing in front of me, slowly removing her panties, slow and seducing. She would then throw the worn out panties onto my miserable face, which I would die to smell. I would lay there, gripping the panties tight within my teeth, like an obedient dog, Then she would come sit beside me, sponging my forehead and looking deeply at me, with those beautiful blue eyes, and she would ask me, in her tempting sweet velvet voice,

"Do you want to sniff my ass slave?"

Now, I felt like, that is the moment, I have lived for. To be bound, with the look of a pervert on my face, worshipping my mistress.

During the first day, she initiated the talk. At first, I had felt it so hard to talk to her, but within a week, I was feeling comfortable. She was very talkative, and I still don't know what trait she has found interesting in me, that she started to stick around me always; during the lunch, in the lab and during the evening walks to home. She lived just a block away from me, and it was during our talks during the walks to college that I got to know her more. And she was one of the rarest person to whom I have revealed my secret.

Not about my deviant passions; not about the whips and the chains, but about my income.

Even though an orphan and a loner, I was the richest guy in the college. My money came from my research stuff, which I sold to a pharmaceutical giant for twenty million dollars.

With my surplus supply of money and with my fear about the girls slowly vanishing, I began spending more time with Rachel; bunking classes and going for the movies, and spending time travelling. Always in those moments, I considered her my goddess, whom I worshipped in all ways.

Then one twilight, she decided to drop in at my place.

For a loner like me, a doorbell at that time was highly improbable.

When I opened up the door, I saw Rachel, smiling at me in her elegant black dress.

I felt powerless, and I felt like dropping to my knees.

Without waiting for my invitation and the other pleasantries, she walked inside. I slammed the door behind me.

The rest of the story happened in my bedroom. Just as I had expected it to happen.

By the time I had went to kitchen and prepared something for her to drink, she had went through my diary, which was laying spread eagle on my escritoire. The diary in which I used to write my wildest dreams with Rachel. By the time I got back from the kitchen, I saw her reading it, and then she looked at me, and for my wonder, still wearing that gorgeous smile.

Without a word, I dropped to my knees, as if acted upon by a demonic charm. She walked to me, not with a look of surprise, but of anticipation; and then stopped right where I was standing, her stockings just inches away from my face. I looked up and caught the meaningful stare she threw me, and then acknowledging it, I bent down slowly, and kissed her high heels. I just waited for her response, slyly forgetting how awful the predicament was. She then reached down, caught the hair at the back of my head and pulled me up. When I looked at her, she gave me a smile, breathtaking indeed, a smile of satisfaction.

I bent down, now a slave to my beautiful goddess, and kissed her heels again. She caught my hair again and dragged me to the cot. Then, as I had seen in my wildest dreams, she let me lick her pussy. She cummed into my mouth at its end. She then gave me the honor of being her seat. She sat and smothered me with her pussy for more than half an hour. Never in my life before I been this fond of getting strangled.

The aroma of air that rushed past her ass and pussy, saturating my nostrils, was intoxicating. She would rise up for one or two seconds, then would settle onto my face, trying desperate to take in the air. After an hour of face sitting session, she allowed me to shove my tongue into her beautiful ass. She held me tight into her ass as she moaned in ecstasy, and then she allowed me to worship her feet for a while.

During the night, she took her laptop, and while sitting on my face, she told me she was going to transfer all my money to her account, and she told me to beg to her to do so. Then she raised her sweaty pussy off my face, and I begged, "My mistress, please take all my money, I submit to you, for a lifetime of servitude."

I saw the gleam in her eyes impaling me. I saw Rachel phasing from being my beautiful best friend to my lifetime mistress.

She gave me some seconds to enter my pin number, and then she sat right back right into my face again, and then moaned, and fingered while she was on my face, to another orgasm.

117

Sex with a Psychopath: The Stalker Finds Himself Chained Up

I've been sitting here for over an hour. The last person, I think an assistant manager, locks the place up and leaves for the night. No more hair appointments today. No girlfriend...

The street lights in the alley hum and buzz as they flicker on, illuminating piles of old shit, broken pallets, wet boxes, and my resting spot in the alley across the street. The stink of greasy food cooking in someone's home escapes from the nearby windows. Enough of this. I look at my phone. 8:23pm... This is unlike her. I've been watching this one for a month. My green eyed goddess. She never deviates. She's always so predictable. Alarm at 5AM, then 30 minutes to wake and shower, never eats breakfast. Minutes later, I watch her pull her blond hair back in a ponytail before running down the steps of her building at 6AM. I will tell her to drink more water. Her skin will get dry... I lick my lips. I snap back to reality as a man and his dog pass by me, out for a walk in the evening breeze. The dog sniffs my pants leg and the man, a stinking, fat, ape of a man, pulls back on the leash. He sees me. A smile gathers in his eyes but quickly dies before the muscles in his face fully engage. He looks down quickly and walks a little faster down the sidewalk, away from me. I take this as my cue to leave. Where was she?

I walk a block to my car. I shut my door and calmly drive the three miles to her apartment. I met her here for the first time. She didn't close her blinds. I know that she wanted me to see her. I leaned against the wall looking in as she dropped her towel. Her nipples were so pink and her tits so wet from the shower. She stared out of the window and I could almost believe she was looking right into my eyes. I felt myself get hard and rubbed my cock through my jeans. She walked away from the window and I saw with pleasure a full bush and firm ass. I knew her cunt was wet, too. I immediately wanted to fuck her. I could imagine how tight she would be. I could imagine my cum dripping out of her pussy, down her leg. What man wouldn't? I knew she was special. She was better, she deserved more than a few drinks at the bar and a hard fuck in the lady's room. I wasn't wrong about her. Not like that last woman, that bitter disappointment. I'd done so much for her. I knew that bitch better than her own mother. She rejected me so I sent her away. The 5th one. I must have been wrong about all of them.

But, no one is like my green-eyed beauty. She would understand what an honor it was that out of all women she was the one I wanted. And, I let my thoughts wander again. Her place is dark. The curtains drawn tight. This is very unlike her. She lives on routine. I sigh and try to think of all the places she could be. I have watched her. She has no friends or family nearby. She is perfect for me on so many levels. Made for me. Mine with no distractions. I wonder... what if something happened to her? Would anyone notice? I start to feel a little worried and, for the first time ever, I cross the street to her apartment. I hop up on the curb and walk to the back of the building. The ladder to the fire escape is easy to reach and I pull it down, trying to make as little noise as possible. First, second floor, I'm noisy, but love requires boldness, right?

Her window is open... I pause. The curtains move softly in the breeze. I can smell bleach and vanilla and HER, I breathe deeply. A door opens in the alley below me. Two men are talking in Spanish. I catch a few words but the conversation doesn't interest me. They need to leave. I can't move until they do. I sit for ages. It's fully dark now and I hear someone on the street saying goodbye and then the putter of a small car driving away. A cat maows and mrmraws nearby then falls silent. More time passes and even the moon falls out of view. I slowly move, my legs are stiff and protest as I crawl to the open window. In all this time I've never heard a sound from the apartment. It's so quiet.

I push back the fabric and step inside, my feet land on the floor. Her floor. I catch movement off to the right, but when I turn to look there's nothing there. What's wrong with me? I'm not going to start jumping at shadows. I need to calm down and savor this moment. How many times have I dreamed of this, of being here?

I realize I'm in her bedroom. I expected to see neatness and I'm not disappointed. There is not a single pair of dirty panties, or anything else, on the floor anywhere. There isn't even a glass on the nightstand. There is a hamper in the corner. Empty. So much for that. Her closet has a few items wrapped in plastic and an old jacket. It smells like lavender and vanilla. I sit down on the bed. It's firm, nice. It's covered by a thick cotton blanket and three of those round bed pillows women seem to like. She slept naked here. I remember... The first time I'd seen her, she sat on the bed and dried her hair with her towel. She reached over and shut her curtains, but I knew, I could imagine her laying back with her legs spread. Her right hand starts to pull at her nipples, teasing them, rolling them, while her left hand goes down to her pussy. Her fingers glide over her clit and her fingertips slip inside and stretch the walls of her vagina. She pumps her wet, slippery fingers in and out, arching her back ever so slightly. Her fingers slip out and begin to rub her clit. Again and again, she pulls and rubs her breasts, pinching her nipples as she fingers her clit. The wetness runs out of her, over her pulsing asshole, to the bed. Her face gets red and her breath comes quickly and she gasps as her orgasm hits her hard. She bites her lip with her perfect white teeth and forcefully bucks her ass up and down on the bed. As she comes, her fingers find her hole again and she fucks herself through her orgasm. She leans back, satisfied, and licks her fingers. Oh sweet memories...

My hand is stroking my cock and in seconds my cum is making a little puddle on her nice white blanket. I imagine taking a hot handful of it and smearing it on her tits. She's going to pay for making me worry like this. I dress and walk into the kitchen. There are no dishes in the sink. The only sign of recent life is a quarter loaf of rye bread on the counter. The refrigerator has a half bottle of wine and what smells like a Reuben sandwich, Probably from the deli on the corner, Stan's. From the light of the fridge I catch sight of a piece of paper on the floor in the corner. I stoop to retrieve it and hit my head on the table. This had better be worth it. Something is written on what's obviously an oil stained fast food bag. A corner of one anyway. Nasty. All it says is:

6PM tonight 555-867-5309 J

J? Who the fuck is J? What is a J? My thoughts race and my blood is boiling. I'm angry like never before. She is MINE. How DARE she?! I crumple the paper and smash my fist against the counter. How dare she?! I'm so lost in my rage that I never hear her soft footsteps or see the axe handle swinging until it's much too late to get out of the way. My world goes white and pain comes to stay like a living thing in my head. I fall hard and roll to my back. Before I pass out... Pressure. A small foot on my chest.

###

"About damn time. I've been looking forward to meeting you, Alex. Do you have any idea how long I've been watching you?" She grins and I lose my contact with the world. I taste blood. What the hell is this? There is something over my eyes. I move my head and a tight band of pain squeezes my temples. More blood. I try to sit up but can't move. Something tight is around my chest and... I can't move my arms. I think those are tied, too. No, metal. Handcuffs? She Handcuffed me?? The BITCH! I try to kick and realize that my feet are tied down, too. I remember what happened and the rage bubbles to the surface. Doesn't she know who I am? I try to speak but something has been stuffed in to my mouth. I tear at it with my teeth. I hear a muffled growling and realize that it's coming from me. Stop. Control. I get quiet and listen. I am the Alpha. I am better than this. Where am I? This wasn't how it was supposed to happen.

I am on her bed. I can feel the texture of the blanket on my cheek. The fucking bitch hit me and tied me to her bed. Her bed... None of this is right.

"He's awake, Anna." It has to be a woman. I lunge toward the voice, getting nowhere. I feel what can only be the blade of a knife on my neck. I can feel it cutting into me. I feel someone sit on the bed beside me and my blindfold is pulled away. The room is dark but I can see Her. A knife clutched in her hand. My Beauty. Why was the other one calling her Anna? Her mail was addressed to Susan. Her name was Susan, wasn't it? The other woman got up and walked out of the room.

"He's all yours, sweetie." I hear a door close in another room. Even like this I am captivated by her. This is my prize. My reward. Why was I tied up like this? She was the one destined for chains, bound. She should be begging me to pull her hair as I fuck her from behind. That is our Story!

"I know who you are, Alex. I know what you are." Her finger trails down my neck. "You killed five women. I watched you with the last one. I saw you squatting like a dog beside a bench in the park, watching her. I followed you back and forth to her house for days and you never noticed. Alex, understand. You are mine. You are made for me. We are the same." She climbs on top of me. Her weight feels amazing. She slips her knife under my gag and it falls away.

"Beauty..." She silences me with her tongue in my mouth. She tastes rich, musky. Her teeth capture my tongue and I wince as she bites down. What in the hell am I doing?! I turn my head away. "Let me go. Untie me!"

She laughs, "I don't think so! Do you really want to stop? We've both been waiting for so long..." She leans back and starts grinding her ass against my cock.

Her pussy feels hot through my jeans. I feel my cock grow tight against the fabric. She feels it too and presses against my erection while rolling her hips side to side. I close my eyes. I can play this game, too. But, who will end up on top? She shifts and I hear her on the floor beside the bed. I open my eyes as she stands with her hands pulling down the waist band of her shorts, her little red shorts. Her panties fall away, too. I can see wetness glistening in her bush. I want to bury my face there and bite. She unbuttons her shirt slowly as she walks to the foot of the bed. Her bra matches her panties and they both end up together on the floor. Her nipples are small and hard. I want to bite those, too.

"Let me go." I say, trying to breathe. My cock is painfully hard in my pants. I'm going to pin her to the bed and shove it up her ass.

She bites her lip, the sexiest thing I've ever seen, and calmly answers, "Nope." Then, she crawls up my legs like a wild animal, a tiger on the prowl, and presses her face against the bulge in my pants. Her hot breath makes me gasp. I scream when she bites me. Oh Fucking God I want Her! She unzips my pants and my cock pops out like a nasty jack in the box. She grabs it and squeezes it. A drop of juice appears at the tip and with the gentlest of motions, she licks it off. I want to be inside of her, now. She reaches in my pants and begins to cradle my balls as she continues to squeeze my cock. Her lips brush against the shaft and it jerks in her hand. She smiles and licks the entire length of me from balls to tip. She licks me again and then I feel her mouth envelop me. I feel her tongue rubbing against my head, it circles the tip, probes the hole, before my cock plunges down her throat. I can feel her lips at the base as she pulls at my balls, kneading them in her hand. Her lips slide up my shaft and with a wet plopping noise, my cock exits her mouth. Spit drips down her chin.

"Your cock is huge... Do you still want me to let you go?" she breathes.

"Yes..."

"What will you do if I untie you?"

"What do you think? I'll make you pay." Pay she would. I watch as she unties my legs. she doesn't make a sound and neither do I. The strap across my chest is removed and I still hold still. My eyes fix on hers... When My arms are free I stand up. My cock is throbbing and knows exactly where it wants to go. I grab

Her and push her down on the bed. This will not be easy for her. I haven't forgotten what her and her friend, can't forget about her, have done to me. My teeth find her hard little nipples and I bite down. She cries out but I stop her cry with my mouth on hers. I kiss her hard and force my tongue in her mouth, gaging her. She arches her back and opens her legs to me. I feel her wet bush against my cock, moving side to side. I can feel how much she wants me. Her hot pussy is begging to be filled. But not yet. I shift position and flip her on her face. She gasps with the sudden movement. I grab her legs and find her pussy with my mouth. She tastes just like I knew she would, sweet and tangy, perfect. I get my finger wet in her pussy and with a twist, slip it hard into her tiny little asshole. I hear a muffled cry from the pillows. My finger moves in and out, hard and fast in but slowly out. Her pussy starts to drip with her excitement.

I part her pussy lips and lap it up with my tongue as I slip a second finger in her ass. My other hand finds her tits and I start pulling her nipples. She groans and strains to press her ass tighter against my fingers. I push her down on her face. I grab her legs and pull her to the edge of the bed. She looks back at me with huge eyes as I stroke my cock. I lift her a bit and guide my shaft deep into her hot pussy. I go in hard. I drive it into her. She throws her head back, her mouth wide open. She's taking all of me. I gather her hair in my fist and pull her head back.

I hiss, "Is this what you wanted?" into her ear. "Answer me." I spank her ass leaving a nice red spot. She makes a noise that I take for agreement. Not enough. "Answer me, now." I pinch her nipple.

"Yes, Oh SHIT, Yes!" I feel myself cum. My cock pulsates and jumps inside of her, deep inside of her. I bite her neck, my orgasm pinning her to the bed. She was mine. The door opens and a tall black woman walks in. The gun is pointed at my face. She says, "What the actual fuck?" and cocks the hammer.

Total Penectomy: How I Became a Proper Slave

Being a first-year resident at a large city hospital can be a real bitch. They work you half to death, and there's no time for a life besides work. That's why some of the residents date each other. And that's how I met Rachel.

I remember the first time I saw her. We were making our rounds together, and I couldn't believe how beautiful she was. She was average height, but that was the only thing average about her. Long flowing brown hair, stunning green eyes, and a great body. All the other guys noticed her too, and she got a lot of come-ons. But she rejected all of them with a little smile.

I figured I didn't have a chance with Rachel. I'm an average-looking guy, and very shy. But I got the shock of my life at the end of our rounds one grueling day. We had both pulled a double shift, and all I wanted to do was crawl into bed and sleep. That is until Rachel came over to me and said, " Rob, I really need you to come back to my apartment right now and give me a good fuck." My mouth must have dropped open because Rachel laughed out loud. "I'm serious. Can you come with me now?" I babbled yes, and before long I was in her apartment as excited as I had ever been.

Rachel's body was just as fabulous as I had imagined. Her firm breasts were topped by luscious nipples that just begged to be sucked. Her pussy was shaven bare. I could barely get my clothes off fast enough, and my cock was pointing straight at the ceiling when I did. All I wanted to do was slip it into her and start pumping, but Rachel had other ideas.

"No screwing until you get my motor running, Rob," she said, plopping into an easy chair. "Get down on your knees." A second later my head was buried in her snatch, and my tongue was coaxing her clit out of its hiding place.

"Ooo, that's nice, " she moaned, wrapping her gorgeous long legs around my waist. My face was soon covered with her pussy juice, and she was pushing her cunt into my face in a rocking motion. Rachel was holding my head in place with both hands. Her clit was swollen to twice its original size. "Oh Yes!" she screamed, as her legs held me so tight I almost couldn't breathe. I swear she came like a man, because a spurt of liquid hit me right in the middle of my face.

After catching her breath, she spread her legs wide. "Well, let's get it over with," she said, making it obvious that she found the task unpleasant. I eagerly pushed my cock into her slippery vagina, and she tightened her snatch muscles as I moved in and out. I was so excited, and she manipulated her cunt so expertly, that I spurted my cum in less than a minute. As soon as I pulled my cock out of her, Rachel got up and climbed into her bed. "Don't forget to turn out the light off when you leave," she said dismissively, turning away from me.

I sheepishly pulled on my clothes and left as Rachel fell asleep. That started the pattern for our relationship. Rachel made no pretense of an emotional connection between us. I was just an easy way for her to come to orgasm. For a while she let me put my cock into her cunt, but then she stopped allowing it. I was expected to bring her to climax first, then I could jerk off while looking at her lounging there naked. It was a little disappointing, but I was willing to do it just so I could be with Rachel. She was the most gorgeous woman I had ever had sex with, and I was obsessed by her. Before long, Rachel became more demanding. She starting making me clean her apartment and run errands, using my own money to buy her groceries. While I was washing dishes and mopping the floor, I couldn't wear anything but a leather strap tied around my balls. If I displeased her in any way, she swatted my bare ass with her hand. Once I accidentally broke a vase that she was particularly fond of, and she put me over her lap and beat my ass with a hair brush. By the time it was over, tears were running down my face, and welts were rising on my buttocks.

Our sex life became more degrading. I was no longer allowed to cum in her presence. Our activities in bed consisted of me bringing her to orgasm with my tongue and lips. Once, when she had her period, I had to take her tampon out with my teeth and perform cunnilingus. The taste of her blood mixed with pussy juices was disgusting at first, but I grew to enjoy it. Rachel sometime even had me lick her asshole. On Saturday nights, she would invite some girl friends over to use me. I'd spend the evening naked, performing cunnilingus and analingus on the women. I would bury my face in their moist, juicy cunts as their juices ran down my face while they quivered and quaked in ecstasy. After they had reached their orgasms, I had to spend the rest of the evening on the floor, massaging their feet and sucking their toes while they chatted among themselves.

At the hospital, everything seemed the same as we went about our rounds. But after work, I was Rachel's slave. She dictated everything I did. Even my bowels weren't mine to control. Each morning she gave me a large enema, and after I was cleaned out she stuck a butt plug up my ass. I wasn't allowed to remove it until I submitted to my next enema. Then she began modifying my body. Rachel felt that I needed piercings to always remind me of my servitude. First, she had curved rods inserted into my nipples. Then, the underside of my cock was pierced, with half a dozen small rings running along the urethra, from the base to just below the head of my cock. Not long afterward, Rachel decided to deny me the ability to have orgasms. A large captive ring was put through my pisshole, with an equally large ring inserted into the base of my scrotum. The two rings were then locked together, keeping my cock permanently pointed downward. Whenever I became sexually aroused, the erection pulled on the rings, causing great pain in my cock head. Thus, the erection would quickly disappear. This also meant that now I had to sit on the toilet to piss.

Since we were both studying to become surgeons, Rachel was able to bring home surgical instruments. She circumcised me, then gradually began widening my pisshole. None of this was done with anesthesia, but I had to sit there and try not to flinch as she cut into my cock. If I made too much of a fuss, she would stop and put me over her knee, and administer a good spanking with her hairbrush.

Then came the day that changed my life forever. We were both scheduled to assist a surgery in urology. "A very sad case," the surgeon told us. "A young man, only 24, with penis cancer. We will need to remove the penis entirely." I could see Rachel's eyes light up. The idea of cutting some guy's cock off seemed to appeal to her greatly, and I started to sweat. The patient was wheeled into the operating room, and put under general anesthesia. His penis was taped to his stomach. A catheter was threaded into his cock, and urine flowed out of the tube into a collection bag hanging from the side of the operating table. His shaven crotch was swabbed with a brown disinfectant, and while the doctor pulled on his surgical gloves, a tray of steel instruments was wheeled over to the table. I watched Rachel as the surgeon began cutting into the guy's cock. Every stroke of his scalpel seemed to excite her more. When the severed penis was dropped into a stainless steel bowl, an expression of ecstasy could be seen even through her surgical mask. I looked at the poor guy on the operating table, and realized that he was the same age as me. It was like I was looking at my own future. That night, Rachel was more passionate during sex than I had ever seen her. She reached orgasm several times, moaning and shouting loudly. Afterwards, I massaged her feet, licking and sucking her toes as she always required after sex. While I performed that task, she picked up her phone and called Susan, her best friend. "Oh, it was incredible watching that guy's cock get cut off!" she raved. "I can't wait until I do that to Rob." I kept sucking Rachel's toes even as she chatted away, describing how I would soon lose my penis. Although the thought horrified me, I knew that I was now completely under Rachel's thumb. Life without her was unthinkable, so I would submit to anything she wanted.

"Oh yes, I'll leave his balls intact," she said. "That way his sexual drive will remain, even though he can't reach orgasm. It will keep him totally devoted to me." She smiled down at me, and began stroking my captive cock with her glistening toes. My penis began to swell, producing a growing ache in my cock head. I grimaced in pain, causing Rachel to throw her head back and laugh. "Don't worry, Rob. You won't have to worry about that much longer," she told me. The next few days I was in a constant state of fear. Would Rachel forget about the whole idea? Or was she really serious about giving me a penectomy?

Rachel gave no indication as to her intentions. I continued serving her as always, waiting for her decision. We arrived home Saturday after our shifts at the hospital. I noticed Rachel was carrying a black bag, and wondered what she had brought home. An hour later, the doorbell rang, and several of her girlfriends came into the apartment. They all seemed to be excited, chattering with Rachel and each other. I performed my usual tasks, sitting on the floor naked while licking their pussies and assholes. After an hour or so, when all the women had reached orgasm, Rachel stood up and made an announcement. "Okay, everybody! Time to go into the bedroom!" Her friends eagerly jumped up and hurried into Rachel's room. I followed behind them, and my heart stopped when I saw Rachel's bed. It was covered with a plastic sheet. Nylon ropes were tied to each of the four bed posts, and sitting next to the bed was a steel tray with a variety of surgical implements. I was going to lose my cock that very evening!

"Okay, Rob! Up on the bed!", Rachel said cheerfully. I reluctantly climbed onto the plastic sheet, and held my arms over my head. Susan and Rachel's other friends quickly tied the nylon ropes around my wrists and ankles. I was totally spread-eagled, my legs far apart. Rachel placed a pillow under my butt, elevating my crotch even higher. Rachel pulled on a pair of surgical gloves and lifted a hypodermic needle from the tray. I felt a sharp sting in my scrotum, then a gradual numbness began spreading through my cock and balls. Susan used a pair of shears to cut the rings holding my cock in place. After swabbing a brown liquid up and down my penis, she picked up a scalpel. Her friend's ooed and ahhed when they saw her holding the instrument up.

"Total penectomy," Rachel said, placing the scalpel against the base of my penis. "Much of the penis isn't visible. It's necessary to go inside the body to remove all of it." I craned my neck to watch as Rachel pushed the blade into my cock, drawing a spurt of blood. Her friends giggled and chatted excitedly as she cut around the circumference of my penis. "It's also necessary to tie these blood vessels off in order to prevent him from bleeding to death," Rachel said, methodically performing the task. I could see that my cock was half-severed, lying flat on my stomach, its head pointed at me. A few seconds later, Rachel grasped the head, lifted it straight up, and sliced through the rest of the shaft. My penis was now separated from my body.

A cheer went up as Rachel held my lifeless cock high in the air. She smiled and dropped it into the stainless steel bowl sitting on the tray. Then she continued the surgery, digging deeper into my crotch to remove the remnants of my cock.

"I'm now going to re-route his urethra," Rachel told her friends. "I'll create a new opening near his anus. He'll piss just like all of us now." The women laughed as Rachel worked. I could do nothing but wait for her to finish. I had long ago surrendered all control over my own body to Rachel. The surgery took just over an hour. I could see she had expertly stitched up the opening where my cock had formerly been. Rachel gave me several more shots in my crotch area to keep me numb.

Then my ropes were untied, and I was led, shaky and weak, to a bed in the other room. "He'll need several hours of sleep, now," Rachel told them, shutting the door. My enslavement is now total. Rachel was right – my sexual drive is unchanged, but there's nothing I can do to relieve it. My only satisfaction now comes from serving Rachel and her friends.

"Oh, things are so much better now!" she said on the phone to Susan as I massaged her bare foot. "I don't have to worry about him leaking semen onto the carpet. And I don't have to look at that ugly cock – unless I want to." She smiled and turned her head toward the table in the corner of the room. A jar sat on top, my penis suspended in a preserving liquid. Small rings still protruded from its underside. Rachel took her other foot and rubbed it against the scar in my crotch, admiring her work. She'll make a fine surgeon, I thought, as I sucked her toe.

Needle Play and Getting Castrated at the BDSM Club (A Horror Erotica)

I have been into the SM scene for many years. Unfortunately I have to keep this from my wife as she was born in England, and has all the sexual inhibitions of the English. I have PA and frenum piercings in my cock. The PA I have stretched to size 0. I can leave these piercings without jewelry in for quite long periods, and quickly re-stretch them back to size. Both my nipples are also pierced to size 10, but I can only leave these without jewelry for up to a month, and then must re-stretch them from size 14 to 10 gradually over about a week. A few years ago, my wife and I had a huge row over my body piercings and since then, I only put jewelry in my piercings about once a month, and then usually over a few days, just to keep them from closing over.

We have two male dogs, and my wife has had both of them castrated by a lady vet, who is a friend of hers. My wife told me, during this row, that if I didn't stop piercing myself, she would reduce my "urges" by castrating me. I thought she was joking and laughed in her face. I am a member of a SM club, which has regular parties once a month. I usually put my piercings in about five days before the party night so that they can stretch out without hurting when being manipulated. My wife thinks that this is a regular night out with the boys, drinking.

The club night is usually great. It is expected that all slaves disrobe completely, and many of the Mistresses are available for sessions. Some of these can be quite intense, but not quite as satisfying as a private session, except for the exhibitionist part of the scene. I enjoy being the subject of a scene with an audience, eyeing out my piercings. Those new to the SM scene, without piercings, are usually quite bug eyed. At one of these parties last year, I was in a scene with a Mistress who liked piercing her slaves, and she proceeded to insert about fifty needles through my cock skin from head to ball sac. I thought that one of the guys watching, whom I had not seen at the club before, was going to pass out. His eyes were fixed on my cock with its forest of needles sticking out of it, and his own erect cock was twitching and dripping with pre-cum. One of the Mistresses noticed this and, quick as a flash, whacked his cock head with the riding crop she was carrying. He immediately yelped, doubled over, and clutched at his cock, whereupon she whacked him across the backside. Everyone in the room cracked up laughing.

However, all my fun at these parties was soon to come to an end. I booked at the club for a scene with my regular Mistress, Mistress Sophia. I had been seeing her for about two years, every ten to fifteen days, and we had developed a scene that gave me great pleasure. That night, the scene started as before. I was tied spread-eagled fashion, legs and arms apart. My balls were tightly bound in one bunch, and stretched by attaching them to the leg stretcher bar between my ankles. A line was attached to the ring in my penis, and stretched by attaching the line to my nipple rings. My nipple rings then had a line tied between them, and the line was placed in my mouth so that I could stretch the nipples by applying backward pressure of my neck. A ball gag was then placed in my mouth, and tightly secured. Hot candle wax was then be slowly and liberally dripped onto my cock and balls until a thick cover of wax had been built up. Mistress Sophia then came to the part that she enjoyed. Using a light multi-stranded whip, she proceeded to expertly remove the wax from my balls and cock with the whip. Each whack of the whip across my balls, stretched as they were, felt like a boot kick, and I needed all my concentration not to pass out. Finally Mistress Sophia decided that she had removed all the wax from my cock and balls and untied my balls and my cock. Whilst I was recovering, Mistress Sophia prepared the next part of the scene. Carefully she swabbed the underside and head of my cock with antiseptic solution. Taking out a box of 21 gauge hypodermic needles, she removed a strip of needles from the box, peeled back the wrapping and inserted each needle in turn under my frenum piercing down my cock shaft. This process continued until twenty needles had been inserted in a row. Now came what Mistress Sophia liked to call the "Crown of Thorns." She inserted a needle under the crown of my cock head, until the point poked out through the head, like dydoe piercing. Evenly spacing the needles, she inserted a row of needles until the needlepoints surrounded my cock head. Each needle produced a momentary burning pain until the point exited the skin, and was pushed right up to the needle hub. The endorphin rush after each needle insertion was tremendous, and the adrenalin coursing through my arteries made my temples pound.

The next part was the one I liked most. Mistress Sophia applied a rubber emasculator ring to my balls, making sure that it was positioned high up so as not pinch any cords other than the two main ones. Normally she would time the remainder of the scene, so that the emasculator ring was not on for more than 20 minutes. Mistress Sophia left the room and after a few minutes, she returned with two other Mistresses, both of whom were wearing leather masks, so that their identities were hidden. The two new Mistresses approached the bench and carefully inspected Mistress Sophia's handiwork. They appeared to especially like the "Crown of Thorns," which was looking quite fierce with the raging hard on that I had developed with the close inspection of my cock and balls by these two attractive new Mistresses.

Normally in the next part of the scene, Mistress Sophia would remove the needles and start to slowly masturbate me until I was close to cumming. She would then stop, slide the blunt side of a pair of nurse's scissors between the emasculator ring and the skin, and then continue with the masturbation. This would progress until the moment of my climax, and she would time the climax to coincide with the cutting of the emasculator ring. The result of the sudden restoration of blood to the balls is a combination of pleasure and pain that is quite indescribable, but totally addictive. My fantasy has always been to be castrated at the moment of climax. I fantasized that this ring cutting was the closest that one could get to imitate the feeling of cumming and being castrated at the same time. This time, however, the scene did not follow the normal procedure. The two new Mistresses watched as Mistress Sophia removed the needles and swabbed the needle holes. The cock head bled quite a lot, so it took some time and pressure to stop the bleeding. By this time, the ache in my balls and lower stomach told me that emasculator ring should be removed soon. I have read that about twenty minutes does not usually result in any damage to the balls. Some men have regularly gone as long as an hour without harmful results, but longer than that would probably result in permanent damage. Definitely four hours and you were a eunuch! The two Mistresses moved to the corner of the room, turned their backs on me, removed their masks and lit up cigarettes. Mistress Sophia came over to me, wiped my brow, since I was now starting to sweat quite a lot from the ache in my belly and balls and gently stroked my cock. More than an hour had elapsed and if the band was not removed soon, I would be a eunuch. Strangely this thought did not scare me, but made my cock twitch. Suddenly, the two new Mistresses turned around and I was confronted by my wife and her friend, the lady vet.

My wife approached the bench and said: "Did you think I didn't know what you were up to? I followed you here some time ago and decided to find out about the BDSM scene myself. I'm now a fully fledged Mistress here, and it's time that you became my slave. Since you have fantasized about being castrated and neglected me, you will now pay for that neglect. You know that our two dogs have empty ball sacs, and how they got that way? Well I have decided that there should now be three empty ball sacs in the house. Mistress Sophia and the owner of the club have agreed that we can castrate you, and you will become a house slave."

"Wow", I thought, "this is going to be some fantasy. My frigid wife has finally found out about sex!" The lady vet approached the bench and rolled out a pouch of stainless steel instruments and medical supplies. She filled a hypodermic syringe with liquid from a vial, quickly swabbed my balls, and plunged the needle up to the hub directly into my balls. I drew a breath in shock from the pain, and she paused to look at my response. Slowly and carefully, she started injecting the fluid from the syringe into my balls, looking deeply into my eyes as she did so. Slowly some of the pain lifted and I felt a slight feeling of numbness around my balls. My wife walked over, a riding crop in her hand. She suddenly brought the end of the crop directly down on my balls, still held in the grip of the emasculator band and now a deep purple colour. The pain was bad, but not as intense as it normally would have been without the local anesthetic the lady vet had injected into my balls. Satisfied that the local anesthetic had the desired effect, she nodded to the lady vet. My wife told me that she had asked her friend not to give me a full dose of local anesthetic, as she wanted me to feel her bite off my balls.

"She must be joking," I thought, "they'll stop soon, and we'll have a good laugh about this." The lady vet approached with a scalpel in her hand. Shaking my head from side to side, I tried to indicate that the game had gone far enough. The gag stopped me from crying out and I was helpless. The lady vet quickly drew the scalpel vertically down one ball, and then the other. She pushed the scrotum tissue away and then dissected the ball away from the connective tissue in the scrotum, leaving it hanging by its cords on my thigh. She repeated this procedure on the other ball, and then tightly tied some suture thread first around the cord of the left ball, and then the right. She leaned over to me and whispered in my ear: "You are now a eunuch, your balls will soon be dead. All that is necessary is for them to be removed." My wife approached the bench, and I watched as she bent down and sucked my dissected right ball into her mouth. She slowly started to stroke my cock, which by this time had grown to the largest erection I had ever had. The lady vet got into the act and sucked my cock head into her mouth. My cock head had swollen so big from my enormous erection that she had to open her mouth wide to get the head into her mouth. The combined attention of the two Mistresses was too much, and within a few minutes I could feel the climax building deep in my belly. The lady vet pulled my cock head out of her mouth and watched. As my cock started throbbing, ready to climax, I felt a quick pull deep in my groin and a sharp intense feeling of pleasure. My cock erupted with a huge orgasm, spurting semen over my belly. My wife stood up from between my legs, and as she bent down to kiss me, she pushed something into my mouth with her tongue.

"Keep this warm for me, slave, I'll want it later." I realized the soft oval rubbery object in my mouth was my right ball. It tasted slightly salty. I pushed it with my tongue between my cheek and my teeth, so as not to swallow it. The three Mistresses moved away and lit up cigarettes. "Perhaps they are going to leave me with one ball," I thought to myself. Then I looked up into the mirror and saw my purple left ball, still attached by its cord, lying on my thigh. I remembered that the lady vet had tied off the cord and whispered in my ear that I was already a eunuch. It was too late, they were going to do it! No more castration fantasies for me, this was the real thing. Their smoke break over, my wife bent down again between my legs and this time took the remaining left ball in her mouth. The lady vet sucked up my now flaccid cock into her mouth and within a few minutes my cock was hard again. My wife's sucking and tugging on my naked ball, and the lady vet sucking on my cock soon had me ready to climax again.

"Slowly," I thought, "make it last". The lady vet pulled away from my cock and started to kiss me passionately. She tasted of cum and as she stuck her tongue in my mouth. I realized that she wanted my severed ball in her mouth, and pushed it into her mouth with my tongue. She pushed it back, and soon we were pushing my severed ball backwards and forwards between our mouths. My climax built up and finally exploded. As it did, I felt another tug and an incredible feeling of ecstasy, bordering on pain. The lady vet pulled back from her passionate "ball kisses" with my severed right ball still in her mouth. My wife reached into her mouth and pulled out my newly severed left ball between her thumb and forefinger. She dipped the ball into the dollops of cum that covered my belly and rolled it around until it was covered in cum, and the popped it into Mistress Sophia's mouth. The lady vet also coated my right ball with cum, and placed it into my wife's mouth. The lady vet then walked back to her medical tools.

She carefully swabbed my scrotum and the severed cord ends, which had been in my wife's mouth, with alcohol, checked that the cords were still tied off, trimmed the cords neatly and cauterized them. She then cut away the rubber emasculator ring, which had kept the cords from popping back into my scrotum after my wife had bitten my balls off. Finally she neatly stitched up the two vertical cuts in my now empty ball sac. Mistress Sophia walked over to me, kissed me and pushed my left ball from her mouth into mine. My wife did the same with the right ball. Whilst I rolled my two severed balls around in my mouth, Mistress Sofia untied me and handed me a towel to clean up, together with a bottle for the balls. I slowly, and somewhat reluctantly, dropped my balls into the bottle and handed it to the lady vet, who filled it with preserving fluid. All the blood in the two balls had been sucked out, and they were no longer purple, but a pinky translucent white. Looking at my balls floating in the clear preservative solution, my cock twitched again. My wife looked at the lady vet with a slight smile on her face.

"I think we should start planning the next phase of our slave's conversion."

"We'll start the female hormone injections tomorrow", the lady vet replied, "and I'll start reading up on male to female surgical conversion, and do a few experiments in my surgery. I like the idea of turning his cock inside out to make a vagina. We'll be able to use our strap-on dildos to both fuck him, or should I say her, at the same time. After all, his cock is of no use to us anymore, now that he's castrated.".

As I toweled off. I looked down at my empty ball sac. I recognized the lady vet's handiwork. My ball sac looked just like the empty ball sacs of our two dogs. My wife had been right, she now had three empty ball sacs in the house. I wondered what other plans she had for me.

Fantasy, Sci-fi, Surrealism, Religion, and the Just Plain Weird

The Death Knight and Paladin: An Erotic Fantasy

"Saidrym Noel, I want to take you as my wife, for now and forever." Myrdias' words rang out in her head as she drifted in and out of sleep. She sat behind Myrdias on his bronze drake, Nursis, with her arms wrapped around him tightly.

For the past several months she wandered Azeroth alone, performing errands and missions for this person and that and aiding in the cataclysm relief. She had been separated from Myrdias by Lady Liadrin, a previously unknown feeling to her; they had never spent more than a week apart from each other in their entire lives. It had driven herself to hysterics and near the point of insanity pondering his whereabouts and his well-being. Taking a short break for her mental health, she found herself in Mount Hyjal, and this is where Myrdias finally returned to her.

Except… he wasn't the same man he was when they departed eight months earlier. His aura was darker, more jaded, and his eyes no longer glowed the bright green natural to the Sin'dorei. Instead, they pulsed an unknown combination of blue and green, the blue possessed by the Lich King's death knights. In addition, a voice spoke to her telepathically, a female's voice that she had never heard before. As they took solace in the high branches of Nordrassil, Myrdias removed his armor, exposing his once perfect flesh to be marred with scars, one in particular upon his left breast, blackened with evil.

"I died in Icecrown, Saidrym." She remembered him telling her. She cried fiercely at the realization. The blue eyes, the scar, his death. She knew that he was no longer a servitor of the Light like she, but a death knight, damned to undeath for as long as he existed. She was upset, empty, hollow, disappointed because she knew this wouldn't have happened if she had been there, and betrayed, hurt, and angered by this unknown female voice that helped tell Myrdias' story. As the tale unfolded, she learned the voice was Myrdias' rune blade, and that Myrdias was the first and only hybrid of paladin and death knight, thanks to the blessing of the Naaru, A'dal. Myrdias had been brought back to life, but some aspects of his unlife lingered. It was a fact of life that Saidrym constantly tried to cope with, and at times, failed miserably.

As they arrived in Silvermoon City, she was fast asleep. Myrdias slowly slipped off the drake and caught her in his arms, carrying her into their seldom-used apartment. He gently took off her clothes and laid her in their bed. He stripped out of his clothes as well and lay beside her, stroking her hair and face, caressing her body softly, and exploring all her injuries she had sustained since he had been gone, which amounted to more than he expected.

"She's been careless without me here… I can't imagine by choice, but more accidental recklessness… I don't know why she didn't chose to heal these herself…" He sighed and muttered a few words. His hand glowed brightly and the wounds healed over. He slid down into the bed, taking her into his arms, falling asleep as deeply as she.

The next thing she knew, she was stirring in her bed with Myrdias snuggling her close to him. It had been too long since she could lie in his arms, she thought. Slowly, she crept out of bed and pulled on a simple white gown and slippers, wrapped her head and hair up in a white scarf, and made her way out into the city to find breakfast for them. The sunlight shone brightly in her eyes as she stepped into the street. She breathed in deeply, savoring the fresh air, tinged with salt from the nearby sea. The city emanated magic, and she took a moment to take in her surroundings and enjoy it; it felt like it had been ages since she visited her home. As she walked through the streets and toward the grocer, she saw a woman with a young child beside her and large bump on her torso. Pain gripped at her heart as she held her basket tightly.

"To want something I can never have…" She thought to herself, pushing back the tears. She softly touched her own stomach in yearning as she watched the woman. There was something familiar about her; she just couldn't place it. Saidrym browsed the fruits and vegetables, placing a few items in her basket.

"Bloodmaster Xaebel…?" A small, female voice called out. Saidrym jerked her head up, pulling her scarf around her face tighter, and looked around. The woman that Saidrym had been eyeing was calling her. "Bloodmaster Luna, right?" The woman walked over to her and Saidrym slowly let her scarf loosen.

"May I ask who you are?"

"Xelika Maernrae, wife of Aelemar Maernrae. You instructed him while you served here in the Blood Knight order. I would never forget you; your presence is quite commanding. Aelemar always said that about you… Are you still a Blood

Knight? I haven't seen you for some time. And what of your mate, Sol?" Saidrym shifted her weight. She had not expected someone to remember her from her days of being a Blood Knight, let alone by her alias. She opened her mouth to speak, and then closed it quickly before thinking over her words.

"Yes, I remember him and you both. I see that you have children now; that's joyous to know. And no, I'm not a part of the Blood Knights any longer. Sol and I were both honorably discharged over a year ago to pursue our own interests." She kept up the performance; she couldn't risk anyone knowing that they had gone by fake names; that information could fall into the wrong hands. "How is Aelemar doing? I imagine you've seen him recently." She smirked and gestured to Xelika's stomach. The woman blushed deeply.

"He's doing well, helping in the Firelands. I haven't heard from him in a few months though. I'm due in the next month; I wish he could be here for his birth." She rubbed her bump tenderly and smiled. Saidrym bit her tongue, forcing her jealousy back. She stepped forward and placed her hand on the woman's stomach.

"Tae ci shi shaeraer." The woman smiled widely. "I know it's not much, but my blessing is all I can give. I must be off now though; give my regards to your husband." Saidrym turned and adjusted her scarf, finished buying her groceries and headed home.

Once there, she removed her scarf, tying her hair up, and rolled her sleeves to prepare breakfast. Peering into the bedroom, she saw Myrdias sound asleep in their bed, his long platinum strands flung around him like a halo. She sighed happily, glad to have him home, and went back to cooking. She prepared a simple meal of vegetable-filled omelets, biscuits with honey, fresh fruit, and juice, and carried it into the bedroom, placing it on the dresser. She crawled into the bed and cuddled close to Myrdias, softly kissing and caressing him to wake him up. He stirred, pulling her closer to him and tried to go back to sleep.

"My love..." She whispered, letting her lips graze his ear. A smile curled onto his lips as he fluttered his eyes open. "Good morning, my love." She let her lips fall upon his and kissed him deeply as if to fully wake him up. He returned the kiss and then pulled away, sitting up and letting the sheet fall away to his hips. She glanced at him as she got up, taking in his toned, muscular body. The fire in the pit of her stomach burned and the wetness grew between her legs, and at that point she realized how long it had been since she had lain with him. "I hope you're hungry. I made breakfast." She handed him a plate and set his juice on the nightstand before sitting in front of him with her own plate.

"Ahh… It's been so long since I've had your cooking. I can say that was one thing that I missed. And I only recently began to eat real food when I was recovering in Shattrath; while I was in Icecrown, I was eating mere soldier's rations." Saidrym made a face at his comment and continued to eat. She too had neglected food for the most part, only eating when she had to or was prodded to by Katasia, so she savored every bite of this meal. "What did you want to do today?" He asked as he finished his breakfast. Saidrym swallowed her last bite and took the dishes to the kitchen, returning quickly.

"It has been an awful long time since we've seen each other… And we do have tons of things to catch up on…" She smirked and straddled him in bed, pinning his hands down. "I would be completely content to start by catching up… physically." Myrdias' eyes lit up as he realized what she was saying. "I think perhaps we should spend the day relaxing, forget about the outside world, and just focus on one another." She stood up and pulled off her slippers and gown, laying the latter neatly on the dresser, exposing her naked form. Her nipples were like hard pebbles atop her luscious breasts. "And speaking of relaxing, I think that the first step is a nice, long, hot bath. I know that I haven't had that luxury for longer than I can remember, and I imagine the same for you." She turned and headed towards the bathroom, turning her head to wink, and shaking her rear to entice him to come with her.

The bathroom was nearly as big as the bedroom; it was something that Saidrym had expressly wanted when they purchased their apartment. It was similar in color scheme to the bedroom as well, bathed in rich reds, brilliant blues, and prominent purples. There were the normal things that a bathroom held, plus a vanity that Saidrym had only used a handful of times and the crowning glory of the entire room - a whirlpool-type bathtub big enough to fit several people. She knelt on the edge and twisted the knobs, testing the water with her hand until it was perfect, and then poured a rose-colored substance into the stream, creating bubbles instantly. She stepped into the tub and let herself sink in as it filled. Her hair was still tied up in a messy bun, but several tendrils had fallen down, framing her face. She closed her eyes and leaned back, sighing. A moment later, the water sloshed and she felt Myrdias immerse in front of her. She opened her eyes and smiled, drawing him towards her and wrapping her legs around him. When the tub filled, she turned the knobs off with her toes, and reached up to grab a sponge from a shelf. Pouring a different liquid than before on it, she started to gently rub Myrdias' shoulders and back. She set the sponge aside and began to knead and massage his shoulders; the tense knots were abundant and she cringed every time she hit one.

"Ahh… Saidrym…" he said as she worked the knots out. His head slumped forward and she let her fingers extend to his neck and the bottom of his head. As she finished the massage, she slid around, facing him, and picked up the sponge again. Dabbing at his chest, she paused when she came near his scar. He grabbed her hand and tilted her face up to look at him. "It doesn't hurt anymore… You can touch it. Don't be afraid, love." Her hand shook slightly as she pressed the sponge onto his chest again and across the scar. She moved down slowly, cleaning his torso, arms, hands, legs, and feet. She dropped the sponge and rubbed a little soap on her hands, reaching under the water and gently stroking his cock.

He jerked forward at her touch, and then relaxed and leaned back, giving her plenty of room to work, groaning softly. She continued to rub him for several minutes before pulling back and grinning up at him.

"You… tease…" he growled as he moved towards her. He took the sponge that she had abandoned and started to clean her; his fingertips extended over the sides as he dragged them over her skin, making her shiver. He let his hands glide over her breasts; he rolled her nipples in between his fingertips and groped at them, making Saidrym moan softly. He bent his head down, taking her nipple into his mouth. She gasped in surprise and pulled his head closer to her. He switched to the other side, but only lingered a moment before continuing to wash her. As he reached her legs he slowly ran his fingers in circles on the inside of her thigh, making her spread her legs apart. He let his hands brush up against her nether lips a few times and drew back.

"That's… not fair…" she hissed at him. He smirked back at her.

"Sure it is. You did it to me; I'm just returning the favor, love." She stood and stepped out the tub, wrapping herself in a towel, and Myrdias followed her. Saidrym could feel the fire burning stronger than ever and she was dripping down her leg, not bath water, but the wetness from her pussy. It had been nearly a year since she had fucked Myrdias and her body was crying out for it. She could only imagine that his was doing the same. He stepped toward her and took her in his arms, holding her close to him. As he leaned down to kiss her she dropped her towel to the floor, pushing her body against his. She reached up, running her hands through his hair, pushing her tongue into his mouth as he did the same. He leaned into her, pushing her backwards into the bed, landing on top of her. He laid a trail of eager kisses from her mouth down her jaw and throat, across her chest and stomach and along her very long legs.

"Nnnnggg…" she groaned in frustration. She loved having Myrdias home and adored all the affection she was receiving; any other day she would welcome it and beg him not to stop. But there was only one thing on her mind this particular morning. She wanted to fuck him, and she wanted it right now. What was more, she thought of her meeting with the pregnant Xelika, and yearned to be with child. She pulled Myrdias to her, her eyes pulsing wildly.

"Take me, Myrdias… Take me and do what you will." She released him and moved her legs to allow him to get closer, receptive to whatever he wanted to do. He lay atop of her and kissed her deeply, letting his hands explore her form. He fondled her breasts, this time with more force, biting and sucking on her nipples. He reached down with one hand between her legs, caressing and teasing her. Suddenly, he plunged two of his fingers inside her, causing her to scream out and jolt forward. He moved down as he fingered her and lightly licked her outer lips, making her quiver. "Oh… by the Sunwell… Myrdias, you can't tease me as such…" At her words, he snaked his tongue inside her pussy, flicking it over her clit as he pumped his fingers in and out of her. She grabbed the bed sheets in her hands, twitching and moaning as he ate her pussy. She could feel the orgasm building up but she didn't want to cum like this; she needed his cock inside her. "Fffff…" She stuttered, unable to get the words out as he pleasured her. "Fuck me, Myrdias, fuck me. Fuck me now!" She commanded of him; she knew her place and knew better than to make such commands but desperate times called for desperate measures. He stopped and pulled away and already her pussy felt empty. He moved up and she could see his erect cock. She pushed him up and sat on the edge of the bed, taking it into her mouth with a quickness he had never seen before.

"Sai… You don't have too…" He stroked her hair and pushed her head further down; his actions said otherwise. She twisted her tongue around his cock, and pulled back.

"But I do." Wild lust danced in her eyes as she wrapped her lips around his cock again, taking it down to the base in one swift action. She gagged and could feel the drool seeping from her lips, but she continued to bob her head and let him fuck her mouth. She reached with one hand and began to gently fondle his balls. After several minutes, he put his hands on her shoulders and shoved her backwards onto the bed. Mounting her, he took the tip of his cock and teased her clit, rubbing it all over her pussy, covering it in her juices. Without warning, he slammed his cock inside her, causing her to cry out, followed by a low moan in her throat as he began to thrust into her, stroking her pussy with his cock. She wrapped her arms around him, digging her nails into his back and dragging them down. She gripped his hips, pulling him into her as far as he could. She was on the verge of her orgasm. He reached down and began to massage her clit with his thumb, which sent Saidrym right over the edge. She screamed and cried out, and bucked against him, her pussy tightening around his cock. Her back arched as the orgasm slammed into her like tidal waves of pleasure. Myrdias bent close to her, gripping her shoulders as he felt his orgasm come as well. Burying his face in her neck and hair, his body began to spasm as he shot his thick, ropey seed inside of her. He groaned as he came, his breath hot on Saidrym's neck. Her moans dulled down as her climax finished and his body released the tension.

When they finished, Saidrym smiled as if she was drunk on their love. She curled up, wrapping her arm around Myrdias, and rested her head on his chest. He pulled the blankets up, and softly stroked her hair to lull her to sleep. The sounds of rain from outside, pattering on the roof and roads, intensifying his own sleepiness.

"Saidrym… my princess… You're my kind of rain." he murmured to her as her breaths deepened and they both fell asleep.

Tentacle Monster in the Pond

It was a hot, sticky day in Dixon, Montana, when Sabrina Maccaul left her home in Ravencrest Apartments for the nearby pond. The apartment complex where she had been living for the past six months did not have a pool. She was unable to afford to live in a place in town that was that luxurious. She could have taken a shower, but she was sick and tired of having to wait forever for her roommates Laurie and Tessa to vacate the bathroom so that she could even take a shower and get ready for work. It was hot and sticky with no end in sight for her for quite some time, being that it was a day in early July, and so Sabrina's best bet at cooling off from the heat was to walk down to that pond and to wade in the cool waters there. She had done so on a few other occasions. The pond water was fairly clear, obscured by trees, and far enough away from the highway that she would be able to ditch her clothes completely before sinking into the blue green waters to cool herself off.

Sabrina walked briskly to get to her destination, but not so fast that she made herself even hotter than she already was. When she finally came up to the fork in the road that led to the shallow pond, Sabrina began following the dirt road to the pond like she had done many times before, and like she would undoubtedly do many times again.

Sabrina paused by the still waters, glancing around her out of habit, just to make sure someone had not decided to come to the pond to try their luck at fishing. As she scanned the area, she knew inwardly that the chances of a fisherman in this area were really rather low. This was private property, and very few people would trespass here. Sabrina knew the older couple that owned this land, however, and so she wasn't trespassing by being here. Although if Mr. and Mrs. Kempton knew that she skinny dipped in here, and did not wade in the pool with her bikini on, it was quite likely that they would revoke their permission for her to be there. The couple currently resided several states away though, and so being caught with her pants down by the owners of this property really wasn't that likely. However, a part of her always hesitated before disrobing here. After all, someone coming upon her in the nude was not completely outside of the realm of possibility, and she had no idea what she was going to do if that occurred.

Sabrina pulled her sea-green Magaschoni top over her head, folding it perfect before lying it on the ground beside her khaki colored sandals. Sabrina was not wearing a brassiere underneath her shirt, and once the shirt was off, her firm perky breasts peaked out like a proud peacock. Next, she slid the off brand spandex figure forming mini-skirt off of her, and folded it up, laying it on top of her shirt. She wore no underwear as well, and once the skirt was peeled away, Sabrina revealed a shaved mound with the ever slight moist glistening at the netherlips.

As Sabrina slowly made her way into the pond, she found the water slightly colder than she anticipated. She walked proudly as she waded into the waters, which she had discovered the very first time she had visited this place, were deeper than they appeared to be. In fact the pond came up to the chest of the five foot four inch beauty, barely covering her swollen pink nipples when she entered the water au naturel.

Sabrina leaned back, soaking her hair thoroughly, enjoying the offering of mother nature, and the immediate cooling effect this pond had on her. It took a few minutes for the water's motion to settle again, and in those moments, she closed her eyes, and just allowed herself to take in the myriad of sensations. That was when she felt something swim around her feet.

Immediately she came up, spoiling the waters serenity as she jumped back at the unexpected companion to her swim. It carefully made its way to the surface, this sick green tentacle creature. It was like nothing Sabrina had ever seen before. Most people, girls in particular, would have vacated the pool immediately upon such a strange discovery. After all people feared what they didn't understand. However Sabrina wasn't most people. She had a curious streak that was a mile long. After withdrawing just a few feet, she finally stilled herself and carefully watched the tentacle as it snaked its way towards her.

"Do not be afraid." The male voice spoke clearly in her mind, smoothly reassuring her that she would come to no harm. It was a few seconds before she realized that the voice that she heard was coming from the tentacle. Sabrina watched the creature's movements with even more curiosity as it began to swim around her in circles, shaking its tail like a rattle snake.

The tentacle rubbed gently up against her leg before stopping its trek a stone's throw in front of her. "You are beautiful, Sabrina."

"How do you know my name?" Sabrina asked as she conscientiously moved closer, reaching out to touch the tentacle with one hand. Even though the tentacle looked as though it would feel gross and slippery the surface of the creature felt hard and rubbery, more like one of her dildos might feel. Once she touched the tentacle and that thought entered her mind, it felt utterly ridiculous to her, yet at the same time, it was a thought she found herself unable to banish.

"You are wondering what I would feel like in between your legs, Sabrina?" The tentacle spoke in a husky seductive voice to the naked beauty that stood before him. The tentacle coiled around in a snake like manner again before lightly brushing against her inner thigh. "You could find out." The tentacle paused. "I can make you feel things you have never felt before. You only need to say the word, Sabrina."

The tentacle began to swim to the shore, near the neat pile of clothes that Sabrina had left there. She only hesitated for a moment before following the creature, and laying down with her legs spread open to receive the monster's offering.

The tentacle slowly climbed up her wet, naked form, its head reaching for her, and its tail slowly slipping down to her slick wet mound. The tentacle circled her left breast, licking her nipple in an impossibly fast motion, while his tail end slowly breached her opening.

The tentacles textures and pattern elicited a wealth of sensations from Sabrina, just as the monster had promised that he would. As the tentacle sank deeper into her womanhood, it moved to her other breast, playing with the other nipple and giving it the same sensitive treatment the other had had.

The tentacle continued to give her breasts the prized treatment, as if she were a goddess worthy of worship, while shoving his tail end into her entrance harder and deeper, until her soft moans of pleasure turned into downright screams, and the sensations were so overwhelming that she could barely stand them.

While the tentacle continued to fuck her senseless, it wrapped itself tightly around her naked form like a python, circling around her and teasing some of her more sensitive regions. The tentacle kept up this movement until he finally had a release of his own, which it deposited deep within Sabrina. Once the tentacle was through, it turned in the direction of the pond, and began to swim away without another word.

Rapture: Demon Ravishes An Angel

As the Holy War raged on, an entirely different war took place in the abandoned Vatican. An sensual battle between angel and demon.

The Rapture was in full swing as souls were harvested, but the fight for the scorching of the land caused certain reunions that only hellfire and brimstone could forge together once more. When Lucifer fell he did not fall alone, thousands of angels took off their angelic feathers in exchange for the dark powers of the Seven Deadly Sins. Sage was one of these angels to fall, his belief in Lucifer, the archangel, sent him spiraling down to the depths of Hell. and this forced him to forget his Heavenly love, the angel known as Gilead.

An immeasurable amount of time had passed from then until the Rapture, the war for the souls of earth, but as it turned out, they were destined to meet once more.

"Is this not fitting? To have our reunion in the Holy Palace? A palace built for those to serve and repent to the Holy Lord. All its silks and riches as men buy their way into the Heavens… or so they thought." Sage chuckled as he took a silken rope from a cardinal's habit. His beloved Gilead had returned to him on this fiery middle ground, her body as pure and beautiful as ever. Her legs spread as she was laid flat back against the Pope's holy bed. Taking the rope in both hands and making it taut, he gently and teasingly rubbed it up and down her clit. Each nodule of the rope rubbing her sweetness caused her legs to shudder and her body to writhe softly in ecstasy. Her mind couldn't focus on the sounds of destruction outside or even the thoughts in her head telling her that this was wrong.

Even without Sage's hands completely touching her she couldn't resist his temptation. Now that he served the Netherlord, he was somehow even more arousing. The rope becoming wet and slick as she grew more and more aroused with each bump of knots. Gilead rolled her hips up, aching for more personal attention.

Sage was never one to deny her, at least not in the days of old, but now, with his darkness wanting to show itself to the fullest extent, he couldn't help but make her suffer a little longer. She had ignored answering his questions initially, but soon she knew she'd find herself begging for his attention, a much more in depth yearning. Sage smirked at this before using the rope to tie Gilead's hands to the backboard. He reached over to the night stand and grabbed the Holy Bible. "You know… This sure has started a lot of pain and suffering…perhaps you'd like to relive some of it with me?" He flipped through several pages before stopping and reading, "Corinthians 6:18… Flee from sexual immorality. Every other sin a person commits is outside the body, but the sexually immoral person sins against his own body… my, my… shall you sin against your own body, Gilead?" He ripped out the passage and slowly dragged it down across her pale breasts. He then quickly used the passage to create a paper cut across her breast. She bit down hard on her bottom lip with a small whimper as she could feel the paper slice through her skin.

Sage reveled in the sight of his Gilead. From her crowning honey blonde hair, her gentle and pure green eyes of the earth, to the serene sculpting of her angelic form. She was just as he had remembered her. He flipped through for another passage, "Matthew 5:28… But I say to you that everyone who looks at a woman with lustful intent has already committed adultery with her in his heart… Aren't I the guilty one?" He gave a sinister chuckle before cutting her across her stomach with the passage. Her green eyes looked up at his of the deepest blue seas, "John 1:9…." She panted as her needs make her inner thighs tingle. He shook his head softly, side to side as he flipped to the page with a smirk and a laugh to follow allowing his onyx locks to fall across his tanned shoulders. "If we confess our sins, he is faithful and just to forgive us our sins and to cleanse us from all unrighteousness… Good job, Gilead… always looking to defend that Holy Kingdom, aren't you?" Sage grinned as he ripped out the passage and made sure to drag the passage across her throat before giving her a long paper cut, her blood creating a sweet smell in the air.

The teasing became almost too much as Sage found the sight of her body with cuts, bondage, and blood seeping into the fabric below to be more than enticing. "You know… I heard some of these religious ladies say that they don't believe in fellatio because the mouth was meant for worship and prayers. If that were true though then why did Father make a woman's lips look so much like the lips below? Confusing isn't it?" He grinned before straddling her chest. After grabbing a fistful of her hair he pushed his arousal in between her plush pink lips. Her lips massaging up and down his length as he forced her head up and down his cock. Her tongue massaged at the underside of the head as she applied pressure to the thick vein she could follow every time he forced her head back and forth. Sage moaned loudly as he let his head roll back and close his eyes enjoying the tightness of her throat and the heat of her mouth. He jerked his hips as he felt her use her teeth to scrape against his cock. He slapped her after pulling his cock out of the hot mouth. "Come now... I know Father said it's a sin to waste a man's seed but that doesn't mean you have to go feral."

Gilead licked at her swollen lips before purring at Sage's discomfort. She wasn't an angel of many words but when she used her mouth, whatever the case, it was truly dangerous. But Sage was also a quick wit and always eager to go head to head with her, thus landing them in the divide they were in now in this Holy War. "Then the Lord knows how to rescue the godly from trials, and to keep the unrighteous under punishment until the Day of Judgment... That day is here now Gilead... I think Father is turning a blind eye right now." Sage joked as he ripped out the passage and used it to paper cut straight up Gilead clit. His mouth immediately descended onto the bleeding tender bit causing her to tremble in pleasure and pain. His tongue pressing against the bleeding slit, tasting her sweetness. His hands pressed down on her thighs to keep her in place as he dominated her. Gilead felt her nails digging into the palms of her hands as he flicked his tongue over her sweetness repeatedly. She cried out for him before biting into the pillow.

Sage pulling away from her for a moment to tease, "Not calling out for Him to see you? Good girl..." Sage pulled away fully to gaze over her torment before shoving himself fully into her weakened form. Hearing the angel cry stirred up a hellfire within him greater than he'd ever known. She was tight and pure. His nails dragging down her sides, slicing her open in small slits like the paper cuts. Her body was his Holy War and blood was all over the field, her slickness making the need feel more intense as he began pounding into her. The slamming of the backboard was less than background music as the focus between the two was like that of the earth and sky in their eyes. Keeping himself steady he pulled one of her legs over his shoulder to allow him further penetration as his free hand began to carve into the exposed inner thigh. Gilead began tossing her head back and forth as pain and pleasure was more rewarding than she could've ever imagined. Yanking her hands free from restraints she grabbed Sage's freehand and pressed it hard against her stomach, "Outside are the dogs and sorcerers and the sexually immoral and murderers and idolaters, and everyone who loves and practices falsehood… In here though…" She continued as she pressed his hand down harder, causing a bruise. "Feel yourself move within me…" Gilead's quoting of Revelations brought a wide grin to Sage's face as well as feeling his erection stab right into her Holy Sheath. He came with nothing but a wide smile on his face. Gilead sitting up, letting his member slip from her lips, she forced him down. "I think it's time for your Holy Retribution."

Sage smirked at this before pinning her back down. "Women are born of pure sin aren't they? Perhaps if you plan on using your Holy powers on me I can only fight back with my newly inherited darkness…" Sage smirked before letting his body shift from that of an incubus to that of a succubus. His once male form now entirely female. His eyes still that of the ocean and sky and his hair still that of an ebony rose. Sage's body now with full round breasts and a wet and slick slit between her legs. Gilead pinned Sage down, their breasts pressing against each other, the blood from Gilead's wounds smearing against Sage's tanned body, their lips crashing against each other in a fiery and lustful passion, their tongues massaging against each other as they fought for dominance. Sage's hands gripped at Gilead's firm buttocks and let her nails scrape at the wet flesh between her legs. Gilead reached up to the headboard and ripped off the golden cross that rested there as if to bless the sleeper with its encrusted rubies that mocked the blood of Christ. Gilead slapped Sage across the face, hard. The demon now needing a moment to refocus but was granted no reprieve as Gilead shoved the long end of the cross inside Sage's heat. The rubies scraping against the pleasure center of Sage's darkness causing her to belt out a loud moan.

Gilead began using the cross to fuck the demon just the same as Sage had been doing to her with the body of a man before. Sage gripped the pillows, nails tearing into the fabric as her toes curled in multiple orgasms as she accepted every golden inch. Screaming in sheer pleasure as the rubies rubbed themselves inside her just right. Her hips rising and falling at hoping to have the cross reach deep within her at a new more penetrating angle with each thrust. Gilead held a gleam of dark pleasure in her eyes as she continued to use the cross to fuck Sage before letting her hand grip at one of Sage's pert breasts. She would not leave the other breast neglected though as he brought her lips down to suckle and nip at the rosy teat.

"AHhhh nghh… HARDER!" Sage cried out laced with unhindered need. Gilead complied making sure to shove the cross in harder, the feeling of blood running across her fingers hardly a care as of course a demon would require pain to truly experience an orgasm. The bloodied golden cross mixed with Gilead's sucking and biting was enough to make Sage shudder hard, the force of her orgasm forcing the cross out with a wave of blood and cum as she squirted out into Gilead's bloodied palm. Sage's body calmed down with heavy pants and closed eyes as she crashed happily with her orgasm.

Gilead was grinning before, but now her face became masked with concern. Blinding white lights streaked across the sky. The war was coming closer to their debauchery. Sage shifted her body back to that of a male. All the blood and secretions splayed all over the two. Their time together was ending… they would have to meet up elsewhere if this was to continue. As Gilead turned around to look from the window back at her dark desire, she sighed. Sage had already left, the pain of losing him again overcoming her. She looked over her body and soon found herself smirking as she looked at her inner left thigh. There in her own flesh Sage had carved out a message: "Proverbs 4:23 Keep your heart with all vigilance, for from it flows the springs of life."

The Television: Becoming a Sissy in a Digital World

I responded to the Craigslist ad on Thursday and didn't get a request until Sunday. I had already masturbated that day but figured it would be okay to get sucked off again. Not my fault it would take longer than usual. After a few responses, it was clarified that the door would be unlocked and I would walk in and sit on the futon where I would get blown by a cougar with a great rack. So even though I was relatively nervous because this was my first time meeting somebody from Craigslist, I opened the door.

When I walked in, nobody was there, so I made my way to the futon as directed. I heard porn playing in the bedroom so I went to check it out. No one seemed to be in the room. I started watching the porn and whacking it. It seemed like a relatively regular solo masturbation session of a woman, but as it moved up to the face, it seemed familiar. It was the lady from the Craigslist ad. She said, "You should have been patient."

I was already very hot but this made me nervous and horny at the same time. She told me to join her, and I responded, "I don't know what you're talking about, you told me to come in and sit on the futon." That's when I noticed that she was sitting on the same futon as was in the other room. Naturally I went to the other room, and still no one was there, so I ended up going back to the bedroom. This time she was back in the room, and leaned over licked my ear and whispered, "Cum with me." I felt a slight pull on my cock and thought it was her hand.

At that moment I was sucked into her pussy and could see outside of it. She seemed to walk right into the television where I was spit back out of her pussy. She said, "This is where you belong." Of course at this point I was freaking out, but she pulled my pants down and started rubbing my cock. She spit on it and licked the underside of the shaft up to the tip. I had forgotten about all of my worries as she started to worship my cock. I also noticed that it was a few inches larger than normal, and her breasts were bigger than before. I immediately spurted a little bit of pre-cum. She licked it up and asked for more and more, and as if it was her dream, she took my whole cock in her throat.

I heard her gagging and instantly I blew the biggest load I ever have. She pulled her mouth from my cock and gargled my jizz in her mouth. She then started to kiss me, transferring my own cum to my mouth. It was still hot and delicious, like cookies and cream ice cream. She told me to swallow it all but I didn't want to because it tasted so good. She slapped me and told me that there was plenty of cum and time left to enjoy. I remembered where I was when she told me we have forever so swallowed the cum.

That's when four large men came into the room. I had never had the urge to suck a cock before but looking at their huge cocks something overcame me and I got on my knees. I started to kiss one of the cocks and she told me I was a good little sissy. My cock got hard again as soon as I started kissing this man's cock. I wanted all of it, forever. After spinning my tongue around the top of his penis I stiffened it out and took it all in my throat and brought my mouth back up making rapid sideways gestures with my tongue while I came back up. I looked back at the woman and she was mounting me. As soon as I saw her I felt a deep penetration. It was glorious and painful, I had never felt anything like it before. I was worshipping the man's cock at the same time, and I noticed that another man was penetrating her from behind. The fourth man sat on a chair in the corner videotaping us and masturbating. Of course, I assumed the woman was wearing a strap on, but after fucking me good and hard she pulled out and forcefully removed the man's cock from my mouth and told him to leave. She said, "You're only going to be my sissy boy." I begged for her jizz, knowing this was my fate.

She blew a glorious load all over my face. It stung my eyes and dripped down to my mouth and tasted like cotton candy. I told her I wanted more and she said I would get more when she was ready. She picked me up and put me on the futon. My body had gone completely limp. She positioned me so my legs were up on the wall and my head was inverted hanging off of the futon. She started fucking my throat. It hurt but I still enjoyed it. All I wanted was to suck her cock and taste her beautiful cum. She let me play with her soft boobs. I rubbed them and scratched them and this made her scream. She clamped her teeth down on my cock drawing just a slight amount of blood. She continued to fuck my face until my throat went completely numb. She shot load after load into my throat and enjoyed it more every time.

I grabbed her ass and thrusted her cock further and faster into my mouth. She jerked my cock which was elevated above the futon and I released my load and it fell onto my chest. I wiped it up with my hands and tried to put it in her mouth.

She said, "You're the cum dumpster here, you eat it." So I licked my fingers until they were clean. It was as if I couldn't quit cumming on my chest though. So she licked it off my chest and spit it into my mouth.

I said, "Master I want your cum though." She told me I didn't deserve it, which made me want it even more. I tried to grab her cock and put it into my mouth but she pushed me away. I fell limp onto the ground and she tied me to the futon. She put a gagging ball into my mouth.

She said, "I told you, it's my decision when you get cum." She jerked her own cock and came on the top of my head. She got behind me and rubbed it all in. She continued to jerk it and get more and more cum in my hair. She told me it was the best shampoo. She rubbed it all into my hair and left the room. She was going to the bathroom, where she filled up a bucket full of cold water and then poured it onto my hair. She told me I didn't deserve to get to drink her cum anymore and left me in the room cold and alone.

The Tomes of Abadoth: A Fantasy Erotica with Tentacles, Nobility, and a "New Money" Maiden

A tall, handsome man astride a horse rode along the overgrown path overlooking the small whaling village of Rathington. Lord Robert Rathbone, as he was known to his subjects, quickened his horse's pace, knowing that today was a day of great importance. She would be waiting for him there. The cool island wind whipped through his thick black hair about shoulder length, underneath his warm wool coat was a strong body packed with muscle, rather unusual for a man of his birth. However, Robert was no ordinary noble, not seeing fit to merely read about the professions that brought in his tax money, but preferring to go out on the fishing boats himself. It made the people of the village see him as one of them.

He saw no reason to be standoffish as many of his noble peers chose to do, he attracted much less suspicion that way, and suspicion was a commodity that he could do well to avoid. Especially as the day came closer... As his horse brought him nearer to the old mansion that had sat dilapidated on the hill for more years than many in the village below could even count. Robert's thoughts drifted to those of the young lady this fateful evening hinged so much upon.

Miss Elizabeth Shelley, she wasn't much for intelligent conversation, but that wouldn't matter that much this evening. It was her body that mattered the most to Robert. He first laid eyes upon her at a meeting for the nobles... that in recent years had been invaded in a sense by "hangers on" as it would be. Elizabeth's family was in the latter category; they were merchants from a village a few miles over from Rathington. They were "new money," and they so desperately wanted to join the nobility, but money could not buy blood. Elizabeth was just like her parents, she wanted to marry into nobility so bad she could taste it. Thankfully, for Robert, she was just what he needed. She was wearing a classic velvet trimmed dress, her ample breasts nearly spilled out of her corset; so desperate she was to catch a nobleman. Her scarlet hair fell just to the middle of her back, spreading out on top of her pale ivory skin, the skin of a girl that had never had to spend a day in the sun.

When Robert laid his eyes upon her, he knew she was a good candidate, almost to the letter as the texts suggest. But she had to be tested first and of course, Robert found her very pleasing to the eye. Robert saw his opportunity during a lull in the music; he introduced himself putting emphasis on his title. Robert knew the type, and he knew how to play people. The moment the word "Lord" left his lips, he noted how Elizabeth's eyes lit up, and he knew this would be much easier than he initially thought. After more idle small talk with her, Robert knew that he needed to strike now. They were both desperate; however, Elizabeth knew not what this fateful encounter would mean for her later. Lord Rathbone pulled her into a private side room of the manor for her "exam." He made his advance upon her, showering her ivory skin with moist kisses. Despite her conservative veneer, she was very receptive, seeing the title of lady in her future.

Robert had a different future in mind of course... Her corset yielded to his penknife, as her ample breasts spilled forth, the sight of her perky nipples served to enlarge the bulge in Rathbone's trousers. Soon, her dress lay at her feet, baring her whole body to Robert. He gazed upon her voluptuous form, taking note of the fiery red patch just above her secret garden. "Just as the tomes say," Robert whispered as he lifted her up, laying her across a nearby table. Robert began kissing her neck, working his way down her ivory temple until he reached her swollen, receptive clitoris. She was curious what he was doing at first, but she quickly realized that his actions were those of a man much more experienced than she. Elizabeth gave herself over to the pleasurable feelings of his tongue on her button. Robert knew that this evening would give her a crash course in sexual deviancy to the nubile young girl. Her body shook with an orgasm as Robert finished up with his oral handiwork. Now it was time for him to have some fun himself; he could contain his lust for her no longer. He dropped his pants, exposing his sizable manhood, nearly nine inches, making Elizabeth gasp at the sight. A slight smirk grew across his face. "This is nothing compared to what lays in store for you in the future." Robert thought.

He moved forward, between her welcoming legs and slid his manhood within her, her moistness pleasing him. He could feel her muscles massaging him from within as they desperately tried to mute their sounds of pleasure so as not to be debased by any unsuspecting guest walking in upon them wound together pleasing one another. Their actions were beginning to leave a moist spot upon the table. Robert's sizeable manhood filled Elizabeth's small canal, but he could not climax yet. He had to know how receptive she was to debasement. He rolled her over, and gazed upon her beautiful posterior before probing her surely virgin ground. He found no protests from her, so he continued his progress until she enveloped him. Elizabeth winced from this new exploration, but found it somewhat pleasurable, and once Robert began rubbing her button, she found herself in absolute ecstasy. Finally, unable to contain himself, and essentially seeing the examination as complete Robert extracted himself and issued himself over her back as she shivered with a great orgasm.

Robert planted a kiss on her lips and left her with a note, instructing her to meet him in two weeks at the abandoned manor he was now approaching… The sun sat below the horizon as Robert stepped off of his horse and up onto the porch. Robert noted that he was the first to arrive. So he stepped inside and began to prepare for the arrival of the others. He moved about the mansion, laying out the arcane ingredients that the others would need, and lighting the oil lamps that he had brought to the old manor earlier in the week. Soon after this, the others in the Order arrived. Five other men clad in black robes stepped into the room, their pale skin worried Robert somewhat, but he knew that the reward would be worth the strange company.

"Is everything prepared?" the head of the group rasped to Robert. "Yes of course, she has only yet to arrive." Robert carefully replied.

"You should pray that she comes soon, the alignment will not last through the night, as I am sure you know the texts say." The reply sent a shiver down Robert's spine, but he knew the power would be worth it. Just as Robert began to worry, a set of light raps at the door filled the air around the group. Lord Rathbone motioned for the members of the Order to hide, as his mind began to work on how the evening should proceed. Robert invited her in, and wasted no time in warming her up with his touch. In no time, they were pawing at one another, and soon, Robert could enjoy the touch of her soft skin once again. He wanted to enjoy her once more before the Order could begin the ritual. He slid his member inside her and they both gave a simultaneous gasp at the rush of pleasure they both felt. His hips began pumping inside her, as her fluids spilled forth onto the old floor of the manor, her body soon rocked with an orgasm, and just as Robert was soon to follow, the members of the order stepped forth, now unrobed.

Elizabeth gasped, first at the sight of the previously unknown watchers, and secondly at the appearance of the men. Their ethereal bodies were covered in muscles, even greater than those of Robert, and their members were all as great as Robert's, if not larger. Robert asked Elizabeth if she would be willing to please these men too, and seeing this as a challenge for admission into the inner circle of nobility she heartily accepted.

"THEN THE RITUAL BEGINS!" Bellowed on of the Order. They formed a circle around both Elizabeth and Robert, and began making incantations. An ethereal portal opened above their heads, but strangely Elizabeth was not scared. She somehow felt what was going to happen would be a great thing. Robert, on the other hand, was becoming more terrified by the minute. This wasn't what the Order had said would happen at all. He was told that this ritual would make him a king over all, that there would be a session of group sex, but it appeared they were summoning some otherworldly being. As the ritual progressed, tentacles slithered out from the portal, and Elizabeth found herself excited at their presence.

The slimy tentacles slid up her smooth legs, tickling her slightly, until they slid inside her. She enjoyed the new sensation of these tentacles, they seemed to know every inch of her body and she felt pleasure like she had never felt before. Finally, the other end of the creature attached to the tentacles came through, one of the Order bellowed, "BEHOLD, ABADOTH, OUR GOD."

Robert looked at the creature, and could not comprehend it, he laid down in tears. His last sight was of those in the Order doing the same thing. Elizabeth, on the other hand, saw beauty and love in the writhing mass of tentacles and eyeballs that was now exploring her entire body. She felt no revulsion, only love. At that point, the creature made contact with her.

"At last my love, we can be together, come with me and be my Queen over the earth. I shall be a consummate lover. Just say yes. It is thanks to these fools that misread my tomes that I have been brought into this world. I have them to thank for bringing us together."

For you see, the tomes that Robert and the Order had thought would bring them power, were actually describing Abadoth's one true love. For that, he spared them. And till the end of time, Abadoth and Elizabeth ruled over the entirety of earth.

Summoning the Demon Succubus through the Power of Orgasm: An Erotic Fantasy

"I wish you didn't have to go. I'm going to miss you." Tarja stroked Johan's thick blond hair.

The warrior embraced his young wife. "You will be coming with me, though." He released her and smiled. She made a sour face.

"Only the vaguest of terms. I probably won't even remember it." She shivered.

"I'm not sure I want to." Johan started a little.

"What – what do you mean?" Tarja gave him a look.

"You think women don't know what those demons are? Why you use them for guardians on long journeys? Why the summoning ceremony involves –"

"All right, all right. That's enough."

Embarrassment warred with a kind of contrition on his face. Tarja shook her head. "We understand, love." A strange little smile played on her lips. "Women have their own rituals."

Johan looked decidedly uncomfortable at that revelation. "Yet you're volunteering to be the Avatar."

"Of course. It frightens me, but I'd rather it be my body underneath it all. And if I die, well…then I won't have to wait in vain for your return."

Johan sighed and embraced her again. "We'll both return, my love." A knock on the door interrupted whatever else the two would have said. Johan opened it to reveal the shaman, holding a bundle of mail. He greeted them with a silent nod, then beckoned to Tarja. She followed the man, whose grey hair was the only sign of his advanced age, leaving Johan in their small quarters. The shaman led her to another small room in the hold. She could hear the fierce northern winter winds raging outside. She imagined it was the voice of the approaching army, the clatter of tree branches their swords. Her husband had been chosen to make the arduous journey to seek help…and she had volunteered as the vehicle for his companion and protector.

They had both been instructed in the ritual beforehand, so she knew what she was to do. The shaman left her with the bundle, not having said a word for the duration. Tarja unfurled the two pieces of mail. They really couldn't be called "armor", not when they barely covered her breasts and pussy, leaving everything else bare. It wasn't meant to afford protection, really; the guardian demon that the ritual would summon was nearly impervious to physical harm. Her flesh, she knew, would be changed once the demon was housed in her. For now, the outfit was cold, and she shivered. She looked down at her body, the soft, pale flesh made paler still by the cold, her nipples standing out against the metal links. Her breasts were ample enough that the mail fit well; these demons were known to be well-endowed, and she was perversely pleased that her own body measured up, as it were. She was already lithe and muscular from a lifetime of hard living and weapons training; they said the ritual worked best when the demon didn't have to remake too much of your body.

She drew a deep breath, then faced the door and steeled herself for the shaman's return. When he had next opened the door, the old man was dressed in his ritual robes, and, still silent, lead Tarja into yet another room. This one was bare of furniture except for a huge, upstanding wooden cross. The two solid oak boards that made it up were identical in length and width, joined flush in the middle to form a huge X. The ends of the boards had iron shackles affixed to them. Tarja walked to the huge thing and spread her arms and legs against it. The shaman closed the shackles around her wrists and ankles so that she was held fast, her back against the wood. The man nodded, then opened the door to the room. Johan walked in and stood before Tarja. They exchanged smiles as the shaman began the chants for the summoning ritual.

Tarja felt a pit of warmth start to grow inside her body, finally driving away the chill. It spread from deep within her chest through her limbs and face, making her flush. Her pussy tingled with it, and she could feel the wetness of arousal starting to drip out of her. The warmth continued to spread, her nipples beginning to tingle themselves, pressing upwards against the chain mail. She was suddenly glad of her bonds, as her muscles went weak with the force of her desire. She moaned softly, suddenly aware of Johan's presence before her. His lips brushed her ear, and she thought she heard him whisper "I love you."

Then she felt his hands caressing the tops of her thighs, and she lost herself in the wave of lust the final words of the ritual called down on her. Johan moved the falls of chain mail on her breasts aside, flicking his tongue over her right nipple and squeezing her left between his fingers. She closed her eyes and cried out, pressing her hips against his as much as her bonds would allow. She felt his cock straining against his leather breeches. Johan ran his tongue from her breast to her neck, her skin quivering under his ministrations. His hands massaged her breasts, and traced the contours of her ear, and his hands slid down her body, caressing her hips and making the fall of chain mail clink and tremble. His fingers snaked beneath the tiny metal links, delicately tracing the pink folds of flesh just peeking out from the cleft between her thighs. His fingers came away wet, and she felt her own arousal on her skin as Johan pinched her nipples again. The slick juices made his fingers slide faster than before, making his pinch harder. She gasped at the exquisite pain. "She's almost ready." The low voice of the shaman swirled around her without really penetrating the fog of pleasure.

Johan dropped to his knees in front of her, lifting her chain mail and running his tongue along the pink folds of her pussy. She panted, twisting against her restraints in pleasure. The tip of his tongue found her clit, flicking lightly and slowly. Tarja's breath came faster, her mouth open in cooing cries. Johan increased his rhythm, his tongue flicking faster. Tarja felt her muscles tighten, and she gasped deeply and cried out, throwing her head back as white-hot fire exploded through her body, an orgasm more powerful than any she had experienced before. A tiny corner of her mind decided that she knew why women volunteered for this. Alexa felt an inescapable tug at her being. The demoness looked up from the succubus she'd been torturing, and groaned. "Sorry, honey, I'm being summoned."

"Too bad," replied the succubus around the gag in her mouth, and wiggled her ass as Alexa faded from the demonic realm.

"Withstand it this time, ok? We were just getting to my favorite part. I do so love a cat o' nine tails." Alexa jerked, her consciousness suddenly restored. The transition to the human realm was always a little unpleasant. She blinked and shook her new body. The body looked like hers – mostly human, pale skin, black wings now furled against a wooden cross, tiny goatlike horns curling out of her forehead. Her hair was black with a few blue strands, although the human's hair had probably been blond. Northerners tended to favor this ritual, she knew. Her hooves clacked against the stone floor. After she left, either by breaking free of the ritual bonds or by being released at the end of whatever task these humans assigned her, the original owner would return, and her body be restored. Although there were certain points in the ritual that would preclude that....

She looked around the ritual room. An old, iron-spined shaman stood in one corner, quietly chanting. Alexa could feel the power swirling around him, ready to be invested in the physical component of the binding ritual. The warrior stood in front of her. He was handsome, for a human. She looked appraisingly at the bulge in his breeches. That wasn't bad for a human, either. Her favorite incubi put him to shame, of course, but he wasn't bad. He looked far too gentle to perform the ritual, though. She smiled and flicked her tail. "Well, warrior, what are you waiting for?" Alexa wiggled as seductively – and contemptuously – as the shackles on her wrists and ankles would allow. Magically reinforced, of course, or they would never be able to hold her. The warrior shook his head. He knew that if he touched her before the shaman finished the ritual, it would free her, and trap Tarja's soul in the shadow-world, a limbo between the realms of the living and dead. Behind him, the shaman finished his chant, and Alexa felt the power swirling around him flow to stand poised behind the warrior.

"Now, demon –"

"Alexa."

"Alexa. I am Johan. I must undertake a dangerous journey, and move quickly. You will accompany me, keep me safe from harm, and return here. Then you will be freed."

"Make me."

Johan smiled a little, and approached her. Alexa bared her teeth as he lifted the falls of chain mail on her breasts, larger even than Tarja's. He produced a pair of small steel clips. He bent over her chest, teasing her nipples with his tongue and teeth until they hardened and stood out from her breasts. He opened the clips and slipped them onto her pink nipples. The sharp pain made her hiss a little. Demons of her type didn't like pain very much…unless they were the ones causing it, of course. Johan tweaked the clips, causing her to shudder.

"Alexa, will you bend to my will?"

"You don't have the balls," she sneered. Johan picked up a short, thick length of black leather. He flicked his wrist gently, the strap cracking against her right breast. She gasped, and felt the gathered power strengthen. She knew that the power would grow with every erg of pain she felt, until it would overwhelm her. She could give in, of course, and save herself the pain, but…well, there was always the chance she could withstand it, and sometimes, too, the game could be fun. Johan snapped the leather strap over her other breast, and her shoulders jerked in response. He did it again, harder this time. She snarled at him, and his hand shot out and cracked against her cheek. She blinked in surprise at the slap. That was a new one on her.

"Alexa, will you bend to my will?"

"No." He switched his attentions to her thighs now, delivering swat after swat, the pain increasing with every crack of the leather. If she were human Alexa would have had tears standing in her eyes. As it was, she could feel the power behind the warrior building to a crescendo.

"Take her." The shaman's voice was barely above a murmur, but it carried clearly across the room. Johan pressed his body against Alexa's, his breeches dropping to the floor. She felt his cock sliding against her pussy. She grunted, the pain and endorphins fogging her brain. This was the final physical component. Her defenses were eroded by the pain, and now pleasure from Johan's cock sliding into her. He pulled on the clips fastened to her nipples, and when she threw her head back in a moan, he nipped the side of her neck. Alexa felt her muscles go to water, her bonds now holding her up. Johan thrust into her, his cock swiftly becoming slick from her juices. Alexa realized that she was aroused despite herself, and knew that the ritual would overcome her. She felt pleasure building in her pussy, and she thrust against him as much as she could.

"Alexa, will you bend to my will?" Johan's voice was heavy with his own panting breaths. When she couldn't answer, he grunted in satisfaction. He bit her neck harder, thrusting faster until he was slamming his cock into her put to the hilt.

With another grunt, he pulled out of her, and she felt his cum splatter against her hips and stomach, the pent-up power cresting over her will and binding her to the task Johan desired of her. He shuddered and straightened, looking her in her eyes, and she had the distinct impression he was looking past her. Well, no matter. She was bound for the time being. That succubus would just have to wait. Although this one was no slouch, either. She looked at him from under her eyelashes. This journey might be fun, after all.

Slaves of God: A Priest, Two Inmates, and Six Officers Cleanse the Souls of the Damned (A Religious Erotica)

The preacher regularly visited the jail where I worked to speak with inmates, lead various religious groups, things of that nature. It was with inmates who had been caught in or accused of sexual acts that he took special interest in helping. When one of the female inmates suffered anal prolapse from having been fucked so many times, suspicions were raised as she had been isolated for some time only seeing the preacher. Monitoring their next one on one session from the security room, myself and three other guards watched on as the pastor stood up, blessing the inmate, and bent her over the cold metal table in there. Using a dental dam he opened up her asshole, using his fingers to pull her cheek like a fishhook.

One of the officers watching with immediately wanted to stop this. We quickly talked him down, as she was not fighting it, agreeing to see what happened after a few more moments. Using his entire fist in her ass, pumping it in and out as she bucked around seemingly in pleasure. One of my fellow officers commented, "All of our cocks could fit in her ass!"

We laughed, most of us probably semi hard. A few more minutes of this they were done, he said a prayer before dry humping her, grinding his cock through his pants on her feet, until pulling his small swollen prick out and screaming as he ejaculated, squeezing her dirty feet together and shooting a load of cum up her legs. The following day when he returned to do his sessions, instead of just letting him in the cell and leaving, I went in with him. Nervous, he asked if there was a reason. I simply stated that this was a new policy. I was going to view his cleansing policy, which he was obligated by god to carry out. The female inmate immediately kneeled before him as he hurriedly said a prayer blessing her.

"Today you will repent," he said. She leapt forward to his genitals, magnetically. The preacher grabbed her hair, pulling it back causing her to moan in discomfort, "Not now, your time will come my dear."

He asked me if I was a follower of God, and I replied that I was and willing to help any way he needed. I said that I was devoted to the Lord's divine ways. The pastor insisted that I go get another specific female inmate, whom I went and retrieved from her cell. Once inside, the preacher relieved me of my police baton, giving it to one of the inmates to fuck the other. As he stood there watching them reciting bible verses, he urged me to "spit my sins" into the ass of the inmate now being penetrated by my police baton. Filling her ass with spit as she pressed her pussy back into the baton, the pastor and I took turns drooling spit into her hole. Frantically he repeated the same bible verse, over and over as the cell door opened and the three fellow officers I had been watching with the day before entered, joined by two more officers. The preacher dropped to his knees, still repeating the verses as the guards walked right past him and pulled their cocks out, waving them in the faces of the female inmates. Two officers quickly mounted one of the female inmates, pressing their dicks together and slowly sliding both in her ass.

The preacher, now inches away from their pricks filling her, whispered how she was doing the good of God. The other three officers and I feasted on the other inmate, picking her up with one of us filling her ass, the other in her vagina, her holding a stiff rod in each hand as she melted all over the horny officers. The cell filled with moans and the preacher's prayers and encouragements, the inmates bent over the tables, one of my fellow officers used his handcuffs to lock the inmates to the tables. The pastor excitedly explained they were slaves of God, and this was divine intervention in their lives.

We took turns fucking the women, while other officer's face fucked them, sometimes two cocks pressing together competing to get into the inmates needy mouths or one of their holes. The preacher, kneeling next to the women, said we were to cleanse him. That the semen belonged to God, and he was the only one pure enough to receive such. One by one we fucked the inmates until ready to cum, then ejaculated on the preacher's face, shaking every drop of cum of at his face until all six cocks had came on him.

"THIS HOUSE IS NOW CLEAN," he commenced, collapsing as if some spirit had sucked every inch of energy from his being. The inmates cooed in pleasure rubbing all over the officers, who cummed out dicks now were being tucked back into their pants. Having done the work of God, we returned the inmates to their respective cells vowing to continue the good deeds.

Forbidden Love and the Escape: An Erotic Tale

The moonlight streamed into the rundown wooden shack near the back of Elizabeth's house, illuminating the two lovers with its rays of silver light. Their skin, clammy with sweat from the acts of passion which they had undergone, was dried by the cool night air. Trevor's callused hand slid across the back of Elizabeth's nape, sweeping aside her long blonde hair and touching her satin smooth skin as she gave out a long, deep sigh of pleasure. It was at that moment that they heard a noise from the large Manor house; it was a sound which shocked and immobilized them, causing them to freeze, embracing each other in their arms. "Is it your father?" inquired Trevor with a slight tremble in his voice "

If it is, he shall never find us here, my love" replied Elizabeth, clasping her lovers hand over her bosom.

"If he finds me here then I shall be dead, but I shall die a happy man," Trevor whispered in her ear before sliding his free hand over to grasp her tightly in his arm. Laying down on the straw covered ground they kissed, passionately and ferociously, aroused by the thought that Elizabeth's father could walk in on them at any time. Trevor slowly moved his hand down Elizabeth's waist, stroking the milky white skin gently, causing her to gasp with delight. His hand slowly made its way down to her crotch where he felt her wetness, dripping down on his fingers; he raised his fingers up and smelt the musky odour of them before reaching back down.

Elizabeth moaned impatiently, longing for his touch, she didn't need to make another sound as he moved his finger back down towards her loins as she moved her hips in a wild gyrating fashion, grinding against his fingers. With his spare hand, Trevor cupped her small yet perky breasts and felt the hot, sticky skin against his own. Elizabeth gave out another small moan as he started to grasp her nipple against his thumb and forefinger, slowly squeezing them and making them hard and aroused. Trevor gave her another passionate kiss, licking the top of her breasts, causing Elizabeth to grab onto his fingers and rub them vigorously against her thick fleshy folds. Trevor responded in kind by slowly penetrating Elizabeth with his fingers, causing her to give out small periodic sighs of satisfaction as he slowly moved upwards towards her clitoris. Trevor felt the clitoris touching his fingers and heard the massive grunt that Elizabeth gave out when he touched it.

He felt the small, pink dot touching his fingers, and tried to comprehend how such a petite object could give his lover so much pleasure as he slowly rubbed it with his index finger. Whimpering desperately, Elizabeth started convulsing around his fingers, dripping his hand in her juices and staining the straw covered ground with a damp patch. As the star struck lovers were engaged in this act of passion, the door slowly creaked open and the tip of a twelve gauge double barrelled shotgun poked in. A pair of worn riding boots made the hay covered wooden floor creak beneath them and finally, a weathered old face stared at the two nubile youths, disappointment dulling his rugged features. A small gasp arose from the two figures entwined together as they saw the dark figure of the man in the doorway, his shotgun pointed directly at them.

Elizabeth scooted backwards in a panic, trying desperately to cover herself up with a few mangled rags lying on the floor whilst Trevor lay still, his eyes wide open, like a doe caught between the lights of a car.

"I am disappointed Elizabeth, disobeying me, going behind my back to have sexual liaisons with this farmhand? Do you have any idea what this will do to our family image if it was ever bought to the light of day?" the man gruffly said in a sombre tone as he threw a small leather bag on the floor of the shack.

Elizabeth looked up in desperation at the man, and then pleaded with him, her tone frantic, "Uncle, please, do not tell my father. He will kill Trevor, and for what, a family name? You must have been young once too, you must have known true love and how it can make you do foolish things out of passion."

"Do you think you can keep this all a secret? Continue meeting out here, sneaking out in the darkness of the night, hiding in the shadows.", as he said this, for a moment, his harsh look weakened.

"Please Uncle, there must be some alternative, you always told me that no matter how grim things looks that there would always be a silver lining somewhere, if you look hard enough for it.", Elizabeth replied in a diminutive manner.

"When I was around your age, I went through this... phase, as well. It was my mother who offered me this alternative, albeit in a less dramatic fashion," he said with a chuckle as he stared at the still exposed youth trembling in fear on the ground.

"In this leather bag, you will find five hundred Sterling Pounds, a change of clothes for the both of you and two saddlebags with food and water. Out back, I've prepared two horses; one of them is Betsy, your favourite mare. Ride hard and fast to London, go to the docklands and purchase two tickets aboard HMAS Allison, bound to Australia. You and Trevor can make a new life for yourselves in this new land, it will be tough but at least you will be together. The alternative is that I dismiss Trevor for a small incident that will happen tomorrow, and you will never attempt to make contact with him again or I will have to deal out some lead justice," a sad look dawned on his face as he said this.

Elizabeth looked at her Uncle with a bleak smile on her face, tears streaming down her cheeks, as she embraced him for what may be the last time. "Do visit us in Perth if you find the time", she whispered into his ear as Trevor picked the bag off the floor, trying to regain some composure over his shaking form. The two lovers dressed quickly under the stream of moonlight pouring in through the windows, a determined look on their faces. Today was the start of a new chapter in their lives, today they were bound for a new land.

After the War

Chris Walker was tired of the war, and the end of it marked a new phase in his life. He was in his mid-40s, but sometimes felt like he was in his 60s. He had risen to a high position in the defense forces that had defended the Los Angeles area against the Chinese invasion, and when the peace was settled, he was given his choice of assignments in the peace forces. The U.S. was no longer a complete nation, and various areas separated into their own territories. The use of nuclear weapons had killed many millions, made some areas uninhabitable, and resulted in massive changes to weather patterns and climate.

Nuclear winter had settled over the world, and many of those who weren't killed in the fighting and the nuclear attacks were dying of starvation. Chris chose to occupy a portion of the low mountainous area northeast of Los Angeles, that was to be a buffer area, and his domain alone. He would be responsible for controlling who passed through his area, and would have complete authority over those people during their time in his area of responsibility.

He had lost his family early on in the war, and had felt their loss heavily in the early part of the war 2 years prior, but their memory was dimmer now; especially after all of the suffering and killing of the intervening time. The sector that would belong to Chris, like the other boundary zones, had been roughly marked in 5 square mile sectors, but no clearing had been performed. It would be up to Chris to conduct his own clearing work.

The rules were simple. No unauthorized people were to inhabit the boundary zones, and the guardian of each zone had total authority in his sector. Chris thought that the isolation would be a welcome thing, and when he arrived in his sector, he looked forward to the simplicity of his task. Chris had no idea where he was going to settle permanently, in his sector. He had some camping supplies, plenty of food and armament, and he plunged into his area late in the morning, that August day. He decided to begin by travelling along the perimeter of his area, and from the point of entry in the southwest corner, he headed due north. The terrain was fairly rough, and after he had proceeded about ½ a mile, he came across a dwelling. Smoke came from the chimney, and Chris took some time to observe the place. No one was visible, and after 15 minutes of watching, he circled the small home and finally called out to the occupants to show themselves.

A petite woman came to the door, and he asked her who lived there. She said that she was alone, which might or might not be true, and Chris asked her to lay down on the doorstep with her hands stretched out from her sides. As he was preparing to approach the house, he heard a rustling in the bushes to his left, and he took care to shield himself as much as possible, by adjusting his position next to a large pine tree. A man yelled from the area of the noise, demanding to know what Chris was doing there, and when Chris said that he had come to clear out all occupants, the man swore, and then came out of hiding. He carried a shotgun, and said that if Chris didn't leave, he'd be a dead man. As the man advanced toward Chris, Chris leveled his assault rifle and as the woman screamed a warning, Chris fired a short burst that put the man down immediately. The woman ran toward the man, and Chris intercepted her before she could reach the shotgun. The man was dead, and the woman seemed upset, but calm.

"He didn't have to try that!" Chris noted. "I would have let you both leave." The woman didn't seem to hear, at first.

"What am I going to do now?" she asked.

"Whatever you were doing before", Chris replied, "you just have to find somewhere else to do it." She slapped him, hard, and was winding up for another slap when he caught her arm. She struggled against his grasp, and when she could make no progress in pulling away, she leaned in and tried to bite him. Chris slapped her, as she had slapped him, and then she tried to kick him. As Chris used his arms and legs to block her attempts at attack, he began to forget his humanity, and just came to feel like an animal, struggling with another animal.

Her dress was pulled up when he had her arms pinned over her head, and the sight of her thighs ignited something in him. She was an attractive woman, and though petite, she had nice muscular thighs. She had the kind of thighs men joke about wanting to have wrapped around their neck, choking them to death, if they do indeed have to die at some point. She saw him looking at her legs, and began to struggle harder, knowing that he was beginning to think of taking her. Chris had never done anything against a woman's will, other than stealing a few kisses; but times were different now, and he hadn't had sex in months.

She squirmed harder, and somehow it just made her breasts all the more juicy, underneath that fabric. She was lean! He grabbed her around her waist, and stood up, and then carried her into the house. He locked the door behind him, and took her into the living room, where there was a decent-looking leather sofa next to the railing that led upstairs. He threw her onto the sofa, and took off his knapsack. There was a set of handcuffs in one of the exterior pockets, which he dug out and clipped onto her left hand. He looped the other cuff through the handrail, and then cuffed her right hand.

She wasn't screaming, which he thought was strange, just struggling against his efforts. She kept trying to kick him, and he just kept growing more and more enamored with her muscular little thighs. He couldn't help himself, and said, "The more you kick, the lovelier your legs are." She stopped kicking, at that, and when she stopped, Chris kneeled down on the floor at the end of the sofa, and pulled her panties down her thighs, and off at her feet. He hadn't had his head between a woman's legs in over a year, and it felt so good to him!

She started squirming again, and tried to kick, but he wrapped his arms around the back of her legs, and just pressed his nose into her pussy. It was not washed and perfumed, at all, but it smelled like home. He dove into that gaping pussy like a penguin into ice water. He didn't give a single thought to his acts, from the perspective of a man and a woman. As much as he would want to have said that he had remained human, during the war, the only thoughts he had now were the joys a man senses when he has nose and his tongue and his cheeks as deep as he can sink them, into a woman's cunt, and the sense that it's not deep enough, ever.

God, she tasted good! He looked like a starved cat, at a full milk dish. At some point, she got tired of struggling, and she just lay there. She wasn't enjoying it, but she had run out of energy to stop him. Chris sucked and nuzzled and licked her pussy for 10 minutes, and finally noticed the firmness in his dick, stretching his camouflage trousers tightly. He stood up, dropped his trousers and underwear, and spread her legs wide enough to open her lips. She was about as wet as a Louisiana swamp, not from her own juice flow, but from all of his licking. She didn't seem to mind that he was about to fuck her. She just lay there, with her hands in the cuffs above her head, breathing gently. Her breasts were lifted by her arm position, filling out the loose dress top, and he kneeled down between her thighs and pulled her dress up around her shoulders. She had a very slight amount of tummy fat, below her navel, which reminded him that she must have had at least one child, but otherwise she was pretty taut. When he uncovered her tits, he was surprised by how much they reminded him of cantaloupes. He loved cantaloupes! He normally didn't lick his cantaloupes, back when he used to eat them; but these cantaloupes were made for licking.

With the aroma of her pussy filling his nostrils, and his hard dick throbbing a bit, he still got the urge to get down on those full tits, and suck some more. He began fingering her pussy with one hand, as he sucked her tits. She just lay there, not struggling, or protesting. He looked up at her, from time to time, and sometimes she just stared off into the ceiling, while at other times she seemed to be considering him. Sucking tits is a nice thing to do, but it's not as stimulating as having one's face as deep as one can press it into a woman's cunt, and Chris began to get the urge to get back into her. She didn't put up any resistance as he kneeled on the couch and spread her legs. She looked at him, and at his hard dick, and then looked away. It was a good-sized dick, but not anything massive; just a normal, hard, pulsing, horny, rigid dick that hadn't been sucked or fondled or fucked in months. He licked his fingers and rubbed some saliva on the tip of his shaft, and raised her hips up to bring her pussy lips to the level of his penis. And then he plowed into her.

She uttered a slight groan, and he started banging her like a fucking rock drummer on a cocktail of uppers. She took it like a highway under a jack hammer. It wasn't violent in a hurtful way. No… it was just violent. It didn't matter what she looked like. She could have been a 250 lb porker with buck teeth. She had a greased pussy, and her legs were spread for him. Sometimes, when a man hasn't had sex for a while, he cums quicker than normal when he gets his dick in a woman. But when it's been a long time, sometimes the orgasm takes a while to happen. Like the semen can't even remember which way it has to go. Sperm headquarters has to draw a hand-written map for each sperm, and the guy feels like he'll have a fucking heart attack, before he pours his load into her. And that's what happened to Chris. He was lost in the feeling of fucking this pussy. She was there for him. This was his pussy! There had never been any pussy but this pussy. He inhaled it, he exhaled it, he lived off of it, and he drank it.

And now, he was doing what had to be done, by fucking the living shit out of it. He finally became aware that the girl was uttering a continual stream of "uh", "uh", "uh", "uh", "uh"s, with every stroke that he delivered. It wasn't a sensual grunt, at all. No, she was simply responding to being torn apart by a jack hammer that was stuck on full strength. He suddenly realized that his groin was a bit sore, from hammering her ass. And then he wondered about her handcuffs, and asked, "Are you ok?", as he continued thrusting, with less gusto. She nodded, and seemed to intimate that she wasn't offended by this act. He slowed his rate of thrusts some more, and looked at her face as he continued fucking her. Her hair looked like it hadn't been washed in a couple of weeks. He pushed into her a bit harder, and she groaned a bit. She had a pretty face, even with no makeup. He gently fucked her, and enjoyed feeling her pussy as it sucked his cock in and out. He slowed his rate down significantly, and purposely noted the sensation of the tip of his cock as it nearly parted from her pussy lips, feeling the cool air on his shaft, and the heat of her cunt as it caressed the tip of his dick. There was a hint of longing in her eyes, as if to say, "I want you back inside of me", and he thrust firmly back up into her until his balls were pressed against her ass. She didn't say anything, but he could see that she was content to be fucked like this. It felt good, knowing that the woman who you're fucking is content to have your dick in her cunt. It wasn't rape, any more. She wanted his dick in her, even if she wasn't saying so. They began to share more and more eye contact, though they said nothing more, for the moment. He just kept rocking his dick into her, and she kept taking it. Part of him just wanted to keep fucking this sweet piece of ass. He wondered if she would suck his load, or let him titty fuck her. He wondered if she would let him sleep with her again, or if she would return to her former state and be combative. Hard to say… he just knew that at the moment, fucking her was the only thing that he wanted to do. He liked women with tight figures and nice tits. Her thighs were really, really, really sexy. He thought about cumming on her thighs, and wondered if she would think that was weird.

Who cares what she thinks! Chris noticed that his arms were getting tired of holding her ass in the air. She was light, but still… he had been fucking her for at least 12 minutes straight. She sure could hold her wetness. His thigh muscles began to tense up, and he dropped her ass back onto the sofa. "I haven't had sex in months," he said to her. "My sex muscles are out of shape!"

She smirked slightly, and said "I didn't notice." There was a bit of an awkward silence, as Chris considered how to finish the fucking that he wanted so badly, and felt the soreness creeping in to his muscles.

"Do you like doggy-style," she asked. "Turn me over, and fuck me like that. Just fuck me until you cum." Chris took note off her handcuffs, and rolled her slowly to allow her hands time to rotate and not get clipped too tightly as she turned. He positioned her knees at the right places so that he could fuck her comfortably, and noticed that his dick had softened a bit.

"What's wrong?" she whispered, when he wasn't back in her immediately?

"Oh, nothing… I'm just a bit tired and out of practice."

"Rub your cock on my pussy lips. If that doesn't get you going, I'm sure we can think of something else that will. I want you to finish me." Just listening to her soft voice seemed to instill some firmness into Chris. He took his semi-firm dick in hand, and leaned into her until he was rubbing the head of his dick back and forth over her pussy lips. He took his time, and noted the warmth between her legs again. He looked down at her ass. A little scrawny, no wonder his groin felt sore. She needed some meat on her. He loved a woman whose ass shivered, when he was banging her like a dog. The rolling waves were a poor imitation of a woman's undulating tits, when she's getting fucked, but watching the ass rock as you hammer a babe from behind is still a sweet thing to see. He was getting hard again, and was anxious to get his rod back into her hot cunt.

"C'mon, boy… fuck me! Get your dick back into my pussy, and give it to me like you mean it. You started this shit, now FINISH IT. FUCK ME like a man, or get off!" Chris pressed his dick back into her soft flesh. She was hot, and wet! Her ass quivered as he fucked her, and although it was slight, he could see little wavelets roll across her ass as his cock pressed into her and his thighs slammed against her legs. She wasn't making any noise, but she was pushing against him and showing some interest in being on his pole. She began to meet his thrusts with her own, and he felt her reaching her hand between her legs and fingering her clit as he stroked her pussy with all of his strength. She began to moan, and let out intermittent gasps and sighs; "Yeah, yeah… fuck me, right there", and "ohhhhhhh, oooooooh yeah!", and all of a sudden, he was raging with that hot flash that meant he was about to cum. She could feel his cock grow a bit harder, and his thrusts get even stronger, and knew he was about to pour his juice into her. She was on the verge of an orgasm as well, and the feeling of his cock squirting its hot love lava into her pushed her into her own sweet nirvana of delight. He kept stroking her pussy as he spewed his milk into her blazing cunt, and she sucked it all in like a hungry cub. He rolled her over and began kissing her, just because it seemed like the thing to do, and she didn't mind. As he caressed her tits, his cum slowly trickled from her swollen lips.

Being Granted Immortality from a Tentacle Monster: An Erotic Fantasy

"It's your shot at eternal life and you want to pass it up?" Amber grabbed a box of salt off the store shelf and dropped it in with the other odds and ends she had been collecting in their basket.

"First of all, you said the video you secretly took of us having drunk sex was going to make us immortal. Secondly, I don't believe in magic," said Kim. She looked away from her goth friend and leaned her head back as if there would be a divine confirmation that she was right about magic. Instead there was a monitor showing the two of them shopping for groceries.

Kim gave a small spin and her dark blue skirt flailed out around her as she turned. The girl in the monitor was only a half second behind. Kim looked around for the camera and leaned towards it to see how much of her 36C cleavage was visible to what ever perv had set up the security. She wasn't surprised that she could almost see down to her belly button. She was wearing a loose dark blue blouse to match her skirt. She brushed back her brown hair behind one ear and caught Amber staring at her in silence.

"I don't even know why I hid the camera in your room. I should have used a damn tripod," said Amber. "Besides, I said the video would immortalize us, not make us immortal. We were on the site's top ten viewed for almost two months. That video's never going away. Especially not after you finished it all off by squirting to the wall."

Kim scowled at her friend, but still couldn't take her eyes off the monitor above them. Even dressed in all black, Amber looked stunning. Thicker than Kim, she made up for it with her 44DD breasts and the bodice she wore to show them off. Amber's hair was naturally black, although she had none between her legs to prove it. She had been Kim's best friend since high school, when she had started claiming she was Wiccan, and the two had hooked up when Kim came back from college for the summer.

"Do you think they watch all the tapes?" Kim asked idly. She closed in on Amber and slid a hand along her lover's ass. The sharp squeeze was enough to make Amber forget her friend's slight against magic.

"I don't think they watch them unless someone steals something," said Amber. She looked up and down the isle, but no one was around. Checking the monitor showed that there was no one around for several isles. She turned to Kim and pulled Kim to her body as she gave her a deep kiss.

Their lips locked and unlocked and one tongue slid against the other. Kim's tongue was hungry and eager while Amber's was inviting. Amber closed her eyes and moaned into Kim's mouth when she felt her lover's hand slip under the loose waistband of her skirt and pull at the thong she was wearing. The garment was already feeling a bit damp, as it always got when she was this close to Kim, and it slid easily between her lips to rub along her clit.

Amber gasped for air and wrapped an arm around Kim. She grabbed at her back and became weak in the knees. She wanted Kim to feel just as weak, so she used her free hand to pull up Kim's top and brought her lips to Kim's nipples.

"You naughty girl," Kim hissed in Amber's ear. She arched her back so that Amber would have better access to her breasts. Her hand never let go of Amber's thong, but it did ease the tension slightly so that she could pull again.

"Pussy," whispered Amber. She sucked hard on Kim's nipple and pulled back until it popped out of her mouth. "Too afraid to get your finger's wet?"

"It's on, Bitch." Kim let go of Amber's thong and brought her hand to the front of her friend's skirt. She moved her hand under the hem and tugged the thong down till it hung just above Amber's knees.

Kim's fingers slid along Amber's bare pussy. She found the slit she had become so familiar with over the past few summer months, and parted them with ease. Amber kissed her way over to Kim's other breast and started leaving dark suck marks on her lover's light colored skin. Each bruise blossomed out, racing towards the next, as she chained them along and around her breasts.

"Fuck," grunted Amber. Kim had found her clit and it had already been throbbing from the thong play. Amber let go of Kim and grabbed on to the cart for support.

Free of Amber's mouth, Kim didn't hesitate for even a moment. She sank down to her knees and flipped up her Wiccan friend's skirt.

Her tongue was free to explore the tasty folds now that both of her hands were free to open up Amber's pussy lips. She sucked and licked at the flesh, and threw caution to the wind as the loud sounds of her eating out Amber could be heard by pretty much anyone in the silent store. Amber's legs shuddered again as she came into Kim's mouth.

Kim pressed her tongue deep into her love and buried her nose up against Amber's clit as she willingly drank her friend dry of her juices. Amber's moan was muffled by her own arm as she tried to keep some level of modesty. Deep bite marks indented her skin when she brought the arm away from her mouth.

"I think I earned this." Kim pulled Amber's thong down her legs and off of her feet before she getting up off her knees. She stuck the thong into her purse and gave her recovering lover a sultry smile.

"Is that," Amber was still having trouble thinking straight. Standing and talking were proving to be a bit difficult for her. "Yea, I had something witty to say there."

The two girls got the rest of the items off the list and brought them to check out. Everyone they walked by stared at them, but no one had the courage to say anything. The cashier didn't even make eye contact with Amber when she paid.

"The machine says you have to hit a button," Amber said. She spun around the credit card machine to face the spaced out cashier. He looked into her eyes, blinked a few times, then finally looked like he was paying attention.

"Sorry, my fault. It's free." He voided out the checked items and he couldn't help but smile. "Just feel free to shop here any time."

Kim and Amber loaded the bags into the trunk of the car. "Well we know at least someone will be looking at the video."

"Don't you want to make a pentagram or something? It's just a circle," said Kim. She walked around the outside of the large circle that was lit by a fire in the center. She already had reservations about starting a fire in the woods, but her and Amber had spent a good fifteen minutes clearing the surrounding area.

"The salt is to keep the summoned from leaving the circle. It'll kind of look like a slug. Did I mention that?" asked Amber. She tossed the box into a trash bag and picked up a bowl she had used to mix the store bought ingredients.

"You said it could have as many arms as Shiva and a face of a mermaid. None of what you said makes any sense because you also say that you are going to summon this thing with magic. What kind of Wiccan magic is this?" asked Kim.

"Not Wiccan magic. That stuff is more about," Amber took a deep breath and adjusted her bodice before shaking her head. "Look, it's demon magic. Just leave it at that and never speak a word of what happens tonight."

Amber tossed a pinch of the mixture into the fire and it changed from its dark orange coloring to a pink flame.

"How did you do that?" Kim took a step back from her friend. Amber grabbed from the bowl once more and tossed even more onto the fire. The color shifted to blue and then green. Color flowed out from the fire in waves. Kim felt like she was seeing the birth of a rainbow at midnight.

"Arise. I summon you from realms unknown. Nameless one of the ice cold star. Arise." Amber held her arms out in front of the fire. The fire went out and smoke blew out of the fire pit and stopped at the salt like as if it were a glass wall.

Kim reached out with her hand and pushed through the wall of smoke. She was too afraid to take another step forward, but a hand from inside the smoke grabbed her and pulled her in. Not a hand. It was something else. She thought of it as a hand because that was the only way her mind would make sense of it. Once inside the smoke she saw it for what it really was. A long tapering vine of flesh that moved like it had no bones. A tentacle.

It continued to pull her though the smoke until Kim was certain that she was going to be pulled out the other side. A pocket of air opened up and Kim let out the breath she had been holding in ever since entering the circle.

"Where's Amber?" Asked Kim. She still couldn't see much except for the smoke and a green pulsing light that came from further into the cloud.

"She is with me," said a voice that sounded like whispers all repeating the same words. "You breached the circle."

"I," Kim stopped speaking as a second tentacle was wrapping it's self along her ankle and sliding up her thy. "I did. I am here with Amber. She promised to make me immortal. Is that why you are here?"

"Yes. I can grant you the immortality you seek. Only if you can give of yourself to prove you are a worthy addition to my," the whispers paused as the tentacle sliding up Kim's leg reached her panties. The vine like tentacle was very deft in its movements as it slipped past Kim's panties and rubbed along her pussy. "My concubine."

Kim's breath caught in her throat. There were so many questions on her lips, but from the moment the tentacle had grabbed her by the wrist, she had felt a heat growing inside her that had only been matched by her feelings for Amber. That heat grew into a need. She ground her hips down on the tentacle when she felt it's touch on her pussy. She took a step forward and slid her lips along the vine.

"Take me. If that's all it takes to live forever with Amber, then it's an honor to serve you," said Kim.

Amber was roughly three minutes ahead of her love. She knew the ritual. She was aware of what was wanted of her, and when the smoke had started, she had taken off all her clothes. She stood there naked and walked forward, towards the center of the green light. She was stopped by the tangling mess of tentacles that protruded from the demon. She fell into the mass of vines and was delivered into a sensory overload of pleasure. Tentacles wrapped themselves around her body and covered her like a mummy.

Once inside the mass she could hear the demon talking to Kim. She couldn't concentrate on what was being said. Several tentacles had already worked their way into her pussy and were busy filling every inch of her with their touch. It pulsed and throbbed inside her in a way no man ever could. Amber moaned loudly, and in that moment her mouth was filled with a new tentacle. It slid down her throat and opened up to fill her lungs with the purest air she had ever tasted. The tentacle was still small enough to close her mouth around. Once she did she licked the tentacle and bobbed her head on it.

The vines wrapping around her spread her open and every hole was filled. She pushed her body down on the tentacles even as they pushed up to fill her ass and pussy. The wrapping tentacles squeezed her breast tight and she could feel small mouths latch onto her nipples. The suction on her nipples were too powerful to ignore. She came and held nothing back. Her moan morphed into a scream of extacy.

Kim was suspended above the ground. Her arms and legs were held up and bound by tentacles and her hips moved in a rhythm that closely matched her pounding heart beat. A vine had wrapped around her eyes and she could see nothing. When she heard Amber's climax, she pulled at the tentacles for the first time and found that they would give if she wanted to move her arms.

"Amber? Where are you? Show me Amber. I promise you won't regret it," said Kim.

The green light pulsed and Kim felt her very core being moved as her body was pulled further in along the vines. The tentacles that had already snaked their way into her body moved along with her. She was stopped before her friend and lowered down to the ground. Amber lay there wrapped up in tentacles like a burn victim on life support, but only if that burn victim's only medicine was extacy. She writhed and squirmed on the ground. Moans and grunts of pleasure were the only sound in the air other than the sliding sound the tentacle made as they moved against one another.

"Amber, you look so beautiful," said Kim. Tears pricked at Kim's eyes as she saw her friend completely in her element. When they had been in high school, Amber had been an outcast for indulging in her Wiccan calling. Now, as Amber lay before her in a place others would never even conceive of, she looked at peace. No longer did her body look guarded or her head held up in a defiant look down her nose at the rest of the world. She was home.

Kim struggled to walk towards her friend. The tentacles were deep inside her now and white liquid leaked out the tips causing her thighs to become slick from the cum that the demon slowly secreted into her. Her own pleasure kept building with each step she took. She took her last step toward Amber and fell onto her as she also fell off the building cliff of the climax that now radiated out from her core and into every facet of her being.

The tentacles opened up for the two women to embrace each other and then closed again over them. Kim and Amber let exhaustion take them.

The two woke up the next morning in the woods, naked, and embracing. Amber slowly moved a hand down Kim's back. Kim's eyes fluttered open and she lifted her head from Amber's soft breasts.

"Did that really happen?" asked Kim. The fire was out, cinders having burned out sometime in the night, and the two lay naked inside the salt circle.

"You tell me." Amber brought Kim's hand down to between her legs and just above where her naked pussy laid bare. Where it had been a hairless beauty the night before, it now had a raised tattoo of a leaf. Kim pulled her hand back to herself and felt down along her own stomach. She stopped just above her pussy and closed her eyes. She didn't need to see it. She laid her head back down on Amber's chest.

Ejaculation Studies: An Erotic Science and Cumshot Fantasy

The signature was complete. Payment was made. My time on the schedule was booked. "See you soon, have a great time," she said with a smile. She was Dr. Saunders, a stunning beauty doing sexual research on male masturbation. She appeared quite modest in her white lab coat and large black framed glasses, but her youthful grace and energy shined through beautifully. I doubt hideously ugly people are drawn to sexology.

The study sounded easy, just relax in a vacation setting and masturbate as often as possible while being regularly examined for physiological and emotional effects. From the consent form, I gathered it was to gain data on a wide variety of healthy male sexual responses to establish a baseline for treating impotence. It was a confidential project, but I doubt any man would brag about something so personal. It was weird knowing I'd be paid well for simply relaxing and enjoying something fun and healthy. There'd be no cause for embarrassment during the study since medical professionals were very familiar with male behavior and anatomy.

I was a little concerned I'd lose a sense of specialness by publically jacking off to excess, but presumed my health wouldn't suffer. The day came. The beautiful, beautiful day. Nothing much happened at first. I checked in to the small island resort and was notified to be ready in the morning. No problem. God, there were a lot of beautiful women around. It was at the height of summer and the sight of their suntanned bodies glistening beside the elegant pool was fascinating. They were all very healthy too. Unnaturally so, as if the normal population of obese people was filtered out. I wondered if women were involved in their own similar research studies? Come to think of it, I didn't see any men. Not that I wanted to. It was hard to believe so many powerful Amazon beauties could randomly be on vacation there and then. I had a nice, peaceful night's sleep with several erections.

I had been "saving up" for about 10 days, so I was very ready to have orgasms and ejaculate hard. I wanted to do a good job for the study, not show up drained and lacking interest. There's something great about just stopping sexual activity for a while. Not even touching my penis. Just quickly toweling it off after a shower. Letting my hormones and sperm count build and build. Letting my pleasure chemicals accumulate day by day in my brain. Letting the easy to burn out pleasure receptors rest and recover. Letting the anticipation of sexual power and bliss slowly burn higher and higher without exploding. The longest I'd lasted was two weeks, and that particular orgasm was practically as intense as my first one ever. The semen just blasted through me. My balls and cock were primed for an extended, shuddering release of come and hot erotic energy. So I was quite interested in getting on with the project!

I wasn't quite clear on the procedure, but assumed I'd simply fill out forms honestly a few times a day, describing and rating my experiences. I was naked and feeling great in the hotel bed. The bedding was clean and white. The room was quiet. My cock was hard and ready to go. I reached down and CLICK! My door opened and a tall nude woman walked in. "Hi. Stop what you're doing please," she said with a smile.

"Uh, OK."

"I'm here to help you masturbate." I gave her a slightly confused look in the golden morning light.

"Here's what will happen. Ever heard of body shots?"

"Um, no."

"OK. Well, I'm going to get into the bed and take any position you want. You will masturbate and ejaculate on me. My body, my face, my back, my hair, my tits, whatever. Sound good?"

I was incredibly turned on. "Yes." I could barely talk, not believing what was happening. The way this tanned, black haired, friendly woman spoke so frankly about masturbating and ejaculating was unlike any female behavior I'd thought possible. She was putting me first and wanting me to have the best experience possible. I didn't have to play any games or work up the courage to talk to her. She was just here for my pleasure, and seemed quite happy to serve my needs.

"Ready? What position you want to try?" she asked with a grin.

"Um, how about plain old doggy style," I replied.

"Love it." I watched her sexily crawl into position and raise her ass. God, she was perfect. So firm and beautifully curved. No tattoos, no implants, no sagging flesh. Such a tiny waist. Her natural breasts hung forward as she crouched down on her elbows. What to say about jacking off? I loved it! I had never imagined a woman doing this, or suggesting doing this. Sex was always about fucking and trying in vain to merge bodies. This was 3D, full resolution, live action porno, far beyond anything I'd imagined was remotely possible in sexuality. It was so simple, it's no wonder I hadn't stumbled into the fantasy on my own. Masturbating felt great. My erection was easily twice as strong as normal.

When she looked back, she smiled and said, "Slow it down. No need not to savor me." Exactly the right words. What was the rush? I'd never have a first body shot again, so I took my time. She looked so fantastic in the bright morning light of that luxurious private room. My God. I was in heaven, hardly believing this was happening to me. I began to notice the hypnotic motion of her upper body as she breathed harder. Every fucking thing about her was perfect. Maybe, I thought, the institute chose her with knowledge of my preferred type. The problem with sex is that you're visually too close and can't appreciate nudity. This solved it.

"Come on, I'm ready for your come." The pleasure rose. I felt like I could just ride this wave higher and higher, gazing into her dazzling naked beauty and jacking off my uncircumcised penis like a teenager enjoying Penthouse magazine for the first time. This was sex reborn! Weird, yes, but incredibly satisfying. There was all the pleasure of being naked and playing with my penis, controlling the feedback of pleasure and sensitivity in perfect sync with my moment to moment needs, and basically, psychologically, having sex with her while she was still unknown and untouched, still a fantasy figure rather than a "partner" with all the relationship baggage that entailed.

I came. Really, really came. All over her back. Onto the nape of her tanned neck. Some come landed in her shiny black hair. I had enough to spray a few times onto her ass cheeks. Oh it was wonderful. So wonderful.

"Mmmm," was all she said as my hot come rested on her hot body. Now what? I wondered, ready to collapse after one of the biggest orgasms of my life. Certainly the greatest.

"Okay. Very good. That's ejaculation session number one. I'm Tracy. Hope you give me a good rating."

"You were wonderful," I said, catching my breath. Tracy turned and sat on the bed, not worrying about getting come on the freshly laundered cotton sheets. I couldn't believe she was so comfortable with what had just happened.

"All right. That was the normal morning routine here. There's a space for requests at the bottom of the rating form. Take your time, I suspect you'll need at least 3 hours of recovery after that." I was very grateful, but didn't quite know what to do. Should I have kissed her in thanks? No. Had to keep a professional distance, which just happened to be incredibly erotically charged after the body shot.

She paused and enjoyed my confusion. "Well, see you soon. You were great." She rose gracefully and walked toward the door. I watched her body flow through the space, a sacred creation of divine feminine wonder. Wonder I had just happily defiled. She made no effort to clean my come off her back and ass. The motion of those white globs and streaks on her tanned skin was the most beautiful sight I had been privileged to see in my sexual life. She clicked open the door, gave one last sexy look over her shoulder, paused, and walked out into the hall. The vision of her lively blue eyes, tanned skin, and my come was transcendent. I could say the rest of my week was just as great, but having a dozen women lined up on sex furniture by the pool as I jacked off anytime I felt like, politely controlling them so I could aim my ejaculations straight at their perfect pink assholes got close to topping my special time with Tracy. To science!

Intense Humiliation and Cuckolds

How I Became a Cuckold Husband: A Humiliation Erotica Story

I'm not sure how my life ended up this way; it all happened overnight. I had no chance to see it coming. My wife Alice and I had been married for only a year when she first brought up the idea that would change everything. She said she had just received an email from an "old friend" from college and it got her thinking that maybe everything wasn't right in our marriage. I was shocked, she had never really talked much about her old boyfriends and although we didn't bang like porn stars, I had thought our sex life was very good or at least it was for me. My wife was younger than I by about 5 years, she is 25 and I am 30. She was very into fitness and had an excellent body, firm C cup tits and a thick juicy ass that seemed to pop out of the spandex "yoga pants" she would wear not only to the gym, but around the house, out on errands, and actually most of the time. I often felt like the luckiest guy on earth during that first year of marriage; little did I know things were about to change forever.

She told me getting in contact with Fred, her first sexual partner, made her begin to question how things were going in our marriage. I was worried and nervous, I could tell there were times when sex seemed like a labor for her that she was just going through the motions to please me but thought maybe things would improve. Little did I know since emailing Fred she had begun coming up with her own plan for improving her sex life. She asked if I truly loved her. I said I did, to which she applied that if I truly loved her I would be willing to do whatever it took to please her. I hesitated a bit, confused, I still wasn't sure what she was getting at. It was then she told me that she either wanted a divorce, or for me to let her begin seeing Fred again. I was shocked, angry, and jealous... but also a little bit turned on. I told her I would have to think about it to which she replied by sitting down on my lap and saying, "You will have a lot to think about honey, but I know this is right for me and if you truly love me you will see that it is too." Well that was that, I didn't have much of a choice to make, Alice had made up her mind and I could tell she wouldn't be budging on this, so I reluctantly agreed. I was sure the excitement of an adulterous fling would die down after she went through with it, looking back that seems like a naive thing to think, but how was I to know what Alice was capable of or what was in store.

The night she first met up with Fred she dressed up in a way that I hadn't seen since our honeymoon. Heels, makeup, red lipstick, a short tight-fitting dress, and her hair all done up. She was a hot mess. She spent hours in the bathroom getting ready, the whole time I was jealous and couldn't help but try to bother her, rattling the locked handle of the bathroom door. "LEAVE ME ALONE, I'M GETTING READY" she'd shout. It turned me on more than I thought it would. After finally emerging from the bathroom, my dick instantly got hard and my jaw dropped. I could not believe how much effort she had put in to getting ready or how gorgeous she looked. She saw my reaction and told me to sit on the bed and get naked. Obviously I did as she said, I was excited because she had never been as commanding as she was right then. It was very much a turn on. So I stripped down and got onto the bed, my cock hard as a rock. She told me that I was lucky to have ever gotten with a woman as beautiful as her, and I just nodded. She then climbed into the bed with me and grabbed my cock by the shaft, quite firmly.

"This cock doesn't please me" she said. "I never told you about Fred, but his cock was so much nicer than yours I was craving it the moment he emailed me. You're a good husband and a nice guy, but you can't possibly turn a woman on or please a woman the way Fred does." I was surprised at how much this was turning me on. She gave me a deep kiss, released my cock from her grip, and got off the bed. She stood at the foot of the bed and told me to masturbate. I did and I must have cum in 45 seconds. She grinned and teased me a bit, telling me to lick up my cum to clean it up. I don't know what came over me, but I did. I could tell how amusing this was for her, and she couldn't contain her laughter. "I'm going to tell Fred what you just did, in fact, who knows who I might tell... it's just too adorable to keep secret. You would really do anything I asked of you, wouldn't you?"

"Yes ma'am." I said, embarrassed but knowing my place.

"Good. I'm glad. That makes me very happy. Now I've got to meet with Fred, I probably won't be home tonight, but if you want to fuck me when I get back you will do what I say," and she reached into the closet and pulled out some rope. She tied me to the bed by the ankles and by my left wrist. "I'm leaving your hand untied so you can jack off while I'm out getting railed by my new lover."

I couldn't believe this, she had never seemed into S&M or being dominate, but I didn't know what else to say so again I just muttered "Yes ma'am" and she left the room, closing the door, leaving me bewildered and naked tied to the bed. It had only been moments since I came, but I could already feel the blood returning to my cock. It was going to be a long night.

After about a half hour, I began stroking my cock again, thinking of my beautiful wife and all the raunchy sex she was having with her ex-lover. I hadn't been so aroused in a long time. I was officially a cuckold, and I can't say that I didn't love it. I thought about it for hours, knowing that when she got back she would likely tell me all about it. I didn't expect what would eventually happen. I fell asleep, but a few hours later, around 3AM, I heard someone enter the house. I was immediately elated to hear her arrive, then I heard his voice, and my gut dropped. She had brought him home, into my home. We hadn't talked about this and I didn't know what to make of it. The most frustrating part is that maybe ten minutes passed of them being there, chatting in the living room, and they still hadn't come to check on me.

I began to shout "Honey? Are you back?" I could tell this annoyed her, because they got quiet but didn't respond. I yelled some more, and then I heard them talk for a moment. Then I heard the door open: but it wasn't Alice, it was Fred. He opened the door and was standing in the doorway, buff naked. He was a tall, muscular guy with a massive 8 inch porn star cock. I couldn't believe it was actually that large. If his cock was an arm, it made mine look like a thumb at best. He said, "Alice told me to come in here and make sure you were alright," as he approached the bed, where I was still tied up, covered in my own cum. I had a bad feeling about this, but was also very turned on and my dick was getting hard just looking at this stud approaching me in my own bedroom, seeing me look like a total bitch tied up in my bed. I knew what was coming next, I closed my eyes and next thing I know Fred was on the bed with me, both hands grabbing the back of my head and a split second later a giant cock in my mouth. I didn't know what to do so I just opened up and let him force it in my mouth.

Before I could make heads or tails of the situation, I heard Alice come into the room and start giggling. "Holy shit," she said. "You weren't joking Fred, he really seems to be enjoying it."

And I kind of was… the panic and the rush, being tied up and having my face stuffed with this stranger's massive rod was a unique and pleasurable feeling.

"I'm a take charge kind of guy," Fred said as he was forcing my head up and down on his shaft, gripping me by my hair and moaning in pleasure. I was gagging and choking a little bit on his cock, but I began to kind of like it and get into it. I wanted to please this man and I wasn't sure why. "He is our bitch now, Alice, I think we've broken him."

"This is so fucking hot, I'm glad you decided we should come back here Fred," Alice said climbing onto the bed and beginning to caress Fred's fit body. The whole thing seemed surreal. She began making out with Fred, both of them hovering over me as he continued to force feed me his shaft. At this point I began touching my cock and stroking it. Almost immediately Alice took notice.

"Nuh uh uh" she said as forcefully yanked my hand away and tied it up using the last bit of rope. I was now completely immobile, strapped to the bed. I had never seen this much energy from Alice, she seemed thrilled. I was almost scared at how much I was enjoying the whole scenario. In less than 24 hours, everything had changed, my wife and I's vanilla sex life was over, and I was now being used and being forced to do something I had never considered. The loss of control was a huge rush, and I wondered what would happen next as I began to slobber and suck on Fred's cock more and more willingly.

"Don't cum in his mouth, Fred," Alice begged him. I was upset by this; I had kind of been hoping he would. "I want your cum in me; I need it in my pussy," she said, with a frank sincerity.

"Oh yeah you want this cock in you now?" Fred replied. "You want me to fuck you in front of your husband?"

She didn't have to answer, it was more of a whimper, a longing for his cock was detectable in the tone of her response. And with little hesitation, Fred took his cock out of my mouth and turned around. They began fucking right on top of me, Fred's muscular ass right in my face. It was suddenly like I wasn't there at all. I was helpless, but what I saw was something I liked very much. My wife was behaving in a way I had never seen or expected her to. She was totally his plaything, as they began to hump faster Fred moved back a bit, intentionally stuffing his ass right in my face.

"Tell him to lick my asshole, Alice," he said, but he didn't have to, it just seemed like the natural thing to do. I was tossing this stranger's salad as he pounded my wife. And I loved it. This went on for maybe ten minutes, I would lick until I was gasping for air. I had an overwhelming desire to please them any way possible, and in my constricted state this was all I could do. They continued fucking until Fred let out a huge moan and I could tell he was cumming. It was a furious moment… he gripped her tight and seemed to crush into her. She too began to moan, but Fred pulled off of her and lifted her up, taking control of her thin perfect body and setting her down practically right on my face.

"Oh my god." She whimpered. I felt her wet pussy on my face, I began licking, lapping up cum and pussy juice. Their combined taste was something I had never imagined and can hardly describe. It was one of the best tastes I had ever experienced. I licked her pussy until she began to moan, I could tell she was cumming. I had never been able to make her cum on my own with either my cock or my tongue, and I was happy that she was able to get off so easily. It was then that I realized I was still a very lucky guy. The exasperation and ecstasy in Alice's eyes said it all. She was overwhelmed by pleasure, you could tell even she hadn't expected the night to turn out as wild as it had. I was a changed man from then on; a cuckold.

This whole event transpired in about an hour, by 4AM Alice was untying me. She told me that she was too tired to help get me off, and asked if her and Fred could sleep in the bed. I said that was OK, and went out to the couch. I was a little disappointed, I thought my oral performance on them both deserved some reciprocation, but I wasn't exactly in a place to express my feelings. I began to jack off, thinking the night was over and that was that. And for me it was, but as I was stroking, I heard the unmistakable sounds of passion coming from the bedroom. I got off the couch and went to the door. It was locked. I took the hint and went back to the couch where I finished masturbating and passed out. I fell asleep to the sounds of them in the throes of lovemaking, jealous but also content and satisfied. It felt good to know that the woman I loved was being pleased in a way that I couldn't.

I awoke to Alice and Fred standing over me, looking down on the couch. They were both fully clothed, which made me feel a little embarrassed as I was naked without so much as a blanket. Fred said thanks for letting him fuck my wife, and Alice asked if I would be able to get used to my new role. I told him that the pleasure was mine and that I would be able to get used to being a cuckold. Alice then kissed me and told me I had been a good boy. She said she would reward me by fucking me soon, but not now because her pussy was too sore. I couldn't argue with that, in fact, I can't argue with Alice much period these days. She has become a new woman, one I seek to please in any way possible. I thanked Fred for what he had done for my wife, and said I hoped to be able to please him again to which he replied "Maybe, if you're a good boy."

This all happened a few weeks ago, Alice and Fred still see each other very often, though she still says that her pussy is too sore for me to fuck her I think it's just an excuse-she has no use for my puny cock now that she's had a taste of Fred's. I've taken to eating her out after he visits, but I've yet to watch them fuck again or to suck on Fred's cock. I think they gave me a little taste of that to break me in, and I must say it worked. I have been on my best behavior, doing whatever they ask; doing laundry, cooking, mixing drinks, doing dishes, running to the store, and leaving the house when they want privacy. It's strange but it's all the biggest rush ever, and I must say I am pleased with how things have turned out. I only hope if I keep up this behavior Alice and Fred will decide to let me watch, maybe Fred will let me suck on his cock again too. It seems pathetic, but I can tell this is what's best for me and her. Seeing her this happy makes it totally worth it, and the feelings I have for her have only grown stronger.

Big Black Dick Cream Pies My Sexy Latina Wife

Well basically it just went something like this. My wife and I watched couple of videos some time ago with a few different guys and girls and some was supposed to be wives that do it with these guys that all had black cocks. I asked my wife if she would ever want to or consider doing it with another guy. She, like most women out there, said no. My wife is from Peru and is pretty traditional at times and not so much at other times. Well, I know how most Peruvian women are, and I knew that it would not be easy to ever get her to go through with something such as going down on a black guy that had a huge cock, let alone allow him to put it in her.

So after about two years had gone by, I finally decided to post an ad on craigslist stating that we are looking for a black man to watch us by webcam having sex. We got tons of emails and offers from a lot of crackpots and men pretending to be black but not really. So one day, me and my wife were drinking and just hanging out, and she finally agreed to do sex live on the webcam. We logged into the cam program and start making out and things started getting hot. Keep in mind that at this time I only wanted people to see us and not for her to see them.

While kissing and touching on my wife, I placed her hand on my cock. So here is my Latin wife, 27 years old, hot, thick body, little tits, and a great fat ass standing at only 5'1 in height with long brown hair. She was pretty buzzed and this black guy was online watching what we were doing and rubbing his big dick.

I sucked on her tits, kissing on her neck in between, and she had her hand on my cock still, stroking it. She just sat there kind of turned on and a bit nervous at what was starting to happen here. She was not really into black guys, but she didn't know the guy looking at us was black (as yet). I knew she would never show her pussy and body or even get into that position unless I kind of helped it along. I asked her right then if she was alright or if she wanted to stop what was going on altogether. I was serious, and she knew I was, and that seem to make her feel a lot more comfortable. So she kept her hand on my cock and moved it up and down a little while I kissed on her. Then he asked her if he could see her kiss it. So she waited for a few moments, adjusted herself, and slowly moved to her knees.

She started by kissing my cockhead a little and then began to lick it a little, and finally started to suck on it a little bit. I got pretty hard and big in a short time. She was really sucking on me and for a while when I then pulled her shorts off, and she was kind of reluctant about it. She would let me rub her pussy through her lacy panties while she sucked on my cock. He tried to send an invitation for us to see him, but she said she would not like that. We all agreed that it was a cool experience. He told her how much of a hot body she had and how sexy she looked with her little lacy panties on and about how well she sucked on my cock. He told her that he loved her nice full lips and how great they must feel.

We drank a bit more and chatted about our experiences and the experience that we just had. By now my wife was a bit more buzzed and said that she had a good time. I could tell at this point that she was a bit buzzed, so I said that before he logged off I wanted her to see who she was talking. So I told him to invite us again to see his webcam. The cam came up and appeared a man stroking a huge black dick much longer and thicker than mine. I could see her face filled with shock but at the same time lust. She started to lick her lips and touch her breasts and move her hips so that her fingers would go in a bit more and more every time she was moving to the motion, imaging his cock moving in a little and out a little. She started to moan and make little cries. I could not believe that I was watching my little Latina wife masturbating to this big black guy. I could not believe that she was even letting this black guy she had just met do this with her. I have to admit it was kind of crazy to see her do this. It was like a dream come true. She was saying how good it felt, and he was asking her if she liked his cock. She would answer in a whimpering affirmative. He would tell her to say that she wanted to feel his big cock inside of her and she would. He asked her if she liked his black cock inside her, and she would say yes in a somewhat out of breath voice, and he would tell her to say it, so she did. She started to shake as I could tell as she was cumming. She must have cum at least three times before she got up.

Our first time was a little by accident and little of me scheming to get my wife to try this. I had been suggesting the idea to her for over five years, but since we are Latino Catholic, it's something that she had a huge problem with. I decided to contact men on craigslist show them her photo and see which men were interested. She is a real thick light skin Latina woman... there were a few rejections, however I settled on one guy that I knew she would like. We arranged to meet at a mall close to home. I made sure my wife had a bit of wine to drink before going out… otherwise she would not be open to any ideas. I also asked her to take off her panties. He had requested that she wear a long sun dress. She was gonna be in for a good surprise!

We went to the mall and I texted the guy that we would meet in the food court. When we got there… sure enough he was there. He was just as his photo and as he described. Black (medium skin tone) about 5'10", medium build, and a little grey in his short hair… He was a little older than us. I let out a huge HEY! Like if I had known him all my life. He did the same. I introduced him to my wife as an old friend, and we all started walking around the mall and talking.

I was waiting for him to make his move. He said, "Bro, you never told me you had such a beautiful wife. You were hiding her from me since you know us black guys love big asses." We all laughed. We kept walking, but I saw both of them slow down a bit, and he had his hands on her ass, touching. Then I saw them giggling together and him leaning in to tell her somethings. I couldn't hear. Then I saw him grab his crotch. He was wearing grey/silver basketball shorts an you could see the outline of his dick… like a big pipe. Both of them could not wait, and they started walking faster to one of the major dept. stores. I followed them. They went to a fitting room and told me to wait outside and keep watch in case someone came by. I could see movement, mostly his body, and I heard moans of, "Ayy papi… dispacio por favour… be gentle… be slow…"

After about an hour and a half, they both came out smiling. He gave her a huge kiss and told us to give him a call anytime, that he lives only 10 minutes away, and he's free to meet up often. After he left I quickly asked my wife what happened? How was it? She couldn't stop smiling! She said she had something to show me, but in the car. We walked to the car. We both got in… She lifted her dress an showed me a huge glob of cum between her legs.

Cuckold Husband Watches as His Wife is Impregnated by Five Black Men

My wife and I are involved in a cuckold/hot wife relationship in which she can do whatever she wants with anyone and I watch. She loves fucking all types of different men, but her favorite are black guys with huge cocks. Often times she comes home with a sore and abused pussy full of cum and she makes me lick it all better.

Just to give you a little background, she is 5'6" with long legs, jet black hair and 36D tits. In addition she has her pussy shaven with a nice little faint landing strip. Recently she has shown a fascination with going bareback. However, that is against our rules.

One night we were walking back from a nice restaurant, but it was located in a dangerous part of the city. My sexy wife was wearing a nice evening blouse, jeans, and heels. Underneath that she had a leopard print bra and a sheer black thong. When we walked past the one house there were 5 black men sitting on the porch. One of them whistled and said, "Where are you going? Get that pretty white ass back here."

I was worried for our safety so I tried to keep things moving toward our car. However, my wife had other ideas. She walked right up on the porch and in the middle of them. This obviously cued them to the fact she was down for whatever they wanted. One of the men asked her, "Do you want a drink?"

She said sure and followed the man inside. While the other four followed behind them the last one said you stay out here white boy. All I could do is peak in through a window as all five men sized up my wife. I heard music get turned on, and I saw my wife stand up. My cock was rock hard because I knew what was coming next. In one swell motion she pulled her shirt off exposing her big tits and leopard print bra. Two of the men swarmed towards her and they each fondled a breast over her bra. One of them unclipped the clasp and her bra fell to the floor exposing her massive tits to the men. This is where things really took off. A third man now walked up and tugged at the button on her jeans. He slid his hand down the front and rubbed her pussy while kissing her.

Then the fourth man walked up and said,"Time to ruin this little white bitch". He pulled out his cock and it was 6 inches soft with the girth of a soda can. My wife's eyes were fixated on it and she looked like a bitch in heat. She instantly dropped to her knees and sucked it to life. At first she toyed with the head licking and sucking it, but eventually, had as much as she could handle in her pretty little mouth. He pulled her off his dick by her hair and moved her to the sofa. He tugged on the thighs of her already unbuttoned pants and pulled them off. She was lying in front of him only wearing a little thong.

He looked at her and said, "Bitch, you on the pill?"

She replied, "No."

"Perfect," he said with a big grin. The he pulled her little thong to the side and placed his now 9" member right in between my wife's waiting legs. He swirled it around her soaking wet slit and I knew she had taken it all the way when I saw her eyes open wide. We always agreed that she would play safe, but there she was like I wasn't even there breaking our preset rules. The man just went to town on her little pussy, stretching it more and more with each thrust. Then all of a sudden I look and there is now a black cock in her mouth. Within seconds of the cock hitting her mouth her body spasmed, and I could tell she was coming. There were two men in her and three others jerking off watching with me as I stood outside.

Shortly after her orgasm, I saw the black man's balls tighten. My stomach tightened because I knew he was going to flood her pussy. This was exciting and all, but I did not want to see her get pregnant. Then the man grunted and started pumping his seed into my wife. He pulled out and immediately took her thong and placed it back over her pussy. Why I don't know, but he grinned at me through the window and walked to the door. He threw open the door and grabbed me by the back of my neck. He threw me in between my wife's legs and pulled her thong to the side again. His cum started running out and he looked at me and said,"Lick that shit up white boy".

I hesitated and then closed my eyes and went to town. This had gone way further than I had ever thought. Once I cleaned her up, she dressed and gave all five men her phone number. They all come over on a regular basis. Turns out she is currently four months pregnant, and we do not know who the father is, just that the baby is black.

Eight Cocks for my Wife

March was here again. Amy, my wife, was so hard to buy birthday gifts for. This year, I decided to blow her mind!! We have a fairly open marriage, and often go to swingers clubs. I knew she fantasized about having several men fuck her at the same time, so I decided this year; I would give her a gangbang for her birthday.

I called up several of my friends that I knew had been drooling over her huge tits at the pool every summer, and I called some of the folks that we swung with on a regular basis. By the time I was done making the "guest list," I had gathered 7 horny cocks to fill my wife with.

Her birthday came, and I took her out to dinner. After we ate, I told her that her gift was waiting at home for her, and we went back to the house. When we walked in, all seven guys were sitting in the den drinking beer and waiting on her. She looked at me questioningly, and I explained what was going on… you could tell by the look on her face that her pussy was already dripping in anticipation.

She immediately started shedding clothes, as she had already had quite a bit of wine at the restaurant. She was kind enough to ask me to start fucking her first, and I obliged. I started off, though, by eating that sweet wet pussy. After she came, I quickly shoved my cock in her sweet, wet cunt, and she let out a gasp. Then, my best friend since high school shoved his cock down her throat. She hungrily swallowed his entire cock, and held it for about 7 seconds. Then her head was bobbing back and forth as I fucked her brains out. As the crowd began to gather around, she soon had a cock in each hand, one in her mouth, and mine still in her pussy… I knew I was about to pop, so I easily slid my cock in her ass and fingered her pussy while I exploded a huge load of cum in her asshole. As soon as I pulled out, one of our swinger friends was right inside that beautiful pussy.

She was sucking her 3rd cock of the night, and had had so many different cocks in her hand that she had lost count. One guy already came all over her face as she sucked his cock. She also still had my cum dripping out of her asshole too. It didn't take long for two other friends of mine to start fucking her at the same time. James had his cock buried balls deep in her asshole while Bo was pounding her pussy as fast as he could. They both came at the same time, as did Scott who had his cock in her mouth. She had cum dripping out of every hole she could think of.

Her face and tits were covered in extreme amounts of cum, and she was smiling! I had chosen the right gift! Now, I couldn't wait for my birthday to get here!

Your Complete Humiliation: Taken by 20 Men as Cheerleader's Taunt

It is early in the AM and you enter my room slowly and quietly, thinking you'll surprise me with a box of chocolates and flowers before I wake up. You hear some noises, some giggling, moaning, so you figured I left the TV on before bed.

As you crack open the door, the light is off, but the sun is shining through the window, and the curtains are open wide. You see my pom poms on my desk, and my cheerleading outfit draped over the chair.

You open the door completely, only to see me on all fours on the bed, naked, my tits hanging down and bouncing as a man behind me pounds me hard. His naked torso glistening with sweat, his chest and abs ripped and tan.

The flowers and chocolates fall out your hands and onto the floor, you are standing in the doorway, mouth open a little, completely stunned.

I look back at the guy fucking me and we both turn to look at you and start to laugh hysterically. "I told you he was a complete dork!" I say as he continues to pound me. There you stand in the doorway, your red and black plaid vest over a white button down shirt tucked into your tan trousers. Your face is pimpled and you're wearing your big, thick black glasses.

"He looks like a complete loser, you were right! And totally wimpy, I could easily take him." The hot man says as he continues to pound me. His hands gripping into my ass cheeks as he pulls me into him, forcing his cock harder and deeper inside of me, making me scream louder with each thrust.

"Oh Gerald, I forgot to introduce you, this is Bobby, the STAR quarterback, not a math league dork like you." I giggle. Bobby pulls out of me and walks right over to you, lightly smacking your glasses off your face. I stand up, completely naked off my bed and walk into the hallway. You hear me shout "he's here ladies!"

Bobby continues to laugh as he pushes you onto the bed. His 9 inch dick still erect, now right in front of you. You can't help but look at it, so much bigger than yours. His body much more muscular and stronger, and you understand why your girlfriend would want such a stud fucking her, and why she's never let you fuck her, in fact, you've barely seen her naked.

With Bobby standing in front of you, you didn't notice 5 girls who had come in to the bedroom. All are giggling and wearing sexy nighties. "So this is him? Oh my god! He is a dork!" One of the girls screams out and points at you laughing. Another girl says "Oh, this is going to be fun! Get him on the ground Bobby."

Bobby grabs your shirt and pulls you to the ground. You're so wimpy that you don't even try to resist, not sure what is going to happen, but knowing that it's not going to be good.

I stand over your face, my feet on either side of your head. I crouch down and look between my legs down at you. "You've never seen a pussy before have you, Gerald? Well you're going to see tons today, because we're going to have fun with you!" I crouch down completely and sit my pussy down on your face. "Eat up, you know you want to!" You start to lick me and taste my wetness, not realizing that it's not only my cum, but Bobby's as well. I start to laugh more. "Do you like that Gerald?" I ask nicely.

You nod your head and continue to eat me. "Oh, and by the way, you're not only eating my cum, but you're eating Bobby's!" You stop eating and I stand up and smack you across your face. "Did I say to stop eating!!" I crouch down again and hover my pussy about an inch from your face, and squeeze out the rest of his cum, as Bobby holds open your mouth, making sure the thick creamy load drips directly onto your tongue.

My dorm mates are all laughing so hysterically, pointing, snapping pictures with their cell phones and talking amongst each other.

"You're going to do whatever these girls want, that means whatever will amuse them! So I hope you're prepared, the RAs are gone for the day and we have the entire floor to ourselves! So scream and cry as loud as you want little loser boy, because no one's going to hear you. Oh, and the football team is coming over later to play with you as well!"

I continue to laugh and move from you. I sit down next to your and touch your face lightly, then smack it hard, and continue to laugh. "What a fucking loser you are, I can't believe you'd just sit here and take this! Man, I wonder what we could get away with!?" I say as I look over at Bobby and give him a big smile.

"So we talked about this before, I'm wondering, do I make you suck his cock before or after I make you eat my ass?" Your eyes widen with terror, but your cock says something different.

I stare at your dick. "Ok, let's ask the little pee pee." I take off your pants, pulling them down hard, and your tiny little dick pops out. "Do you want to suck Bobby's cock, and maybe even the whole football team?" Your cock twitches a little. "Or would you like to eat my asshole and THEN suck Bobby's dick?" Your cock twitches even more. "We have a winner!"

I face your cock as I stand over your face again. You are looking right up at my ass as it lowers down onto your mouth. You can't help but do as you're told, licking and tonguing my asshole. "Good boy, that's how you do it! Do as your told you fucking loser bitch. God, you are such a pathetic, worthless little shit, we are going to have too much fun using you. And if you're a good boy, you might get this every weekend! Aren't you happy you are dating a cheerleader!?"

You can't say or do anything but lay there, your shirt and vest still on, your glasses broken on the floor next to you, and your trousers pulled to your ankles. No one's playing with your dick, but it continues to throb. Your tongue is deep inside my ass and you can't get enough.

As your tongue is deep inside my ass, all of a sudden you feel something wet dripping down your chin, onto your lips, and into your mouth. You stop tonguing me for a second to see what it is. You taste it, it's salty and warm, then you smell it and realize that I have just leaned back, and let some piss dribble out of my pussy and into your mouth.

I don't let up grinding down on top of you and grab ahold of your balls hard and say "Don't stop little boy, I'm so close to cuming, I just had to pee a little to do it." I laugh and the girls laugh around me. You don't know what's come over you, you can't help but obey everything I say and you know you'll do the same for my girlfriends.

You have no idea what's going to come next, but you do know you'll be doing it all!!

I stay on your face for another minute, after you have drank my piss and eaten my asshole and I've cum all over your face. Finally, I stand up, you see all the girls laughing at you, their hands over their face. "I thought he had a white shirt?" One of the girls says as she continues to laugh. You look down, seeing your shirt stained yellow from my piss. All that dripped out of your mouth is either on your shirt or on the floor.

"Eww…" I say as I kick you in the side. "There's fucking piss on my floor!! Clean it up bitch!" Bobby grabs your shirt and pulls you up off your back and pushes you on your face in the floor. Bobby crouches on the floor next to you, grabs ahold of your face and pushes it into the piss on the floor. "Lick it bitch." He says, as he holds a fist full of your hair. You immediately start licking it up like a little kitty cat licking up milk.

"Hahaha, could you be any more pathetic?!" I say as I kick you lightly again. "Actually, I have a GREAT idea what will make you more pathetic." I walk over to Bobby, who's still standing in the room naked and start to whisper in his ear. He walks over to one of the girls and whispers to her. She giggles and runs out of the room.

"Ok girls, now to really get Gerald's little dick jumping. Turn over Gerald." I step out of the way and the girls start to take off their clothing. Each is absolutely gorgeous and varying in "sizes." Five girls stand in front of you, one's a C cup, a D cup, a DD cup, a B cup, and me the B as well. There's shaved pussies and hairy ones; blondes, brunettes, and even a red head (and yes, her carpet matches the little runway of her drapes).

You think that you're finally going to have the fantasy of a life time, you're going to get to eat and fuck each of these girls. You start to stand up and I take my foot and put it right on your chest, pushing you back onto the ground. "No no little boy, you stay right there, your surprise is coming and will be here shortly."

"In the mean time, Bobby, are you ready?" I look down at his cock and then back at you. You look up at me confused. "Get on your knees boy!" I lean down and scream into your face. You fucking pathetic geek, you are so worthless, and always will be, now service your superior jock's cock.

You are frozen on your knees, your face right in line with this 8 inch dick. So much bigger than your tiny little 5 incher. "Open up little boy, you know you want it, besides, you need to practice!"

"What? Practice for what?" You stutter.

I don't say a word, I just laugh and say "Open wide!" and I smack the back of your head, making your lips touch his cock. Bobby is standing in front of you, his cock only partially erect, and he's stroking it.

You don't know what comes over you, but you open your mouth slowly, and as you do, he holds onto the shaft and pushes the head into your mouth. "Suck boy!" Bobby yells out. You're looking up at him, just the head in your mouth, not doing anything. "Suck it or I'll make you wish you did!"

You start to suck on just the head, but Bobby pushes his dick farther into your mouth. You can feel it grow bigger in your mouth until 6 inches are inside, and it is hitting the back of your throat. You gag a little and we all continue to laugh.

"Are you ready for one of your surprises?" I ask you, my face next to yours as that cock slides in and out?

You're on your knees next to the bed and one of the girls pulls up a chair and stands on it, while another stands on the bed. They both lean back a little and spread their pussy lips. Their pussies are basically about a foot over your face. You are focused on sucking Bobby's dick and don't even realize that about 5 other guys walk in with the girl who left the room. All are in their football uniforms. What you don't realize is that another 20 are outside in the hallway, stripping down.

As you look up at the girls above you, something wet hits your eye. You close both eyes and then feel the warm stream on your face and then 2 streams. You open your eyes again to see 2 golden streams criss crossing over your face. The girls are emptying their bladder on your face and you are drinking it as it falls onto Bobby's cock and you suck it into your mouth along with the cock.

"Good boy, but don't get too full when Bobby cums, because there's plenty more where that came from!" I turn and look at all the guys standing around me and the ones in the hallway.

"Oh, don't worry, you're not only going to get your mouth fucked," I giggle sinisterly. "and of course you'll get to wash anything you take in your mouth with the girls piss!"

You suck on Bobby harder and harder, being forced to take the entire 9 inches into your mouth. He's being rough with you, grabbing your head and pushing it down, basically fucking your face. His balls are slapping up against your chin.

The other guys come closer to you, taking their dicks out, you glance over and see all of their dicks, all different sizes, but all very big, so much larger than yours. Your are intimidated by it, that your dicklet actually shrivels. Even though you are excited, your dick is scared.

"Aww, look at that tiny thing, all shriveled and useless." I point it out to my girlfriends and they all chuckle.

Bobby starts to fuck your face harder and then all of a sudden stops, and without warning, shoots a big creamy load in your mouth. He keeps your face on his cock until he sees that you've swallowed it.

Another jock taps on your back and says "my turn." Bobby pulls his cock out of your mouth and this other guy shoves his in.

"This is going to take forever and I want to cum!" Yells one of the other guys. "You're right," I say, "this is going to take forever, but I have a way to fix that." I tell the guy who's fucking your face to just hold off for a moment.

I then push you onto all fours and have the guy get on his knees in front of you. "Wait, this would work so much better on the bed." You immediately get up on all fours onto the bed, taking off your shirt.

You're on all fours on the bed, your puny tanless body looking so wimpy, almost....girly.

The next guys who are ready to fuck your face move up towards you. Tan, muscular, hard bodied jocks. Instead of both getting in front of you, one gets on his knees behind you. As you wrap your mouth around one of the guys cocks, you feel the other one behind you, pressing his lubed up dick against your asshole.

He presses his dick into your ass, you feel the head spread your asshole wider as it slides in. You let out a squeak as he pushes it in another inch. You have no idea how long his dick is, but you can feel how thick it is as is stretches you out slowly.

Then, without warning, he shoves it in all the way… all 10 inches. His cock hits you so hard and deep, you let out a loud yell that is muffled by the other man's dick in your mouth.

You keep getting pound by each guy until they all have cum in either your mouth or your ass. The whole time, the cheerleaders are making up cheers to humiliate and emasculate you. "Go faggot Go!" "That's right, suck that cock, suck it like a champ!" They are naked and you can look over at them as their tits bounce up and down as they jump around cheering for you.

After only an hour, you've had 20 different men in both your ass and your mouth, and you're filled with cum. But what you don't know, I that I have planned one last surprise for you.

I pat you on the back and start to clap. "Gerald, you've been an amazingly obedient boy, we had no idea we would get so much out of you, but it seems like you would make a great faggot! And you swallowed all those loads without getting sick, I am truly amazed. And therefore, I have a super amazing, present, in fact, I have 2."

I wave the guys over to the bed and they all crowd around you. They pull the bed out from the wall so everyone can stand around the bed. They are all squished together, their cocks out and aimed right at you.

"I think you know exactly what's going to happen, don't you boy." While laying on your back, you look up at me and beg me not to, "haven't I done enough for you my Goddess?" I laugh as you grovel and beg so you don't have to have a cum shower. You have no further objections, and I catch you diddling your small manhood before sheepishly removing your hand from your junk.

"Go boys, he's all yours!" The jocks continue to jack their dicks off until they explode all over you, focusing on your face, but shooting where ever they can, anywhere on your body.

Everyone is laughing at your little wimpy ass as you are covered by 20 loads of creamy, white, jiz.

"Now you can leave Gerald." I tell you nonchalantly.

"But Goddess, can I at least take a shower?" You beg.

"Hahaha, GET THE FUCK OUT!" I yell as I point to the door. The jocks then grab you and drag you down the hall and throw your naked ass covered in jiz into the elevator and watch as the door closes behind you.

You have nothing left to do but walk the long walk back to your car, all naked and pathetic, strangely aroused by the events that just took place.

Sleep With My Wife? Become My Bitch (A Demented BDSM/Feminization Erotica)

Frank Weber took a drink of his ice cold Bloody Mary and savored the taste. Nothing tasted half as good as a red and pulpy cocktail after work—that is except for Sally's hairy pussy. Not only did she make a fine Bloody Mary, but she didn't bleed like a normal woman her age. He smiled to himself, and clicked play on the video he had stored on his computer—a video that recorded the making of his masterpiece. A beautiful blonde appeared on the monitor with an hourglass body and all natural 38D tits that swung as a small male with red hair and a not so small cock fucked her hard doggie style. She moaned almost in rhythm with the thrusts and begged him on with bursts of "fuck me baby…fuck me baby."

Even now, Frank couldn't help but frown when he watched the recording. He had taken it from the small male who could only be described as a man with a pretty face and a massive cock. That was how the blonde—Frank's wife—had described him when caught in the act. Delores, the blonde, now his ex-wife, had taken half his property and dumped the small male with the pretty face and massive cock for a body builder with a massive cock. One thing you could count on Delores putting importance on was the size of a man's cock, thought Frank, as he sipped his Bloody Mary.

Hell, you would have thought my two-inch girth would have kept her at home. The recording switched to another video segment that featured a mattress with no sheet lying on Frank's basement floor. He remembered how he had specially placed the video camera to catch all the action. He smiled as he watched himself appear on the monitor, his arm around the small man's neck. As an ex-Marine, he knew how to easily strangle a man in a headlock, and he had the small, red haired man knocked out in a matter of seconds. Dropping him roughly on the mattress, he literally ripped off the nearly unconscious man's shirt and tugged off his jeans.

The small stud didn't wear underwear. Convenient, Frank thought. Frank had his clothes off in an instant and kicked the red head's legs wide apart. Rolling a condom on his thick cock, he lubed it up, and then spat down on the still unconscious man who had broken up his marriage. "I'm gonna fuck the shit out of your asshole," he said, and then descended on the unmoving body.

"Give it to me," the red head says.

He thrust his well lubed cock into the man's butt hole in one quick violent thrust. Violation and pain were his goal, and he achieved them. The red head tried to raise his head and screamed as Frank's dick thrust in and out of his virgin asshole. Frank's strength and his powerful hand on the red head's throat kept him down and a piece of fuck meat.

"You fucked me… now I'm fucking you bitch," Frank said with menace. "You took away my bitch, fucker," he said. "So, now you're my bitch… like it or not." Frank threw a very powerful thrust against the red head's butt to make his point.

"Tell me you're my bitch… say it!" Frank's powerful hand gripped the red head's throat so tightly that he had difficulty saying anything.

But the red head did manage to screech out, "I'm your bitch…" Reaching over to his pant's pocket, Frank reached in and drew out some pills and fed them to the red head's mouth.

"Swallow them," he ordered. A squeezing of his hand around the red head's throat convinced him to do just that. Letting go of the red head's throat he grabbed his mane of red hair instead and pulled his bitch's head back and thrust violently into his tight asshole and held it there as he felt the intense pleasure of his sperm filling the condom. Roughly pushing the red head's face into the mattress he told him what he had just given him. "You just took your first dose of female hormones, bitch. Get used to it."

As the video played on it revealed that the journey had not always been an easy one—forced feminization rarely goes without some give and take on both sides— but Sean had proved a true submissive and had embraced his role as both maid and fuck meat. As the last video segment appeared Sean was now Sally and had 38D tits, an hourglass figure, and a real pussy all thanks to some rough brain washing and the miracles of female hormones and some expensive surgery in Mexico.

"Would you like a refill, honey?" Sally said sweetly and then glanced over at the computer monitor.

"Oh, God," she said, "every time you watch that thing you rough fuck my ass." She took his glass for a refill. "Please rough fuck my expensive pussy for a change," she said.

"Get upstairs and lube that tight ass hole, bitch," he ordered.

"Not without a kiss, and an 'I love you' I won't," Sally countered.

"You know I love you," he said.

"Yes, I do." She smiled and started to strip as she climbed the stairs. The best looking bitch money can buy, he thought. Isn't life full of strange twists? His cock now stiff and impatient he stood and went upstairs and made love to his red head.

Cum-burgers and Hot Dog Insertions: An Erotic Story with Food Fetish Sex and Cum Eating as an Art Project

"Dude, I'm sorry, I can't do it"

Craig sat with his back against the wall scowling and cursing the day her ever agreed to help his friend Trevor out with his master thesis project. He'd come in thinking it would just be another one of Trevor's weird art projects, maybe he might have to take his shirt off and get pelted in the abs by a paint ball gun again. Or maybe it would be like the time Trevor had convinced him to show up to class naked so that he could video everyone else's reaction. That time was actually kind of fun, until the professor tried to yank Craig out of his seat and ended up getting a handful of his dick. It was their last semester and Craig just wanted to make it through without being the fall guy in yet another of Trevor's crazy ideas.

"C'mon, I'd do it for you man!" Trevor pleaded hoping for some sympathy.

But, Craig just continued scowling "That's because you know I'd never ask you to."

"She's cute though. I mean at least I found a cute girl this time." Trevor protested.

At this, Craig had to laugh. He'd walked into the studio caught one look at the sight in front of him and immediately balked.

"Hard to tell with her face covered in ketchup and mustard"

"IT'S A STATEMENT PIECE!" Trevor insisted, feeling a little insulted.

Despite himself, Craig started to relent.

"You're going to pay my half of the rent for the rest of the year?"

"Yes."

"And all I have to do is fuck her on top of a table covered in hotdogs, cheeseburgers, and condiments?"

"Yes."

"And you're definitely going to pay my half of the rent? I want that part in writing!" Craig insisted.

They shook on it and Craig found himself walking back into the studio shaking his head that he had been talked into yet another of Trevor's crazy schemes. Before him stood the woman who Trevor said he met at the campus library she seemed excited to be taking part in Trevor's "project". He tried to look through all the gobs of ketchup and mustard to see if she was actually cute like Trevor had described, but it was too difficult. The most he could tell was that he liked her hair. It was dark brown, curly, and fell to about mid-shoulder length. He thought for a moment about if she would mind him cumming on her hair.

The woman on the table sat up so that her legs dangled over the edge. "Hi, I'm Anita" She finally spoke up "and you are?"

Craig stammered, he was still trying to get his head in the right place and find a way to make his dick hard enough to commit to doing the deed.

"I'm uh…I'm Craig"

He would have spent the next few minutes staring blankly at her like a deer in headlights if it weren't for Trevor's sudden interruption.

"Alright" he announced accompanied by a pattern of loud clapping. "We've got limited studio time so let's get this thing going okay." He turned his attention to Craig. "Dude, drop your pants already! We gotta be out of here by six."

Craig seemed perplexed and in some sort of daze. He just had his eyes transfixed focusing on the pile of hotdogs on one end of the table where Anita had been resting her head.

Before Craig could even attempt to respond Anita sprung off of the table and began to approach him. Taking him by the hand, she guided Craig toward the table.

"Thank you!" Trevor exclaimed in relief. "I'm rolling now" He informed them while hoisting a massive camera onto his shoulder.

"It's alright." Anita tried to comfort Craig. She rubbed at his crotch gently and tried to feel for his erection.

For his part Craig was still having a hard time getting in to the moment. The room smelled like pork grease and two-day-old over-heated cheese. But then he felt his pants dropping and Anita's hands around his cock. His girth began to grow as she manipulated it inside of her hands. Moving skillfully up and down in a circular motion she'd finally gotten him hard enough for a good fucking.

"Should I put it in her mouth first or are we going to…" before he could finish the question Anita had grabbed a hamburger off the table and began massaging Craig's penis with it. He was confused again. No one said anything about playing with the food.

"This is great!" Trevor insisted. "But uh, lets make it wilder. Really get in to it and maybe wrap his dick with one while you jerk him off."

Anita was eager to do as instructed and quickly grabbed another burger off the table, wrapped it around Craig's dick and began working his pole with her hands again.

"Dude" Craig protested, feeling a mix of arousal and lingering apprehension, "I did not agree to have my dick wrapped in cheese burger lube!"

But Anita knew exactly what she was doing. Before long the pleasure Craig felt took over and it didn't matter what she was doing to get him there. She just kept at it, working the burger around his dick with her hands, watching as Craig threw his head back and his body relaxed. His shaft was definitely a grower. She'd been salivating as she felt it growing and throbbing about in her hands. She could have sworn she heard Craig holding back a soft moan. She knew it was time. She took her hands away and placed the burger off to the side. Lying back on the table she spread her legs to reveal a clean shaven pussy.

"That's fucking fantastic!" Trevor yelped while moving around to get a better camera angle.

Craig couldn't help it now he was hot for this girl like a dog in heat. He kept himself busy stroking his dick while Anita went to work on her pussy, rubbing and fingering herself until her fingers were covered in her own pussy fluids. She was watching Craig as his eyes stayed fixated on the growing thickness of her outer walls.

"You see my pink taco?" she cooed. "Are you going to cover it in your sour cream?"

Anita took both her hands and spread her vagina to show Craig the pleasure cave that awaited him. "Fuck me with your massive sausage!"

He didn't need another word. He took her by the legs and spread her apart shoving his cock into her like a possessive caveman.

"Fucking horny food obsessed slut!" He grunted into her ear. The smack-talk excited both of them.

Craig grabbed for a bottle of mustard and swirled a messy yellow pattern all over Anita's breasts then began to lick it all off as he rammed into her even harder. He picked her up off the table, his dick still inside her, and carried her over to a wall. With Anita's face pressed up against the wall and Craig's body keeping her pressed up against him, he slowly slipped his pole out and smiled as she protested, insisting that he put it back in.

"You like being filled with meat?"

"Yes, I want your meat back inside me!" Anita moaned.

Craig grabbed a hand full of hotdogs off the table and held them up to Anita's lips.

"I wonder how many foot-longs you can take in that tight pussy" he teased.

Anita licked at the hotdogs in Craig's hand. Trevor was still filming and trying to maintain professionalism. This was for the art. It was his statement piece, an examination of food culture and the pleasure associated with eating. He was an ARTIST! But also, he was turned on.

"Yes, please put them in me. I want all your meat inside of me." Anita pleaded as Craig slowly slipped his dick back inside of her pumping harder than ever before. He picked up one hotdog and slowly slipped it in, then a second, then a third, and another, and another until they'd formed a tight semi-circle around his rock hard shaft.

Anita slipped her hands down to her clit and began massaging it gently. "I want to cum all over your German sausage!"

Craig just kept at it working in and out of Anita's wet pussy, keeping her body pressed up against the wall, watching as her pulsating walls sucked the hotdogs further inside of her. Before long her body fell into a pleasure filled spasm and he knew she'd cum. He stepped away, taking all the sausages out of her snatch and watching as she licked and sucked at them moaning with delight at the taste of her own pussy. Feeling satisfied that she'd sucked all the juice off, Anita turned her attention to the throbbing cock before her and took it in her mouth with her hands wrapped around Craig's bare ass. She sucked, and licked, and swirled her tongue around it, following Craig on her knees as he made his way back over to the other end of the table.

Anita turned her attention to Craig's balls. "Those are some massive meatballs!" she teased.

She worked them with her hands while continuing her assault on his cock. Craig's face went flush and they both knew he was going to unload soon. Anita pulled away and grabbed for the cheeseburger she'd been using earlier. She took the top bun off and held it in front of Craig's shaft while he continued working it. Before long Craig had unleashed a massive amount of cum all over the burger patty. He grabbed the burger away from Anita and put the top bun back on. Holding it up to her face, he teased her with it.

"Are you a fast-food loving whore?"

"Yes" Anita hissed.

"Are you going to eat this cum burger?"

"Please! Feed it to me, let me have it!"

Craig finally relented and held the burger out watching as Anita downed it in a series of large bites. When she finished she licked at Craig's dick playfully for a while until the scene seemed to come to a natural end.

"Man!" Trevor declared with excitement. "That was damn fantastic." He was truly pleased with the result. He tried to give Craig a pat on the back, but his friend stepped away. Trevor couldn't really understand why until Anita spoke up.

"Trev, you've got a situation in your pants" she laughed. "You might want to get someone to look at that."

Anita walked off and grabbed her clothes from the corner thanking both Trevor and Craig for a good time. She even gave Trevor a few editing tips before she went off in a hurry to get back home saying she was due for a long bath.

Craig put his pants back on and looked down at his shirt covered in ketchup and mustard stains. That was a new shirt, he'd never get the stains to come out. Also, he'd allowed Trevor to talk him into yet another crazy idea. He took another look at his shirt, well at least this time he'd have something to remember it by.

Trevor was busy packing up his equipment and trying desperately to ignore the raging boner still bulging against the fabric of his pants.

"Just give me a second" he called out, "and I'll be ready to go."

But Craig was having none of it. They'd walked to the studio from their apartment and He was not walking anywhere with Trevor in his current condition.

"Dude no way, I'm not going anywhere with you like that." Craig teased. "Go handle your business in the bathroom."

With that Craig left deciding to walk back to the apartment on his own. To tell the truth, Trevor was glad. He'd been hoping Craig would leave him by himself, they still had a half hour of studio time left. When he felt comfortable no one would disturb him, Trevor undid his zipper and unleashed his veiny Johnson, walking over to the table where the food was he pointed his cock toward the pile of hamburgers and went to work. He stroked his cock methodically, closing his eyes in concentration and jerking until his cum came splurging out spreading his load all over every item left on the table.

"For the art!" he moaned in relief. He shook the last drops out of his dick and stuffed it back inside his pants. Zipping back up he sighed one last time "For the art."

The Boss Is Hungry:
My Boss Made Me Fuck Her For My Raise

Well it was just another workday, and it seemed like everything was going the same boring way it always had on a Wednesday. Of course being hump day, that was definitely a light at the end of the tunnel. So I thought…

Just then my boss called me into her office. *Oh boy what now?* Seems like I always getting into trouble at my work, even for doing the littlest thing wrong. This time, though, when I was called to her office, she came to my cubical and looked at me and smiled. Maybe I was getting a raise? I could only wish.

Following behind her in that tight spandex skirt always got me so fucking horny and hard in my pants. As we went into her office, I noticed that she shut the door behind me. This only happen to other employees if they are going to get fired or get a raise; I was hoping for the better of the two, but wouldn't be surprised either way!

As I sat down in the chair in front of her desk, she positioned herself in front of me, sitting on the desktop itself. She kept looking at me as if I knew what she was going to say to me. Of course I wanted to say, "So am I in here for a raise?"

Before I was able to say anything, she started removing her work jacket as if she were getting ready for a beating. Then she started unbuttoning her blouse all the way down to her stomach. At this point I was getting very uncomfortable, confused, but hard at the same time. I could feel my cock throbbing in my pants, and it was clearly becoming very noticeable to her eyes that I was getting hard.

She then got up and walked by me and locked the office door. Coming up behind me while I was sitting in the chair, she started to rub her breasts on the back of my head and neck. I could smell her sweet perfume and feel her hair falling around my back neck. Oh my, I was getting so fucking hard and could feel my heart beating in my cock. Not to mention the feeling of my cock tighter in my pants as she kept rubbing her large breasts on the back of my neck.

She walked in front of me and said, "Do you know how long I've been wanting to suck and fuck your dick?"

I was in shock, knowing this was my boss talking to me like this. Falling to her knees, she scooted close in front of me and started to unbutton and unzip my pants. At this point, I was so fucking hard and horny for her I couldn't stand it.

She pulled down my pants down to my ankles and proceeded to put her hand in through the hole of my black satin boxers, pulling my dick out and touching it with the tip of her index finger. pubbing my pre-cum around on my cock head and saying, "Oh you are definitely getting a raise today, aren't you? Your dick is so fucking hard and much bigger than I imagined."

At this point it was all I could do to keep composed, so I just smiled at her gracefully.

She started leaning her head in towards my cock, licking off the pre-cum and stroking my cock firmly with her hand. I could not believe I was in the office with my boss and she was doing this to me. But it was all I could do to just sit back and let her do what she wanted. After all, she is my boss!

She started sucking harder on my head, and I could feel her tongue twisting around my dick head. God it drove me fucking crazy! I couldn't help but to start moving my hips up and down as she guided my cock deeper into her mouth with her hand, sucking on me as she kept stroking me at the same time. I could tell I wanted to climax so bad, but I didn't want the pleasure to end. Just then she got up and turned around and took down her skirt, no panties at all underneath.

This only meant one thing to me, she wanted me too fuck her hard and deep.

She then leaned over onto the front of her desk and took off her blouse all the way and threw it across the office, at the same time her skirt fell to her ankles. I could feel her wet pussy dripping for my dick to slide into her. As she stretched her legs wide open, allowing me to have my way with her from behind. I then wrapped my arms around her waist and moved my hands up to her tits and began to hold them firmly flicking my fingertips on the edges of her nipples. Causing her to be even more aroused, I then kissed the back of her neck at the same time. I could tell I was driving her crazy with anticipation for my cock to go into her wet pussy.

Before I was even able to finally slide myself into her she reached back with her right hand and forced my dick into her. Her fuck box was so wet and warm with anticipation for my hard dick. It was all I could do to not make too much noise banging up against her wet pussy, hearing the slapping sound of our pre-cum mixing, drenching my balls in wetness. She then started screaming louder in anticipation as if she were about to cum. As she screamed more I pushed harder and deeper into her pussy. I couldn't help but to let go of her tits and grab onto her long hair as a guiding tool, or as if I were riding a horse and those were the reins. With each thrust I could feel my cock hit deeper into her slit. Fucking deeper and harder 'til she said, "Cum, baby cum!"

Just as I pushed one last time deep into her, she started shaking in excitement and screamed as I shot my load deep into her wet pussy. I could feel her pussy so wet as cum shot out around the base of my cock. Knowing that we couldn't have gotten any deeper with each other.

She then rested herself on the desk and said, "By the way you got your raise. That's all I need to tell you."

As she pulled her skirt back up, I then pulled my pants up from my ankles and gained my composure. Once I was dressed she said, "Thank you for coming to see me in my office about your rise. You can go now."

That I did, with a smile on my face.

Can You Bark Like A Dog?:
Depositing His Seed In A Curvy Bombshell

"Jesus… she's here… hey, it on?"

Mark's friend Lucas was still silently pressing buttons on the laptop. Mark was sitting casually waiting on an answer, but his patience wore thin as he sat himself up with a serious stare.

"Ok, its good." Getting up with a giddy twist, he walked over and threw himself, almost pushing Jason off the couch. Lucas got a fiery of a look from Jason, but Lucas ignored it.

It only took a few minutes before they heard the knock. Lucas went to get it ardently.

She strode in with swaying hips. They were big against the tightness of her pants, snug as can be, devoid of air. Mark licked his lips in anticipation.

He could not wait to put his keys in this ignition. He, like all men, loved to test a new ride, but he was no fool. A prudent driver Mark was.

Glittering like gold was her façade of a necklace. Her face blinded him with its light tones, the light of the small apartment shone off her skin like a disco ball.

Hopefully she could take him to the moon. Pink and white windbreaker over her curves… the only thing that seemed real was her confidence.

She knew she was the center of attention when she walked in. Three dudes in the room besides Mark, nobody was looking at anything else except her. The girl called Marie.

"Yo, you should have been here hours ago, babe."

Her eyes twinkled as she stepped up to the coffee table that separated her from Mark and his friend Neil, next to him.

"Calm down, I am here now."

"Ah, well hmmm. Sit. We all here."

She obliged, Lucas went to the laptop to play some tunes. All of them sat down. Liquor was pouring and food was eaten. Mark started grimacing as parcel after parcel of food came out of his fridge. Shaking his head, he though, *this better be worth it.* She was avoiding the alcohol; smart chick.

She was Jason's friend. But he just chilled silently. Lucas was talking with her about anything that came to mind. But she just shook her head. He was so close if someone walked in they could be mistaken for a couple.

He tried touching her often.

She did not cry out over it, but smoothly kept moving her body to avoid his touch. Jason was snickering at the sight.

Neil actually became the butler of all them, yet he did not seem to mind.

Mark was trying to move the conversation towards anything more laid back, but Lucas was a real pussy.

Mark knew on that day Lucas was a terrible candidate for clubbing with. Mark would rather go to the club with a homeless dude, his chances of getting female's phone numbers would be higher.

"Yo, Lucas go get me a flask of rum across the street." He did not want to leave. Jason goaded him into it much to his awkward complaints.

Marie chuckled as they both left. It was only Mark and Neil now… *it should be easier now.*

Marie said it perfectly. "He thirsty…"

"Who him, nah he drinks Kool-Aid every day. He is good, fantastic even."

Marie laughed. Neil sat down coming from the kitchen.

"He probably was drunk." Marie chipped in.

"Sure he was, on you," Neil retorted.

"Really?"

"Well, you ain't ugly." Marie stared at Mark adoringly but slit her eyes at him like he insulted her. But he knew she was just playing the game.

"So what am I then?"

"You tell me, better yet show me." Mark was not sure how she would react to that. She only got up and started dancing to the music. Rolling with motion, the tension soared into his loins.

She kept it up and started gyrating her body in many contortions. It was more like she was twirling sections of her body to the music, she was genuinely dancing. She was no freak. It had form and function to it.

When she finished, she was sweating. Her short hair rebounded effortlessly, suspended in curls.

"I like it. You are the free spirited type?"

"Ain't just a pretty face…"

"Whoa…" was all Neil could say.

"What other talents you have?"

"Many."

"Can you act like a dog?"

She stared at him as Neil burst into laughter.

"I ain't no bitch, man."

"Nah, it is not like that. Women are always calling me a dog, but I always tell them being a dog is very difficult."

"Really?"

"Ya, actually wait." Mark laid his drink down and started woofing like a Rottweiler.

WOOF!

WOOF!

Aruuuu!

Now Neil and her were laughing.

"Try it."

She looked sideways, but after a second gave a half hearted attempt at a bark.

"Come on, girl, give me a real dog. I want to hear you, woman." Orating like some aleck preacher, Mark had her smiling.

"Alright alright."

Woof

Woof

"Alright, sister, that is what I am talking about." They were all laughing.

She came to sit back down. Neil leaned back lazily in his chair.

"Yo, you down to give me a piece of that dance?"

"If you want a piece come and get it." With a smug smile, her shrug only intensified his desire to get close. Mark got up as she jumped back and started dancing, twirling her body relentlessly. He could not get a hold so he had to roll with it.

He grabbed her sides and elevated himself, rising to the occasion.

Their bodies touched, she pressed on contact. Lavishly the throbbing ached, traveled in him like lightening. He never felt gyrations like this before, his soul moved in tandem with her.

No, this was not enough for him. Holding her now, he smoothly tugged her towards him. Lips on the side of her ear, a breath escaped the heat of the moment.

"Come here."

He fell back and she turned with the passion of a million cougars. Mark walked back and used his fingers telling her to come and get her dessert.

Sitting on the coffee table now, she came up to him in a twirl. He could have sworn the wind cascaded with her and flew into his face.

She grabbed his shoulders and began rubbing her pelvis into his. The feeling was vivacious and mighty was his hold as he tried to maintain his composure on the table. A few things fell off as she pushed into him, Mark kept his balance as her passion corroded his sanity.

Neil smiled as he got up and made a beeline for the door. He only gave Mark a thumbs up before closing it. Marie looked behind her distracted by the closed door. Mark held on her face from the bottom of her chin.

"Jesus, yo, mmm, show me that beast in you."

She hopped slightly and came up with his body more.

"What…"

"Yo, go out and show me that dog in you. Baby, give me that and I will suck that pussy dry, I swear to god!"

"Scouts honor?" Mark laid her back and let herself suspend in his strong arms as he swept her in a round motion.

"Marie I ain't no scout, I'm a soldier."

She chuckled as she came up to face level and dismounted him. She dropped to the floor in a split which really turned Mark on.

As she curved her back, raising her behind. Mark held his member for dear life. Beating like his heart, he felt like he was having a heart attack or something just as traumatic.

That bounce, the vibrations lingered in his mind, hypnotizing him. She started barking with each shake of her behind. He was drunk as his eyes pierced the denim pants and vaporized it. Imagination took over and gripped him, licking his ego, smoothing his ambition.

He desired to mount that mountain. The allure of her crawl to him kept him on edge. Enter the predator she tensed and gyrated her behind, and he felt like the prey. But the question had to be who the real predator was? It must be him. Mark was the prey leading the predator into the trap of a champion hunter.

She held onto his legs and drew herself up, the smile on her face said it all. Fervent, her fingers dug into his skin and made him more aroused.

She lunged up in one movement and her body fell into his. Her bottom slid across his pelvis, riding up his foreskin. Her face was close, and he seized her from the back. Marie breathed hard, as he drew off the windbreaker over her head.

Such haste infected them, like rabid beasts. The windbreaker flew like it was the fourth of July. With such candor and rapid speed, Mark's shirt disappeared in the wind.

She pushed him back, torso falling on the sofa. Over him, with a docile look she slid her hand up his belly to his chest.

She swept it low quickly and unfastened her pants and drew it off over him. Magnetic tension tingled in his hands as he watched with bated breath.

He could not hold himself anymore, he gripped her and pushed her pelvis up to his chest.

Almost ripping her red panties off, he laid his hands on the element of his desire. Hairs on his hand tingled with a current.

The beauty of it was glamorous, drawing her in, his tongue blessed her eloquently. The moans were like a melody, an ensemble to his soul.

He drew her in, she levitated with her hand strength, he dug in. She grinded on him in joy, he lapped it up. Pushing her down on his pelvis, she gripped him roughly and pressed against his body hard.

Lifting herself, she went to work and took off his pants this time. She took his greatness and graced her tongue on his member. He fell back as she ravaged him masterfully. Leaving him with the luster of her saliva offering, he was on a high that needed relief.

"Marie come here…"

He need not say no more; she mounted him. He could feel it the tight embrace of her body in both places, she kissed him on the face. He held her as she rode him with emphatic yield. His zeal was matched by her gleeful eyes.

She felt his chest and massaged him as he went it. They only got faster and moved more erratic. Like a sassy girl of the night, she bounced with more vigor as he held her breast.

Caught in the overgrowing pain of their desires, she cried. He groaned at the throbbing tension, too much, gushing a flood of liquid blessing into her body.

She contorted as her body inflowing into the course of these powerful emotions.

When all was said and done, they clothed, and she bathed before she left. She enjoyed it and was eager to meet Mark again. That he would make sure of. Mark had carried her home and was impatient to get home and see what he produced.

When he returned, Jason and Neil were on the couch playing a card game. Mark instantly heard moaning. Jason only looked at him with a curious brow.

"What's up man, you carried her home?"

"Ya…." Mark noted his laptop was missing and wondered where was it.

He still heard that moaning… actually it sounded familiar.

"Yo, where Lucas?"

Neil chuckled as Jason pointed into the side room and said. "Fapping to you my nigga."

"Hey, hell no, Lucas give me my laptop, man! What you take this for?"

After Mark retrieved his laptop by force from Lucas, he ran him out of his apartment.

Mark got himself something to eat, as Neil went home and Jason fell asleep watching football recaps. Mark sat in his room munching on a chocolate bar as he watched his recorded video. The angle was good this time.

Watching it over, he had to admit, he really enjoyed this experience.

The fact that he was going to see more of her, the anticipation was palpable, licking his lips. He edited the video and rendered it in the form he wanted.

Uploading another clip to his porn star portfolio, the porn site he was a part of was always teeming with real content from real people. His fans were definitely going to love this one. This pretty girl named Marie was going to be a star.

Lesbian, Gay, Bisexual, Trans… and Futanari!

Picking Up a Hitch-Hiker: A Gay Erotic Story With Cumshots and Groupsex

As I was headed home from work on a sleepy residential street, I saw a 20-something young man sticking his thumb out to say he needed a lift. He looked like he'd been through some heavy exercise, like jogging, and he didn't have a shirt on. Drops of sweat glistened on his bare chest. He wasn't a bodybuilder or anything like that, but his body was toned and I felt myself getting a boner as soon as I saw him.

Normally I'm afraid of giving stranger rides, and I'm not even sure it's legal to hitchhike. As a gay man especially, I don't feel safe letting a macho-looking guy into my car. He might kill me! But there was something about his soulful brown eyes, his smile. I threw caution to the wind, stopped my car, and pressed the button to move the passenger-side window down. "Need a lift?" I asked.

My voice is super high, and I think he knew immediately that I'm gay. I thought maybe he smiled a little. Wishful thinking?

"Yeah, man, I just got done with my run, and I found out I need to be back home now because my girlfriend's coming over and I forget about it." His voice was a pleasant baritone – deep but not frightening.

"Where do you live?"

"Corners Point." That was about two exits away on the freeway. I could get there in about 15 minutes and then get home within a half hour of that. Not too bad.

"Hop on in." As he entered, I saw he had a shirt folded up hanging out of his shorts. I breathed a sigh of relief. I could ask him to put it on so I wouldn't be staring at his body the whole ride. I felt like I would come in my pants just looking at him otherwise. "Um, do you mind putting on your shirt?"

He grinned. "You checking me out?" He raised his arms and flexed his biceps, then brought them down and flexed again, his pecs flaring. I obviously followed his every move, because he grinned again. There was nothing more I wanted to do right then than jack off. I imagined him kissing me surprisingly delicately before a river of white semen erupted from me, and spilled out of my pants spurting out all over those glistening muscles.

"Um, no, I, um …"

"Just playin' with you, dude. Of course I'll put my shirt on." What a relief. As he put on his reddish orange T-shirt, I caught a glance of his hairy armpits and imagined myself sniffing them or licking them. Is that a fetish? I don't know. Anyway, he put the shirt on and climbed into my car. He was a little dude, even shorter than me, about 5 feet two inches, but he filled out that size S T-shirt. You could see his arm muscles stretching out against the fabric every time he moved, and his chest seemed barely contained as well. But I had to drive, had to get that out of my mind! He gave me directions to his home, and somehow I managed to make it there without completely embarrassing myself. I even merged on the exit okay in rush hour traffic.

We made small talk on the way there. His name was Pablo, and he did freelance work in IT. He had just graduated from the university nearby, and still lived alone in the same apartment. Brains and brawn? Almost too good to be true. We got there and he told me to come on in with him because he wanted to pay me for the ride. I told him, "No, it was my pleasure."

"I bet it was," he said, cockily.

"Come in, I can give you some more pleasure."

"Uh, okay, sure," I replied, without stopping to think. What the fuck! Was this some kind of dream? Why had he said that? People only talk like that in porn movies and erotic lit. I came with him into his apartment. It was a neat, organized kind of place. Exactly what I would expect from a guy like him. Just then, Pablo got a call on his cell phone.

"Hey, baby, I made it back … What? … Yeah, give me 30 minutes."

"I can go, your girlfriend's coming over," I said, worried what I had gotten myself into. What was this straight boy trying to do to me? Pablo didn't say anything. He just came over and kissed me. It lasted almost a minute. Our tongues locked. He was pretty sensual and sensitive for a masculine guy. I melted. I would let him do anything to me. I didn't dare hope. He unbuttoned my dress shirt and ran his mouth down my hairless Asian chest, breathing soft breaths. He didn't seem to mind that I'm a little out of shape.

"Wh -- What about your girlfriend?"

"What she doesn't know can't hurt her."

"Are you bi?"

"No way. I'm straight, but you're so so hot." I could tell he was serious, which was really surprising. He took his shirt and his shorts off, and he was standing there in just his underwear. I did the same. He led me to his bedroom and closed the door. I lay flat on his bed and he lay on top of me, kissing. Then we rolled over and I was on top. I rubbed my penis against his thigh and ran my hand down his chest. He shivered with excitement and said he was about to come. I ran my tongue around his nipples. I put my hands around his penis and stroked it hard, up and down, up and down. A little bit of precum came out and then a fountain of white splurging all over his chest and my hands.

He kissed me again and then he worked on my penis with his hands. I had a release and one of the best orgasms I ever had. Just then I heard someone turning the key to get into the apartment.

"Your girlfriend has a key? Fuck!!" He just smiled at me. He did nothing to clean himself off, put his clothes on, anything. He just lay on the bed staring at me with his beautiful eyes. I got up and tried to find where I'd put my pants. The door to the bedroom opened and Pablo's girlfriend stood there in shock. Then she laughed and laughed. I was thinking she'd gone hysterical. I was so embarrassed.

"There's nothing hotter than two boys kissing," she said. "I knew I had a catch when I found you, Pablo." Pablo turned back to me and kissed me again. His girlfriend, Elaine, squeed. It was weird as fuck, but I dug it. Elaine ended up getting into bed with us, and Pablo had sex with first her, then me, then back to her again, and so on and so forth. I even copped a feel of Elaine's breast and she touched my penis. It was an orgy, but also the best night of my life. The next morning, Pablo told me to call him if I ever wanted to do it again. And that's what I'm going to do as soon as I've finished writing this story.

THE END (or is it the beginning?)

My First Bisexual Threesome with Another Man

My first threesome was one of the greatest times of my life. As a closeted bisexual male in my late teens I had always wanted to see most of my friends naked, but I didn't want to be exposed as bi so I never had attempted a peek before. A little about me and my friends first: I was 19, 5'8", 150 pounds, slender but muscular, and had always been cute and able to get girls easily. My roommate and best friend Marc was 18 5'11" and 190 pounds. Very muscular body, great looks that all the girls loved and from what I could tell through jeans and shorts a very large package.

One Friday night we had our usual keg party after work and all of our friends showed up to drink. One girl in particular named Sam came who I had been sleeping with on and off, and I knew she was a for sure thing. 5' 3" 130 pounds a little thick but not chubby and very large C cup breast. As the party went on late into the night people drank on, some passed out on couches, and most left. I noticed Marc hadn't found a girl and that it was just the 3 of us left awake. I started to get ready for bed Sam coming with me we had already started a little foreplay of kissing a rubbing when Marc in his drunken state said, "Can I come to bed with you guys? I'm scare of the dark." I expected her to get mad but she got a seductive smile and said sure.

I was so excited I knew I would finally get a chance to see him naked but I wasn't 100% sure that's what would happen. We all went to my bed and laid down, Marc being totally drunk didn't hesitate in stripping down to his boxers and Sam didn't seem to find it awkward so I did the same. We all laid on top of the covers for a second Sam in the middle with me to her left and Marc to her right. I started to grope her breast and kiss he neck for a moment and whispered in her ear, "You don't have to do this if you don't want," still unsure of her intentions. She giggled. I looked up to notice the two of them with their hands in each others underwear. I then felt her other hand start to grab my already throbbing cock. I was quite decent size myself 6 1/2 inches and very thick. I am circumcised and have quite a large head which makes girls go wild. Sam jerked us both for a minute me trying to sneak a peak over at Marc but my view was blocked by Sam's arm.

I was so horny I felt like I might cum just from the simple jacking she was doing so I shifted directions and motioned for Marc to move his hand so I could undo her pants, I got my glimpse he was not huge but maybe 5 3/4 inches and relatively not that thick. I had pictured him much larger than me but I was still satisfied in seeing it. I undid her pants and started to take them off still sporting a huge boner through my boxers. I started to slowly rub her sweet pussy through her panties I could feel how wet she was, I pulled her panties off and dove hard head first between her legs. I started to really get her going when I noticed Marc's boxers coming all the way of and his dick start to go in her mouth. I was enjoying watching her suck him more than my licking of her vagina.

He kept looking at me with a big smile. He motioned that we should switch places I agreed I sat up and pulled my boxers down and let Sam start sucking on me while she was on all fours. Marc got behind her and started to fuck her doggy style. She was screaming in pleasure, but her screams were muffled by my dick filling up her mouth. This's lasted for only 2-3 minutes when I came in her mouth. I tried to hold it in for as long as possible but watching that sexy man plow this girl who was blowing me was too much and I couldn't take it anymore.

Almost 10 second later I saw him pull out and he spun her around also cumming in her mouth. She looked so satisfied after swallowing every last drop of both loads. Satisfied we all got up and put our underwear back on, Marc went to his room and Sam and I cuddled into bed and fell she stated she needed to hurry up and catch some sleep because it was already 3 a.m. and she had to be to work at 8. I obliged and went straight to sleep, I was dreamt about the 3 way and visualized it all again when I started to realize I was actually being sucked. It wasn't just in my dream. Without opening my eyes I said to Sam, "Don't you have to be to work soon? What time is it?"

No response just long deep swallows of my cock so I popped my head up to find not Sam but Marc sucking my cock and Sam nowhere in the room. I was stunned but enjoying it, he looked up at me and said, "I could tell by the way you looked at me last night this is what you really wanted!"

I could barely speak. It was my dream come true. Before I could mutter something out he said, Don't worry nobody else is here. Sam went to work and nobody will ever know we are bi." I couldn't believe it! Why had I not done this sooner? We sucked each other off for about 3 minutes before we each blew our loads on each other, and he simply got up and walked out of my room. We never spoke of it or had any type of sexual relation again. We moved out from our place and went separate ways 2 months later, each of us taking jobs in different towns and eventually we lost contact. But I always wonder if he thinks about me and would do it again.

Getting a Facial from a She-Male: A Gay and Transsexual Erotica Story

I'm a graduate student and being a teaching assistant barely covers the rent for my shitty little apartment, so I also work at a coffee shop near my place. I live near Boystown, which means it is pretty safe, and I don't have to worry about walking home late after a closing shift. Sure I would get the occasional whistle, but I had never really had any gay interest. It was Thursday, and it had been a week from hell. All I could do was hope for the weekend to arrive. But first I needed to get through tonight's closing shift, then I could start making plans for my weekend. It was turning out to be a slow shift; the unrelenting rain was keeping people inside tonight, and there were only a few people occupying the sofas.

Should be an easy close tonight, I thought to myself.

"Excuse me," said a soft voice, bringing me back to reality. "Could I please get a green tea?" I looked up and immediately was lost in the deepest of green eyes.

"Err um, yeah sure, sorry of course..." I stumbled. "Could I have a name for your order?" I asked.

"Sam, but I'm not too worried about somebody taking it." She said as she looked around the empty coffee shop.

"Oh yeah, sorry. Force of habit." I said as I turned red. She laughed a small giggle and said thanks before she turned away. She had a great smile, and I couldn't help but stare at her tight ass as she walked away. I made her drink right away handing it to her with some mumbled compliments.

I spent the rest of my shift kicking myself for not being smoother. Finally it was time to close up. There were only a couple people left in the shop, but to my disappointment, no sign of Sam. After sending the last person on their way I locked up the doors and got ready for the final duties. First job was to make sure the bathrooms were clean. I grabbed the handle of the first door only to find it locked. I knocked on the door as I said, "We are all closed up; I've got to get you on your way." But there was no response.

Assuming someone had locked the door by mistake I unlocked the door with my keys and opened it. Standing in the middle of the bathroom was a brunette with long hair and a fantastic ass.

"Excuse me miss but I've got to ask you to go. We are closed." As she turned around to face me I was once again met by those deep green eyes. "Sure, but I could use a little help. " Sam said softly as she turned her eyes downward. I followed her gaze down past her breasts, past her stomach, and was immediately breathless when I saw her jeans opened wide revealing a meaty seven inch rock hard cock.

"Oh my..." was all I could think, but I couldn't look away. She slowly started stroking it in front of me running her tongue over her ruby red lips.

"I got so turned on and just couldn't help myself. You were so cute out there. Would you like to give me a hand?"

I felt like I was in a trance. I couldn't look away but felt myself moving closer. I was inches from her. I ran my hand up her leg slowly, running my nails along every stitch in the seam of her jeans. I gently stroked my fingers along the shaft of her cock, and as she let out a deep sigh I circled my hand around her and started stroking. Not saying a word I increased my pace. She leaned back against the sink breathing heavier.

I felt her pulse quickening in the warmth of her cock in my hand. I loved the sensation of it on my skin. As she tilted her head back she took in a deep breath "Oh god... I'm going to cum" She said. I don't know why but I immediately dropped to my knees and took spurt after spurt of her gorgeous sticky cum on my face. As I got back to my feet, still covered in cum, Sam zipped up her pants, kissed me on the cheek, and moaned, "That was fun. Thanks!" She slipped her phone number into my back pocket and slipped out of the bathroom.

Lesbians in Jail

Marina. She was everything I wish I was. I catch myself analyzing her so closely. Everyone was terrified as she had this quiet intensity about her. It was intriguing actually. Marina didn't trust anyone but herself. A long time ago, her cell mate overdosed on heroin. That cell mate was undoubtedly the only person that Marina ever loved. I used to hear them in the middle of night whispering and breathing heavy. Every night I lay in bed thinking about them two over and over again.

My name is Jamie and the reason why I am here is because I robbed stores. That is all I was good at. Of course, I gave up personal training to be a fugitive, that is. "Hey. You mind giving me a spot over here?" My eyes had an afterglow of excitement.

Instantaneously, I responded, "Yes, anything you want, Marina". Her arms were folded and her eyes traveled from my breasts to my eyes. I felt myself becoming wet. Marina took over the smith machine and loaded it with as much weight as she could handle. I was stunned at her power and determination to lift it. I stood behind her in the event she needed guidance. I quickly grabbed my water bottle and noticed Marina's nipples were hard. I choked on the water that left my mouth. The water sprayed on her bare skin and found its way down her sports bra. Marina's eyes closed at that moment, following a moan from her voice.

I stood up in front of her just about to apologize. Marina pulled my spandex shorts towards her sweaty olive body, then reached her hand down to touch my drenched pussy. Our lips met passionately and our arms wrapped around each other's waists. Marina picked me up and walked me over to her cell bunk. All I could smell was notes of sandalwood and musk. God, Marina was beautiful. I could stare into those green eyes forever.

I decided I was going to dominate her. It was my turn to be her. I pinned her down tightly, ripped off her white wife beater, and suctioned my mouth of her breasts. Marina's back arched farther and farther. Immediately, I removed her panty and mine, her legs parallel up in the air, my pussy massaged her pussy until she climaxed. I inserted my finger inside her as I yearned to feel her warm glaze. Marina commanded that I stand up and fallback against the wall of the cell. Her head between my legs, I had a feeling someone was watching.

The female prison guard had heard us. Esther was not so bad looking herself. I was too turned on to quit. I wanted her to make me cum. Marina traveled in circles around my clit, leaving not a single spot unattended. Esther chimed from the shadows, "Girls, I'm afraid you have to stop. This is my shift and I cannot allow you two having sex. Unless... "

Esther walked over to the bars and unlocked the cell. Esther paced back and forth with her nightstick in her hand then slapping the palm of her hand with it. Esther walked over to me and placed the nightstick between my breasts. I did not know how to react. Marina wiped her mouth, defensively protecting me. Esther cuffs both Marina and I, forced us to our knees, and to face opposite directions. Guiding in the nightstick, she directs us each to fuck an end of it. Once she's seen enough, she forced me to lick her pussy until she has an orgasm. Unceremoniously, she finished, uncuffed us, zipped up and left.

Paco's Christmas Futanari Surprise (Homosexual and Shemale Erotica)

One brisk Monday morning, Paco woke up to discover that it was only two days until Christmas! And that meant most of his clients would be gone for the Holidays. He stepped out onto the porch of a little shack house behind a medium-sized apartment building in Los Angeles and surveyed the day. His trusty shopping cart was loaded up with his reliable mop bucket, broom, dustpan, cleaning supplies, sponges, everything that a personal housemaid would need. He was a relatively good-looking Hispanic young man at the age of thirty-six; he was also a little bit slow on the uptake when it came to social cues, which was why he was reduced to cleaning houses instead of rolling big with the homies at the casino.

His first assignment of the day had already been prearranged on the previous day via text message, so the apartment was somewhat clean with minimal effort required on his part. The next was a "usual" Monday cleaning in a unit located in the big apartment building, which required him to kind of loiter down the street until he saw someone he knew come in or out. They would of course get the door for him since he didn't know the code (nor could anyone give it to him under penalty of eviction) and he could continue to earn.

This usual client's name was Josh, who lived in a one-bedroom apartment and rented out his living room to someone else to help offset the rent. Paco figured that Josh was gay due to the emphasis on useless furniture and a nice but bare kitchen contrasted with a lavish bedroom complete with waterbed, big-screen TV, and a little weiner dog named Buddy. Being an older Asian man, Buddy must be his security animal.

Paco always started with the bedroom first in order to get all the dog hair out of the way before tackling the easier jobs of the bathroom and kitchen, but as soon as he opened the front door leading into the unit, the dog ran out and past him, squealing high-pitched as if it were hurt. It didn't appear hurt, however, and Paco started after it to try and catch it. Just then a young black woman appeared in the doorway of Josh's apartment. "Hey! Help me! I think my friend is hurt!"

"But I have to get the dog—"

"I'll get him! He'll come to me, just come in and go look at my friend, please?"

She stepped aside, reaching her arm out to gesture him in. Paco took the bait and he didn't take two steps inside before she closed the door behind them and locked it.

"Hey, what—" She put her hand on his throat and squeezed.

"In the bedroom. Now." She walked him backwards through the living room, which was dark due to drawn windows but Paco could see that the couch had been torn through and all the kitchen drawers had been emptied. The fridge was wide open. The Christmas tree still stood but there were torn wrapping paper everywhere. Empty stockings laid on the floor beneath lines of scotch tape like grave markers on the wall. Then he was in the bedroom where he saw an unfamiliar younger Hispanic dude semi-passed out on the bed with his pants around his feet.

"Who is this, Bobby?" Paco thought Bobby looked tired and sleepy, too naïve to realize that it was because Bobby had been drugged.

He mumbled, "That's Josh's cleaning guy. Comes every Monday."

"Well, he's gonna clean you out." The black woman reached behind her jacket in a fluid motion and brought out a gun. Paco knew nothing about makes or models, just that they were serious business.

"What's your name, Josh's cleaning guy?"

"Paco," he murmured as if he were someone else.

"Okay, well, Paco, Bobby here and his boyfriend Josh owe us money and screwed my boy over. You're in the wrong place at the wrong time." She wiggled her gun. "Pants off."

Paco did as he was told. He didn't want to get shot, after all. Once they were on the floor, she smiled. "Yeah, I think I'll take that. Bend over next to Bobby." The gun wiggled again. He obeyed her, and he heard her unbutton her pants. Then he heard some rustling and felt a warm fleshy throbbing thing slide up and down between his ass cheeks. Is that what he thought it was? He heard the faint slapping of saliva as she licked her palm to lube up her dick.

Paco had never heard of shemales, being naïve to the underground forays of the internet, but that didn't stop him from clenching when she tried to press her dick against his asshole. "Relax," she whispered. "And after I do you, you're gonna do him."

"I'm no queer," his voice quavered. "Please, don't put it in me, don't make me do this?" He felt a cold circle against the back of his neck.

"Relax. Your. Spinchter." Closing his eyes, he grunted as he made as if to go number two. He felt the hard throbbing helmet probe just inside him, followed by the wet squishy sound of saliva being spat from her puckered lips to dribble down her shaft. She made her fingers slippery and then felt them rudely jam up inside his butthole, making him feel all wet and nasty. He tried to make her calm down by relaxing more, sighing audibly as he did so, but that only made her put the hand holding the gun on the small of his back as one finger suddenly slipped in up to the second knuckle. "Ahh," she sighed in his ear. "Now you're ready."

Then he felt the gun move back up to his neck as she attempted to penetrate him again. It went in deeper and he gritted his teeth as he tried to push so he could let her in more – his mind racing, "just get it over with, make it over soon, then I run and tell the police, don't fight or I'll die." He couldn't suppress a gasp, however, when she slid her hard throbbing cock all the way up his ass to the hilt. His eyes locked the gazed stare of Bobby's next to him, yet Bobby was still too far gone to really register what was going on. He noticed that he was drooling. Paco thought Bobby could be an extra, or a small-time movie star, even. He wondered if Josh was at work or on Holiday or just out running errands. Or otherwise unavailable. Then he felt her withdraw, her cock sliding out of his asshole like an uncontrolled dump, and Paco was surprised to find that he actually sort of liked it! And then she brutally rammed home again. Paco thought at first about how to escape, but the gun pointed at him in various ways turned those ideas off really quick.

When he felt her hand reach around to feel his flaccid cock and bounce his balls, her expert textured touch managed to awake it to its full stiff state of arousal. It was a shameful boner, but she knew how to tingle his glands to bring him to the edge of orgasm. She immediately took her hand away as soon as she saw that he was about to get lost in the throes of ecstasy and refocused her attention on getting hers first.

Being completely filled and somewhat vacated and then completely filled over and over again at a rapid rate while hoping, waiting for her to bring him off, was beginning to wear on Paco's mind until she suddenly stiffened. Knowing all too well what was coming, he braced himself for the hot sticky jets of cum shooting deep inside his rectum, breathing heavily through his nose as he clenched his teeth. The black woman sighed raspily in deep satisfaction before withdrawing slowly. Then her hand was back on his cock, which was semi-hard.

"Now it's your turn. Get behind Bobby." All of a sudden Bobby groaned. Through his drug-induced sleep paralysis he was trying to resist but all he could do is try to make sense through the puddle of drool that was pooling into one cheek and spilling over onto the bed. Paco was grabbed by his collar and pulled back up onto his feet, his clenching ass stinging from the recent friction. Since she had lubed up with spit, Paco was going to feel the water blisters in the morning. But for now, he had noticed that Bobby's pants had somehow completely fallen off his feet because the woman kicked them away and kicked his legs apart. Then she looked at Paco and waved her gun.

Taking a deep breath, Paco stepped behind Bobby and put his hands on the stranger's hips. Was this guy Josh's boyfriend or just a buddy? He figured the latter, most likely a dog-walker or something. How did this woman play into the situation? Did she know Josh? Or Bobby? Who was this person that they had screwed over?

He muttered, "I'm gonna need some help, maybe if you touch me—"

"You touch yourself, I'm done with you." She leaned back against the doorway and crossed one arm over her chest, resting her gun hand into the crook of her elbow.

"On Donner, On Blitzen, Come on, Paco, On Bobby, get bitzen!" He closed his eyes as he spat onto his palm and tried to think about the girl whose apartment he cleaned on Thursdays, the cute redhead who worked for the adult movie industry and had naked pictures of herself lying around on the counter sometimes. He had fantasized exclusively about her whenever he had masturbated over the past three years and hers was the face he tried to conjure up now, but it was replaced instead with the visage of this black shemale's, her heavy eyelids and addictive crooked smile.

He tried to emulate the attention on his glands as she had earlier, and found the correct groove. "Okay, now IN Bobby." Remembering why he had been masturbating in the first place, he placed the tip of his slippery cock against Bobby's asshole and spiraled it inside, working his hips around and around until he plunged in with almost a fall. Bobby groaned meekly in a mixture of utter dismay and resignation. Paco glanced at the woman, who was smiling as she watched and gave him a little chins-up, and he closed his eyes and thought about her sucking him. Yes, that's it, maybe she would suck him and let him fuck her ass, with her cock against his as they did it missionary style. He could probably even see her breasts and suck on them as he jerked her off. Those would be fun and new exciting things to try for Christmas!

It was the image of her cock against his that brought him over. He pretended that Bobby was her, and when his ballsack slapped against the back of Bobby's, he got closer and closer until he exploded a load of his own deep inside this hot clean-cut stud on the bed. Paco was sighing in satisfaction as well as relief that it was almost over, while Bobby was sighing in a weak, continuous sob. The woman clapped as best as she could while exercising trigger discipline.

"Bravo! You boys did good! Now Paco, it's time for you to have a drink with Bobby." There was a huge purse lying on the floor, and she bent to pick up a half-empty bottle of Pepsi Holiday Spice.

"Set Bobby up and hold his head up so I can get some more of this down his throat, and then you're gonna drink some." The gun never left the line of fire to Paco and with a little struggle, Bobby was leaned back into the crook of his elbow with his head lolled back. He was croaking continuously, whether in protest or in dismay Paco couldn't tell. What was going to happen to them? He could try to knock the gun out of her hand and run, but what if she had a back-up piece or a knife? And then she answered for him.

"Bobby's here to use Josh's shower and you're here to clean Josh's house. So that leaves Josh unaccounted for. You two are going to have some fun when he gets home." She tipped some of the soda mixed with whatever drugged him into his mouth as his head was tilted back, ensuring that it went down his throat without choking him. Once she felt she had given him enough, she handed the remaining thirds of the bottle to him. "Drink up."

"But won't you have enough left for Josh?" asked Paco in a futile attempt to delay the inevitable.

"When I'm done with him, I won't need to drug you guys anymore. Drink up." The dose was a little stronger for Bobby this time, thus knocking him completely under. Paco fell asleep as well, and waited to wake up.

Double Penetration with the (Secretly Gay) Judge, Servant, and Escort Girl

Kelly was a tall sinewy blonde. Her long legs and thin frame coupled with her full breasts made her one of the most requested escorts in the office. All of the escorts at this service were required to keep the dates clean. There was a specific rule about no sex with the customers. Kelly had figured a way around this. She simply explained to her clients that she would be happy to assist them with their larger needs, but she would have to do it off the clock.

Most men were willing to pay her under the table for work she would do between the sheets. Kelly remembered this client specifically. He was a politician, elected in a nearby community to be the president judge. When during dinner, he had laughed at Kelly's joke, he put his hand on Kelly's thigh. Kelly crossed her legs and trapped his hand, she pressed her thighs together tightly as she explained that in order for this to go further, he would need to call her when she was not working for the escort service.

She slowly pulled his sweaty palm from between her squeezed thighs, jotted a cell phone number down on the palm of his hand and finished her paid escort date. When she left, she hugged the judge a little too tightly, pressing against him, and she could feel his manhood rising. She KNEW he would be calling. It was no surprise to her that she got the call on her cell phone before she had finished at the escort service for the day. She knew that the judge had wanted more of her, and she made a time to meet him later that same night.

When she arrived at the address they had agreed on, she rang the bell. The door was opened by a much younger man who led her to the judge's private bedroom. When she stepped inside, she could see the judge was naked on the bed and waiting for her. The judge asked Kelly to make him a drink from the bar in the room, and she moved to do just that. While she was mixing the drink, the judge asked the younger man if he found Kelly attractive. He nodded indicating that he did. Then the judge asked if the younger man would like to join them for the evening. The younger man hesitated. Kelly, in the spirit of helping out, took the younger man into her arms and kissed him deeply. She rubbed his cock through his pants and whispered, "Oh please..." into the young man's ear. He simply couldn't resist and he began rubbing Kelly everywhere. He cupped her full breasts through her dress and his hand felt its way to her wet slit.

The three got completely naked and slipped into the bed. Kelly began sucking the judge's cock. She guided the younger man's face between her thighs and he started to lick the juices from her pussy. The judge took the young man's cock into his hand, and the younger man started to protest. Kelly simply assured the young man that he was not gay. He was not doing anything gay by allowing the judge to pleasure him. After all, the young man was not sucking cock. He was eating pussy. Before long, the protests stopped, and the three of them had made a pleasure triangle. Kelly sucked at the judge's hard cock, and she could feel the pulse in it with her tongue. The young man was quite good at eating pussy, and he lapped at Kelly's until she exploded with cum. The judge was sucking at the young man's cock, his secret pleasure. The young man came and the judge swallowed the salty hot liquid and continued to suck him hard again. Once the young man was ready, Kelly slid herself on top of him and pulled his cock deep inside of her. She then spread her ass inviting the judge inside as well. Once he pushed into her, the judge screamed in pleasure, "Oh! I feel it, I feel his cock rubbing mine!"

The Futanari Curse and a Pussy Like Vodka: A Fantasy Erotica with Futanari, Anal Sex, and Clit Licking

It was a cold night and Sarah was running late. She'd promised to meet Alice, her friend, at a nightclub in town 10 minutes ago.

"Sorry I'm late," she said as she arrived at the club.

Alice smiled and said, "That's OK. I'm just glad you arrived!"

Alice was a voluptuous girl to say the least. She had short brown hair and wore bright red lipstick. Sarah, on the other hand, was a much classier sort of woman. She was thin with legs that went on forever, large breasts, and a beautiful face. She'd been working hard all week and was looking forward to having a well-deserved night off. Little did she know that tonight would be a night she'd never forget.

Sarah and Alice were both quickly ushered into the nightclub by the bouncers and they walked down a flight of stairs. Another bouncer stood at the bottom of the door and held it open as he saw them coming, and they walked straight through. It was your typical venue. The music was blaring and the whole room was packed full of people dancing. Alice and Sarah joined in straight away. A guy watched as Sarah danced. She noticed and decided to tease him. She hitched up her skirt, stuck her ass out and began to gyrate her hips slowly to the music. She could tell he wanted her. He started to make his way over.

"Sorry, not interested," Sarah shouted, and then walked away. She giggled to herself and made her way over to the bar to grab a drink. She sat down and looked around for Alice, but couldn't see her anywhere.

"Is this seat taken?" asked a sultry voice.

Sarah turned around. She was speechless. A tall lady stood over her. She had long jet-black hair, exotic green eyes, full luscious lips and high cheekbones. She was the most beautiful woman Sarah had ever seen. Sarah slowly looked down at her cleavage. She wore a tight black dress, barely covering her huge breasts, which were inches away from Sarah's face. She couldn't take her eyes off them. They looked so smooth and soft and to her amazement, they suddenly began to grow as the lady breathed in. Sarah's mouth dropped.

"I'm up here," said the lady.

"I-I," Sarah stuttered, and quickly looked up.

"I'm gonna go ahead and take a seat," said the lady. She sat down next to Sarah. "My name is Anya by the way."

"I'm Sarah, a pleasure to meet you," said Sarah, finally returning to normal.

Anya smiled, and then looked over at the drinks deciding which one to choose. Sarah couldn't help herself; she found Anya strangely attractive, and she had to get another look at her body. While Anya sat waiting for her drink, Sarah began to stare at her crossed legs. They were beautiful, long, and hairless. She followed them up to her crotch, but it was covered by her dress.

"You wanna see my pussy, don't you sweetie?" asked Anya.

"What? NO!" exclaimed Sarah, ashamed that she had been caught looking.

"It's OK, I don't mind," said Anya. She looked around to see if anyone was looking, then lifted her skirt with one hand and pulled the front of her panties down with the other.

Sarah's eyes were locked in amazement. Anya's pussy was the sexiest thing Sarah had ever seen. It was hairless and covered in moist glistening pussy juice. There was a small black star tattooed just above her clit. Without knowing, Sarah began to bite one side of her lower lip wondering what Anya's pussy would taste like.

"You wanna lick it, don't you sweetie?" asked Anya.

"I-I," Sarah stuttered again and began to blush.

"Follow me," Said Anya.

She took Sarah's hand and led her through the crowd. They came to a door hidden on the side of the wall. Anya gently pushed and it gave way to a set of stairs. As they walked up, Sarah's heart began to beat faster. She was nervous but also excited. She was an open-minded type of girl, but she'd never been with a woman before.

They came to a room at the top of the stairs, and Anya opened the door and pulled Sarah inside.

"I've never scored so quickly," Sarah joked. "The last boyfriend I had was a real asshole."

"I don't care," said Anya.

"I'm sorry?" asked Sarah, surprised at her rudeness.

"Did you come to talk or to eat my pussy?" asked Anya as she lit a cigarette.

"How dare you!" said Sarah, "I've never been so insulted. I'm leaving."

"Suit yourself," said Anya casually. "I guess you don't want any vodka."

"What?" Sarah asked in confusion.

"My pussy juice is alcoholic," said Anya. "Vodka to be exact."

"Bullshit!" Sarah said, laughing hysterically.

"Don't believe me?" asked Anya. "Try some, what's the worst that could happen? Just one long lick, and if you don't like the taste, you can go, no hard feelings."

Anya pulled down her panties, sat back on the bed and opened her legs.

"OK," said Sarah.

After hesitating for a moment she slowly went over. Her heart was pounding. She sat on the bed, brought her face close to Anya's pussy and admired it for a moment. The tight pale mound was covered in beads of pussy juice. She stuck out her tongue and gave a long lick all the way up. She poked her head out from between Anya's legs and looked at her in amazement.

"You were right!" she exclaimed. "It does taste like vodka!"

She began to quickly lap it up like a thirsty dog. Anya began moaning with pleasure.

"Do you want bourbon?" asked Anya.

"You're kidding me," said Sarah.

"Nope," replied Anya. "Just press the button."

Sarah pressed her finger on Anya's clit and juice began to pour out of her pussy. Sarah immediately began to lap it up. It did indeed taste like bourbon. Anya began moaning again.

A few minutes had passed and Sarah was a little drunk.

"Thank you," said Sarah. "Now it's my turn to give you a gift."

She stuck her tongue out as far as she could and headed towards Anya's clit intending to give it a good licking. Anya realized this and her face went white.

"No no no," shouted Anya. "Whatever you do don-"

It was too late. Sarah had already rubbed her tongue over Anya's clit and began sucking it. Anya began to have an orgasm and Sarah smiled knowing that she had returned the favor, but something wasn't right. She could feel Anya's clit growing in her mouth. It felt like it was an inch longer. She kept probing it all over with her tongue. It kept growing. 3, 4, 5… inches. She immediately pulled away and stared at it. 6, 7, 8 inches. She couldn't believe what she was seeing, it was still growing. 9, 10, 11 inches. Sarah began to freak out, jumped off the bed in horror and shuffled back into a corner. It finally stopped growing at 13 inches.

Sarah slowly came forward, looking at it closely. It was a cock. There were veins running along the shaft and it throbbed continuously. She immediately became wet, but this was too weird.

"I dunno what you are," Sarah said, "but I'm leaving."

"Wait, don't go," said Anya in desperation. "Only you can make it go away."

"What do you mean?" asked Sarah.

"It's a long story," continued Anya. "Basically a curse was put on me and the only way to get rid of this cock is if I cum."

Sarah thought for a moment.

"So why don't you just jerk yourself off?" she asked.

"Because the curse doesn't work like that," explained Anya. "I have to cum inside the person who licked my clit, otherwise I will have a cock forever."

"This is crazy!" said Sarah. "I've never had anything that big in me before. The biggest I had is 5 inches, and yours is almost as thick as my wrist too."

"Please," begged Anya. "We have to try. I'd do the same for you."

Sarah thought for a while. She stared at Anya's big throbbing cock; pre-cum had been seeping out in anticipation. It was turning her on.

"Sure, why not," she said.

Sarah sat on the bed on all fours, and stuck out her ass in the doggy position. Anya smiled and was just about to put her cock in Sarah's ass.

"What are you doing?" asked Sarah in surprise.

"I have to come in your ass in order to break the spell," replied Anya.

"Seriously?" asked Sarah. "I've never been fucked in the ass. Why didn't you tell me before?"

"I didn't think it was important," replied Anya.

They both paused for a moment.

"OK," said Sarah. "But take it easy. Don't go too deep OK?"

"I have to," replied Anya. "I have to cum inside you balls deep in order to break the spell."

"Are you serious!?" asked Sarah angrily. "Well, if it will break the spell. I guess it was my fault."

Anya smiled and pushed the huge head of her cock into Sarah's asshole. Sarah let out a huge scream and began to orgasm. Her asshole was squeezing Anya's cock.

"Are you OK, honey?" asked Anya.

"Yes," replied Sarah. "It's OK, keep going."

Anya grabbed Sarah's hips and pushed her cock a few more inches into Sarah's tight ass. Sarah let out another scream and began to orgasm again.

"Oh god," Anya moaned. "You're so tight, I can feel your heartbeat. We're halfway there. How are you holding up, sweetie?"

"I'm OK," said Sarah. "Please keep going."

Anya tried to push her huge cock deeper, but it wouldn't budge.

"What's wrong?" Sarah asked.

"Your ass is too tight," Anya replied. "I can't go any further."

"Grab my shoulders," commanded Sarah.

"What?" Anya asked, surprised at Sarah's change in tone.

"You heard me," continued Sarah. "Grab my shoulders and ram it in with everything you've got."

Anya did as she said. She put one hand on each shoulder and pushed Sarah into her cock and thrust her hips forward as hard as she could. Her cock finally squeezed through and her balls reached the base of Sarah's ass. Sarah let out a scream full of ecstasy and tears of joy rolled down her eyes. Her whole body began to shake in pleasure. Anya could feel Sarah's tight asshole constantly squeezing her cock as she orgasmed, and this made Anya cum. Her cock began to throb violently and then exploded inside Sarah.

Sarah could feel Anya's cum filling her up. It felt ice cold. That and the throbbing of her cock made Sarah orgasm once again.

Once her orgasm was over, she realized that Anya had not budged. Her cock was still balls deep in Sarah's ass and it was still squirting out huge amounts of cum. Sarah could feel that her ass was almost full of Anya's cum and since Anya's cock was firmly screwed into her ass, there was nowhere else for the cum to go. She could feel it filling her stomach, then her chest all the way to her throat. It started to spray out from her nose and ears. Sarah opened her mouth and huge amounts of cum came gushing out. Sarah tasted it. It tasted like vanilla ice cream.

Anya's orgasm finally began to subside. She pulled out her cock from Sarah's ass and let out a huge sigh.

"Hahaha, I'm free! I can't believe you fell for that," said Anya.

"What do you mean?" asked Sarah.

"You were right," explained Anya. "To make my cock disappear, all I have to do is jerk it 'till I cum, but if I cum in the ass of the person who licked my clit and made it appear, then I pass on my curse to her."

She quickly pulled her panties back up and ran off. Sarah sat on the bed contemplating what she had just been told. After a while a smile grew on her face.

"Sarah! There you are!" shouted Alice. "Where have you been?"

"Do you wanna try some ice-cream?" asked Sarah.

Suck The Futanari: An Erotic Story about a Girl and a Hermaphrodite

Tiffany was walking down the street, minding her own business, when she realized that she was on Saints Boulevard. An ironic name, this was the place that hookers and trannies hung out. What was interesting is that a friend she had known from high school, Sara, was there. Sara used to be ruddy, too much of a bookworm for Tiffany to notice. But she had changed. Her brunette hair was pulled back into a bun, something that Sara exuded confidence with.

Something must have been in the air, because Tiffany, the popular girl, felt no judgment from talking to Sara on Saints Boulevard.

"Whatcha doin' here bookworm?" Tiffany said jestingly. A lot of things chimed in Sara. Mom and dad never let me hang out here in high school. and for good reason. I just saw a used heroin needle , actually two, down the alley. But I like this.

"Tiffany, I've changed," said Sara.

"How so?" asked Tiffany.

"For starters, I'm more assertive. Tiffany, I want to be honest. I want to hang out with you tonight".

Tiffany agreed, because it was a strange, wonderful night. Sara took Tiffany to a bar that looked straight out of the Matrix movie. It was more welcoming, because everyone wearing BDSM attire had wacky smiles to match the oddly provocative air of the night. They all minded their own business. Sara got a few shots of Soco Lime, and Tiffany had a beer.

They talked about high school, and some of the men they had dated. Tiffany was a little woozy when Sara offered to Tiffany to finish off her shot; she didn't want it, and hated to waste a good Soco Lime. Tiffany agreed, thinking strangely that there may be a rape drug in there, but there wasn't.

"Okay, as I mentioned, Tiffany, I'm more assertive. Let's go back to my apartment and hang out." Too drunk to resist, Tiffany agreed, again. "Okay, I'm having fun, let's continue," she said. As Tiffany entered Sara's apartment, she noticed how neat it was. Minimal. The only thing that spoke in the room was the Dark blue wallpaper with pink accents. The window at the side of the room was adequate, but the kind that didn't have any onlookers.

"Tiffany, I know you like me, and I need you to do two things for me. If you do these, I'm going to be your friend for life. The first is that you need to suck my cock."

"Sara, why didn't you tell me that you had a futanari cock going on?"

"Because this adds to the surprise. Don't you like me telling you just now? Don't you feel a bit uneasy, violated, hot, and your clit walls getting wet? Give in! That's what made me amazing, and not a bookworm anymore. That's what made me assertive! Give in! Suck my cock!"

Sara could hardly resist herself. Whether or not there was anything in those soco limes was hard to know. But she did know that she was more drunk than she had let on. That damn strange wispy wind on Saints Boulevard had struck again.

"Okay Sara, I will, but my fellatio isn't as good as it was in high school."

"I'll walk you through it, again, for the first time," said Sara. Tiffany noticed that Sara's cock was bigger than she had expected. Paralleling the surprise at Sara, the introvert, becoming more social was the fact that her futanari cock was bigger than the ones Tiffany had seen on the internet. Scared, but excited, she licked the tip, timidly, but gaining confidence. Sara let out a mild, growing, groan, and her cock was getting a bit bigger.

Tiffany got excited and her instincts carried in. She began to lick the shaft. Surprisingly, because Sara was acting like the dominant one, Sara released a load all over Tiffany's face. Sara was surprised how fast she had cum, but she knew what to do next.

"Okay Tiffany, we're not done yet. I want you to lick my balls." Tiffany was confused, and a bit mad.

"But Sara, no offense, but you don't have balls. "

"Yet. Yet. Yet. Yet. Yet." Like a Seance, Sara repeated the word "yet" five times. "Here's what is going to happen Tiffany. I'm glad you asked. You are going to lick where my balls will be in the future. After I come again, you are going to pay for my surgery, so that I can get balls. All I ask after that is that you lick my real balls at that time. I lied earlier. I'm giving you a choice to become my sex partner. It's better that way. So you understand, Tiffany, after you pay for my surgery, and lick my balls one time, you have the option of enjoying me as your sexual partner. I'll be yours forever. But in this, I give you the option. IN this, I am not the dominatrix. You have the choice. One might say, you are choosing men, or me. I will not influence you either way."

Sara knew what she had to do. Her mind was made up......

Chance Encounter with a Transvestite: Sucking My Futanari Mistress' Cock

As I walked into the hotel bar, I was immediately drawn to the beautiful woman at the end of the bar. She was tall, about 5'11", Asian, with soft yellow brown skin, black almond shaped eyes, and a friendly smile. She was wearing a tight black dress and had legs for miles. I sat down and asked the bartender to send her a drink.

Once she got the drink, she looked over and smiled. She slowly slinked over next to me, putting her hand on my shoulder. "Hi, I am Yoko," she said.

Her voice was smoky but friendly.

"Hi, I am Bob," I stammered out. I was nervous. My mouth was dry and I became flush.

"Are you looking for a date, Bob?" she asked.

I was shocked by how forward she was, and I started to stutter something out. She quickly reached for my crotch and led me out of the bar by my hardening cock.

Yoko took me to her suite. She kissed me passionately and told me to lie back while she gets more comfortable. I loosened my tie, took off my shoes and socks, and sat on the bed. Yoko walked back into the room wearing only a black lace bra and panty set.

"You look gorgeous!" I said with some enthusiasm.

"Thank you sweetie," she said to me.

She leaned over and kissed me deeply, our tongues dancing with one another. It was a slow moving, exploratory and sensual kiss. Our kiss grew hotter as it went on.

She undid her bra and it fell to the floor. Her breasts jutted outward, fake but beautiful, and I kissed and licked the sides of her beautiful breasts as I traveled down her front side. She told me to get on my knees in front of her. The rug was rough on my knees and my 6" cock was rock hard. She pushed my face tight to her silk panties. They were wet and surprisingly full. Yoko giggled sweetly and pulled down her panties.

Very soon it apparent what her big surprise was! She had a good 9" of thick veiny uncut shecock. She said, "Are you just gonna keep staring or suck it?"

I protested and tried to explain that there was some sort of misunderstanding here. She laughed and slapped my face with her cock.

Yoko said, "You are gonna suck my big cock and I am going to stretch that white ass of yours." She reached over and held my nose while she pressed her cock to my lips. I started having trouble breathing and my mouth shot open. Yoko rammed her cock home into my open mouth. Without realizing it, I have swallowed all Yoko's 9 inches.

The feeling in my throat was tight and I started to choke and panic. Yoko said, "You better be a good cocksucker and take all my cum down your throat." Then she slapped my face. I was completely at her mercy and decide that I better cooperate. I kissed her cock and then started to swallow it. I work it slowly in and out of my mouth, taking more and more, until her balls were slapping my chin.

Yoko muttered, "Oh my god, you are an incredible cocksucking slut." She began thrusting quickly as her strong hands held my head. "I am fucking your face, whore," she whispered.

"Yoko, would you fill my throat with your hot cum?" I weakly asked.

"Sure, bitch," she replied. She pinched my nose again and buried all 9" down my throat, further into my mouth and down my throat. Yoko pushed until her cock sank as deep as it could possibly go. Soon Yoko was fucking my mouth so hard and fast that I forgot about everything but her throbbing cock. I didn't think about whether I was gay or straight, I just wanted to please my mistress. She was pulling on my ears with both hands and ramming her cock down my throat, withdrawing it to the tip and then ramming it all the way in, over and over.

She started to shutter with the beginning of a powerful orgasm but quickly pulled out. Yoko said, "You aren't getting off that easy... next time." She smothered her belly against my face, all 9" down my throat. Yoko pumped my mouth full of hot salty cum. More than I can ever believe I could swallow. Yoko slapped my face and said, "Swallow it all, slut." I did as I was told and collapsed on the floor. Yoko pulled up her panties then leaned over and reached into my pocket, almost bringing me to orgasm when she brushes up against my hard cock. She pulled out my wallet and took all my cash. She threw my wallet back in my face and told me to get the fuck out. I shuffled off painfully with a jutting erection, blue balls, and a face glazed with she cum. Just before she slammed the door shut, Yoko shouted, "Be back next Thursday at 9, and bring more money."

I am ashamed to admit that I will be there.

Gangbanging A She-Male in Vegas: How I Fucked A Trans-Sexual He-She In The Ass With Another Guy (At The Same Time!)

I had never been to Vegas, and I was very excited to spend some time in sin city for the week. I had just spent the day strolling around town and gambling away some money. After a long day I came back to the hotel room to shower up and wind down. I was hoping to get up early the next morning for some more sight-seeing. While in bed I just couldn't get any sleep and body was raging with hormones. I was thinking about back at home all the girls online that I look up and lust after and decided that I should go out to get some action.

I put some clothes on and went to a bar. I didn't want to get any whisky dick so I did my best to stay sober and just ordered one drink so that I could remember my night. As I was looking around the bar one chick caught my eye. She had the thickest looking ass, for a white girl, that I had ever seen and perfect hips. She was also a tall goddess around 5'10. Me being only 5'6 I second guessed myself into talking to her. Then later I said to myself *to hell with it* and had the courage to go up and talk to her. She was so feminine in the way that she handled herself, and I asked if I could buy her a drink. She accepted, and we chatted for a while. Later while I went to the bathroom and came back another guy was talking to her. I felt betrayed that she was talking to someone else while I wasn't around. But she still showed interest in me. To my shock she revealed to me that she wanted both of us tonight. I was not used to that, me being strict with who I choose to sleep with and how. But I couldn't resist her thick ass. The three of us took a cab to drive us to a nearby hotel.

My heart was beating and I didn't know if it was because I was nervous or because of how horny I was or maybe a mixture of both. Me and the other guy, named Axel, sat at the bed waiting for her. She decided to give us each a lap dance. She started kissing me with her thick luscious lips. She started unzipping Axel's pants and pulled out his already hard cock out. Her lips slowly teasing his cock. Then she unzipped my pants and started to tease my cock. My cock was so hard that I couldn't believe it. Then she started showing her oral skills by putting both our cocks in her mouth at the same time. I was feeling a bit strange by having another man's cock touching mine, but it felt good. I withdrew when I felt that I was about to come. She kept slobbering all over Axel's cock and kept dipping his dick hole on her tonsils.

I wanted to take advantage of every inch of her body. I took off her pants and her ass looked so gorgeous with her thong. I looked closer and me and Axel were both SHOCKED. We were messing with a shemale this whole time. I felt angered that I was deceived. I was about to leave just because of the shame of it, but Axel said, "FUCK it… ass is ass." He had a point, to some extent, and I couldn't waste a perfectly good hard on. She kept sucking Axel's cock and pleasing him. Sucking his cock balls to chin deep. Even though she had a package just hanging from there, her ASS still looked hot. I couldn't resist and I let go of my inhibitions. I stuck my tongue deep into her tight asshole. Licking her rim hole just made me harder and harder. I wanted to plow that ass of hers. I kept sticking my tongue deeper into her asshole while she moaned on Axel's cock. I couldn't resist any more and started going to deep in her ass.

I didn't care about anything I went condom free. My bare tip of my cock started teasing her asshole. You could see it was easy aroused as it kept pulsating and loosening up. Her cock was getting hard too and it was a sight to see her big thick booty with her cock and balls just hanging there. When her asshole started loosening up I started going in slowly. All of this rush inside of me was something new. I pushed my cock completely in and started thrusting in and out. Her cock started getting stiff and hey moans getting louder. A girl's pussy couldn't compare to this ass of hers. It was just so tight and juicy. My cock head kept pumping inside the edges of her ass. Axel wanted to dig in too and we switched spots. He started beating her asshole too. She was so horny that she didn't care that my cock was in her ass and started sucking my cock right away. She was salivating for cock tonight and we were there to please that craving of hers. She wanted to lubricate our cocks with saliva for more pumping action in her ass. She wanted TWO cocks in her ass this time. I thought for a minute that this might cross the line for me. But then I said to myself you only live once. She sat on my cock and started passionately kissing me. Her ass all jiggly bouncing on top of my balls. Axel got behind her and slid his cock inside her ass while my cock was inside. MY cock was throbbing by now. This felt so good. We kept fucking her ass real hard and fast. She wanted it harder and faster. She wanted us to tear her ass. SHE WANTED COCK. Her cock was being sandwiched between my abs and her sexy flat stomach. It kept going back and forth between my stomach and hers while me and Axel's cocks were pulsating inside her ass. We were all getting very sweaty and hot. Then I felt something on Axel's cock vein or something pulsating as if something was about to shoot up. He started coming hard inside of her. This got me very turned on and couldn't last much longer. I started fucking her ass harder while Axel's cummed cock was still in there. Axel's cum provided me with more lubrication and his come was all over my cock. I groaned hard and she moaned hard as both came at the same time. She came from sliding her cock between our stomachs and me inside of her ass. Her ass was fully cummed. And her cock craving was satisfied.

Stuffing my Stocking: A Gay Erotica for the Holidays

Finals were over and my last class was about to let out for Christmas break. My name is Patrick and this is my first semester away from home at college and man has it been fucking fun. Before I get to into the story, let me describe myself a little bit.

I'm 19 years old about 5'9 140 pounds and pretty damn toned. I've got dirty blond hair and what most people tell me are stunning green eyes. Most girls, and more importantly guys, think I'm hot.

Anyway back to my story. Ever since going away to college, I've been having fun with every guy I can find. My first semester has been full of dick in every hole in my body but now it's coming to an end, and I have to go home for Christmas. See my family doesn't know how much of a cock slut I have become. Shit, they don't even know that I like cock, so I wasn't look forward to being stuck with my family and not being able to get my tight little ass stuffed.

I got home two days before Christmas, still bummed out all my fuck buddies were back at school and I was stuck with the family. There was the usual hugs and kisses from the family. My mom was gushing over how much she missed me. My dad asked me, "So how did your finals go?"

I responded, "Well it was hard, but I came through in the end. "

"Good", my dad replied, "Always glad to see you working hard."

Little did he know what I was working so hard on! After I got all my things back in my old room and settled in, my parents called me on down to the living room. When I got there, I saw a family that my parents had been friends with for years.

"Hey Patrick, you remember Mr. Jones don't you?" my dad asked.

I walked up to him and shook his hand. "Of course dad, I'm not as old as you are."

"Well Patrick, if you remember me I'm sure you'll remember Bobby!" Mr. Jones said. How could I forget that fine piece of ass? He was a couple of years older than me and was a fantasy of my jerk off sessions for years, and over time, he had only gotten finer. He walked up to me and gave me a big hug. Bobby was about 6'2", brown hair, crystal blue eyes, and fucking ripped. I'm no slouch, but he was like a god compared to me.

"Hey Patrick, how have you been bro?" Bobby asked me.

I barely stuttered out my answer, "F..f..fine man, how 'bout you?"

"Oh, you know, same old shit. Just got my own place, and we're having an ugly sweater party tomorrow if you want to come chill."

I looked over at my dad asking for permission with my eyes, "Sure why the hell not. Don't want you to be bored and not come back home ever again," dad said.

"Sweet, I'll see you there!" Bobby said before they left.

After hanging with the family for the rest of the afternoon I ran up the stairs to get some sleep. Tomorrow couldn't come soon enough. Hopefully there would be drinking and I could seduce the guy I've been wanting to get in the sack for years. I jerked off thinking about it that night and blew the biggest load of my life.

The next morning I picked out the ugliest sweater I could find and then got ready for the party, at around six, I borrowed the extra car and headed on over to his house. When I got there I knocked and he just yelled, "COME ON IN."

As I stepped through the door, I noticed that no one was over yet so I figured I was the first one. "I'll be out in a sec," Bobby said, "Just getting myself ready."

When he came out of his room he was wearing nothing but a cock ring and a huge hard on! It was nine inches of uncut cock. "I remembered the way you used to look at me Patrick. I know you've always wanted this, so merry Christmas," he said with the hottest smirk on his face.

I looked at his toned body and his big meat and could not believe my eyes, "W..w..what about the party" I managed to get out.

"We are the party." He walked over to me and whispered, "I know you've always wanted this, baby." Without hesitation I took his cock into my mouth. I've sucked a lot of cock over the past semester, but this one was huge and it took some work to get it down my throat. I sucked and swirled my tongue over the giant head, pulling his foreskin back as I jerked him off at the same time. I was in heaven, and he was just drooling precum down my throat.

"Oh yeah take that cock like the good little slut you are," he said as he grabbed my hair and began to slowly fuck my throat. After about 15 minutes of slow fucking my throat, he pulled out and rubbed his drool covered dick all over my face. He picked me up and threw me on the couch, put my legs on his shoulders, and began rubbing his dick on my ass.

"You ready for my cock baby? God, I want to fuck you so bad," without even speaking, I reached down and grabbed his cock and shoved myself all the way down on it. It hurt a bit, but luckily I was an experienced cock hound. After that he grinned at me and pinned my arms down and started to slowly fuck me. He was moaning loudly about how tight my ass was and how much he loved his dick inside of me. I was in pure heaven moaning at every hard thrust. I don't know for how long he impaled me on his cock, but it seemed like forever. I was loving every second of it; suddenly he decided to pick up his pace and really rail my ass. His cock was thrusting in and out in and out, and I was screaming in pleasure.

After about 15 minutes of this he started really nailing my prostate with his cock, it wasn't long before I could feel my balls start to boil. "Oh god I'm going to cum," I shouted. As I was yelling this he really picked up his pace. It was like the animal in this gorgeous hunk took over. As I shot cum all over my own chest and face he grunted loudly and thrust as hard as any dick has ever thrust into me as he let out a growl of satisfaction, his cum coating the inside of my ass. After slowly pulling out, we both lay together on the couch, his flaccid cock up against my wrecked hole. He whispered into my ear, "Just wait until tomorrow when you get the rest of your presents." God I could not wait to see what he had in store for me. His stocking stuffing was turning out to be the best fucking Christmas present ever.

Gay Puppy Play for the Prince

The Prince was not disposed to sitting regally with an adult composure in his throne. Not when he was alone, at least. After all, at 19, he was hardly to be expected to hold the wisdom of a ruler already. Instead he lounged, legs draped over one arm of the throne with an elbow leaning against the other. He knew that he had appointments today, but simply could not be bothered to care enough to put on the dull facade of nobility. Besides, these were not state matters. That was his father's business. That which came to the Prince was limited to that which affected him directly and those appointments, he set up himself.

A doorman walked briskly in from across the great hall. He looked like a paper doll for the strange appearance of his thin, wobbling limbs. He stopped five meters from the throne. "Sire…" The doorman's voice was far stronger than it seemed, and the sound carried well despite his deep bow. "The first applicant is here. Shall I let him in?"

The Prince pushed the heavy gold crown he wore further up his forehead, mussing his wavy brown hair. "What do you think of him? Think I'll approve?" He asked, languidly turning his head to the doll-like servant and staring at him with eyes like coal.

"I… I…? Sire…?" The doorman froze.

"Oh, stop. I'm only joking. Yes, let the poor man in. Heaven knows he'll have to prove himself one way or another. Go on!" With a wave of the Prince's hand, the doorman rushed off, back across the hall. Silence. "Let's hope this one's not just another waste of my time," the Prince muttered to nobody in particular.

The doors to the great hall opened again, and this time a handsome young man of 21 walked through. He stood tall, though not with swagger. There was a quietness about him that just seemed to float out like pollen from a flower. He stopped five meters from the throne and knelt on one knee.

"Thank you for allowing me, my Prince." The Prince took a good look at the youth before him, assessing how much of his demeanor was fear and how much was reverence.

"Stand."

The young man did. His gaze was averted, though, obscuring his eyes behind long eyelashes.

"Tell me, why are you here? What do you want?" The Prince knew damn well why this subject was there, but he wanted to see him squirm a bit. The young man hesitated, unsure if this was a test. "Go on, tell me. What do you hope to gain?"

"I… I wish to belong to you, my Prince. Please, allow me to be your dog." Stammering then blurting out his words, the boy could not help but feel the Prince's gaze bore into him. He shivered and, steeling his courage, looked the Prince in the eye to show how much he wanted this.

"Well, there's something of an audition process for that, so I certainly hope you're worth my time." The Prince swung his legs around and sat up straight in his throne. His lips curled slightly into a small, arrogant smile. "The first thing to know, of course, is that I demand not only respect, not only fealty required of most subjects, but absolute loyalty. If you are to hunt and work for me, you must understand that you are mine, above all. You will belong to me. Minor disciplinary problems will be dealt with by me personally, through punishment I feel is appropriate. But lack of loyalty will have you flogged and sent to the dungeons with the rest of the treacherous creatures who sully my land. No appeals, no second chances. Is that understood?"

The young man nodded, finding his gaze again at the floor.

"And you still want to belong to me, then?"

"Yes, my Prince. Very much." The young man felt his hands trembling slightly, despite his resolve. His heart pounded fast in his chest.

"Very well. A few questions, then, before we get to task." The Prince crossed his legs and leaned back in his throne. "Can you hunt?"

"Yes, my Prince."

"Good. Can you work in a team?"

"Yes, my Prince."

"And you swear, on penalty of imprisonment that, if I take you on, you will not back out like a coward?"

"Yes! Please, let me serve you, my Prince. I'll be the best hound you've ever had! I'll serve you so well." Without meaning to, the young man found himself kneeling again, like a knight asking to serve his king. Begging to serve. The realization sent a rush through his spine, and it took all of his composure to keep from squirming with excitement. The Prince eyed the young man, assessing this sudden burst of reverence. His tiny smirk widened into a grin. This one had potential.

"I think it's a bit early to decide just yet," he finally said. "I only choose my dogs among the most worthy and able, you know. The most fit and healthy, ready to do my bidding at a moment's notice. I'll have to get a good look at you, you know. Really decide if you're up to the job." The Prince stood up and walked towards the young man kneeling before him. The man found himself staring directly at the Prince's boot and could feel his heart pounding even faster. His breath grew shallow. "Look at me." It took a moment for the man to steel his courage and look up at the Prince's face. And as he did so, the Prince knelt in front of him to get a good look. But where the young man's face showed worship and even a little fear, his Prince's eyes were critical. He grasped the young man's face in one hand, noting his bone structure and the texture of his skin.

He looks at me as though I were a racehorse, the young man thought. *Or a dog.* The thought filled him with excitement.

With his hand still firmly grabbing the young man's face, the Prince leaned in a bit and spoke. "I want to get a better look at you. I'm going to go and sit back down. In the meantime, you're going to strip for me. Is that understood?" The young man could only stare at him in surprise. The Prince's grip on his face tightened and he let out a small whimper. "I said, 'is that understood?'"

"Y-yes, my Prince."

"Good. Now be quick. I don't have all day, and you're hardly the only one who wants to serve me." The Prince let go of the young man's face and stood up. After a moment of silent shock, the young man quickly fumbled at his clothes, trying to hurry and be finished by the time the Prince was seated back in his throne. He didn't quite get done in time, but that meant the Prince got to see him finish removing his pants, revealing shapely legs, sharp hipbones, and a very attractive, half-hard cock. The young man stood up as straight and tall as he could, but still could not help but avert his eyes. Again, the Prince lazily crossed his legs and leaned on one arm of the throne.

"Not bad," he said at last.

"Thank you, my Prince."

"I think you have a lot of potential, you know. You really want to serve me, don't you?"

The young man's cock grew harder and a tiny shiver ran down his back. "Yes, my Prince, I do. Very much."

"Good boy. It's nice to see one so eager." The praise brought a flush of red to the young man's cheeks, and he could not help a tiny smile. The Prince, however, was not finished. "That said, it takes more than that to be one of my dogs. I need to see firsthand what you are capable of. You're going to do something for me."

"Anything, my Prince! I'll do whatever you wish." In his adoration, the young man overcame his nerves and looked the Prince right in the eye.

"I need to see how capable you are of finesse, of being able to take things into your mouth without damaging them. And typically, I would just have you tested on somebody else, but I have a feeling that you've got promise. How does a dog pick things up?"

"With his mouth, my Prince."

"That's right. So I'm going to test if you have the necessary skills to do what is expected of you. Come closer." The young man stood and approached slowly, eyes widening as he saw that the Prince was undoing his own pants. "I need to see how much ability you exhibit with that mouth of yours, so you're going to suck my cock for a bit. You'll have to be strong enough to see it through to the end, but soft enough to do a good job. Now get back on your knees." The Prince uncrossed his legs completely and set one foot on the arm of his throne. He undid the last of the buttons on his pants and slowly ran his hand up the shaft of his cock, admiring the sight before him. Similarly, the young man knelt and stared in awe at the handsome young Prince looking down at him with those dark, endlessly confident eyes. "Oh, and one last thing," the Prince added, before the young man could get started. "You won't be allowed to touch yourself while you do this. A good dog has restraint, after all."

The restriction only made the young man's cock even harder, more desperate for touch. "Yes, my Prince. I'll be a good dog for you."

"I certainly hope so. You can get started now." Without hesitation, the young man took the Prince's cock in one hand and kissed along the shaft, licking gently as he went. The Prince's breathing caught on each flick of the young man's tongue, and he found himself gasping quietly in spite of himself. The young man felt a wave of elation fill his heart. Here he was, serving his Prince like he had dreamed! Being a good boy for him. A good dog. Emboldened by his excitement, he took the Prince's cock into his mouth, feeling it twitch as the Prince sighed with pleasure. The young man took his other hand off of his own leg to avoid temptation and, moving closer, wrapped his arm around the Prince's hips. He could taste the precum dripping from the Prince's cock and found himself sucking even harder, hoping to hear even more sighs and moans. The Prince placed one hand over his own mouth, trying to suppress the noise he was making, and glanced down at the young man between his legs. He seemed to be filled with a single-minded drive, a total reverence and dedication. He wanted nothing more than to serve. This thought only made the Prince all the more aroused, and made the stimulation all the more exciting. He placed his other hand in the young man's hair, gripping it firmly, but not tightly. Not just yet. The young man became aware at the precum now pooling on his legs from his own cock, at his own moans being muffled by the task at hand. The hand in his hair only made him more excited, more aroused, and he started moving faster and putting more focus from his tongue on the spot just under the glands that made the Prince twitch and gasp each time he touched it.

The Prince found it impossible not to thrust gently into the young man's mouth as he went. He tightened his grip on the young man's hair. The arousal crept up the Prince's hips and spread into his spine. It seemed as though his entire body was feeling the electrifying pleasure and yearning need. The Prince let out a moan as the young man went even faster and harder. "Don't fucking stop," he found himself saying through the moans and gasps. "Don't you fucking stop. Oh, fuck..." The young man let out a small whimpering moan as he kept at it, trying his best to not allow temptation to sway him from his purpose. His cock was so hard, and so desperate to be touched. He could hardly bear it. The Prince could feel the pressure building inside of him, knew that it would only be a matter of minutes before this would have to be over.

This boy is perfect, he thought. I *could very well pass him right now*. But there was no point in cutting off such a wonderful experience. The young man never once backed down or asked to stop. And in a short time, the Prince, feeling the urgency in his body's reactions, gripped the young man's hair tighter and thrust into his mouth with more vigor. "I'm getting close… I'm gonna..." The Prince was unable to finish his sentence. With a loud, high-pitched moan, he came into the young man's mouth. The young man, hardly one to quit now, swallowed all he could and did not stop until the Prince was shaking. Finally, he pulled back and sat demurely on his knees before him. The Prince looked at him for a fairly long time before catching his breath.

"I think it's fairly safe to say you've proven yourself. So congratulations, you should be proud. I'll take you on." The young man's face brightened up with excitement. "Thank you, my Prince! Oh, thank you. I won't let you down!"

"I know you won't. If you'll collect your clothes and speak to the doorman again, he'll set you up. I look forward to your service." The young man stood up, bowed deeply, collected his clothes, and started to turn to the door. "Oh, and one last thing!"

"Yes, my Prince?"

"If you still want something done about that," the Prince pointed to the young man's cock, still hard and dripping. "I can come by later. So that moratorium on touching yourself still applies, for now."

"Thank you, my Prince! I would love that." The young man bowed again, and hurried out the door. The Prince did up his pants again, sat up straight, and adjusted the crown atop his head with a smile.

Anal Sex and Butt Stuff

Romp on the Beach: Sex and Anal Play with a Stranger off the Internet

Mark picked me up at midnight. For hours I have been trying to stop the butterflies from dancing in my stomach. We met the night before. He was the first of my online dating experiences. I was nervous and excited. I ran out the door, and jumped into his green SUV. He reeked of confidence and sexuality. His arms were muscular and heavily tattooed. We drove around to the North Shore of Oahu, and made small talk about how amazing it was that we hit it off so quickly. I wasn't sure what was going to happen, but the anticipation was driving me up the wall. He picked a very quiet beach. Remote with no houses in sight, and pulled over. He reached across the seat, and kissed me. His lips touched mine, and immediately sent fire through my belly. I could feel my pussy getting wet. I wanted him. I could only hope at this point he wanted me back.

We walked hand in hand down to the beach. He had conveniently packed a large blanket. After spreading it out, we sat down close to each other. The beach was perfect tonight. The moon was bright, and the waves were so loudly crashing down around us. I was nervous, and just gazing out into the water, afraid to look him in the eyes.

We talked about everything. Kids, Marriage, Love. He told me how beautiful I was. He could not understand why I was single. Why I was online dating.

Finally I gathered enough courage to kiss him again. I pushed him down on the blanket, and sat on top of him. My wet pussy was pressed against his jeans. I aggressively kissed him. Sucking on his tongue and lips. His hands were roaming all over my body. With every touch, he was driving my body more and more insane. He rolled me over, and allowed his body to hoover over mine. He had his knee in between my legs. He kissed my neck and my ears, so sweetly. He pulled my dress down to my waist. Mark started to caress my breast through my bra while continuing to kiss my lips. He pulled my bra straps down one at a time. He very gently placed his hands on the clasp behind my back. He looked at my eyes, and I knew that he was silently asking me if what he was doing was okay. I just nodded my head. I did not want to say anything in fear of ruining the moment. With one move of his skilled hand, my bra was laying on the blanket. I was now almost naked on the beach, while Mark was still fully dressed.

He took one of my nipples into his mouth.   My entire body had become an electrical current.   He sucked gently and expertly.   His hand was massaging my other nipple.   They were so hard.   He was switching back and forth to give both of my nipples the attention they needed.   The breeze was perfectly hitting the wetness.   I wanted Mark, and he knew it.   I could feel the moisture coming down inside of my pussy.   My panties were now evidently wet.   With his mouth on my nipple, he took his hand and placed them inside of my panties.   I moaned, for it had been years since I have been touched this way.

I wanted him to make me cum.   I needed an orgasm.   Mark dipped his index finger into my wetness.   He very slowly and perfectly started rubbing my clit.   He would wait until I was almost to climax, and stop to dip his finger into my pussy again.   I did not know how much more I could take.   I needed my control back. As much as I wanted to cum, I knew that once I did, Mark had me, I would belong to him.

I removed his hand, and rolled over on top of him.   I placed his hands behind his back.   I began unbuckling his belt with my teeth.   I had never done this before, and I realized that it is quite easy.   I unbuttoned his pants, slowly.   I wanted him to want me as badly as I wanted him.   I pulled his pants down to his knees.   To my pleasant surprise he wasn't wearing any underwear.   I sat back and just took in the sight of his amazing cock.   It was one of the nicest ones I have ever seen.   I couldn't wait to get that in my mouth.

I immediately stuck his dick in my mouth.   I wanted it to touch the back of my throat.   My goal was to touch his balls with my tongue and gag on his dick at the same time.   What a lovely fucking dick he had.   I started bobbing my head and at the same time grasping him firmly at the base of his cock.   My split was all over him.   Sucking his dick turned me on more than Mark touching me would ever do.   I knew he was close to cumming, and I wanted to swallow every drop of his juice.

Abruptly, he stopped me.   He rolled me over, and got behind me.   Mark ripped my panties and he struggled to get them off.   He took my arms and pulled them behind my back, holding them with one strong hand, and had my hair wrapped tightly around his other fist.   The first moment of penetration was crazy.   I wanted to explode all around him.   He was slamming inside of me.   It was so hard, so fast, and so fucking amazing.   His balls were slapping my already sensitive clit.   He let go of my arms, and placed my hands in front on me on my clit.   I had no clue what was coming next.

He pulled out of my pussy, and pushed my head down into the blanket.   My pussy felt empty and my ass was in the air.   He started tonguing my ass. Jamming his tongue in and out, and at the same time fingering my pussy.   I was going to cum.   I couldn't stop it this time.   My body started tensing up and I started shaking.   I let myself release.   I started moaning and squirming.   Mark replaced his tongue with his thumb.   He very slowing starting working it in and out of my ass.

All of the sudden he jammed his dick back inside of my pussy.   I knew that he wouldn't last much longer.   He kept pumping away.   I was going to cum again.   I couldn't stop shaking. I felt full.   His dick in my pussy and thumb in my ass was exactly what I needed.   Mark pulled his dick out and flipped me over.   He sprayed my face with warm salty semen.   I stuck my tongue out hoping to get a taste of him.

After he was done, he started licking his own cum off of my face.   He would rotate from licking my face, to kissing me.   I had never before that moment tasted a man's cum from his own tongue.

After he had me cleaned up, he helped me put my bra back on, and pulled my dress back up.   We folded up the blanket and started walking back to the car. There was nothing but silence.   I didn't know what to say.   That was one of the best, and most erotic sexual experiences I had ever had.

As we pulled away from the beach, my only thoughts were about how many other men there were on that dating site.   With this as my first date, I can only imagine how much sex I was going to have.   I waited years for this experience, and it was amazing, but I couldn't wait to get back home, and answer another man's email. I have a feeling, my pussy will never be lonely again.

All Holes With The Fuck Buddy

"I would much rather have your sister," bare-chested Keith whispered in her ear.

"Well, she doesn't want you, so you better settle for…." Before she could finish the sentence, he had flung her on his bed. He did not even kiss her. He immediately started to grope her. He ran his fingers between her legs. Through her pants, he could feel her wet, hot, eager pussy. Her leg quivered, she wanted nothing more than for him to fuck her, and the harder he would do it the better! No man had fucked her in over two years, so there was no way in hell that she would go for two more years without the touch of a man!

Keith was all that she needed; her main desire, at the moment. Oh yes, she wanted to come over and over on his dick.

"Aw…" she moaned.

"You want it, don't you! You really want this dick!"

"Fuck, yes, and it's about time that you give it to me!"

"Not just yet, Susan, if you want it in your pussy you have to get it in the other two holes first!"

"You drive a hard bargain, but sure, whatever you want." She moved gently from underneath him to take an upmost position. She took off his pants and his boxers, "You won't need these, Keith."

He smiled, "Will you….Oh…yes baby…That is so fucking good!" Her lips hugged his dick like a sloth on the branches of a tree. "Yes, honey, suck me dry!"

"That's just what I intend to do, baby!" Damn, his dick was so warm and delicious like freshly baked pastry. She could suck him forever. Ten minutes later, he decided to take charge. Instead of laying her on the bed, he bent her over on her knees. Unbuttoned her pants, took them off, removed and sniffed her panties. Patting her on the ass, he said, "Now, you are gonna get it!"

He tore her blouse off of her luscious skin. He stroked her breast and pressed his dick firmly against her butt cheek. "Are you ready?"

"Yes, Keithy baby." He pushed the entirety of his dick directly into her ass. "Fuck! This shit hurts, but I kinda like it."

"Of course you do!"

"Gosh, you are so fucking huge! I love a big dick; it's my favorite kind."

"I'm a size 11 baby! So enjoy!" He fucked her so long and so hard, she felt like she was about to pass out, but she was enjoying it.

"Ok, that's enough. Now, I will give you what I promised you, right after I eat up that pussy of yours!" She laid on the bed and opened her legs. "You have a beautiful pussy."

She chuckled, "To think that you would have preferred my sister's."

He smirked, "I still want to fuck her, but will fuck you first" He started to play with her pussy. He rubbed her clit with one finger, then two. She was really wet. He shoved both fingers inside of her warm crabby. Her legs trembled from all the excitement. He stroked her pussy. "I'm really going to enjoy fucking you," he said. He, then, dove down right in the middle of her beautiful pink vagina. He started to eat that pussy like it was nobody else's business. She moaned and groaned. He pushed his tongue inside her pussy and started to tongue-fuck her.

Fuck this man can eat, she thought to herself. A few minutes later, she felt it. She knew it. She was about to explode. She could not help it! Hot goo burst out of her cunny hole, right in his mouth and down his throat.

"Ok, that's it! I've made you cum. Now, it's my turn." She felt his warm dick as it pressed against her inner thigh as he prepared it for its destination.

"Are you sure that your small hole can handle this entire dick!"

"Well, if my ass could handle it, there is no reason that my cunny can't. Besides, I want you. All of you, and…Fuck!"

"What? Is it too much? Thought you could handle it!" He proceeded to fuck her. It did hurt her like hell at first, but afterwards; she had no problem accepting the full cock! They were both hot, wet and dripping with sweat. He raised her legs above his shoulder for better penetration. Gosh, she loved every inch of him.

Now, he was a really good fuck buddy. He really knew how to make her pussy water. In fact, she came over and over on his fat, long dick. Each time she came, he felt more inspired; he intensified the fucking.

"I want it doggy style!" she exclaimed. "I want to feel your entire depth in my pussy, and I want you to fuck me as hard as you can!" She positioned on the bed for him. He rubbed his fingers over her pussy from behind to test her level of wetness.

"Are you sure that this is what you want?

"Yes, please. Give me, everything."

"Okay, at your request." With one great push, the entire 11inches went in.

She screamed bloody hell from pain and delight. He bumped and grind her cunny. Her liquid combined with his sweat flowed down her legs. His balls were all wet, dripping with her pour. They fucked for two hours and then, he grabbed hold of his dick, squeezed it very tightly to prevent his precious contents from spilling. He lowered her on the pillow and he shoved his thickness in her mouth, "Suck it; I want to feel my dick touch the back of your throat."

She complied. She gave him a deep throated suck. As he exploded into her mouth, she could feel his sticky wet warmness going down her throat. She savored his taste. They both laid in bed tired from all the excitement of the day. He played with her breasts, and looked at her, "Today was fun. Maybe we can fuck again sometime soon." She smiled in agreement.

"Next time, Susan, bring your sister along with you!"

Anal Pleasures with a Demon Whore from a Costume Party: An Erotic Story with Snowballing

He woke up to the sound of his alarm clock buzzing around on his side table. He reached over without a thought and slapped the "snooze" button and rolled back on his side. It was a Friday, and he was going to a party later that night with a few of the guys from work. The alarm clock started its dreadful buzzing again and fell off the table. Annoyed, James finally got out of his bed and walked to the bathroom to shave and clean up. Before leaving the bathroom to get dressed, he looked in the mirror and decided to keep his bed-head hairdo and smiled and winked at himself. He shut off the light, marched into his room, and grabbed his white dress shirt with his crimson tie and threw on his beige slacks. He sighed a relief as he marked today's date with a red "X" and chugged out of the gallon of orange juice. Then he grabbed his keys and started out the door to his boring office job.

James couldn't get something off his mind while he was on his daily commute to work. The thought that today was going to be different. He felt that the day was going faster than usual. There was barely any traffic, and he was excited to go to the party later that night with Will and Frankie from work. It was a costume party, and he already planned on being a firefighter. Will was dressing up as a Cop, and Frankie would be Abraham Lincoln.

As soon as the clock on his computer hit 4:30, He saved his document and ran out the door to his car and sped home. As soon as he got home, he kicked off his shoes and tossed his keys on the table. He raced up his stairs to his closet and took off all his clothes and jumped in the shower and started washing his hair and chest, then slowly went down to his dick. He knew he would be around women tonight and has the chance to get some, so he starts scrubbing his dick. He always enjoyed washing his dick. He would always put extra shampoo on his hands and would start jacking off. It was his favorite guilty pleasure. He would always think about Christina, the receptionist from work who always wears those sexy V-necks with her double D breasts practically hanging out of her shirt. He moaned softly and started jerking off faster and imagined her sucking his dick while it's between her big and voluptuous breasts. And then right before he blew his load in her mouth, she pulled it out and made him cum all over her cute little face. He came all over his hands and let out a soft and long moan.

He washed himself off as fast as he possibly could and got out to put on his costume. He rushed as he pulled on his yellow fireman jacket over his white t-shirt and kept it unbuttoned while he pulled on his suspenders and grabbed his hat. He was out the door to the party.

He pulled up to the party and saw Will and Frankie waiting outside. He ran over to them and they all walked inside together. There were people everywhere, tons. People he never met before, but there was a girl, dressed up like some kind of demon-whore. She was gorgeous, and she saw him too. He couldn't take his eyes off her. About an hour passed, and he finally built up the courage to walk up to her and ask her name.

"Hey" James said, "I couldn't help but stare. I hope I didn't offend you."

The demon-whore lady chuckled. "It's alright! I usually don't like be stared at by creeps, but you can watch me for as long as you want. I'm Maia."

James smiled, then replied "I'm James. What kind of name is Maia?"

"Beats me!" Maia said. "You could ask my parents, but I don't think my folks would like you."

James opened his mouth to talk but realized it would get drowned out by the loud music that was playing. He smiled and grabbed her by the hand and pulled her outside of the building. Maia followed willingly and stopped as soon as they got outside and pulled him to her and kissed him. James pulled back in shock and stared at her seductive smile, grabbed her firm ass, looked at her curiously. She closed her eyes and bit her lip softly when he touched her ass. When he stopped she looked at him and smiled.

"Take me somewhere... private," she said as seductive as she possibly could. James couldn't help but run to his car and open the door for her. She stepped in and smiled at his generosity, and he shut the door behind her. He jumped in the driver's seat and drove her home. All the way home, she had her hand on his thigh rubbing his dick as he drove. When they got to his house, he picked her up over his shoulder and brought her to his room. He threw her on the bed and started kissing her while he pulled down his pants. Her costume was very thin and she clearly had nothing on under it. He started slowly reaching for her breasts, and she grabbed him and threw him on the bed. She laughed at him, and grabbed his tie from the clothes he wore to work that morning. She looked down at him and grabbed his hands and put them together and tied them with his tie.

James willingly let her tie him up because it was something he always wanted to do. She looked down at him and rubbed his dick through his underwear. All she could think about is how hard and big it was and how it would fit in her tight asshole. "I'm your master now, and you'll treat me as such." She proclaimed. "Understand?"

He looked up at her, this beautiful woman he hadn't even known for more than about 2 hours had him tied up and all he could say was "Yes, Master Maia."

"Good." She straddled him and started rubbing the crotch of her costume against his hard dick in its cloth confinement. She loved it. She grabbed both his hands and started to suck on his fingers as if she was sucking on his hard delicious dick. Her pussy was getting wet. Fast. She pulled him off the bed and on to his knees and stood in-front of him.

"Take off my panties" She ordered "with your teeth." James looked up at her shyly, then leaned in slowly, and bit her panties and pulled them down to her ankles. She lifted her feet out of them. She pulled them from James' mouth and smacked him across the face with them. She pushed his head back against the bed and sat on his mouth. Making sure her wet pussy was on his lips, and before she could tell her new little toy to start eating her out, she could feel his tongue inside her... his long, thick, and wet tongue just wiggling around inside her. She couldn't help but let out a loud squeal. James noticed and kept licking her, trying to explore her and find her "G-spot." She noticed he liked her juices and teasingly stood up all the way and spread her ass cheeks.

All she could feel was his tongue against her asshole and she loved it. She fell to her knees and put her ass in the air to let him keep licking her. He took this as a chance to make her his toy now. He broke free of the tie and teasingly forced his tongue into her asshole, his cock just stood straight up. He pulled his tongue back into his mouth and spanked her tight, firm ass. He took his long and hard dick, meanwhile she starts to look back confused, and he starts to smack his dick against her asshole. Maia lets out a small moan. "Please stop beating around the bush and pound me," she begged.

James bit his lip and pushed the head of his dick against her ass and tried to force it in, but it was too tight so he decided to start fucking her tight and dripping pussy. He started slow, forcing his entire dick inside her as she moaned softly when he her skin touched his balls. Then slowly pulled the entire dick out and then slowly, but progressively, faster. Maia was moaning, begging for more, with her face against the floor. James forced his finger into her tight ass and started fingering her. Maia started moaning louder and panting faster, and saying she's going to cum. James pulled out and flipped her on her back. He began to smack her pussy softly watching her facial expression hoping she will cum for him.

"Mmmm... James, I want you to eat my cum right out of me," Maia proclaimed. James willingly starts licking her pussy and fingering her asshole again, hoping to loosen it up. She wiggled around and let out a loud squeal and came on his mouth. He smiled as she let out a loud sigh of relief and laid back as James cleans up all of her delicious cum. She starts to get up and crawl on the bed, meanwhile James forced his dick into her asshole.

"You thought we were done? You must not know me all that well" James said as he started pounding her tight asshole as hard as he could. Maia let out the loudest moan she made all night and started fucking him as hard as she could. She loved his large and hard dick in her tight ass. She didn't even care if he came inside her. She wanted his cum. She wanted him. James noticed her increased enthusiasm and let her take control while he tried to hold his cum in. She started moaning louder and fucked him harder, making sure his dick went as deep as possible. James couldn't hold in his moans and began to start moaning her name louder. She heard him and it made her want him more. She started pounding him harder and harder. James couldn't handle it and moaned as he filled her ass with his cum. He got on his knees and started sucking on her asshole and sucking his cum out. Once he got a mouthful, he started kissing her, moving it all to her mouth. They made out back and forth like this for about 10 minutes before she swallowed it.

My Girlfriend's Anal Virginity

One winter I was at home enjoying my whiskey and watching a movie when I received a call from my girlfriend at around midnight. I could tell by her voice that she was feeling nasty as she told me that she wanted to see me immediately. I told her I'd be there within the hour

I finished my drink as my mind began running. She was living with her parents and an older sister, and it was one in the morning almost by the time I arrived. When I texted her, she said she'd be down in just a minute. I was waiting in my car when she came down in a rush, swung open the passenger side door, and leaned over the seat. She started kissing me all over, and her hands were everywhere. I was wearing my shorts, so she had an easy time as she started feeling my cock, which had been hard since the first phone call. She started rubbing my cock over the shorts, and then she finally pulled it out.

She whispered in my ear saying that, "You have a huge cock," and then she went lower and started kissing my cock all over and finally sucking it deep in her mouth, sucking it like a lollypop. While I was enjoying her talents and moaning with joy, she went deeper and ended up licking my balls with my cock down her throat. I took a large grab at her ass, and was pleased to find that she was only wearing pajamas without any panties. My hand went even lower as I caressed her, and I started rubbing a finger on her asshole. She was closing and opening her butt hole when my finger was feeling it, which I assumed meant that she was enjoying it a lot.

Then she whispered in my ears, "Fuck me, please."

I lifted her legs high in the car, her pussy lips wide open, and I could literally see the juices dripping. I started licking her pussy, and after a moment I slid a digit into her tight butthole. She kept on saying, "Fuck me please."

Finally I inserted my cock in her pussy very slowly, as I knew she was most likely a virgin. While I was fucking her back and forth her pussy was making noises, wet noises. I kept on fucking her for 6 to 7 minutes. Then I told her go doggy style at the back seat of the car. She agreed , spreading her ass wide open as if she wanted it in her ass. I could clearly see her asshole closing and opening as I continued prodding into her tight vagina. Finally my cock was wet enough for her tight ass. I plunged my cock in her butthole without any further warning. She was moaning , then she said, "Fuck me harder!"

I rammed my cock as far down as it could go within her asshole. She yelped in a bit of pain, but began wracking her body as I rubbed on her clit and continued pounding away. As she had an earth shattering orgasm, I spilled my seed inside her virgin asshole and kept pounding until she begged me to stop.

Sucking Swittles Out of Her Butthole: An Erotica with Anal Candy Insertion and Anal Sex

Bite-Size Gabriella was a sizzling hot petite girl that worked at my dentist's office. My visits had become more frequent because of an obsession with candy taking its toll on my teeth. I don't know where she was from, but her exotic look suggested a Latin American persuasion. A perfect 5'4", 100 LB, thick little 22 year-old body, straight black hair and emerald green eyes. If Helen of Troy caused a war, this girl would cause a war of the worlds.

She was always friendly and smiled but I would never get a chance to talk to her much because it was a high volume practice. One day I saw her while I was jogging and started chatting with her. She had this sexy Spanish accent that would give anyone a bulge in the pants. After speaking a while, I talked her into going to dinner. I made sure to take her to Garibaldi's on 8th, one of the classiest restaurants in town. I had to impress the hell out of her right off the bat. No room for fuck-ups.

So we talked and had a sumptuous lobster dinner. I had the waiter bring us a bottle of Dauphin Noir that I knew would put us both in a good, relaxed mood. The whole time all I could think about is stuffing my 8" cock into this hottie. So I pay for dinner and give the waiter a generous tip, and we walk out laughing, hand in hand. We get in the car and out of nowhere, Gabriella leans over and kisses me and starts stroking my cock, which had been hard ever since I picked her up.

I'm kinda looking around to make sure no one creeps up on us, like some cop or something. I suddenly hear a zipping sound and then feel her thick Latin lips wrapping around my dick head. I was actually a bit shocked. I did not know she liked me THAT much. She just kept sucking on my cock while her tongue massaged my flesh. Holy fuck, this girl could suck! So I ask her if she wants to go to my house for a bit more privacy. Reluctantly, she took my cock out of her hungry mouth, and we drove off. The whole way she is rubbing her pussy and moaning, and I'm just hauling ass trying to get home without crashing or getting a ticket so I can just pound her tanned little ass.

When we got home, I ripped off her clothes and laid her on the bed and told her to just be still. She had a puzzled look on her face. I go in the drawer and pull out a bag of Swittles bite size candy, my favorite. I also pull out the watermelon flavored lubricant I had gotten in the mail a few days before. I just start slurping and her on her little clit while I finger fuck her anus with the lube. You have never seen a more gorgeous pussy than her waxed little cunt. I open the bag of Swittles and start stuffing her tight, creamy asshole with them slowly. She is just losing it.

After I made her cum hard, I started licking her asshole and begging for my candy back. So she's moaning as she squeezes the Swittles slowly into my mouth. Then I just started sucking the candy out and you could just see the juice just oozing out of her hot little twat. Now, I would SUCK a hot girl's asshole plain, but I'm a candy freak so it made it all the more sublime. By now her waxed little pussy is just pure cream and my thick, 8" cock is like portland concrete. I start fucking her tight little cunt and I can barely stuff my cock in there.

In the meantime, I unwrap a watermelon Sharms lollipop and start twirling it between her thick, juicy Latin lips. She is zombied out in ecstasy. I stop fucking her for a second so I can suck on her clit some more while I twirl the lollipop in and out of her tender, creamy little asshole. She's just jerking from the intense pleasure. She let out a shriek and a squirt of thick juice out of her pussy. All of a sudden she grabs my stiff cock and starts working it up her ass. I thought I was gonna die. I was actually kinda surprised I had actually gotten this far. Now, this is just insane. As I'm stuffing her tight asshole, I can see my dick is covered in blue, red and all the other Swittles colors. After a while, I sat up, leaned back, and started bouncing her hot Latin ass hard on my cock.

What a delicious little fuck! I felt the most spine-tingling sensation as I plunged my cock deeper inside her, and she was almost drooling from the intensity. After about 10 minutes though, I could barely hold my cum. She told me to pull out for a second to stop from ejaculating. Then she laid me back and started deep throating my dick nice and slow. I mean, I could actually feel it going down her throat. Her lips were covered in Swittles juice. It only took about 5 minutes for me to ejaculate in a most explosive way.

She jerked back a bit but just kept sucking and swallowing until I was so sensitive I had to beg her to stop. I never saw a drop of cum and trust me, it felt like I shot a gallon of semen. She rubbed my cock on her precious tanned face and kissed it a few times. I was literally on the verge of tears. In my 43 years, I have NEVER fucked a girl that was hotter, sexier, or more willing to do ANYTHING than Gabriella.

Afterwards, we both just plopped down and fell asleep. After about an hour I feel something on my cock and when I open my eyes, there she was deepthroating my thick cock again. In my head I'm like: "Holy fuck! Here we go again and I'm all out of Swittles, shit!"